TRULY EVIL

MARK HARDIE

sphere

SPHERE

First published in Great Britain in 2017 by Sphere

1 3 5 7 9 10 8 6 4 2

A CIP catalogue record for this book
is available from the British Library.

Hardback ISBN 978-0-7515-6862-2
Trade Paperback ISBN 978-0-7515-6210-1

Typeset in Caslon by M Rules
Printed and bound in Great Britain by
Clays Ltd, St Ives plc

Papers used by Sphere are from well-managed forests
and other responsible sources.

Sphere
An imprint of
Little, Brown Book Group
Carmelite House
50 Victoria Embankment
London EC4Y 0DZ

An Hachette UK Company
www.hachette.co.uk

www.littlebrown.co.uk

For Debbie

Prologue

I

The tide was coming in. His feet sinking as the silt became softer, less definite. Rivulets of advancing water reflecting the sickly dawn over the estuary. The air damp and chill, the haze yet to be burnt off by the warmth of the sun, so his stinging and streaming eyes could not make out the other side of the river, although he knew its contours and dimensions by heart. The county of Essex at his back. Somewhere in front of him, beyond the mist, lay Kent. In the occasional lull between gusts of a buffeting wind which had numbed and frozen his ears came the distant clanging of halyards on masts. The screech of seagulls.

The cold wind bit into his flesh, flapping his damp clothes around his body. His hands constricted into chafed and chapped claws. He looked down once again at the figure half-submerged in the mud. The eyes and mouth open. Grey silt had gathered and then cracked on the skin so that now it seemed more like a statue than a human being. Sandflies already hovered. Lining up to kiss the eyes. Mourning relatives filing past to give their last respects to someone they hated or hardly knew. A tiny translucent crab scuttled from the mouth, grains of sand dislodged by its claws. He took a deep breath, stepped closer and put the sole of his boot on the face. Applying a steady pressure. Pushing it under the mud. The slight sucking sound snatched away by a gust of wind. The sea rushing in to fill the space. A pool of brackish water forming. Before that too drained away and was gone.

II

EXTRACT FROM TRANSCRIPT OF SESSION HELD ON 27 JULY

The subject was fairly unresponsive and questions often had to be repeated. The answers were faltering, hesitant, at times monosyllabic, and numerous lengthy silences occurred. The subject was also frequently upset and very confused.

AF: Where are you?

RL: I don't know.

AF: What can you see?

RL: Dark . . . Darkness.

AF: OK. Try to stay calm. Try to relax. Look around you.

RL: OK.

AF: Good. Can you see anything? Anything at all?

RL: Curtains? At a window. A small crack of light . . . they have a . . . weep? No . . . weft? . . . weave. They have a heavy weave.

AF: Nothing else? You can't see anything else?

RL: No.

AF: What can you feel?

RL: Metal. Under my hand. A metal frame. A hospital bed.

AF: What can you smell?

RL: Hospital . . . sweat . . . sleep . . . pain . . . body-stink . . . many bodies.

AF: What can you hear?

RL: Cars? Outside . . . a squeaky wheel . . . metal on metal.

AF: How long have you been here?

RL: Here? I don't know ... weeks? Months? A long time ... for ever. Now ... here now ... before? I don't know before ... I know ... now ... I know here.

AF: Who are you?

RL: I don't know ... I was someone ... before ... I was someone ... before now ... before this room ...

AF: Good. Good. Well done.

PART ONE

Day One

1

Barely half an hour after a fitful night had shuffled uncertainly into a gloomy dawn, Detective Sergeant Frank Pearson sat waiting in his car at traffic lights. The view beyond the windscreen, blank, featureless, dull. It was going to be the sort of day, Pearson felt, when the sky went up and down – but never out of – the greyscale. A fine rain, barely more than a mist, started to fall from the leaden sky. Flicking on the wipers to their lowest setting he sat for a while, listening to the patter of rain on the car roof. The ticking of the indicator. The ponderous clunk and squeak of the windscreen wipers. Finally the lights changed and he swung the car right onto Marine Parade. Past the closed chippies and rock shops. The hushed pubs and bars. The mute arcades. And into the gusting wind off the estuary. The slow sweep of the wipers smearing the needles of rain across the windscreen on their upward arc before halting momentarily then with a shuddering squeal of protest grudgingly clearing his field of vision on their downward trajectory. Passing under the footbridge to the pier. To his right, the restaurants under the arches were shut tight. The chairs and tables put away, the metal shutters down. To his left, a jogger in a hooded waterproof jacket and shorts, head down against the rain and wind. The tide out, the grey expanse of the mudflats exposed. But on the other side of the estuary, the metal tanks of the disused oil refinery were hidden from view.

Reaching Chalkwell, the seafront was already crowded. Haphazardly parked vehicles. Pedestrians in hi-vis jackets. Marked police cars. A solitary ambulance, the yellow banding achingly fluorescent in the dim light. Two uniformed police constables sectioning off the area with blue-and-white tape.

Pearson pulled to a halt. Picked up his dark woollen overcoat from the passenger seat. Climbed out, shrugged it on, slammed the car door. Digging in the pocket for identification, holding the warrant card at shoulder height, nodding to the uniform on duty and ducking under the tape, he made his way towards the sea wall looking for the senior investigating officer. He spotted the over-large, navy anorak. The between-regular-sizes body and habitually ill-fitting clothes of Detective Chief Inspector Martin Roberts. His normally ruddy cheeks were now chapped red, his thinning ginger hair flapping in the swirling wind. Roberts was talking to a senior uniform Pearson recognised as Detective Chief Superintendent Andy Curtis. Between them stood the crime scene manager, dressed in white forensic overalls. Six foot eight and stick thin. A couple having a furtive assignation under a lamppost. As he approached, Roberts turned and nodded. 'Frank.'

'What is that thing?' Curtis asked, indicating a granite obelisk, about fourteen feet high and around forty feet away.

'The Crowstone?' asked Pearson. 'Historically, it marks the limit of the responsibility of the Port of London Authority on the Thames.'

'So,' Curtis asked, 'is she ours or theirs?'

Pearson looked out at the girl. Lying on her stomach, as if in obeisance at the foot of the monolith. Some weird kind of ancient fertility rite. The long black hair fanned out in front of her, obscuring the face from view. The black bra just visible under a ripped grey satin top. The black miniskirt. The boots some kind of wet-look PVC. A path had been marked out with tape from the sea wall to the area around the body and the scene-of-crime officers in paper forensic suits were beginning to erect a tent. Somewhere above the clouds, the drone of a light aircraft.

'Her head may be in London,' said Pearson, 'but her heart is in Essex. She's one of ours.'

A moment later the crime scene manager checked his watch. 'The tide's coming in. We've got maybe an hour, tops.'

'Is there a search team available?' Roberts asked.

'Not sure we'd get one down here in time—'

'Then we'll just have to make do,' Curtis cut in. 'We'll use the uniforms that are already here. I'll get them organised.' Turning on his heel. Taking charge. Striding off purposefully, the CSM in his wake.

'There goes our next chief constable,' Roberts said, shaking his head. Then, to Pearson, 'I've been getting it in the neck for the last ten minutes about "public perception" and "media profile".'

'What's he doing down here anyway?' asked Pearson. 'I've never known brass to turn up at a dump site before.'

'He can smell a public relations disaster,' Roberts said. 'Given the past couple of months, the last thing he needs' – looking towards the beach – 'is a dead girl being washed up on his patch.'

The girl was hidden from view as the white forensic tent was erected around her. Dragging his gaze away Pearson asked, 'Who found her?'

'Dog walker,' said Roberts, nodding towards an elderly man sitting on a bench, a black Labrador at his feet. The dog was asleep. Next to the pair stood a uniformed PC who wasn't, but looked well on his way. Thank God for dog walkers, thought Pearson. What would we do without them? Every wood and lay-by in England would be chock-a-block with corpses. Perhaps the Home Secretary should put them all on the payroll. Or maybe they could work on commission: get paid some kind of finder's fee.

'What did he have to say?'

'Not a lot.'

'Mind if I have a word?'

Roberts shrugged an answer. As Pearson approached, the dog scrambled painfully into a sitting position. Started wagging its tail. He crouched down and scratched the dog under its chin. It flopped down onto its side and exposed its belly. Pearson scratched the damp hair of its chest and patted it, then, looking into the owner's face, said, 'I understand you were the one who found the body?'

'Body?' Swallowing hard. Looking on the verge of tears. The old man stammered, 'Y-yeah,' blinking, 'I found her.'

'You were walking the dog. Do you usually walk your dog this early?'

'Yeah, I'm a bad sleeper. And Harry needs his exercise. He's got arthritis.' The old man reached down and touched the dog's head, as if for reassurance. 'We're usually out as soon as it's light. In the winter he's allowed on the beach. If the tide's in, he likes to swim.' He looked down at the dog, rubbing behind the ear. The dog wagging his tail. A pink, wet tongue lolling out of the side of his mouth. 'You like your swim, don't you, boy, eh?'

'So,' Pearson said, 'can you tell me what happened this morning?' He stood up and, for the first time, the old man met his gaze.

'I've got a place further up, near town.' He waved in the vague

10

direction of the pier. 'We walk down, along the front, down to here. Then we turn around.'

'You follow the same route every day?'

'Pretty much. In the winter we go the other way, towards Shoebury. That's where,' indicating the dog, 'he swims.'

'OK. So you got to here and then what happened?'

'I saw something out by the Crowstone,' lifting a hand towards the beach, 'so I stopped for a minute to see what it was. Then Harry started sort of sniffing the air and whimpering, and that,' swallowing again, 'and that's when I realised what it was. What I was looking at, I mean. That it was a girl out there. A dead girl . . .' Trailing off, he stared out towards the white tent.

After a moment Pearson spoke again. 'Did you phone from here? Do you have a mobile?'

'Yeah.'

'So you were here from the time you saw the bod— the girl until the police arrived?'

'Yeah,' said the old man. Still staring out towards the leaden sky, the grey sand of the beach, the tent, the white-suited SOCOs moving in and out.

'Was there anyone else about?'

'Nah.' Shaking his head. Not looking at Pearson. 'Just us.'

'What about on the walk down? Did you see any other dog walkers?' Pearson thought of the man he'd passed. 'Any joggers? Anyone out for an early morning stroll?'

'Nah. Just us. I've already said all this.'

Pearson looked to the constable – bored rigid, frozen stiff – who nodded in agreement, then turned back to the old man, studying his face for a moment. Finally, patting him on the shoulder, he said, 'OK, chief, I think I'm done here. I'm afraid we're going to need you to make a video statement for us. You just sit tight and

11

we'll arrange transport for you to the police station. I'm sure that we'll be able to look after Harry for you – OK, mate?' He gave a nod over the man's shoulder to the young officer.

Roberts was talking animatedly into a mobile, finishing the call as Pearson walked over, tucking the phone away in the pocket of his anorak. They watched the line of uniformed policemen in silence for a few minutes as they made their slow progress from the tideline to the sea wall, occasionally stooping to load various objects into plastic evidence bags.

'We're going to end up with an awful fucking lot of seaweed,' said Roberts as he hunted again in his anorak pockets. He pulled out a packet of Polos, peeled back the silver paper and offered them to Pearson. Pearson took one and put it into his mouth, catching the scent of wet dog on his fingers. Holding the mint between his teeth. Working his tongue into the hole in the centre. Roberts crunching his mint noisily, saying, 'We're going to have bags full of polystyrene cups, dog-ends, Coke cans, lolly wrappers, all sorts of shit!'

'Not to mention,' Pearson said, 'those little wooden fork things for eating chips. What are they all about?'

Roberts gave him a scathing look. Shook his head. 'You're a fucking silly-arse at times, Pearson.'

Smiling, Pearson finally gave in to temptation and crunched his Polo. Curtis broke away from a group of uniforms and came over.

'We're just going to see if the pathologist can give us any preliminary, sir,' Roberts said to him, 'then we'll head back to the nick.'

'Mind if I tag along?'

They made their way along the beach between the lines of police tape that marked the safe path.

'Who's the pathologist?' Curtis asked. 'Is he up to snuff?'

'She. Patricia Bannister,' Roberts replied. 'She's what you might call "a character".'

A character. That was one way of putting it, Pearson thought. Trish Bannister might pass for attractive. If you ever saw her with make-up, without her steel-rimmed glasses, and with her hair styled in any other way than the habitual severe ponytail. Might. Pearson, however, wouldn't be the one to tell her. But that same brusque, no-nonsense manner, the huge bosom on a slight frame, had made her the object of many an off-colour remark back at the nick.

'Ah yes, I've had dealings with her before.'

Roberts shot Pearson a surreptitious look. Smirking. Eyebrows raised.

At the entrance to the tent Roberts said, 'We need to suit up, sir. If you're planning to go in.'

Inside the tent. They could see the slim back of the pathologist, squatting by the body. Talking quietly to a white-suited SOCO opposite.

Roberts cleared his throat. 'Trish?'

She raised a hand in acknowledgement but carried on her conversation. Beyond her, Pearson could see the top half of the dead girl, now lying on her back, the face only slightly spoiled by its immersion in the salt water. The features small and delicate. The long hair raven black. The remains of thick eyeliner. What might have been black lipstick, though it was difficult to tell on the blue-ing lips. When another minute or two had passed Curtis shifted impatiently. Lifted a cuff to check his watch. Cleared his throat.

'Um, Ms Bannister, have you found anything for us?'

The pathologist stood up. 'Ah yes, Chief Superintendent,' she said, standing to one side and pointing down towards the body. 'I've found you a pair of bollocks.'

2

'I don't want to hear, again, the term "cock in a frock ... "'

Detective Constable Catherine Russell hesitated on the threshold of the incident room. Five minutes early for the morning meeting, but DCI Roberts was already there. Loosening his tie. Undoing the top button of his shirt. Rolling up his sleeves. Slowly scanning the assembled officers.

'Nor do I want to hear "chick with a dick" ... ' Catching sight of Cat loitering uncertainly in the doorway, regretting now her trip outside for a quick fag. Nodding to her, his face stone. As if it were her fault he had started before time.

'Nor do I want to hear the phrase "he-she" ... '

Cat made her way across the room. The smell of newly applied emulsion – magnolia for the walls, and gloss paint – white – for everything else – overpowering. The redecoration the result of a major flood from a burst pipe in the washroom on the next floor. The room was too bright, the light too harsh. The overhead fluorescents on in order to overcome the crepuscular morning outside, but their diffusers lay stacked in one corner, yet to be fitted. And

15

half-built computer workstations sat on top of partly constructed desks lined up against the walls.

'Or "she-male" ...'

Some of the officers had been forced to sit in the open space, their chairs arranged around Roberts in a loose semicircle. It put Cat in mind of afternoons at nursery. Golden Hour. The teacher reading to the children from their favourite book. But the book in question here was the *Murder Investigation Manual*. This, their own Golden Hour. When 'effective early action' could 'result in securing significant material that would otherwise be lost to the investigation'.

Cat slipped behind her desk. Opposite, Pearson sat pinching the bridge of his nose between thumb and forefinger, a telephone balanced in the crook of his neck. Aimlessly doodling on the open notebook in front of him.

'Or "tranny" or any other pejorative terms of that nature,' Roberts went on. 'We are dealing with the loss of a human life here. And, as such, it deserves the same respect as any other human life. Are we all clear on that?'

There was a murmur of assent. Roberts hitched up his trousers and attempted to tuck his shirt in.

'Detective Sergeant Pearson' – nodding in his direction – 'will be Acting Deputy SIO on this investigation.' Roberts paused momentarily as the heads of the new arrivals to the Major Investigation Team looked in Pearson's direction. The team was short of detective inspectors. Had been even before DI Sean Carragher's death. Roberts had approached Pearson, but he'd declined. Cat wondered if it was because of the money. You got paid overtime as a detective constable or a detective sergeant but not as an inspector. It was one of the ironies of the job. Promotion could actually result in a real-term pay cut. Although, of course, it was just as likely that Pearson simply didn't fancy the extra paperwork.

Pearson had watched Cat enter the room. Black trouser suit. White blouse. Shoulder-length brown hair in a loose ponytail. An English rose complexion that tanned well in the summer. He'd pretended to sketch on the notepad, following her progress through the disorderly arrangement of chairs. Trying, as he had every day in the last eight or so weeks, to calculate by her carriage, her body language, whether there might have been any lightening of mood since the death of Carragher. DI Sean Carragher had been the subject of an internal inquiry by the Professional Standards department when his body was found in a burnt-out car in the Ness Road car park. The investigation into his death had been successfully resolved, at least in the eyes of senior-ranking officers; a culprit charged and the honour of the force salvaged. But Cat's relationship with the dead detective had, for her, resulted in a career temporarily in jeopardy, a reputation tarnished, immediate prospects of any advancement in the Job severely damaged, and a deep sense of personal betrayal.

He caught the faint whiff of a recently smoked menthol cigarette. Felt her hazel eyes on him now across the desk.

'Six six eight.' The voice made Pearson jump. He'd been waiting so long for a reply, the phone clamped to a sweaty ear. The request called in because the newly upgraded computerised accounts system was down. Again. He'd almost forgotten what it was he was actually waiting for: a cost-code against which any accrued overtime was to be allocated.

'Ah,' he said, 'the neighbour of the beast.' Shooting a cuff and checking his watch. An old-fashioned Timex on a battered leather wrist-strap.

At the other end of the line, a pause. Then, 'I have absolutely no idea what you're talking about.' The voice, female, was so lacking in enthusiasm, in oxygen, that it could dampen any spark of excitement. An instant antidote to Viagra. Pearson, about to explain the joke, thought better of it, saying instead, 'OK. Thanks,' and putting down the phone.

Looking up he saw the eyes of the room on him. He paused momentarily, allowing notebooks to be opened. Pens to be picked up from desks ...

To Cat, this point in an investigation had always felt a bit distasteful. A little insensitive. Overtime codes and rosters, equating another's misfortune with her own personal gain. It was something that had never sat quite right with her. All the same, though, her notebook was open, her pen was in her hand, as Pearson announced to the room, 'Overtime code six six eight.'

Roberts nodded. Turning back to the room, he said, 'It is, of course, possible that the death might turn out to be non-suspicious. Those of you who are new to the team will, no doubt, become all-too-familiar with my opinion on designating a death as "unexplained". It is ... ' Roberts paused theatrically.

'Utter bollocks!' A handful of officers supplied. In concert. In a studiedly bored tone.

'Because of the circumstances surrounding the deceased,' Roberts continued, 'and until such time as it is proved to the contrary, this will be treated as a suspicious death.' Scratching his chin. 'At this stage we have no positive identification of the deceased. This is likely to come from fingerprinting, a hit on the DNA database – depending, of course, on whether the deceased has been the subject of a prior arrest – or dental checks. A match against a MISPER or a DVI or through public response to a media appeal, if, and when, a media appeal is deemed appropriate.' The original missing person form was called a MISPER1 and the name had somehow stuck. A DVI was a Disaster Victim Identification form, instituted after the tsunamis a decade or so ago, which could be sent to Interpol for matching with MISPERs from other countries.

All standard procedure, Cat knew. As laid down in the *Murder Investigation Manual*. An initial trawl for information. Instigation of the so-called 'Fast-track actions'. Forensic examination of both the body and the scene. A search of the area for any potential weapons or trace evidence. Door-to-door enquiries in the immediate vicinity of the body deposition site. The interviewing of potential witnesses, including the person who had made the call to emergency services. The information collected from these sources would then help to determine any subsequent lines of enquiry. Location of a home address would enable analysis of 'passive data generators'. Intelligence gathered from any mobile telephones or computers. Financial data from debit and credit cards. Lifestyle information such as membership cards. But in reality until, and unless, the victim had been identified the investigation was going nowhere.

'Until we know different,' Roberts continued, 'we will assume that the deceased had chosen to live as a female. As a consequence of this we will refer to her henceforth with the female pronoun "she". And, until such time as her real identity can be established, I think it only right we give her a name.' Putting his hands in his pockets. 'Any suggestions?'

Silence. He sighed, said, 'OK.' Taking a hand out of his pocket. Wiping it down his face. Scratching the back of his head. Thinking. Finally he said, 'Rachel.'

Roberts took the DVD containing the crime-scene video and fitted it into the player. A cue for the lights to be dimmed, the conversation to fade and then die . . .

19

A wide-angle shot of the beach. The girl's body even more slight and frail in that vast expanse of sky and grey silt. The focus narrowing. A measured sweep of the foreshore. An abrupt cut to the body. A slow pan of the girl. The once-silky grey fabric of the top stiffened and dulled by its immersion in salt water. The dark hair, salt-crusted and coarsened, stirred by the breeze, had the look of frayed and tarred hemp. Grit and grains of sand dusted the blue lips, the numbed and bloodless cheeks, and clung to eyelashes above lifeless, blank eyes . . .

The video finished. The lights came up. There was a noticeable change in atmosphere. Suddenly subdued. The general hubbub diminished. The banter forgotten. Roberts stood up, his shirt somehow having become untucked again.

'The key to this case depends on establishing Rachel's true identity. The post-mortem and forensic examination may help us in this respect.' He turned to Pearson. 'Frank, can you attend the PM?'

Pearson nodded. 'Guv.'

'Preliminary examination by the pathologist,' Roberts continued, 'suggests that Rachel had not been in the sea more than a few hours. If, for instance, she was dumped off a boat in the estuary it would seem logical that she entered the water at or around high tide and was washed up at low tide the following morning.' Roberts looked over to DS Alan Laurence. Fat. Balding. His mobile on his desk. Checking the screen. Killing time until his retirement. When, according to Pearson, he planned to open some kind of donkey sanctuary with his missus. Glancing up he saw Roberts looking over and picked up a biro.

'We need to establish times of high and low tides,' Roberts said. 'Sea levels, any unusual currents and so on will have to be checked. River traffic. Commercial. Oil tankers, freight, fishing and pleasure boating will all need to be followed up.'

Laurence nodded. 'Guv.'

Roberts turned back to the room again. 'At the same time, we need to keep an open mind as to the method and original site of body deposition. Was this from a boat? Off the pier? Could the deceased, for instance, have been rolled over the sea wall and then been carried by the tide? Or was she simply placed where she was found? Someone will be tasked with scoping CCTV coverage. That includes the entire length of the seafront, the high street, pubs, clubs and restaurants, also any footage from cameras at garages and private driveways. We need to build a picture of Rachel's last known activities, try to construct a timeline, a map of travel in her last day or so.'

Roberts scratched under an armpit. 'In addition, we need to note all vehicle traffic against Automatic Number Plate Recognition and get lists of names and addresses. Is all that clear?'

He took a packet of Polo mints from his trouser pocket, started to unwrap them, then changed his mind and put them away.

'Rachel was dressed in a provocative manner: miniskirt, skimpy top, black underwear and her boots were of a fetishistic nature. So this may suggest that she might have been working in the sex industry. But, once again, people, let's keep an open mind on this.'

Laurence held up his pen. Roberts looked over. 'Yes? Alan?'

Laurence stood up behind his desk. 'As regards the clothing. The skirt, top and bra are of a type available in several high street retail outlets. The boots are advertised on several sites on the internet. But are also on sale from a local shop. Called, um,' he checked a piece of paper on the desk in front of him, 'Iniquity.'

Roberts was about to turn away but when Laurence made no move to sit down he asked, 'You've got something else?'

21

'Not really, guv,' Laurence cleared his throat, 'just, if you're buying footwear, you'd most likely want to try them on, right?'

'Fair point.' Roberts nodded and Laurence retook his seat. 'Someone will be tasked with visiting the shop, getting till receipts, looking at any CCTV and so on. Did Rachel visit the shop in person? Did she pay by cash or debit or credit card?'

Cat glanced over at Pearson. Knowing this was the sort of work he preferred, out on the street, interviewing people, rather than staying in the incident room, hitting the phones. Or stuck behind a computer. So, despite being Deputy SIO, Pearson would probably allocate this task to himself. Which, hopefully, meant Cat going with him.

'As regards media strategy,' Roberts said, 'unfortunately the press seem to have already got wind of something – I don't want to find out about any leaks to the media coming from within this team. Am I making myself clear?' Doing another slow scan of the assembled officers. 'It has been decided, for the moment, that the sexual alignment of the deceased is subject to non-disclosure. As far as anyone outside this room is concerned, and until we decide to tell them otherwise, we are simply investigating the death of a young girl. Is that understood?'

3

EXTRACT FROM TRANSCRIPT OF SESSION HELD ON 31 AUGUST

The subject was more responsive than on prior occasions and even showed a marked improvement from his previous visit. On the whole, questions only had to be asked once and the answers came more readily. These were, however, still somewhat confused and disjointed. Clarification needed to be sought on more than one occasion. The subject's demeanour was also calmer throughout, although he did become quite distressed at one point. As a result, the session was terminated prematurely.

AF: Where are you?

RL: In the dark . . . Always in the dark.

AF: In the hospital?

RL: Yes.

AF: The same place as before?

RL: Always the same place ... Always in the dark.

AF: Who are you?

RL: I don't know.

AF: How long have you been here?

RL: Always. I have been here ... always. I will be here ... always.

AF: What can you see?

RL: Dark. A curtain. A line of light. The weave of the curtain. Other beds. Other bodies.

AF: What can you hear?

RL: Traffic. Breathing. The sound of an aeroplane. The wheels of a ... trolley ... metal ... on metal ... the needle.

AF: A needle? You can hear a needle?

RL: Yes. The needle is coming ...

AF: You want the needle?

24

RL: No . . . sleep.

AF: Sleep? You want to sleep now?

RL: No.

AF: Sleep is good, yes?

RL: No . . . sleep is bad. Sleep is . . . bad.

AF: OK. OK. Sleep is bad. Then what? After sleep. What comes after sleep?

RL: Pain . . . can't breathe . . . needle . . . needle . . . can't breathe . . . dark . . . then . . . white pain . . . burning . . . the smell.

AF: Good. Good. Tell me about the pain.

RL: Before the pain I was . . . someone. Someone else.

AF: And now? Do you know who you are?

RL: I don't know . . . always the same questions. I don't know . . . why do you all keep asking me the same questions?

AF: OK. It's OK. Don't cry. You're doing really well. I think we'll leave it there for today.

4

Looking up, Cat had been surprised to find the incident room almost full. She hadn't noticed the officers drifting slowly in for the evening meeting, her attention elsewhere for the past twenty minutes or so. Busy on her computer, glancing over every so often at Pearson: sitting in the chair opposite, a phone pressed between his shoulder and his left ear, writing furiously in his A4 Major Investigation notebook. Talking to an expert advisor recommended by the National Crime Agency. Finding out about the process of gender reassignment. And, judging by the frowning, the eye-rubbing, finding out just a little too much. Occasionally underlining. Or crossing out. Or, possibly, just doodling. The counselling: scratching at the back of his neck with his biro. The hormone therapy: fiddling with the phone cord. The surgery: wincing, sucking air in through his teeth, crossing his legs.

Now, he put the receiver down and stood up, addressing the assembled officers, referring every so often to his notes.

'Genetically,' he said, 'the deceased is male. A limited blood

27

screen performed by the pathologist found that both X and Y chromosomes were present. As were heightened levels of oestrogen. This accounts for the secondary female characteristics of the deceased, such as the growth of rudimentary breasts.'

'So ... what?' Roberts asked, dropping his jacket onto a desk, undoing the top button of his shirt and loosening his tie. 'We're talking about someone in the early stages of ... what's the correct terminology these days?'

'Gender reassignment,' Pearson supplied.

Roberts nodded. 'Presumably, in order to do that you'd need to be registered with a GP? Undergo some kind of psychiatric evaluation? Be issued with a prescription for the medication?'

'Depending on what stage of the process she was at, yes.'

'In which case she's likely to be in the healthcare system. Let's follow that up. What kind of medication are we talking about?'

'As far as I can tell,' said Pearson, 'the same kind of pills doctors prescribe post-menopause for HRT, something akin to a contraceptive. But they're readily available from overseas internet pharmacies, so it's possible our deceased was self-administering. You can also get the surgery abroad. The current destination of choice being Thailand.' Pausing. 'But it's also possible that the ultimate goal was not complete transition, just enhancement of female characteristics through hormone replacement.'

'Point taken,' Roberts rubbed his chin, scratched under an armpit, 'but let's say the goal was complete transition and she wanted to avoid going through the healthcare system ... the medication and the surgery is going to be expensive, right? Which might be a motivation for working in the sex industry.'

Crossing the room he opened a window. Cat stared beyond him and into the night. The orange street light outside, by some weird

28

optical illusion – a combination of the condensation-streaked interior and the rain-spattered exterior – was reflected twice in one of the panes. The amber eyes of some primeval beast.

'Any progress on cause of death?'

Pearson flipped back through the pages of his notebook until he found the right place.

'Just give us the gist,' Roberts said. 'It's getting late. We'll put the full report on one of the incident boards later.'

Staring down at his notes, Pearson's mind went back to the post-mortem ...

Bannister had looked up from her examination of the body, addressing a girl in her twenties.

'What is the typical mechanism of drowning?'

She had been introduced to Pearson as Melissa, a trainee pathologist, recently qualified from medical school. Her first day on the job. Bearing up quite well, he thought, although from his position in the viewing gallery above – leaning forward so he could use the handrail to rest his chin on folded arms – her eyes, behind wire-rimmed round glasses, were perhaps a little too wide, her skin a little too pale. Why were so many pathologists female? he wondered. What was the fascination with death for these young girls?

As if learned by rote – Pearson imagined countless nights spent in draughty student digs, wrapped in a duvet, hunched over a textbook – and, with some expectation of less-than-perfect recall, Melissa recited: 'The victim will inhale water into the lungs which will be churned into a foam. This may appear as blood-specked froth at the mouth and nose, or more likely be apparent in the windpipe and lungs. There may be signs of blood and even haemorrhaging of the sinuses.'

29

'Good,' said Bannister. 'Now, would you like to examine our deceased's mouth and airways?'

Bannister stepped back from the stainless steel table, exposing the naked body. The Y-incision had been made. The chest opened. The ribs and internal organs removed. But the scalp had not yet been peeled forward from the skull. Rachel's face was still visible. After a momentary hesitation Melissa took a torch and gently opened the girl's jaw. Bending close. Taking her time. Carefully examining inside the mouth. The throat. The nostrils. Before turning with a worried look on her face and shaking her head at Bannister. 'I can't find any.'

'OK. So can you think of any reason why the foam might not be present?'

Melissa thought for a moment then brightened. 'The action of the water? Maybe it was washed away while she was immersed in the sea?'

'Good.' Bannister nodded. 'Any other indicators we can look for?'

'We could check if the lungs appear swollen, spongy or saturated by water?'

'And how do we test this?'

'Mmm, manually?'

Bannister nodded. 'Go ahead.'

Melissa picked up a lung from a silver specimen tray, holding it in her hands. Squeezing and stretching the moist, pink tissue between latex-covered fingers. Drowning. Not a way Pearson would want to die, given the choice, his knowledge of the sequence of events. The desperate attempt in the first few minutes not to breathe. Followed by the inevitable inhalation of water. The coughing. The spluttering. Gulping in more water which tears and burns the chest and airways. Panic. The natural

30

instinct for survival taking over. Hands clawing ineffectually to gain purchase. Legs thrashing, kicking for the surface. Finally, the fight lost. Slipping away with a feeling of calm and peace from oxygen deprivation into unconsciousness. Cardiac arrest. Brain death. Better a quick exit, a gun in the mouth. A squeeze of the trigger and blow out your brain stem. The burned-out American cop of popular myth. Not that hard to get a gun in this country. If you knew where to go. Who to speak to. The fingers of his right hand strayed to the gold band on the ring finger of his left, applying pressure, turning it around and around. Women favoured an overdose of pills, he had read, in the mistaken belief that they would slip gracefully away. Pearson knew from experience that in many cases the suicide would simply asphyxiate and drown in their own vomit. There was a tenderness, a soreness, in the pad of his left palm. The beginnings of a callus.

'What else might we do?' Bannister asked.

'Could we test the blood and organs for diatoms?'

'We could; diatoms being ... ? And, remember, it's always best to try and couch your observations in layman's terms,' Bannister nodded in Pearson's direction, 'whenever there are observers present in the gallery.'

Melissa looked up at him, blushing slightly. 'They're microscopic algae found both in salt and fresh water.'

'Correct. And what's the purpose of the test?'

'It's an indication of whether someone was alive when they entered the water ... '

'Because?' Bannister prompted.

'If diatoms are present in the organs then it's because they travelled there via the lungs and then the bloodstream.'

*

31

'Although the pathologist will not definitively rule out that drowning may have played a part,' said Pearson, 'she did say that it seems unlikely, as the normal indicators of death by drowning are not present. No foam in the airways. No saturation of the lungs. No expectation that diatoms – microscopic algae – will be found when they test the internal organs and run more complex blood screening.'

'Which means,' Roberts said, 'that she was dead when she entered the water, right? So, what is the likely cause of death?'

'What are the signs of asphyxiation?' Bannister had asked.

'Petechiae?' Melissa ventured tentatively.

Bannister moved aside once again so that Melissa could carry out her examination. The younger woman bent close to the body, gently opening each eyelid in turn, carefully examining the eye. After a minute she looked up and nodded. 'Definite pinpoint haemorrhaging in the conjunctivas.'

'Good.' Catching the movement as Pearson tried, surreptitiously, to check his watch, Bannister said, 'As our guest seems to be in somewhat of a hurry, I think we'll have to postpone our examination of the internal organs for petechiae. However, the presence of petechiae does not, in itself, prove strangulation, nor does the absence of petechiae disprove it. What other indicators of strangulation might you observe?'

'Fracture of the hyoid bone?'

Bannister nodded. 'Correct. In this case, fracture of the hyoid bone is not observed, but this is not uncommon, as it only occurs in less than a third of strangulations. Hanging, for instance, can be administered with surprisingly little force, leaving the hyoid bone intact. The evidence which the uninformed' – Pearson had wondered at this point whether this particular remark might be directed towards him – 'presume to be associated with suicidal hanging – for instance, rope burns or ligature abrasions – might only occur when the body has been left suspended for a number of hours after death. If the ligature is removed at the time of death there may be no external marking of the skin – as in this case. What might we consider doing next?'

'Dissection of the neck?' Melissa suggested.

Bannister selected a scalpel from a tray of instruments, bending over the body, once again obscuring Pearson's view. 'Let's assume then,' she said, 'that our deceased has been strangled. Talk me through the likely mechanism of strangulation.'

'Pressure on the jugular veins would have prevented venous blood returning from the brain' – a hesitation, a glance towards Pearson – 'and the victim would have become unconscious because of the backing up of blood. This would have been followed by depressed respiration and asphyxiation.'

'And how could we prove this?'

'By taking some brain tissue samples?'

'We could.' Then, still bent over the body, but addressing Pearson, 'Only a slight, prolonged pressure is needed to restrict blood flow in this way and limit oxygen delivery.'

'Dissection showed damage to the internal structure of the neck,' said Pearson, 'so our likely cause of death is strangulation. But the pathologist can't say how the strangulation may have occurred.'

'Not definitively,' said Roberts sarcastically.

'In the case of compression of the jugular vein,' Bannister had continued, 'it can take several minutes to lapse into unconsciousness and be completely painless.' She looked from the girl's body and up at Pearson in the viewing gallery. Saying the phrase he was repeating now to the crowded incident room: 'The same mechanism has been observed in the accidental deaths occurring after the practice of autoerotic asphyxiation.'

In the silence that followed Cat glanced, once again, out of the window as the amber-eyed beast expelled its cold, damp breath into the room.

5

It looked, Cat thought, like a photograph of any pretty, fresh-faced young girl. A university student, perhaps, from some foreign, more exotic, country. Someone who you might meet by chance while travelling in your gap year. If it wasn't for the eyes. They were just unreal enough to suggest that there might be something awry with the image. Just that little bit too conspicuously superimposed. The sunken, closed lids overlaid by a slightly crazy, fixed stare.

An artefact of the computer enhancement. The picture had been taken that morning by a SOCO, after the external examination had taken place. After the body had been cleaned and prepared. Before the internal post-mortem had been performed. Cat leant forward and took a cigarette from the packet on her coffee table and put it in her mouth. Or maybe it had been taken after the post-mortem. She ran her fingertip around the outline of the girl. As if she might actually be able to feel whether the likeness had been captured following the cadaver's reconstruction. The skull repaired. The scalp pulled back into place. The empty chest

35

cavity packed with cotton wool and the bagged internal organs restored. The ribs reinstated. The Y-incision sewn back together. The harsh overhead lighting, the camera's flash, the digital remodelling had all conspired to wash out all the colour, the life, from the face of the girl they had found on the beach. Cyane vanishing *into insubstantial rivulets. Nothing solid remained, when lastly the lifeblood coursing her weakened veins was taken over by water* ...

Had she still been at work, had she voiced these opinions aloud, Pearson – staring into his plastic cup, slowly turning it around – might have said, 'Yeah. Best not say anything like that in front of Roberts, eh?' before pitching the empty cup into the bin. Ovid – well, it might be classical literature but it was still all about depravity, wasn't it? Cannibalism. Incest. Rape. Murder ...

Cat picked up the disposable lighter and lit her cigarette. Took an appreciative draw. Put the lighter next to her ashtray on the coffee table. All the indications were that Rachel hadn't drowned. Hadn't spent the final few minutes of her life gulping in lungfuls of cold, salty water in a last, desperate, panic-stricken attempt to survive. Had, instead, been slowly strangled and probably slipped away calmly and relatively painlessly into unconsciousness and then death. Cat exhaled a cloud of blue smoke. Only after her passing had Rachel then been mutilated and laid bare. This was the reality, no matter how respectfully and even reverently the post-mortem had been performed. Once they knew her true identity, of course, the perusal, the scrutiny, the dissection of her private life would begin.

An hour earlier DS Laurence had riffled through the paperwork on his desk, pulling out a sheet of A4 and placing it on top of the pile. Standing up, he had glanced down at his notes and, with the tip of his biro marking his place, addressed the room.

'Low tide was at seventeen fifty-six the previous evening. High tide at oh-oh fifteen. The next low tide was at oh-six thirty-two.'

'Giving us a window,' Roberts said, 'if the body went into the water before or around high tide and came to rest before low tide, of around six or seven hours. What time was it called in?'

'According to our eyewitness he saw the body just before half-seven. The telephone call he made to the emergency services is logged at oh-seven thirty-two.'

'And the pathologist said that Rachel had not been in the water more than three or four hours,' Roberts said, 'which, by the time she examined her, puts it around four or five in the morning, three at the outside, right? Which suggests that she was more than likely dumped where we found her.'

Cat leant forward again, tapping the ash from her cigarette into the ashtray. The death of a young girl now moving into the routine. A procedure to be observed. Facts to be gathered. Processes to be followed. The logging of river traffic had been put on the back-burner for now; Roberts wanting to concentrate in areas where he believed significant material progress might be made. CCTV coverage in the vicinity of the deposition site was non-existent. Footage had been collected from further along the seafront, in the high street and outside pubs, clubs and restaurants. It was now being collated before being allocated to specific officers for viewing.

Cat took a final drag on her cigarette, replaying the crime-scene video in her mind. The camera moving up the body in a slow pan. The boots. The miniskirt. The torn silk top. The small, once beautiful face turned to the camera's cold eye. It was difficult to grasp that Rachel wasn't a girl. Not really. Not yet, anyway. Cat ground out her cigarette in the ashtray and, with an effort, wrenched her eyes away from the photograph. The only photograph in the room. Looking around, she became aware once again of just how devoid of any personality the room, the whole flat, actually was. There was precious little furniture. Two art deco-style brown sofas set at right angles to each other. The wooden coffee table. The flat-screen TV on one wall, the other walls bare. There was nothing whatsoever of a personal nature. None of the objects any normal person might collect as they passed through their lives. The ornaments. The mementoes. The keepsakes . . .

The souvenir pottery houses neatly arranged along the window ledge. Jaywick. Dymchurch. Frinton-on-Sea. The cast-iron Edwardian-style fireplace. The garishly patterned green carpet. It could have been any sitting room from Pearson's childhood. A childhood spent in the East End of London, where a trip to the seaside might only last a matter of days. More usually, just a few hours, but was still something out of the ordinary, something to be celebrated and remembered. A childhood where armchairs still had lace-trimmed headrests and antimacassars and front parlours were 'kept for best'.

Could have been, if it wasn't for the commode. Emptied, he noted, but not cleaned. Not properly, at any rate. The metal hospital-type bed, a call button hanging over the headrest. The ugly NHS wheelchair in which his mother sat, occasionally dabbing at rheumy eyes with a balled-up paper handkerchief. And the smell. The smell of hospitals and retirement homes. The smell of sickness and old age. The smell that had greeted him at the front door. Buzzed in by one of the care assistants. The smell that had followed them across the communal sitting room as they made small talk. Pearson asking where his mother might be. The care assistant saying, 'I think Mrs Pearson stayed in her room after her visitor.' The smell lingering on the stairs as Pearson made his way up. The smell of institutional kitchens and human waste.

'You've had a visitor, I hear,' Pearson had said, entering the room, slipping off his suit jacket and sitting in the armchair.

'No,' his mother replied, 'just you.'

A lie. Obviously. But Pearson didn't have any inclination, any energy to pursue it. Instead passing his mother the family-size bar of Dairy Milk he'd brought and then asked the usual questions. Questions he already knew the answers to.

'How've you been?' Much the same.

'What've you been up to?' Not a lot. A wash. Breakfast. Sitting in a chair. Lunch. Sitting in another, or maybe even the same, chair. Tea. Back to her room. The tedium only broken perhaps by some physiotherapy. Some minor scandal. Or, if she were very lucky, by a punch-up between a couple of the other residents. The questions he asked just to have something to say. The big question ignored, skirted around. When was she going back to her bungalow? In all probability, she wasn't. She wasn't capable of looking after herself at the moment. At least in Pearson's opinion. In the opinion of all the health-care professionals. Probably wouldn't be capable of independent living again. And he couldn't – didn't want to – be her long-term carer. So, as usual, they had quickly run out of things to say to each other. Had sat in silence in the overheated room. The only sounds the blaring television set, the snapping off of squares of chocolate from the bar of Dairy Milk.

Pearson had watched the mechanical movement of his mother's hand between lap and mouth. Clawed. Awkward. As if there were little or no feeling in the unnaturally pink palms and fingertips. The yellowed nails. Noticed, too, the sly looks in his direction, as if he had forgotten something. Something he should have brought in. Something he should have done. Something he should have said, maybe. She wouldn't simply come out and tell him. Just sit and wait until he figured it out for himself. She was concentrating on the telly. Worrying, every so often, at a lock of her thinning hair.

Pearson's mind was back on the investigation. A hair had been found in the folds of the girl's clothing during the 'gross examination' stage of the post-mortem. The body carefully unwrapped from the plastic sheeting wound around her at the scene. Bannister meticulously scrutinising the body before it was undressed—

'You might as well go,' his mother said. Not looking at him. She hadn't been looking at him for some time now, he realised.

'You sure?' Pearson asked. Already getting to his feet, one arm in his suit jacket. 'Do you want me to bring you anything next time?' This question, always asked, always elicited the same response. A request for something, yes. But asked as if it wasn't really that important to her, as if she were doing him a favour. And it never failed to irritate him. If he didn't bring it she would sulk. Even though, half the time, she'd insist, when he did bring whatever she asked for, that she didn't want it. Would swear blind that she'd never asked him to bring it in the first place.

'If you're coming past the fish shop you could get me cod and chips.' She knew he wouldn't be. Knew the fish shop wasn't on his way. Knew he'd have to make a special trip to get it.

'OK,' he said, 'cod and chips it is.' Sliding his other arm into his jacket. 'You sure you don't mind if I go?' But her attention was already back on her programme.

Pearson was halfway down the stairs when it hit him. She'd been to the hairdresser. Or, more likely, a hairdresser had visited the home. Hence the sly looks. The hand constantly going to the newly applied shampoo and set. Or whatever hairdo it was that old women had these days. Some kind of perm, at any rate. He

40

considered for a moment going back. Complimenting her. Saying how nice it looked. Then again, maybe not. Way too late now for that. More than likely, knowing his mother, it would only make matters worse. He'd pay for it next time, fish and chips or not. So, instead, he turned away and headed down the stairs, his mind back, once again, on the case.

6

'Mr Morris would like a word.'

The man who stepped into Frank Pearson's path was big. Too big for the grey suit he wore. He had close-shaven ginger hair. An ineffectual attempt to hide the onset of male pattern baldness. A wide face; young but jowly. The colour of corned beef. The colour, in winter, of the legs of underage miniskirted girls on street corners. He was sweating. Puffing slightly from his jog across the car park. Moving from foot to foot, he settled himself in place, an immovable object. Holding one wrist with the other hand. Cocking his head to one side and slightly backwards; the classic hard-man pose. Pearson had heard the door shut behind him. Had spotted the car as soon as he had exited the retirement home. Then again, how could you miss a white Rolls-Royce with tinted windows? He'd heard the quick footsteps, leather soles scuffing the wet tarmac: had been expecting this. His overcoat collar up against the drizzle, Pearson took a hand from his pocket. Tugging at an earlobe. Smiling. Something he'd seen in a Humphrey Bogart film.

'Is that right?'

The man pursed his lips and nodded over Pearson's shoulder. 'Yeah, he'd like you to take a little ride with us.'

Pearson turned, glancing towards the Roller, then turned back. 'Say please.'

'What?' The other man shifted uneasily. Unwilling to lose face. But unsure of his next move.

'Say please,' Pearson repeated. Heard the sound of an electric window opening behind him.

'Frank, stop fucking about. Just get in the car.' Then, after a pause: 'Please.'

'There you go,' said Pearson, raising his eyebrows at the man in front of him. Smiling again. 'See what politeness gets you?' He said, turning away. The car door opened and Pearson got in.

'What was that all about?'

Jack Morris. Pushing seventy by now, Pearson guessed. His size, though, his sheer physicality, was a presence in the interior of the car. Hair salt and pepper. Eyes seemingly always on the verge of tears. His skin an unnatural grey. And even though he was inside the car he wore a camel-hair overcoat.

Pearson shrugged. 'He only had to say please, Jack.'

Morris shook his head. 'Kids, eh? No fucking manners.' He chuckled. 'I thought Tony was going to have a stroke there. Not the brightest of lads. But he's family – what can you do? My sister's grandson. My great-nephew.'

Pearson felt the suspension shift as Tony eased himself into the front seat. Morris shook his head again. 'Fucking great pudden, more like.'

Looking up, he nodded towards the rear-view mirror and the car moved off. Morris pulled a packet of cigarettes and a slim gold lighter from his inside breast pocket; shivering, he pulled the coat tighter around him. Pearson noticed for the first time how thin the shoulders were under the fabric, the slight tremor in the old man's hands as he lit up. Morris took a deep lungful of smoke, exhaling with satisfaction, took in a wheezy breath which became a wracking cough. There was a nasty scar on his neck, the suggestion of a series of past deep incisions which had healed badly. Leaving the edges red, strangely smooth and shiny. Finally, getting his breath back, Morris took a handkerchief from his coat pocket and dabbed his lips. Took another drag of his cigarette. Looking away. Flicking ash into the ashtray.

'Thought it was you. Recognised you going in,' he said, gazing wistfully at his cigarette. 'You didn't stay long.' He took a last drag, briefly enjoying Pearson's discomfort before grinding out the cigarette. 'Supposed to be giving them up,' he said by way of explanation. 'We've spent a lot of time talking, your mum and me,' indicating out of the car's window with his chin, 'about the old days – catching up.' Pearson said nothing. 'You never knew your dad, did you? He never was much company for her. Not much of a talker, your old man. Bit like you.' Pearson wasn't going to bite. Morris shook his head. 'You've got no idea how it was for her, living with him. What she had to put up with.'

Pearson felt a brief flash of anger. But how much did he really know about his father? After all, he'd left when Pearson was still only a kid. So why should he be bothered by Morris's snide insinuations? Why should he feel any loyalty to his memory? He hadn't really thought about his father in years; had made a point of not thinking about him. All the same, he begrudged hearing it from the likes of Morris.

'Me and your mum were close. Long before your dad came on the scene,' Morris went on. 'Just friends, that's all. But he came along and offered her something I couldn't. He was a lot older than her, a safer option. Things like that mattered in those days. I can't blame her, she was a decent woman, what would she want with . . . with someone like me?'

'Didn't stop you sniffing round, though.'

Morris shook his head again. 'It wasn't like that.'

Pearson remembered his mother saying the same thing: *It's not like that, Frank. We're just good friends.*

Looking down, turning the cigarette packet over and over in his hand, Morris said, 'Did you know I asked her to marry me, after your dad left?'

Pearson snorted. 'Why would she marry you?'

'No, Frank,' Morris said, taking a cigarette out of the packet and looking directly at Pearson, 'the question is: why wouldn't she?' Pearson said nothing. 'Because of you, Frank. You hated me, and she knew it.' He laughed. 'You know, when you make that face you look a lot like her.'

Pearson shook his head. 'I couldn't see you bringing up another man's kid.'

Morris examined his cigarette, rolling it between his fingers, sighed. 'Look, the point is, your mum hasn't got long left. She knows that.' This was news to him. She hadn't said so. 'I just want her to be as comfortable as possible. If that means paying for her to go somewhere else, somewhere better, somewhere more expensive . . .'

'If she wants to go somewhere else, I'll pay for it.' He wouldn't. Pearson couldn't afford it. They both knew it.

'Look,' said Morris, 'the offer's there, right? She doesn't have to know it's me pay—'

'I'll pay for it.'

The car jerked suddenly to a halt, Morris tipping forward almost into Pearson's lap. Someone banged on the car bonnet. A group

46

of teenagers crossed the road in front of the Rolls-Royce. Pissed. Shouting. Giving the occupants of the car the finger. Morris nodded out of the window.

'Look at this lot – no fucking respect! Was a time the name Jack Morris meant something.'

If there was, then Pearson wasn't aware of it. To his knowledge Morris had never been anything other than a reasonably success-ful, if small-time, businessman. The owner of a few local betting shops, a couple of minicab firms. Recently, so he'd heard, acquiring a part interest in one of the clubs in town. All of them cash-rich, offering him a chance to avoid paying tax and VAT: an opportu-nity for money-laundering. He'd always suspected that there was something a bit dodgy about Morris. He'd just never been able to prove it.

'Look at them. They look like they dress out of the fucking Poundshop. What's that all about? It's like a badge of honour nowadays, being poor. When I was a little kid I had to wear hand-me-downs. And I hated every fucking minute of it. It just made me all the more determined to work hard to—'

A shout. A jarring, metallic explosion of liquid and foam as a can of supermarket lager hit the car's side window.

'Was a time,' fumed Morris, 'I'd've got out and give them all a slap.'

Pearson looked out of the window. Kids. The oldest one couldn't have been more than seventeen. Of course, he could get out. Flash his warrant card. Lay down the law. And probably get a load of verbal in return. If it didn't escalate, if he didn't have to call for uniformed assistance, what would be gained? Half an hour of his evening wasted. One of them making the 'wanker' sign as soon as his back was turned. In the end he couldn't be arsed. Not for Morris. The car jerked into action and a minute or so later they turned on to the seafront, following the route Pearson had taken that morning. Morris was toying with his cigarette and lighter again. Pearson hoped he wasn't planning to light another fag. It was already too smoky in the car, his eyes were beginning to sting. To his relief, Morris had second thoughts. He gestured instead with his unlit cigarette out of the window.

'When I was a kid, this was a day out.' Indicating the space. The absence of the elaborate illuminations of the old Southend 'Golden Mile' that used to be strung out beside and above the road. 'Bit of a drive from Bow. We'd come all the way down here in the old man's Austin Seven, just to see the lights. When I was older, a few beers, a bag of chips, a punch-up. Or if I was really lucky a shag under the pier.' Morris lapsed into silence for a few minutes, then leaning forward past Pearson he tapped on the glass partition. It slid open and Morris said, 'Stick the Rolls in the car park here and wait. We'll get out and stretch our legs for a bit.'

Now, thought Pearson, we get to the real reason I'm here. When he looked out of the window, he was surprised to find that they were in the car park by the Crowstone. They got out of the car and walked up, over, then down the steps onto the deserted seafront. All evidence of the day's activities gone. Further up, a foot of blue and white police tape attached to a metal pole, flapping and crackling in the gusting wind. Cupping his hands, Morris finally lit his cigarette. He smoked in silence for a few moments.

'Bad business, all this,' he said, exhaling smoke, pointing out at the Crowstone with his cigarette.

'Yeah,' agreed Pearson, non-committal. It had been a long day. The last thing he wanted to talk about right at the moment was the dead girl.

'These people usually get caught though, right?' Morris prompted.

48

'Mostly,' Pearson said. Even he could hear the doubtful tone in his voice, the tiredness.

'Mostly?' Morris echoed, taking a drag on his cigarette, eyes narrowed against the smoke. 'I thought it was easy these days, what with DNA and all that?'

'DNA's only useful if whoever did it left some on the body or some of the clothing.'

After a minute Morris asked, 'You got a name yet?'

'Not yet.'

'Won't you be able to use DNA to find that out?'

'She'll only be on the database if she's been arrested.'

'But then it's pretty quick, right?'

'It can be done on the same day,' Pearson admitted reluctantly, 'but that costs extra, and there's a squeeze on budgets at the moment.' Then, in an attempt to close the subject, 'Plus we're not even sure that it isn't just an accident. So it won't be top priority, which means you're probably talking a couple of days.'

'And if there's no match?'

Pearson shrugged. 'We can ask them to look for a familial match. See if a member of her family's been arrested.' Irritated suddenly by all the questions, he asked, 'Why are you so interested all of a sudden?'

Morris's turn to shrug this time. 'No reason.'

He took a last drag of his cigarette. Was just about to flick the dog-end out onto the beach, when he seemed to change his mind. Pearson was surprised to see him pinch out the end with his fingers and replace it in the pack. Behind him, there came the sound of leather soles scuffing the pavement and, turning around, he saw Tony standing a little way off, watching them.

'Tony will give you a lift back to your car. I'll stay here a bit.'

Turning back, Pearson saw Morris was looking out across the

estuary, apparently lost in thought. He studied the old man's face for a few moments. The grey skin. The livid scar on his neck. What's your real interest in this? he wondered.

'My offer still stands, Frank,' Morris said, 'about the nursing home. I'd like to help.'

'I'll think about it,' Pearson said. Grudgingly. If Morris heard the resentment in his voice he showed no sign.

Pearson followed Tony back towards the car park. At the top of the concrete steps he stopped briefly and looked back. The old man was still staring out across the river. And from the way he stood, huddled in his overcoat, drawn in on himself, shoulders heaving, Pearson could swear that he was crying.

Day Two

Day Two

7

'So? What?' DCI Roberts asked, rolling a pen across the top of the desk: grey metal, utilitarian, careworn; the bottom drawer sitting slightly proud where the runners were buckled. It was, Cat thought, entirely in keeping with the rest of the building. A three-storey, concrete monstrosity built in the early sixties and badly in need of repair and refurbishment. Roberts was waggling the biro at Pearson.

'You're saying that this Jack Morris is gay? That maybe he's in some kind of relationship with our girl?' Pausing, momentarily. But before Pearson could reply, asking, 'Or maybe he's just paying her for sex?'

They were in Roberts's office. Best described as 'functional', it was dominated by the large desk. To the DCI's left, a three-tier wire in-tray: overflowing. A flat-screen computer monitor, the key-board pushed to one side. To his right, a three-tier wire out-tray: all but empty. On the wall behind, heavy white wooden shelving: cluttered with box files, ring binders, cardboard document wallets and scruffy stacks of papers bound with elastic bands. In the right-hand corner of the room sat a dented filing cabinet, the same grey metal as the desk.

Cat and Pearson sat in the visitors' chairs, only two now usable. There had been a loud crack as Pearson sat down, the orange, moulded-plastic seat coming away from the metal legs, tipping him violently sideways and almost landing him on the floor. Pearson had had to suffer Roberts' shaking head, his exasperated glare, as he swapped the chair with its neighbour.

To Cat, this office always felt gloomy, despite the half-glazed door on one wall, the window opposite. Outside: a bleak square. A red-brick wall. The bare branches of a row of trees. To the right: the council offices, the thirteen-storey tower block; to the left, the magistrates court, the holocaust memorial garden – no more than a raised brick flowerbed containing some bulbs and shrubs. In the centre: the fountain, never holding more than a few inches of water, a low brick wall enclosing three twenty-foot shard-like monoliths of black cement and glass-fibre. Etched in turn with a medieval fisherman, a monk and the symbols of the town crest. It had been designed by one of the nation's most highly rated sculptors. Not that you'd be able to find anyone in Southend who knew it. Or might care, come to that. The view had never been the most inspiring prospect at the best of times. And as the light level outside dimmed, and the rain again started to drum against the glass, it all seemed even more depressing than usual ...

Pearson shrugged. 'I'm not saying that. Just that he was showing an interest, that's all.' But thinking, could Jack Morris be gay? Could he have got it all wrong? Could he have misinterpreted the old man's motives regarding his mother? Had he misjudged Morris all these years? *It's not like that, Frank. We're just good friends.* Is that what his mother had meant? And hadn't Morris himself said, 'What would she want with ... with someone like me?'

54

Roberts asked, 'So you haven't heard any rumours?'

'About Jack Morris being gay? No. But these things don't always necessarily get out, do they?'

'These days?' Roberts said doubtfully, starting to tap the biro on the desk. Frowning. Looking up. 'And remind me again how you know Morris?'

'He's a friend of my mother's. From way back, when we lived in London.'

'And that's all?'

'That's all.'

'It's just, with the other business ...' Roberts gestured vaguely over his shoulder with the pen. As if the 'other business' – the 'other business' being Sean Carragher – was behind him. Probably, thought Pearson, he hoped it was. Roberts held his gaze for half a minute. Then expelled a breath through his nose. 'All right.' Dropping the pen onto the desk, turning away, he opened the top drawer. Took out a packet of Polos. Unwrapping them, he offered the packet to Cat who shook her head. Then to Pearson, who took it from him, peeled back the silver paper and prised out a mint.

Cat watched the two men bringing the mints to their lips. Simultaneously opening their mouths. In unison, crunching down noisily. Roberts was shaking his head.

'Some fucking family you are!' Scanning the desktop for something else to fiddle with, he finally settled on a paper clip. 'First your brother-in-law – what's his name?'

'Terry,' Pearson said.

'Yeah, Terry. Terry Milton, right?'

Pearson nodded. Not, it seemed, entirely comfortable with the direction in which the conversation might be headed.

'And now your mother,' Roberts said. 'Anything else you want to tell me?'

There was a sharp rap on the glass pane of the half-glazed door. Roberts sighed. 'For fuck's sake! Doesn't anyone know the meaning of "Do Not Disturb"?' and then, raising his voice, 'Yes?'

The door opened and DCS Andy Curtis entered. Flicking back and forth between two stapled sheets of A4, apparently engrossed. Or, at least, wanting everyone to believe he was.

'Martin . . .' he said. Then, glancing up, taking in the presence of the two lower-ranking officers, half-risen from their seats. He flapped a hand towards the floor, indicating that they should sit back down, before turning back to Roberts. 'Where are we with this . . . um, body . . . on the beach?'

'Declared a male,' said Roberts.

'Male?'

'The deceased was male at birth,' Roberts nodded, 'halfway through gender reassignment.'

'Ah, well,' Curtis said, trying to regain some ground, 'that would at least explain some of the costs incurred through the Force Forensics Lab. I gather there's also some confusion as regards the cause of death?'

'Asphyxiation due to strangulation,' said Roberts.

'Quite. But, as I understand it, no proof of homicide?'

Roberts said nothing. His hands slipping below the desk. Working the paperclip, Cat guessed.

'All I'm saying, Martin, is should we really be treating this as a suspicious death? Mightn't it just as likely be suicide? Or even accidental? In which case, are these requests strictly necessary?' Brow furrowed, Curtis made a show of studying the top sheet of paper again. 'CCTV footage,' turning to the second sheet, 'door-to-door enquiries, ANPR matches—'

'Any news on the media appeal, sir?' cut in Roberts.

'And that's another thing. Officers tied up answering phones, logging calls on the computer system, when their time might be better deployed elsewhere?' Shaking his head. 'We all need to keep an eye on budgets these days, Martin. The cost in man-hours alone of something like this,' flapping the sheets of paper, 'every force in the country is being encouraged to exercise fiscal restraint, to justify every expenditure. I'm not sure you appreciate the financial pressure being applied by the Home Office.' Curtis's gaze drifted around the room, as if looking for an ally.

Pearson cleared his throat. 'There is still the question of the deposition of the body, sir.'

Frowning momentarily, Curtis nodded for him to carry on.

'Even if the death itself was accidental,' Pearson said, 'the PM shows no water in the lungs. Which indicates that death occurred before the body was immersed in the sea. Which in turn makes it more likely that it was put there by a third party. So even if we don't have a murder, as such, we still have maybe "obstructing a coroner" or "preventing the burial of a body".'

'I've just come from a meeting with the Chief Constable,' Curtis said, turning back to Roberts, not quite ready to concede the point. 'He was very keen to stress the need to produce positive metrics when comparing budgetary expenditure against clear-up rates—'

'There is the political aspect to consider in all this, sir,' Roberts said.

'Go on,' Curtis said, reluctantly snagged by the phrase.

'However hard we try to keep a lid on it, the nature of the victim in this is bound to come out one way or another. Something will get leaked to the press. It always does. It's not going to reflect well on us if it is perceived, in any way, that we haven't tried our damnedest to solve this. The force is already viewed in some quarters as unsympathetic to the LGBT community.'

57

'So what are you saying?'

'Only, sir, that any chance of wrapping up this case quickly will depend on a positive identification of the victim. And that would be much more likely with a media appeal.'

Curtis, clearly in two minds, paused momentarily, then gave a grudging sigh.

'Very well. I'll speak to the Chief Constable. But, as I said, the clock's already ticking on this one.' He checked his watch, then made to leave, opening the door. 'And as far as authorising any other expenditure is concerned,' he half turned, 'just bear in mind what I said, Martin.'

The door closed. Roberts shook his head. '"Positive metrics" my arse. He'd be happy if no cases got solved, just as long as we didn't spend any money. You know what this is all about, don't you?' When Pearson looked blank Roberts went on, 'The Assistant Chief Constable's about to officially announce he's moving on. And Curtis thinks his best route into the job is by confiscating the keys to the fucking stationery cupboards.'

'Trouble is,' said Pearson, 'he's probably right.'

Cat watched as Roberts dropped something on the desk. The paperclip. Now bent and twisted out of shape. A petty, personal act of defiance.

'OK.' Roberts took a sheet of paper from the top of his in-tray. 'We've got the preliminary results back on the hair found in our deceased's clothing.' Laying it in front of him and starting to read, 'A single strand. Definitely human ... ' He turned to Cat. 'How much do you know about hair?'

A straightforward question. A precursor to some piece of proffered information, maybe. Or just an attempt to pass on his professional experience. Probably. So why did she feel like it was some kind of test?

'I know that hair goes through distinct, cyclical phases,' Cat said.

'Which are?'

'The anagen, the catagen and the telogen.'

'And for those of us without the benefit of a university education?'

And there it was again. The inverted snobbery. The idea that attending university, *getting* a degree was something to be looked down upon. A 'soft option' for advancement through the ranks. It was, for her, a corollary of the still predominately male force; the all-boys-together attitude, the laddish culture, the casual chauvinism.

'The growing, transitional and resting phases?' Cat ventured.

Roberts nodded. 'All right, and during which phase does the root contain DNA?'

'Well, in all phases, but it contains the most in the growing phase.'

'Because ... ?'

'The cells are dividing?'

Roberts nodded again, picking up the packet of Polos. Test passed. Unless he was just fed-up. 'As the national database only holds samples of nuclear DNA,' he took a mint out of the wrapper and put it into his mouth, 'for the purposes of getting a match, for it to be of any real fucking use to us, the root has to be attached, as the root is the part that contains the nuclear DNA, right? And guess what? According to the lab, the hair we have does not contain the root, is more than likely in its resting phase and was probably shed naturally.' Roberts exhaled heavily. 'Which means that it could've just as easily got onto the deceased's clothing by some kind of secondary transfer. The owner of the hair sits on a sofa. The hair falls out. Our deceased sits on the same sofa some time later and picks up the hair on her clothing.'

'Plus,' said Pearson, 'hair takes a very long time to decompose. Which means that, although we might be able to place the owner of the hair and our deceased at the same place, we've got no way of knowing how long between the shedding of the hair and the transfer onto the clothing. We could be talking days. Weeks even . . . '

Roberts nodded. 'Just going on visual comparison alone,' picking up the report, he passed it over to Pearson, 'the lab boys think it's unlikely to have belonged to our deceased.'

Pearson scanned the paper for a minute. 'It says here that it's grey.'

8

The shop was the last in a row in a run-down side street just off the main shopping centre. A newsagent. An appliance repair shop. A Chinese supermarket. A launderette. The shop itself: unassuming. The word 'Iniquity' tastefully picked out in gilt script on the glass frontage. Discreetly curtained so that any passers-by could not gawp into its interior. The street, of course, was not unfamiliar. Or the shop, come to that. Pearson had just never paid it much attention before. He turned now and looked across the road at his brother-in-law's club. At night the neon sign would flash a white lozenge-shaped outline with 'HIP' in uppercase, shocking pink in the upper left-hand corner. Then 'gnosis' in lowercase, electric blue cursive script in the bottom right. The whole thing remaining illuminated for a few seconds before it went out and the sequence repeated itself. This morning – damp, miserable, overcast – the tubes were unlit, dull and dirt-flecked from the recent rain. Several soggy, rotting leaves caught up in the framework. A good name for a club, Pearson had to admit. A clever play on words. Although predictably most people missed the point. Pronounced it incorrectly. Or else assumed it was a misspelling. Pearson turned back and shouldered his way inside the shop, holding the door to allow Cat to follow.

Nothing too remarkable in here, Cat thought. The usual array of sex toys. Vibrators. Dildos. Mock-leather riding crops. Fluffy handcuffs. And hanging on racks, somebody's idea – presumably a man – of what passed for 'saucy' outfits and titillating underwear. Nylon. Feathers. PVC. Zips. But nothing you couldn't find in any branch of Ann Summers. The acceptable face of sex nestling alongside the mobile phone stores, coffee bars and pound shops in the high street. The young female assistant barely acknowledged their existence, her eyes flicking up only momentarily from the magazine spread out on the counter. Black, back-combed spiky hair. Heavy, black eyeliner and lipstick. Facial piercings: nose, eyebrow, lower lip. All of which did nothing to disguise the unre-markability of a doughy face with bad skin. A threadbare mohair jumper with a high-neck that, along with her hair, gave her the look of someone who had recently been attacked by a flock of crows.

Pearson didn't mind the make-up. The piercings. Didn't even mind that the displaying of his warrant card prompted nothing more than a sullen look. But he did mind that she insisted on chewing gum with her mouth open. He had to fight the urge to reach across the counter, grab her chin, prise her jaws open, reach into her mouth. Take out the gum and drop it into a bin. Instead he slid out a piece of paper from between the covers of the leather slipcase holding his notebook. Deliberately placing it on top of her magazine – to stop the ostentatious licking of the index finger. The snapping of the pages as she turned them over.

'We're trying to trace an item of clothing,' Pearson said. 'Those boots over there?' Nodding towards a display of fetishwear.

'They're not an exclusive range,' the girl said. Bored. Barely looking at the photograph. 'You could probably get them on the internet.'

'But,' Pearson said, tapping the picture of the wet-look PVC boots, 'they could have been bought from here?'

The girl looked up. 'Could've.' Staring blankly back at him. The black mascara thick. Clumped. The white of one eye slightly bloodshot.

'Would you be able to check the serial numbers against your stock?' Staring. Chewing gum. 'Do you keep till rolls? Computer records?'

She shrugged. 'Dunno. S'pose so.'

'Would it be possible to look at them?'

'The owner deals with all that stuff.'

'Is he in? Could I talk to him?'

'It's *her* day off,' she said, emphasising the 'her'. 'I'm not s'posed to disturb her unless there's an emergency.' Chewing the gum. Blowing a little bubble. Cracking it between her teeth.

Pearson sighed. Opening his notebook, taking out his pen. 'What's your name?' *'Don't tell him, Pike!'* a tiny Captain Mainwaring warned from somewhere in the back of his mind.

'Courtney,' said the girl, watching him write it down.

'Courtney . . . ?' prompted Pearson.

'Woods.'

'OK, Courtney Woods, we're investigating a very serious crime. We need to establish whether these items were bought from this shop, when they were bought and by whom – do you understand? If you don't contact the owner right now I will arrest you for obstruction and you will have to close the shop anyway.' When

63

there was still no reaction, Pearson went on, 'While you're up the nick, Courtney, maybe I'll ring Trading Standards? Get them to have a good look around. Maybe give Customs and Excise a bell? I'm sure they'd be interested in going through your VAT receipts – you do understand about VAT? You got any idea how long it takes to justify your VAT returns for the last seven years? How happy d'you think the owner will be about that? Now, you've got exactly one minute. And then I'm going to nick you. Is that enough of an emergency for you?'

After a moment, just long enough to make her point, she turned her back on him and picked up the phone from the rear counter. Talking too quietly for him to hear what was being said. Shooting him the occasional glance over her shoulder. She put the phone down. Took a flier from the counter top. Scrawled an address on the back and pushed it across to Pearson. He picked it up, folding it and tucking it into his slipcase. He took out another piece of paper and placed it on the open magazine in front of them. Turned it to face the girl.

'Do you recognise this person?'

Rachel. The long, dark hair. The delicate features. The over-large, staring eyes. The slightly unreal quality of the computer-enhanced face.

Pearson saw the girl's lips pucker, her face tighten; she swallowed. He thought some of the colour might have drained from her skin. Difficult to tell with her unhealthy complexion. It was obvious the girl in the photograph was dead. Even if he hadn't said they were investigating a 'serious crime'. Still, looking down, Courtney Woods shook her head.

'So, to your knowledge, she hasn't been in here?'

She shook her head, was still shaking her head as Pearson tucked the photographs back into the slipcase. Hearing the sound of clothes hangers moving along a rail behind him, he turned. After a moment, Cat became aware of his gaze and looked over. Looking back down, she saw under her hand a hanger containing underwear. Leather. With straps and buckles. When she glanced back up, Pearson was grinning, taking the piss. Flushing, embarrassed, Cat glared back and mouthed 'Fuck off!'

9

EXTRACT FROM TRANSCRIPT OF SESSION HELD ON 7 SEPTEMBER

The subject responded well to questions, answering fairly promptly. His memory of events was clearly more detailed. The subject was tense early on and towards the end he became confused and extremely distressed. Again, the session had to be terminated prematurely.

AF: OK. Last time, we spoke about the trolley, do you remember, Richard?

RL: Yes.

AF: You know where you are?

RL: Yes. In the dark.

AF: Yes, that's right. In the dark. In the hospital. Now, Richard, concentrate. On the sounds. On what you can hear.

RL: Breathing ... the sound of a trolley ... the squeaking of a wheel ... metal rattling on metal ... I'm frightened ...

AF: You're frightened? Why are you frightened?

RL: The trolley.

AF: You're frightened of the trolley?

RL: Not the trolley ... what's on the trolley.

AF: OK, Richard. Try to relax. That's it. Now, what's on the trolley?

RL: The needle ... the needles.

AF: The needle? A hypodermic needle?

RL: Yes.

AF: You're going to have an injection?

RL: Yes.

AF: You've had injections before?

68

RL: Yes ... lots of injections ... the needle is bad ...

AF: OK, Richard. You're doing really well. The needle is bad. Why is the needle bad?

RL: Sweat .... drool .... jerking .... thrashing around ...

AF: And then?

RL: Sleep.

AF: The Bad Sleep?

RL: Yes. The Bad Sleep.

AF: OK. Good. So every time you have the needle you have sweating, thrashing and the Bad Sleep.

RL: No.

AF: No?

RL: Not every time.

AF: OK, what happens the other times?

RL: Can't breathe ... suffocating .... can't move ... then ... pain ... burning ... white ...

AF: Where is the pain?

RL: It's here ... it's here ... in this room ... it's here ...

AF: No, I mean where do you feel the pain? Where on your body do you feel the pain?

RL: In my head ... always in my head ... can't think ... before ... I was ... someone ...

AF: Who? Who were you?

RL: I don't know ... I don't know ... someone ... I was ... someone ...

AF: Who, Richard. Who were you?

RL: Really, it's a question I haven't considered ...

AF: What is? What's a question you haven't considered?

RL: I don't know ... I don't know ...

AF: OK, Richard. You're upset. We'll leave it there for now. Good. Good. You're doing really well.

Dr Angela Fitzgerald gathered together the sheets of paper from her desk, placing them carefully in the manila folder, closing it. Looking down, now, at the hands resting on the cover. Big hands. The knuckles over-large, knobbly. The blue veins overlaying them bunched and knotted. Ugly hands connected to prominent wrist bones exposed beneath the cuffs of an expensive navy blue designer suit jacket. She was thin, painfully thin. She had seen it all too often on the faces of patients as she stood up behind her desk to greet them. The look of disquiet. Wondering if she might have an eating disorder. Doubting whether such a psychiatrist, such a human being, would be capable of curing their own particular affliction. Their eyes slipping away from hers and drifting past, finally settling on the wall above and beyond her shoulder. Searching for an answer in the warped and patched plaster, the untold applications of layers of cheerless and neutral paint.

It was part of the reason. A large part of the reason. Maybe the only reason, if she were honest with herself, that she was willing to accept the more difficult cases. Those too far gone to bother passing judgement on others. The kind of patients her colleagues were reluctant to see. The ones who were scarcely able to communicate. Barely able to raise their heads and meet your eyes. The most profoundly disturbed patients, where there was scant prospect of any progress. Where few successes could be claimed. Where there would be little, if any, discernible change in the majority of cases. Patients like Richard Lennon . . .

'Nobody wants to steal your brain, Richard.'

Despite her very best efforts, she had sighed. Even though she knew it was bad form. Not something you were meant to do as a psychiatrist. But, really! Just how many times were you supposed to say the same thing? She took a breath now. Tried to keep the annoyance from her voice. Tried. But wasn't sure she was exactly successful. Putting down her pen, Fitzgerald looked up from the notes she had been making in the manila folder.

'We've been through this before, Richard. Nobody wants to steal your brain. We've spoken about this many, many times, Richard. Remember? You're talking about when you were at Runwell? You remember Runwell? The mental institution?'

She nodded encouragingly as the old man briefly glanced up. She thought of him as an old man although she had actually calculated he was probably only in his sixties. And sixty wasn't that old. Not these days. But Richard Lennon looked older; he could easily have been mistaken for someone in his late seventies. Eighties even. Offering no reaction, looking quickly down again, his elbows planted firmly on the wooden armrests of the chair, he hunched forward. Hands hovering over his lap.

'Professor Corsellis had a collection of brains. Brains that he had taken from dead people, Richard. Brains he had taken when he had performed post-mortems. He was a pathologist. Do you know what a pathologist does, Richard?'

There was no answer. She wasn't sure he was actually listening. And, if he was listening, whether he understood. He just stared at his hands. Not moving. Even if he did understand, chances were she would have to say exactly the same thing the next time she saw him. 'A pathologist looks at dead people, Richard. He tries to find out what happened. To find out why they died. So that he can help people who are alive.'

She looked across at Richard Lennon. At the top of his head, to be exact. The unkempt, thinning grey hair. Saying nothing. Staring down at his lap. Slowly uncurling stiff, arthritic hands. Gradually, deliberately, pointing the trembling index fingers at each other.

'Other doctors used to send him brains, Richard. Brains from dead people. That's what you saw. You told me you'd seen lots of brains in jars. That people were having their brains stolen. Do you remember? Maybe someone told you that? That Professor

Corsellis was stealing brains from people? Another patient, perhaps? Or one of the orderlies?' She had asked him this before. And, like before, she got no answer. 'Professor Corsellis didn't steal people's brains, Richard.'

She watched as the old man began again his wearying ritual. The customary concentration on his index fingers. The tremorous hands inching agonisingly towards each other. Shoulders tense, forearms braced against the wooden armrests of the chair. The fingers almost, almost, meeting. Then the sudden, convulsive spasm. The hands slipping past each other: the habitual failure. Swallowing her irritation, she cleared her throat. Waiting a beat, she said, 'Please believe me, Richard. Nobody wants to steal your brain.'

Not exactly true. Wasn't that precisely what had happened? If not his brain, then his mind had been stolen from him. Or as good as. He had been passed across to her at a departmental meeting, as if he were a curiosity, a challenge, rather than a nuisance. His medical history, his personal background, all but unknown. He had been referred to them via a GP, after concerns had been raised about a deterioration in his mental state by the warden who looked after the sheltered accommodation in which he currently lived. Prior to this, as far as they could tell, he had been a long-stay patient at Runwell Hospital in Wickford. Until Runwell was closed and mental health provision had been transferred to Rochford Hospital. Somehow, but not untypically, he had slipped through the net. All relevant records relating to him: treatment plan, medication regime, original diagnosis, even birth certificate and national insurance number, apparently misplaced or lost. Initially she had approached their weekly therapy sessions with little ambition, optimism or hope of making anything other than the most minimal headway. To her surprise, after a few sessions there

73

was some improvement. Negligible, if she were truthful, but all the same it was something. Later, when they had started making progress, real progress, progress that could actually be measured and quantified; when he had started to slowly recover his shattered memory, it had become something more. A piquing of academic curiosity. A rekindling of long-dormant professional ambition. And hadn't part of it also been a desire to impress hitherto indifferent and cynical peers? And, finally, an unshakeable hubris? In the end hadn't it become less about helping Richard Lennon, her patient, and more about uncovering what had actually happened for her own selfish motives? So, at the end of each session, every session, afraid that he might not want to come again, she would ask the same question . . .

'You'd like to feel better, wouldn't you Richard?'

Richard Lennon would. He would like that. Richard Lennon would like to feel better.

'I'd like to feel better,' Richard Lennon agreed. Richard Lennon concentrated on his hands. Drawing them apart, taking a deep breath and holding it. Richard Lennon. Whenever he heard that name – his name – whenever he heard a voice saying that name, at the same time he heard another name, another voice, saying a different name. He held his breath, steadying himself, before beginning the laborious business of guiding his hands back together. Trying, once again, to get the tip of one index finger to meet the tip of the other. But his fingers, his hands, his whole body, seemed to carry its own current. A low-level rumble in the nervous system. A thrumming vibration in the muscles. A buzzing in the head like tinnitus. Trembling, shuddering, shaking with the effort, the hands approached each other. The fingertips nearly, nearly touching. Then his body gave a wild, involuntary jerk and they slid past. His hands were like poles of a magnet. But north and north. Or south and south. And try as he might he just couldn't get them to meet.

'Richard? You'd like to keep coming, wouldn't you?'

Richard Lennon would. He would like that. Richard Lennon would like to keep coming. Coming back every week. Talking to Dr Fitzgerald. And, right at this moment, Richard Lennon would also like to cry . . .

'There's no need to be upset, Richard,' she said – said every time. 'I'm sure if you keep coming, if we keep talking, you'll feel better. You'd like that, wouldn't you, Richard? You want to feel better, don't you? You want to know . . . why you are the way you are? You want to know what happened, don't you, Richard?'

Richard Lennon, the man who she knew as Richard Lennon, never answered this question. Even though Dr Fitzgerald kept asking it. Convincing him, convincing herself, that he really did want to know what happened, when, in reality, it was probably only her who wanted to know. But, all the same, she asked it. And when she again got no answer, she asked the question. The question solely designed to make him come the next time . . .

10

They stood outside a front door set in a façade of cracked and faded red brickwork in need of repointing; a depiction of the crucifixion in stained and frosted glass on the upper half, oak panelling starting to gap with age below. Somewhere, Cat thought, you might expect to be occupied by a vicar, rather than the owner of a sex shop. And when the door opened she could tell by the look on his face – regret, disappointment, anticlimax – that this woman was not quite what Pearson had been expecting. A latex basque, perhaps, cinched into a waistline that would have left Scarlett O'Hara faint and breathless. Some Manga comic nymphet with black-painted fingernails, black lipstick, heavy black eyeliner, eyebrows plucked into high arches and heavily drawn, glossy black hair with a blue sheen tied into a high pony-tail. She was, by contrast, a little ... unexceptional. Unexciting. Ordinary. Granted, her hair was black. But loose. Odd strands stuck to the damp skin of her forehead. As if they'd caught her in the middle of a workout. Or she wanted it to appear that way. She dabbed delicately at an area of exposed chest with the towel draped around her neck. It was all for effect. The sports bra, the Lycra shorts. The ever-so-slightly flustered manner. They'd been expected. Or maybe, she'd been expecting that Pearson would be on his own.

'Inspector Pearson, isn't it?' she smiled. Small teeth. Pink gums. A heart-shaped ruby in a nose piercing. 'Courtney said you were coming.'

'Actually I'm only a DS,' Pearson said. 'A detective sergeant.' Taking out his warrant card, showing it to her, nodding toward Cat, 'This is Detective Constable Catherine Russell. Miss . . . ?'

After barely a glance in Cat's direction, she said, 'Layla,' shooting him a look that said *Make something of it*. Seemingly certain of a response that wasn't forthcoming, she said anyway, 'Yeah, Eric Clapton has got a lot to answer for.' Smiling again. 'Layla Gilchrist.'

'Can we come in?' Pearson asked, gesturing beyond her with the warrant card before slipping it into his inside breast pocket.

It took Cat a moment to place the smells: baby oil, latex, talcum powder. Newborn odours. She wondered what Pearson's febrile imagination might be conjuring up now. Someone wearing a nappy. But that someone would, no doubt, be around six foot in height with a moustache. Holding down a position as a stockbroker or junior cabinet minister. Or, maybe, a chief constable. Layla Gilchrist showed them into a sitting room which was remarkably, well, 'twee', Cat supposed would best describe it. Nineteen twenties in style. Inlaid plaster panels in the walls with the characteristic double-stepped art deco design, the coving around the ceiling likewise. Ornaments on the mantelpiece. An Egyptian bust. A bronze female in terpsichorean pose. Two Lalique crystal tableaux of ballerinas. The rest of the furnishings – rugs, seat covers, cushions, curtains – were floral. And very definitely Laura

Ashley. Gilchrist sat on a settee and indicated that they should take the two armchairs opposite. Wiping her face with the towel, dabbing again at the area just above her bra, meeting Pearson's gaze, the action intentionally provocative. Cat wasn't sure whether to be amused or annoyed. She settled on annoyed.

Pearson opened his slipcase and took out a piece of paper. 'We're trying to trace who might have bought these items of clothing,' he said, 'and when they may have been bought.' He passed over the paper and Gilchrist scanned it quickly.

'Well, they could be some of my stock.' Looking up at Pearson. 'You know they're available on the internet?'

'Yeah, so your shop assistant said. But we're thinking that, a pair of boots, you're more likely to want to try them on, right?'

'Not one of our top sellers,' she said. 'I'll have to get the item number. What do you want to know?'

'A list of sales for, say ... the past six months?' Pearson said. 'Purchase details? Whether they were bought for cash or by credit card. Name and address of cardholder and so on, if you have them.' He slid the photograph of Rachel out from his slipcase. 'Do you recognise this person, Miss Gilchrist?'

Gilchrist took the photo and looked at it for a moment or so. 'Is she dead?' Eyes flicking back up to Pearson.

'Why would you think she was dead?' Pearson asked.

Gilchrist looked back down at the photograph, her eyes narrowed, lips pursing momentarily.

'Something about the eyes?' Tracing the outline of Rachel's face with a finger. 'And the lighting's all wrong.' Looking back at Pearson again. 'Plus, why else would you be asking me about her?' When Pearson said nothing, she said, 'Is that what this is about? Courtney didn't say on the phone. Just that you wanted to talk to me. She's dead, isn't she?'

After a moment Pearson said, 'I'm afraid so. Do you recognise her? Might she have come into your shop?'

Gilchrist appeared to give it some thought, then she shook her head. 'No. But then I'm not in the shop all the time. Maybe she came in when Courtney was serving?'

'She said she didn't recognise her,' said Pearson.

'Well, Courtney hasn't been there that long. We have a fairly high turnover of staff' – shrugging – 'it's minimum wage. And the type of work … I mean, I would have had their names and addresses at the time, but I wouldn't have kept hold of them.'

Pearson sighed. 'OK.' He held up the photo of the boots. 'Do you think you could check these for us?'

Cat watched Gilchrist move to a writing desk on which stood an open laptop and a wireless printer and start tapping the keys. She had a tattoo on her back. Cat couldn't quite make out what it was meant to represent. It ran down Gilchrist's spine and disappeared into the waistband of her Lycra shorts. Some kind of climbing flower, maybe? But it could just as easily be a chain of stylised, mythological beasts. Or runic characters. Cat still wasn't quite sure. Obviously Pearson wasn't, either. Even though he was spending some time studying it. Had already spent some time studying it as they had followed Gilchrist across the hallway earlier. Pearson became aware that Cat was staring at him. He turned, Cat shook her head, affecting a disappointed, pitying expression. Turning away before he caught the smile that said 'Gotcha!'

11

'You'd like to feel better, wouldn't you, Richard?'
On each occasion, Dr Fitzgerald would adopt the same tone of voice. Casual. Almost nonchalant. As if him not turning up was of absolutely no consequence to her. Glancing up from her notes then, Richard Lennon would be hunched forward. Concentrating on his hands. On getting the index finger of one to touch the index finger of the other. The echo of a half-forgotten action. Some repetitive, menial task. The 'industrial therapy' he had performed as a long-stay mental patient at Runwell, perhaps. But recognising that what he was doing actually related to some previous misremembered real-life activity hadn't made it any easier to watch – but she still watched him: as if this time would be the time he got the fingers to meet. As if somehow this time, by a joint effort of will, he would actually be successful. She had wanted to know, had needed to know what had happened to this old man, to delve further and further back into his past. So, once again she asked the same question. And got the same answer . . .

*

'I'd like to feel better.' Richard Lennon didn't look up. Concentrated, instead, on his fingertips. So that he wouldn't cry. So the noise in his head would quieten a little, although it never quite went away. Dr Fitzgerald was asking another question. He wanted to answer but the words just seemed to get stuck somehow, so he had to push them out, get them out in a rush.

'I can't hear the words – the noise – hissing – gurgling – under water . . .' No; that wasn't it. Wasn't what he wanted to say.

He thought Dr Fitzgerald might be writing something down. But he didn't look up to see if she *was* writing something down. He wanted to say there was something else. He wanted to tell her about the 'something else'. But he couldn't breathe. Couldn't stop himself from shaking. So he concentrated on his hands. The doctor had finished writing the 'something' down. Now she was asking him questions again. Always questions. But he didn't want to answer any more questions . . .

'So, you'd like to keep coming, Richard? Because I have some ideas of different things we could try next time. To find out what happened, Richard? To make you feel better?'

But now, she wasn't at all sure that he did feel better. Wasn't sure that, looking into his past, either of them felt better for what they had found there. She had listened repeatedly to the tapes. Had read and reread the transcripts. Had edited and re-edited the notes on the sessions with the man she still thought of as Richard Lennon. Until the paper was covered with an almost illegible overlayering of her neat, meticulous handwriting. Red on green on blue on black on white. The notes were the result of solid research. Scientific method. Professional experience. There were some assumptions, of course. Some conjecture. Some speculation. Even a little creative licence, if she were truthful. How couldn't there be when you were attempting to piece together the disparate fragments of a shattered mind? All the same, she was certain. Or fairly sure, in any case, that her conclusions were sound. That she had a pretty good idea of what had happened to the old man. Except, she still couldn't believe it. Wasn't quite yet ready to let herself believe it.

Opening her top drawer, she ran her fingertips along the ranks of miniature DATs, selecting one, taking it out, she fitted it into the tape recorder and pressed the 'play' button ...

Richard Lennon, the man who would later come to think of himself as Richard Lennon, lay awake in the near dark. The sour taste of sleep clotted in his mouth. Feeling the slow rise and fall of his chest, the rattle of mucus in his throat and lungs. The sluggish flow of blood in his veins. His limbs leaden, immovable objects. The muscles withered and useless. He had woken, had *been* woken, and found himself in the same bed, the same room. He had always been here. He had always been in this bed. Always been in this room, in this hospital. He couldn't remember a time before being here, couldn't remember a place before being here. Couldn't remember any 'before' at all. Only a 'now'.

He lay for a time, though what length of time it was he couldn't have said, slowly becoming aware of the smell of antiseptic, soap, unwashed human bodies, long-term sleep. Gradually becoming accustomed to the half-light. A glimmer of daylight from a partly open window. Hot, stale air worrying a drab curtain. A pattern of geometric shapes in the heavy weave. Outside, a background hum of traffic. The flow and ebb of accelerating and decelerating vehicles. The hiss of air brakes. The reverberation of an aeroplane engine. And from somewhere inside, from somewhere down a long corridor, the sound of double doors crashing open. The clatter of metal on metal. Doors flapping on their hinges. Rubber wheels on polished linoleum. The rattling of sharp metal objects in shiny metal bowls—

'Mr Lennon? Mr Lennon?'

Richard Lennon heard his name distinctly. But whenever he remembered his name being called, whenever he heard his name now, at the same time, underneath this voice saying this name there was another voice saying another name. Richard Lennon's shoulder was shaken, his right arm turned so the palm faced upwards, his arm flexed. Fingers probing the crook of his elbow for a vein. Richard Lennon knew that the trolley was coming for him. Making its slow, unhurried progress down the long corridor—

'Mr Lennon?' said the voice, the voice by his right arm. 'It's time for your treatment. Mr Lennon? Are you awake?'

The trolley entered the ward. The squeak of the wheel. The rattle of metal on metal as the sharp objects were displaced. Hushed voices in a shared conversation. Richard Lennon moved his lips to answer. But his tongue was furry. A thick liquid curdled in his mouth. So he could not speak, could not answer.

'Would you like some water, Mr Lennon?' asked the voice by his right arm.

Richard Lennon nodded, tried to raise his head, to sit up a little, but didn't have the strength. An arm was wedged behind his neck, lifting his head from the pillow. Leaning forward, his mouth closed around a plastic beaker which was upturned, the water filling his mouth, dribbling down his chin and into the creases of his neck, spilling onto his bedclothes. The arm behind him was withdrawn and Richard Lennon lay back down again, exhausted. A paper towel was wiped across his lips, his chin, under his neck, dabbed on the sheets and blankets.

'Jonathan,' said a voice, a second voice, a voice on his left, 'are we ready?'

The first voice, mumbling an apology, fumbling with Richard Lennon's arm. Swabbing the inside of his elbow with something cold and wet.

'I'm really in rather a hurry,' said a third voice.

'It won't take long,' said the second voice. 'We'll dispense with the niceties. Jonathan, don't bother with that.'

Richard Lennon felt a coldness on his temples. Damp cotton wool. He tried to resist. Tried to clamp his lips together. To clench his teeth . . .

'Induced insulin coma, of course,' said the second voice, 'has the added bonus of making the patient more acquiescent. Even the most resistant become more pliant with long periods of deep sleep.'

Richard Lennon tried to turn his head away. Couldn't quite summon the energy.

'The process,' said the second voice, 'is, of course, being continually refined . . .'

So, instead, Richard Lennon bit down on the gag. Tried to swallow. Began to sweat. A cold sweat that pricked the skin on his forearms. His shins.

'I'm sure you'll find the procedure quite fascinating. Brutal. But fascinating.'

The cold sweat spread to Richard Lennon's chest. His neck. And finally his back. His jaws clicking, his mouth working dumbly, Richard Lennon made no sound . . . although he wanted to scream . . .

'I'm afraid I was unable to come to a definite conclusion,' said the third voice, 'as to any specific clinical diagnosis.'

'While it's true that these therapies have primarily been applied to patients with schizophrenia and depression,' said the second voice, 'I think we can safely say that, whatever was wrong with him, after thirty or forty cycles of treatment he is now almost completely cured.'

'I understand you've had a few casualties?'

'Initially, maybe ten or twelve. Then we stopped the intravenous feeding and allowed them to wake up periodically and found we gained much better survival rates as a result. This one's been in deep sleep ...' A cardboard folder opening. The riffling of paper. Richard Lennon could not rouse himself enough to look at the two men, to even turn his head. Could barely keep his eyes open. 'Ah, here we are,' said the second voice. 'Nearly eighteen weeks.'

'And there's been no significant physical deterioration?'

'Well, that's not really my concern, is it? I understood the focus here to be on the potential applications of the therapy. Agreed?'

'Agreed.'

'One of the areas we have been looking at to optimise the depatterning process is the use of tape loops on a twenty-four-hour basis while the patient experiences insulin coma ...'

Richard Lennon wanted to say something. Wanted to say something to the third voice. Wanted to say something ... But couldn't remember what it was. There was a rummaging under his pillow. A click. A hiss of white noise. A low level gurgling. An alien language spoken under water.

'Sounds like there's a bit of a problem,' said the third voice. Amused.

'I'll get the machine swapped out,' said the second voice negligently. 'The patient probably only needs to undergo one further course of treatment in any case. To all intents and purposes we can regard him as almost totally depatterned.'

'By "depatterned", you mean his memories have been altered in some way?'

'Altered? No.' A click. Richard Lennon felt the machine being replaced under his pillow. 'After the next course of treatment his memory will be completely wiped.'

'So he'll have no memories whatsoever?'

'None at all,' said the second voice, 'a blank page. It'll be a completely fresh start for you.'

'And what happens if we cannot implant a new personality?'

'That's your problem. Really, it's a question I haven't considered.'

12

When Pearson returned with their drinks in two plastic cups, Cat was sitting behind her computer screen, a granary bap on a wrinkled piece of cling film in front of her, extruding a clump of green foliage – rocket, perhaps. He watched her pull it apart and put it into her mouth, the painted fingernails little birds pecking away at the bread. Pearson had the sudden realisation that he was starving. That he hadn't eaten today. He could murder a couple of bacon rolls. But there wasn't time before the team meeting.

'What's this?' Cat asked, picking up the plastic cup and examining the contents.

'It's orangey-red,' Pearson said. 'I've got brown.'

Cat poked at the grainy liquid with a pencil. 'It's like some kind of pond scum mixed with red powder paint. What's it supposed to be?'

'It said "Tomato Soup" on the button. Mine claims to be coffee.'

Cat stirred the soup with a pencil. Took a cautious sip. 'Ow!' Running her tongue along a scalded top lip. 'How do they make it that hot?'

Pearson drank some of his. 'You're lucky. Mine's stone-bollock-cold.' Cat had tried the coffee before. It tasted a bit like dishwater, but not quite as appetising.

'I think I'll give it a miss, if that's OK with you.' She moved the cup to one side of her desk, opened her bottom drawer and took out a plastic bottle of mineral water. Unscrewing the cap. Wheeling herself out from behind her screen. Taking a swig. Screwing the cap back on. 'I've been looking into your girlfriend's background.'

Pearson felt slightly nauseous. Shivered. Someone had left the windows open in an effort to dispel the smells from the room. Paint. Solvent. Carpet tiles. Plastic. But all it had achieved was letting in the cold and dampness from outside.

'My girlfriend?'

'Your girlfriend, the Latex Lady of the Whips. Our friendly neighbourhood dominatrix.'

'I don't know what you mean.' Pearson looked away. Took an interest in the contents of his cup.

'I saw your face when she opened the door. You were gutted. You thought she was going to be some Amazon warrior, all in leather and straps and carrying a whip.' Cat tore off another piece of bread and put it into her mouth.

Pearson looked at the bap on the desk in front of Cat. Definitely rocket. And crayfish tails, by the look of it. Hollandaise sauce. He took a mouthful of the cold, disgusting coffee. There might be a grain of truth in what she said. Might be.

Cat shook her head. 'You know as well as I do that any dominatrix around here is more likely to be some sad, middle-aged old tart...' he didn't like the way she was looking at him, 'with sad, middle-aged punters.'

Pearson smiled. 'She really got under your skin, didn't she?'

She had, Cat had to admit to herself. Why was that exactly? Was it the way she'd been ignored? Totally dismissed as if she weren't important. Gilchrist might have been expecting Pearson, but she obviously wasn't expecting her. And Gilchrist was exactly the sort of woman who didn't bother with other women, only paid men attention. The obvious dabbing of her chest? Making cow eyes at Pearson? The business Gilchrist was in? The way she made her money? Cat wasn't quite sure. But there was something.

Cat said, 'Anyway, it turns out she's a doctor.'

'A doctor?' asked Pearson, looking interested. Making a big thing about it. Aping thoughtful. 'As it happens, I've got a bit of a bad back, perhaps I'll swing by there. And she's sure to have the equipment if I need a bit of traction.'

'Not *that* kind of doctor! She has a doctorate? A PhD in Economics. Did PPE at degree level.' When Pearson looked blank she said slowly, 'Philosophy ... Politics ... and Economics?'

'Philosophy?' He nodded at her. ''S'what you did, isn't it?'

'Psychology, Pearson.' Needled, despite herself. 'How many times have I told you? Psychology!'

'And what's your certificate?'

'It's not a certificate, it's a degree, a first-class honours degree.'

'But you get a certificate, right? So, is a doctorate better than a degree? Or what?'

Cat could feel her face starting to burn. Admitted, albeit grudgingly, 'A doctorate is slightly higher, yes.'

'So, it's the next one up, is it?'

'One or two qualifications higher, yes.'

'One? Or two?'

'All right. Two.' She unscrewed the cap on the bottle of water. Took another swig. Eyed him across the desk. Deadpan. But behind the cup he held in front of his mouth, he might be trying not to laugh. She screwed the cap back on the bottle. Wheeling herself back behind the computer screen.

Smiling to himself, Pearson downed a mouthful of coffee. Immediately wished he hadn't.

'Her dissertation was on ...' Pearson didn't quite catch the next phrase. Wondered if it was actually English. After a moment or two, Cat emerged once again from behind the screen. 'Did you hear what I said?'

'Yep.'

'So, what do you think?'

'About what?' She gave him the hard stare. 'The statistical whatsname? Dunno. Didn't understand a single word.'

'God! You're in a fucking irritating mood today!' She retreated once again behind the screen. A minute or so later she said, 'Ooh, that's interesting ...' She paused. Waiting for a response. After a moment, he bit.

'What is?'

'Well, she starts off by pursuing a career in politics, gets a top degree, works as some kind of political research assistant – you know, one of these unpaid internship things? Her name's come up on a couple of political blogs. So, anyway, she does her masters, then a PhD ...'

'And?'

'Then, she's done for possession of class-A when she's twenty-five. Coke. Got off with a fine.'

'Nothing since then?'

'No,' Cat admitted reluctantly, 'not that I could find.'

'No complaints for ...' Pearson's mind went blank. Cat waited, eyebrows raised. Not helping. 'Keeping a disorderly house?' he said at last.

'What?' Cat smirked. '"Keeping a disorderly house"?' Then,

affecting a very bad stage-school cockney accent, 'She did, guv'nor. But after becoming aware that young Prince Bertie was involved, following an excess of laudanum and gin, Mr Disraeli decided that in the interests of the realm it was better kept on the QT like.'

'All right, all right,' said Pearson, '"controlling prostitution for gain".'

'No.'

'No complaints from neighbours? Parties going on into the early hours? Music being played too loud? Reports of antisocial behaviour?'

'No, nothing. Look, my point is, she gets this doctorate and looks set for a career in politics, so why is she now making a living as some S and M queen out in the sticks?'

'S and M queen? A minute ago you were saying—'

'OK. Running a sex shop.'

Pearson shrugged. 'Getting busted for coke isn't going to do much for your career prospects.'

'You could ride that out, surely.'

'Only if you'd made the right friends. As for what she's doing now – everybody needs a hobby. Perhaps hers is spanking people.' Pearson turned on his own computer as Roberts entered the room. When he looked over, Cat was wrapping up the bap. More than two-thirds uneaten. But before he could say anything, before he could make the offer to take it off her hands, she dropped it into the waste bin.

13

'I'm surprised he let you come,' Cat said.

Placing her glass of white wine on the low-level table and pulling out the leather bucket seat, she sat down, slipping the strap of her handbag off her shoulder and jamming the bag down beside her hip.

'I told Dad I was going on a date,' Vicky said. Smiling apologetically as she took a seat. Glancing sheepishly away across the bar. The town centre pub, one of a nationwide chain, was much like all the other pubs in the town centre. Stripped wooden floors. Pine tables. Leather benches and bucket seats. Whitewashed walls. A compilation of insipid Tamla Motown hits from the sixties playing quietly in the background. It was the sort of pub you wouldn't find her father dead in. Which was its one saving grace. Her sister never could lie convincingly – not to Cat anyway. So now she just told her the truth. Mostly.

Vicky took a large gulp of her wine as Cat studied her face. Her sister was younger than her by a couple of years. But already looking much older. Bags under her eyes from lack of sleep. Skin starting to show the effects of a poor diet.

'How are the girls?' Cat asked.

'Oh, I've got a photo for you, I forgot.'

Vicky bent down to retrieve her handbag from the floor and Cat noticed how dull and lifeless her hair seemed. Saw the split ends and dark roots showing in the blonde. Is this how her own life would have turned out if she had stayed at home? If she hadn't, against her father's wishes, gone on to sixth form at school to do her A-levels? If she hadn't taken a place at a university halfway across the country? Would her life have been that much different from her sister's? A single mum of two. Forced to come back home after a disastrous relationship with a bloke who was now inside. But then, the family still thought more of her sister than they did of Cat.

Vicky finished rummaging in her handbag. 'Here y'are.' She looked at the paper in her hand momentarily and smiled, then held it out to Cat across the table. 'Who do they remind you of?'

The two girls, aged four and five, were smiling at the camera. Both had long, dark hair, as Cat and her sister had had at the same age. Pretty. Fresh-faced. 'Sorry about the colour,' Vicky said, 'the printer cartridge is running out.' The colour, the life had been washed out. The girls had their eyes wide open so as not to be photographed squinting. They reminded Cat of—

'They're growing up to be a pair of little cows,' Vicky said. Cat glanced up from the photograph to see the smile, the hint of pride in her sister's face. 'Mum and Dad spoil them rotten.'

Cat looked back down, saw that the girls were both in Nike trainers, the jeans looked like Next, the jackets, Baby Gap. Cat had already noted that Vicky's own clothes were tatty and washed-out. A loose thread hanging from the bottom of her denim miniskirt.

'Can I keep this?' Cat asked, looking up.

'Course, that's why I brought it.'

'So, what are they up to now?'

'Gracie's just started reception, Lily's in first year of juniors.' Vicky took a sip of her wine. 'God knows what they're up to though. It's like their big secret, y'know? They're full of it for the first week, tell you in intricate detail about every single thing that happened during the day? Now it's all,' shrugging her shoulders, '"I don't know", or the other one, "stuff". "What did you do today?"' – she took another drink, finishing it – "Stuff!"' Vicky smiled. Played with the stem of her empty glass. Looking slightly embarrassed. Wanting another, but not wanting to ask. Not offering to buy one because she couldn't really afford it.

'D'you want another?' Cat asked. Nodding at the glass, her purse already in her hand. Vicky looked down at her glass. As if surprised, now, that it was empty. Looked across at Cat's glass, which was untouched. Hesitated momentarily. Then nodded. Cat took a tenner out of her purse.

'I'll pay.' She'd paid for the first. She'd pay for all of them. 'If you go up the bar.'

When her sister had disappeared, Cat got her phone out of her bag. Checked for messages. Checked the time.

Vicky sat back down again. A quarter of the wine already gone in the journey back from the bar.

'So how are they all?' Cat asked. 'How's Mum?'

'Oh, y'know. Same as ever.'

Cat knew. Harassed. Put upon. Under the thumb. Wanting to get in touch with Cat but not daring to because her dad wouldn't like it.

'And the boys?'

Boys. Their two brothers were in their twenties now but they still all referred to them as 'the boys'. Jason and Darren. You couldn't get more Essex than that.

'Staying out of trouble,' Vicky said. 'Just.'

Meaning: still up to their old tricks, but they hadn't been caught yet. Hadn't been arrested, at least. Cat was surprised she hadn't seen them at the nick. Was waiting for them to turn up one day. Any day. Waiting for the call from the custody sergeant. They had blanked her. Hadn't wanted anything to do with her for years. But that didn't mean they wouldn't drop her name when they were charged. In the hope that, that way, things might go easier for them. In the hope that she might be able to 'just have a word' somehow, and get them off the hook. They were just like her dad. Scaffolders, the three of them. Making a decent living, more than a decent living. But that was never quite enough. All the male members of her family were the same, uncles and cousins included. Chancers. On the fiddle. On the thieve.

'I don't know how,' Vicky said. 'But you know them,' she shrugged, 'they've always lived a charmed life.' Turning her wine glass on the table. Eventually asking, 'How are you?'

Cat looked across at her sister, considering the question, weighing up actually telling her the truth. Confiding in her sister that her career was in limbo. Her reputation in the toilet. That she really didn't know if she belonged any more. That she was thinking of jacking it all in. Saying, instead, 'I'm good. Busy, y'know?' Looking around the bar. The after-work crowd had gone. The few left determined to make a night of it. By the bar, a couple of estate agent types. Looking in their direction. Christ, that was all she needed.

'Have you lost weight?' her sister asked. Cat looked back at her. Vicky was frowning. 'I know I haven't seen you for a while, but you look like you've lost weight to me.'

98

'Maybe a little,' Cat said. 'I told you, I've been busy. D'you want another?' Nodding at her sister's empty glass, getting a twenty out of her purse. 'I'll have one this time.'

When Vicky had gone back to the bar, Cat checked the time on her phone again. Wondering how long she could leave it before making a move.

'Sorry,' Cat said. Vicky was on her fourth, or fifth, glass of wine. Cat had barely started her second. 'I've asked about everyone else, how are you?'

Vicky swallowed. For a moment Cat was afraid her face was about to crumple, then she brightened. She flapped a hand. 'Oh, I didn't tell you, I'm studying!' She gave a half-smile and nodded. 'My GCSEs. English. And maths. To start off with. I'm going to see how it goes, then I might do some more.'

'Well done,' Cat said. Genuinely meaning it.

'Yep,' Vicky said, taking another drink, 'your thicko sister is going back to school!' She gave a little laugh. 'All those years of bunking off ... '

'So,' Cat said, 'what brought this on?'

'My big sister!' Vicky said. 'I was sitting with the girls the other night. We were all snuggled up in bed. Do you remember when Mum and Dad used to go out and you used to babysit?' Yeah, thought Cat, when I was about eight or nine. '"Face washed. Hair brushed. Teeth cleaned. Jim-jams on. Or no story." And then we used to snuggle up on the settee. Do you remember? Winnie-the-Pooh, Doctor Seuss, Peter Rabbit ... ' Vicky seemed to have lost her train of thought.

'So?' Cat prompted.

'So, I'm always telling the girls how proud I am of you. How their Auntie Catherine does a really, really important job. How clever their Auntie Catherine is and how she went to university? So, Gracie looks up at me, with this serious look on her face and asks, "Aren't you clever, Mummy?" Well, clearly I'm not. Not a qualification to my name, can't spell for toffee. So, how the bloody hell am I supposed to help them with their homework when they're older? I said to myself, "Back to school, Vicky, my girl."'

'That's brilliant,' Cat said. 'I'm so pleased for you.'

'Where was it you went?'

'For what?'

'University.'

'Oh, Durham.'

'Where's that?' Vicky asked. 'It's in Wales, isn't it?'

'Maybe,' Cat said, 'you'd better do geography next. It's in England. Up north. Almost as far as you can go north before you're in Scotland.'

And, Cat had wondered at the time, whether that was far enough. Had considered Dundee. Had considered Greenland. The North Pole even. But had settled on Durham because it had a really good reputation for Psychology.

'Seriously,' Vicky said, licking her lips, 'you're my only hope, y'know? That there's something better than ... ' Faltering then. Before the prospect of trying to explain. To describe all the things that should be better than they were. Not quite having the words, the energy. 'I've always looked up to you.' Looking into her glass. Empty. 'You never knew that, did you?' Turning the glass again on the table top. 'You got out, Cat. Durham University.' Shaking her head in admiration.

Cat had got out. Got away from home. From her father. From everything. Only to find herself in another 'situation'. A situation she had barely survived. But that was something else she had kept from her sister, her family. Something very few people knew about.

'My big sister, in the police!' Vicky went on. A smile. Fleeting. Self-conscious. 'Mind you, you were always bloody bossy! But, Cat, you ... you made something of yourself ... '

Across the table, Vicky was looking down into her glass once again. A tear running down her face ...

14

THURSDAY 3 MARCH 1966

He came out of the Shrubbery coffee bar. Too hot, despite the chill of the evening. Struggling for breath. His mouth dry. His head spinning. His heartbeat erratic. Racing. Thumping hard, then skipping a beat. His muscles shaky and weak . . .

The Shrubbery was always the last stop of the night. After the Jacobean. The Black Cat. The Capri. The Shades . . . or had it been the Capri first, then the Jacobean? He couldn't properly remember. He'd taken a couple of leapers first thing. Besides, after a while all the coffee bars blended into one another; the condensation running down the windows, the hiss and gurgle of the coffee machine, the cappuccinos served in glass cups and saucers. Most of them having the same music on the jukebox: The Kinks, the Stones, The Who. Not that he spent a lot of time in any of them. Just stuck his head through the door, whistled to get the attention of anyone he might recognise, tipped his head to indicate that they should go outside.

At the Shrubbery he was a bit more discreet. Sat at the corner table furthest away from the counter. Made sure the owner couldn't see what he was up to. Even allowed himself time for a coffee. The music there was much better. They always had the latest blues and R 'n' B imports from the States. The stuff you didn't get to hear unless you tuned in to one of the pirate radio stations operating just past the mouth of the estuary. The stuff you couldn't get hold of in the shops. Not in the shops in Southend anyway.

When he entered the square and saw the scooter was still there he felt a little better. Every time he went into a bar and left it he was convinced that he'd come back to find it'd been nicked. He patted the handlebars lovingly, then put both his hands on the seat, leaning forward, taking in great lungfuls of air. Slowly breathing in. Holding it for a few seconds. Trying to calm himself . . .

There was another attraction to the Shrubbery, of course. About a week ago he'd gone through the back for a slash – ladies' and gents' toilets, downstairs a private drinking and gambling club – and found an unfamiliar half-open door he'd never noticed before. So, he'd given it a little push . . . and discovered another flight of stairs. He'd run up. Just being nosy. Just to see what might be up there. Reaching the upper landing he'd blundered through a door and into a dimly lit room. Red bulbs in lamps on side tables. Maroon flock wallpaper. A small bar in one corner. The air thick with perfume and cigarette smoke. And all eyes in the room turned in his direction. On the low, velvet sofas: men in suits, women in their underwear: high heels, stockings, garter belts, those fancy corset things, the lot. He'd just stood there. Not moving. Stunned. Then a figure had peeled itself away from the shadows. Some big, ugly bastard with a broken nose, like he'd been a boxer at some time, unfolding his arms and slowly stepping away from the wall on which he'd been leaning. So he'd held his hands up, backed slowly from the room, shutting the door quietly on his way out . . . and then he'd legged it down the stairs.

He'd asked around. In the end, to his surprise, it had been Beverly who had told him what was going on. And that everyone knew it was going on, apart from him. That a whole lot of posh blokes came down regularly from London to visit the brothel upstairs.

He'd made a crack about 'tarts', said something derogatory about women who could have sex for money, and Beverly had surprised him again by saying, 'It's not that much different from being married, is it?'

Beverly Marsh. His girlfriend. He'd first met her on one of his regular trips to the typing pool. A dozen cartons of Peter Stuyvesant cigarettes in a carrier bag. His 'Duty Free' he called them with a knowing wink at the girls. Though he'd never flown abroad, had never been out of Southend. But he knew someone at Southend airport who thieved the cartons and flogged them on the cheap. Then it was just a matter of breaking them up into individual packets of twenty and selling them on at a profit.

'I can offer you a special one-time-only offer,' he'd said to Beverly, after they'd been introduced, 'of one free packet.' But when she'd held out her hand, he'd kept hold of them, 'Providing you do me the great honour of accompanying me to the cinema this Saturday night.' With the other girls giggling and egging her on, Beverly had been too embarrassed to turn him down.

He'd tried the door to the upstairs room again tonight. And found it locked. Leaning heavily against the scooter he took another deep breath. Holding it. Exhaling again. Feeling his pulse gradually slacken. The sweat starting to dry on his body. The confusion in his brain easing slightly. He'd taken another couple of leapers twenty minutes or so ago. 'Just to get him through.' But even as he'd shook them out of the envelope, telling himself he didn't really need them; even as he'd sat there looking at them in his palm, telling himself it was a stupid idea; even as he put them in his mouth, took a gulp of his coffee and swallowed, he knew he was going to regret it. But what could you do? A ten-hour shift at the EKCO radio factory, six days a week: burnt fingers, the overpowering smell of the hot plastic as you pressed it in the moulding machine. And there still wasn't enough money to go round.

The holiday season proper hadn't started yet. He could do two jobs then. The daytime shift at the factory and then working on one of the stalls at the Kursaal. The hook-a-duck. The rifle range. The tip-the-lady-out-of-the-bed. Or one of the rides, maybe. One of the rollercoasters. Or the dodgems. He'd worked the dodgems last year, jumping on and off the back of the cars, chatting up the birds down from London. Course, he hadn't been going out with Beverly then.

What choice did you have? When your old lady was in the loony bin: the 'happy house'. Though the one time he'd been to see her, she hadn't seemed that happy in there. What choice did you have? When you lived with your nan. And *she* 'lived on her nerves'. When she didn't work because she couldn't – or wouldn't – leave the house. There was something not quite right about his family. Something 'not quite right in the head'. Everyone said so. That, after all, is why his old man had finally fucked off. He didn't blame him. Given half the chance he'd be doing the same. So what could you do? Other than leave school as soon as you were allowed, get a job. Take the first poxy job that came your way. Pay the rent, feed the gas and electric meters, pay for the grocery shopping. At least he wasn't still doing the cooking. He got his food out now. In the EKCO canteen during the day with the thousands of others. Grabbing a sandwich – egg, bacon, sausage – on his travels in the evening. He didn't know what his nan did about eating. But by the end of every week there was never any food left in the house.

Even the scooter he was leaning on didn't really belong to him. He'd 'acquired' it on one of his trips to London. Hanging round in Carnaby Street. But some posh Face had started turning up on the silver Vespa GS 160. Taking the piss out of his clobber, decking him in front of some stuck-up public school would-be Jean Shrimpton, who hadn't quite had the looks to carry it off. Finally fed up with it, he'd deliberately got involved in a scuffle with the bloke, let him push him around a bit, knock him to the floor. Put up with the Face sneering down at him, the smug look on the girl's boat race. Only after the two of them had disappeared into one of the boutiques had he opened his hand on the keys to the scooter he'd lifted from the bloke's pocket during the fight. He'd laughed all the way home, imagining the look on the bloke's face when he came out of the shop and found the GS gone ...

Feeling better now, normal, almost, he straightened up. It was the car he noticed first. Black. Brand new. The street lights reflected in the shiny bonnet, playing along the chrome strip on its side. The illuminated radiator badge. An Austin Wolseley. Only then did he see the man standing next to it. A handmade suit. An expensive raincoat. A grey fedora set at a rakish angle. The man slid a silver cigarette case out of his inside pocket, took out a cigarette, snapped the lid shut, tapped the cigarette on the lid. Retrieving a lighter from his overcoat pocket, he lit up. In the flare of the lighter's flame he recognised him as one of the suits he'd seen the week before in the room upstairs.

15

It had seemed like a good idea to come into his brother-in-law's club. An opportunity to talk to Terry. Find out how Ruth was. His wife. His soon-to-be ex-wife, Pearson reminded himself. Had to keep reminding himself. She would be his ex-wife. As soon as one of them could be arsed to get around to making it official. For once, though, Terry Milton wasn't about. And no one knew where he was. Or when he was likely to be back. Not even Tracy, the regular barmaid. The only seemingly permanent fixture throughout all the various incarnations of the club.

Milton had always struck Pearson as a man living out a part. Sitting behind the leather-topped desk, in the wood-panelled office. A glass of Scotch in his hand, or about to be poured from the bottle he kept in the bottom drawer. The stereotype of a club owner. Not the only one, of course. There was Jack Morris, with his ostentatious displays of wealth. The white Rolls-Royce. The chauffeur. The camel-hair overcoat. Even the gold lighter. Playing out the role of the successful businessman.

Pearson eyed the bottle of lager and packet of cheese and

onion crisps on the bar in front of him. They, too, had seemed like a good idea. At the time. Now, he didn't fancy them. He ran his hand around the coolness of the bottle. Fingered the crisps. But couldn't muster the energy to open the bag. The trappings of Morris's success seemed dated somehow. Like the man himself. An anachronism. Pearson pushed the wet label around the bottle of beer. Then there was Tony. The hard man. The shaved head. The macho posturing. The practised cold stare. All of them just living out their lives according to what they thought was expected of them – but wasn't he doing exactly the same? Wasn't he simply living according to somebody else's rules? Performing the tasks required of him? Reading his words from a predetermined script?

'You're a copper, Frank,' Ruth had said. 'You've always been a copper. Whatever happens you can carry on being a copper. It's what you do. It's what you are.'

Was that it? The be-all and end-all of his existence? A copper and no more? Surely there—

'Frank?'

The wet paper label crumpled under his fingers. Rolling it into a ball, leaving it on the counter, Pearson turned towards the voice. A mop of brown hair. Not quite yet the foxed and blotchy complexion of the committed drinker, but getting there. The eyes, though, rather than bloodshot and rheumy, were sly and cunning. Ken Sawyer. Wearing a shirt and tie. A V-necked pullover under a green duffel coat. Had the sartorial elegance of a geography master. And a moustache. Joseph Stalin as a supply teacher. There had always been something Pearson disliked about moustaches. About any kind of facial hair, come to that.

'Ken.' Pearson allowed the journalist a slight nod of acknowledgement. The other man took a large gulp from his pint of beer. And when he sucked the foam from his moustache with his bottom lip Pearson had to turn away.

'Are you working on this murder?' asked Sawyer. Looking for a reaction. Searching Pearson's profile.

'What murder might this be?' Pearson asked. Tone of voice neutral. Expression blank. Turning back towards the hack. Nowadays he worked for the local rag, but at one time he'd worked for one of the big dailies. Rumour had it he'd been encouraged to leave. The precise circumstances surrounding his departure unspecified.

'The girl on the beach?' Sawyer prompted. 'The one on the telly.'

A news report. Pearson turned his attention back to his untouched lager. There had been no actual media appeal. Yet. But they were running out of other options. The hair found in the clothing, belonging to someone other than the deceased, was worthless without the possibility of extracting DNA. The sales records provided by Layla Gilchrist had also resulted in a dead end. Rachel may well have bought the boots from the shop. But if she did then it was for cash. And neither Gilchrist nor Woods had any memory of the girl being in the shop. Or so they claimed. Hours of CCTV footage from the town centre had been reviewed with no luck. Tomorrow they would get the go-ahead for the appeal: Curtis had a meeting scheduled with the Chief Constable, where the Chief Super's misgivings would be weighed against the possibility of any potential future political fallout. The upshot of which would be a reluctant acceptance of Roberts' request. Turning the bottle of beer slowly on the counter, Pearson said nothing.

'There's something ringing a vague bell.' The journalist took a sip of beer, frowning into his pint. 'Something nagging at me . . .'

*

Something about the eyes. The phrase came back to Cat now. Sitting alone – again – hours later, in the sterile silence of her flat. Although it had only been Layla Gilchrist who had actually voiced the doubt, it had been there, too, in the reaction of Courtney Woods. The draining of colour, the tightening of her facial muscles, the puckering of her lips. Cat imagined the rise and fall of her throat, the hard swallow, as she stared fixedly at the photo, shaking her head.

'Is she dead?' Gilchrist had asked, eyes flicking back up to Pearson.

'Why would you think she was dead?'

Looking down again, eyes narrowing, lips pursed, Gilchrist saying, 'Something about the eyes?'

Cat studied the photograph. Traced the outline of Rachel's face with a finger. The eyes didn't quite work. A reasonable match, but it was just obvious enough to make you question the image. And as Gilchrist had said, the lighting was all wrong. Cat's mind went to the photograph in her handbag. Her two nieces: eyes wide, smiling into the camera, the colour bleached out where the toner cartridge was running low. She shivered. Placing the photograph of Rachel carefully on the coffee table next to her mobile phone, she picked up the pack of cigarettes. Taking one out and putting it into her mouth. Dropping the packet back on the table and picking up her lighter. How many more of these photographs would she stare at in her career? she wondered. How many dead girls? How many victims of violent crime? Lighting her cigarette. Taking a drag. Slowly exhaling. Putting the lighter back on the coffee table. Women fixed in time. Unchanging. Their beauty never fading ... while she would get older. Jaded. Cynical—

Christ! Listen to yourself! Is this what your life's come to? Returning home every night to an empty flat. Taking a shower.

Scrutinising yourself in the mirror – that familiar routine come back to haunt her – convincing yourself that you are putting on weight. Unable to motivate yourself to cook. Sitting alone and smoking your fucking brains out, wallowing in self-pity? This was how it had been, even before Sean's death, if she were honest with herself, but since his death it had become worse. There were days now when she could barely even bring herself to talk. Today had been one of her better days. She had even exchanged some banter with Pearson. But her heart hadn't really been in it. And now, in her barren flat, as always, everything had started to crowd in on her again. But this is surely an all-time low, even for you – feeling so sorry for yourself, so pathetic, that you are actually jealous of women who've been murdered? Reaching for the ashtray. Flicking the ash from her cigarette into it. Time you sorted yourself out, girl. Make a decision. Make a go of your career. Or ... pack it all in.

She'd thought about it. Thought very seriously about it. Done nothing but think about it in the last couple of months. Since Sean's death, and what had followed, she didn't feel like she belonged any more. Not in the force. Not anywhere. But she hadn't quite, yet, taken that final step. The question she kept asking herself, though, was: why not? She was sick of the politics. The politicians. The Andy Curtises of this world. For them, the deaths of these girls would always be viewed purely through the prism of possible professional advancement or demotion. Reduced to a calculation of man-hours against clear-up rates. The loss of a human life just another row on a spreadsheet. Drawing on her cigarette. Was that his only involvement in the case? His sole concern? Pearson had told her, after all, that he'd turned up at the body deposition site. Taken an unusual interest in the pathologist's preliminary findings ...

Flicking ash into the ashtray. Would she always view all men – most men – with the same suspicion? Was she always to wonder what they might be truly capable of? Slowly exhaling the blue smoke.

The girl – Cat thought of the deceased, of 'Rachel', as a girl – had been transformed by her death into something more significant, more important, than she would have ever been when she was alive. Not for everyone, admittedly – Pearson, for instance. Roberts – maybe. There were still some in the team who cared. Those who hadn't quite lost all faith in human nature. But, looking around the incident room earlier, she'd wondered exactly how many that might be. Was that an inevitable consequence of the Job? Would she, if she stayed, one day just stop caring? Become inured to the sight of death. Would she, at some point in the future, just view the loss of these girls as something routine? Something mundane and run-of-the-mill? Cat looked down again at the photo on the coffee table. When would she start thinking of the latest victim as just . . .

'Another dead girl,' Sawyer muttered into his pint.

'Stop fishing, Ken.' Pearson picked up his bottle of beer. Took a sip. Wished he hadn't. It was tepid. Flat. Tasting sour somehow. 'You know I can't tell you anything. Not yet.'

'Fair enough.' Sawyer's eyes slid from Pearson's face to the unopened crisps. 'Are you going to eat those?' Pearson pushed the packet towards him. Sawyer opened it and ate a handful. 'I was sorry to hear about your mum.'

'Yeah, thanks.'

'She still in hospital?'

'Retirement home,' Pearson said, turning away, 'at the moment. Rehabilitation.'

Turning back a minute later the flattened crisp packet was on the counter. Sawyer's glass empty. The tattered lace of suds clinging to its sides. Pearson nodded towards it. 'Beer? What is it you drink? Old Foetid Smeg or something, isn't it?'

'Old Speckled Hen,' said Sawyer. 'They don't do it here. I'll have a lager top, cheers.' As Pearson turned back towards the bar, Sawyer added, 'And a couple of bags of pork scratchings?'

Pearson didn't get a drink for himself, wanting to make a move as soon as he could. Sawyer took a gulp of his pint, put the glass on the bar, picked up one of the bags. Frowning again. Whether with the effort of thinking, or the opening of his pork scratchings, Pearson wasn't sure. Finally he got the bag open and poked a few into his mouth.

'Something's still nagging at me. About this girl?' Taking a gulp of beer, shaking his head. 'I'm sure there was another dead girl. Same place. Up by the Crowstone.'

Pearson was suddenly interested. 'Really? When was this?'

'A fair while back.' Pearson waited. 'When was it?' Sawyer mumbled. 'Sixty-five? Sixty-six? Something like that.'

'*Fifty* years ago?'

A moment's pause from Sawyer as he poked more pork scratchings into his mouth. Then a definitive, final, shake of the head. 'Nah. It's gone.'

Pearson dragged his eyes away from the salt, the flecks of crisp, in the other man's facial hair. Checked his watch as Sawyer took another drink. And before his bottom lip came up to deal with the foam in his moustache again, Pearson left.

In her flat, Cat's mobile pinged to indicate an incoming text. She picked it up and read the screen. Frowned. Then read it again. A name from the past. From her time in Durham. Only eight years ago, but it might as well have been a lifetime. It was a name, a person, that she thought had been consigned to that past. That version of herself. Now, it seemed, that same person wanted to get back in contact. And, right at that moment, Cat wasn't sure it was what *she* wanted at all . . .

Day Three

16

Pearson sat in a public shelter on the seafront. Repainted earlier in the season, but already starting to peel and flake after just a few months of wind and salt air. It stood amongst a row of beach huts, the one-time striped pastel, vivid green or vibrant purple boarding of their sides now weathered and drab in the grey autumnal dawn. He ran his hand idly along the slats of the bench, as if he might read the message in the scored surface under his fingers. He was only a couple of hundred yards from where, a few months previously, a colleague had been burned alive in his car. A colleague. Nothing more than that. But a serving police officer, a human being, all the same.

He pulled his overcoat tighter around him. Turned up the collar. Watching the sky begin to lighten over the mudflats. Checked his watch. Not that he was in any real hurry to go in. Roberts had phoned him the previous evening to tell him that they had the go-ahead for a media appeal. To proffer the opinion that the nature of the case would prompt 'every type of fucking nutter' to ring in. And to delegate to Pearson, as deputy SIO, the responsibility of each call received being properly logged, assigned, followed up and investigated. And to acknowledge the fact that from past experience these putative leads would doubtless turn out to be 'a complete fucking waste of time'. In front of the shelter there was a pair of large, metallic rubbish bins. In each a single, empty socket. A sightless eye, and a perforated skull through which dog-ends could be pushed. Perfectly framed between these, the concrete sea wall, a hundred yards or so of sand exposed to the incoming tide. And beyond, the dim outline of the chimneys of the power station across the estuary. Electric pylons. Gasometers. And several tall cranes: the skeletons of monstrous giraffes in the mist ...

Richard Lennon, the man who never was Richard Lennon, sat at a table. A table with a red Formica top. A table in a kitchen with blank walls in a flat in a block of sheltered housing. A bare window with flaking paintwork on its frame. A stainless steel sink and drainer. Three wall cupboards, units underneath. A small fridge and cooker. A bare overhead bulb casting shadows from the objects on the worktop. A toaster. A kettle. A box of tea bags. A cup. If he looked at them – if he looked at anything – for any length of time they began to swirl and move. So he didn't look at them. Just like he didn't look at Dr Fitzgerald. Looked, instead, at his hands. Concentrated on his fingers. On getting the index fingers to touch. To stop the swirling. To stop things moving about. If he concentrated on his hands he could breathe a bit better. Would shake just a little bit less.

The light was on. He had put it on because it was getting dark and he couldn't see properly. So maybe it was night-time. But the lady hadn't been today. Hadn't come and made tea. Hadn't sat at his kitchen table and talked with him. He was pretty sure she hadn't been. Hadn't asked him how things were going with Dr Fitzgerald. He was glad she hadn't been yet because he hadn't seen Dr Fitzgerald. Hadn't gone the last time he was supposed to go. And maybe the lady would be cross. Or the lady would say nothing but she would have that disappointed look on her face. He wasn't going to go to see Dr Fitzgerald again. Or didn't think he would go again. Didn't think he would ever go back. Dr Fitzgerald always asked, 'Richard? You'd like to keep coming, wouldn't you?' And Richard Lennon had. Had wanted to keep going. But now Richard Lennon didn't want to keep going. The light was on. But the lady hadn't been yet – he was pretty sure she hadn't been yet – so maybe it wasn't night-time after all. He stared at the bare bulb. As if it might give him a clue. After a few seconds he had to look away. At the red Formica table top. A green shape wriggling and dancing in front of his eyes. A hiss of white noise in his head. And, muffled, a voice. Telling him something. Something important. He couldn't hear the words, but it was something important. He was sure it was something important . . .

'You want to feel better, don't you, Richard?'

Richard Lennon had wanted to feel better. That's why he had been seeing Dr Fitzgerald, to feel better. But he wasn't sure he did. He wanted to feel better, but now Richard Lennon had begun to remember, he didn't feel better at all . . .

Pearson heard the sound of footsteps to his right. Jack Morris walked past. Standing by the sea wall he reached into his overcoat pocket and pulled out his gold lighter and a pack of cigarettes. Sparking up, lighting his cigarette, taking a long drag. Looking out over the estuary. To his left Pearson heard the familiar scuff of leather soles on concrete. Tony ambled over. Lowered himself onto the sea wall. Crossing his arms he proceeded to try and stare

121

Pearson out. From the corner of his eye Pearson saw Morris turn, and walk slowly over to stand by the shelter.

'There used to be a barrage balloon over there during the war.' He gestured with the hand that held the cigarette, towards the mouth of the river. 'They reckon it caused all sorts of problems for the Allied pilots flying out of the airbase at RAF Rochford. Because of the way the runway was lined up, they had to take off and then do a sharp left or they'd hit it and end up in the drink. Apparently we lost quite a few pilots like that.' Pausing. Taking a drag on his cigarette. 'Can you imagine it, Frank? Jerry flying up the river, our boys scrambling out of Rochford and Hornchurch?' Looking up at the sky. 'Dogfights right over our heads!'

Pearson dragged his eyes away from his staring match with Tony. Yawned.

'I hope you haven't brought me all the way down here to talk about the war, Jack. It's a bit early for history lessons. I assumed you rang me because you had something important to tell me, otherwise I'd have stayed in bed.'

Morris looked away again. Quiet for a while. Smoking his cigarette. Looking past him, further up the beach, Pearson saw an elderly man with a black Labrador. The dog old and overweight. Tail swinging round in circles. Charging into the sea. Snapping at the white tops of waves as if trying to eat them. Was that their witness, the old man who had found Rachel? At this distance it was difficult to be sure.

'I sometimes think that was my problem, Frank,' said Morris. 'Born out of my time. If I'd been old enough to be alive then, to fight in the war ... ' Trailing off. Exhaling a cloud of smoke through his nostrils.

Turning back, Pearson studied the old man. If Morris had been in the war, he'd probably have been involved in some sort of scam.

Nicking stuff from the NAAFI maybe. Selling it on the black market. But he would have ended up in the glasshouse for one reason or another.

'So what's happening with that kid they found up at the Crowstone?' Morris asked. 'Word is you're getting nowhere.'

'Still no ID as yet. There's going to be an appeal to the public today for information.' Searching the old man's face for any kind of reaction. 'Local telly, newspapers. You know the sort of thing. Probably have an ID by the end of the day.' Pearson made a show of looking at his watch. 'Speaking of which – get to the point, Jack, if there is one. I've got to go.' Looking beyond him again, Pearson saw that the figure on the beach, the man who might have been their witness, had gone . . .

Richard Lennon didn't feel better. It had been much better not knowing. That he *wasn't* Richard Lennon. That he wasn't that person but someone else. Or he had been someone else before he was . . .

'Richard Lennon,' he said out loud. Out loud, to himself. But now, when he heard that name, and whenever he had heard the name, for as long as he could remember, he heard another voice saying another name. Even if he said it himself out loud in his kitchen. Even with no one else there, he could hear, underneath, another name. Another voice saying another name. And even if he tried, tried really hard, he couldn't hear the other name. His real name.

He could remember the rubber gag, the searing pain, the white light in his head, the confusion. Sometimes it seemed that it was the only thing that was real and all the rest was—

What? That voice again. Saying something. Something just below the level of his hearing. An insistent voice. Close to his ear. Telling him to do something. Or that he had done something . . .

He had sat down at the table for something. Some reason. The lady hadn't been yet. The lady who sat at the table with him and drank tea and asked him how he was and how it was going with Dr Fitzgerald. Maybe he had sat down at the table to wait for her – he didn't think so – he had sat down at the table for something else. A pair of scissors. On the table in front of him. He didn't remember putting them there. But he must have, he supposed. He picked them up, hands shaking. Fitted his thumb and two fingers into the loops of the handles. Caught his distorted reflection in its surface. Blurred. Anonymous. Unrecognisable. Then, as he opened them, it slipped away. He turned them this way and that, watched as the stark overhead light glinted on the newly sharpened edges. Then he remembered why he had taken them from the drawer . . .

Jack Morris dropped the cigarette and ground it out under his foot, walked over to the bench and sat down next to Pearson. Taking something out of his pocket, offering it to him. A tremor in the old man's hand. Pearson took it from him. A photograph. A young boy. About six or seven, Pearson guessed. Squinting uncertainly into the camera, hands thrust into his back pockets. A stripy polo-shirt buttoned to the neck. Baggy khaki-coloured shorts. Sandals with no socks.

'So?' Pearson asked, holding it out for Morris to take.

'My son,' said Morris, 'Michael.' Pausing. And then, 'Mikey.'

'Again. So?'

'Look at it.'

Pearson looked down again at the photograph. A good-looking boy. A mop of strawberry-blond hair. The features delicate, almost pretty. Suddenly he thought of the grey morning of two days ago, the body of the unidentified girl on the beach.

'You're saying the girl we found on the beach is your son?' he asked, taken aback.

'Yeah.' Morris nodded once. 'You take some DNA from me, you'll get a match. You can do that, right? You said. A "family match" or something?'

'A familial match,' corrected Pearson, distracted. Still looking down at the photo, comparing in his mind the boy's delicate features to those of Rachel. The image turned to the camera in the crime-scene video. The computer-enhanced photograph from the morgue. The as-yet untouched face of the body on the stainless steel table at the post-mortem. There was no doubt about it. The old man was right. It was the same person.

17

'He was such a lovely little boy.'

Jack Morris looked away from Pearson and back down at the photograph, the same photograph he had shown Pearson at the seafront. The same tremor in his hand. After a moment he offered it to Cat, who took it from him, saying nothing. Morris's eyes strayed to the slim, gold lighter balanced on top of the packet of Marlboro on the table in front of him. He'd insisted on taking them out when he'd taken off his overcoat. Despite the 'No Smoking' sign on the door. Had since had to be reminded again that he couldn't actually light up.

The interview room was oppressively hot. A small window with a grille, looking out onto the car park, that couldn't be opened. An over-large, old-fashioned, cast-iron radiator. And somewhere in the building some genius had turned the heating up to maximum. Bare walls painted a deep red. 'Plum,' Cat had pronounced when Pearson had asked what colour she thought it might be – who was he to argue? A metal alarm strip running round each wall at about the height of the seat backs. Four plastic chairs. A newish pine-effect table already scuffed and scratched with the initials of interviewees. Someone had had a late supper the previous night and dumped it in the wastepaper bin. Stale coffee. The congealed fat from a takeaway burger. And a rotting banana. Nothing worse than rotting bananas, as far as Pearson was concerned. Although Morris's aftershave was running it a very close second. Something expensive, granted. But way too much of it. Already slightly queasy, having missed breakfast again. Pearson was making a habit of it lately – not eating during the day. Grabbing a take-away every night on the way home. The combination of the heat and the smells in the room were beginning to seriously turn his stomach.

'"Was a lovely boy"?' Pearson asked. 'When that photo was taken, you mean' – nodding across to where Cat had laid it on the table next to her notepad – 'but not so much later?'

Morris reached for the packet of cigarettes. Repositioned the lighter by an eighth of an inch. Said nothing.

'How old is he there?' Pearson asked.

Morris made a gesture. Something noncommittal. Head moving left and down. Shoulders shifting forward. 'Seven? Eight maybe?' Extending a hand towards the photograph. Hesitating. Cat looking up, nodding that it was OK. Morris picked it up, studied it again. 'London Zoo. He loved the giraffes. Most kids like the monkeys or the penguins, Mikey liked the giraffes.' Morris slipped the photo back into the pocket of the overcoat hanging on the back of his chair.

'So, you thought he might be different,' Pearson said, 'even then. Different from other boys of his age?'

Morris's right hand went to his face. His index and middle finger pressing down on his top lip. The unmistakable pull of the ciga-rette. 'That he was gay, you mean?'

128

Cat looked up from her notes. Something in the tone of the voice. Subtle. Disguised. But there. Disappointment? Disapproval? Distaste even.

'He used to like to try things on,' Morris said, not catching Pearson's eye, 'from the dressing-up box, y'know? Linzi – his mum – put all her old dresses in there, high heels, things she found in charity shops. Hats. A feather boa.' Glancing up briefly at Pearson, as if the other man might be about to find fault. 'Men's stuff as well. Jackets. Ties. Shirts. All sorts. But Mikey – Michael – always liked the girlie stuff ...' Looking away again. As if he, personally, might have something to be ashamed of. 'Wasn't interested in playing football. Preferred cups and saucers. Had some little plastic tea service thing.'

Cat glanced over at Pearson. Maybe she was reading too much into what Morris said. Picking up on things that just weren't there. There was obviously some history between the two. Some resentment. Some animosity. At least on Pearson's part. Maybe because of the old man's relationship with Pearson's mother. Roberts had sensed something, had said as much, in the meeting the previous day. Mind you, he had also wondered if Morris had been gay. If he had been having some kind of tryst with Rachel. Michael. And he'd been totally wide of the mark there. Pearson looked over at her. Nodding almost imperceptibly, a sign that she should take the lead. Cat took a breath. Reminded herself that, whatever any of them may think of him, they were still dealing with a bereaved relative. The father of a possible murder victim.

'And you didn't like that?' she asked. 'That he preferred cups and saucers to football?'

'She was supposed to be his mum!' Morris said. 'She treated him more as some kind of playmate—' He frowned. 'That can't be right, can it?' Looking to Cat for affirmation. Disappointed when it wasn't immediately forthcoming. Looking away again, down at the table. 'I mean, she wasn't just playing. You know, like an adult with a child. It was like she was a child herself.' That gesture again. Head moving left and down. Shoulders shifting forward. Something like a shrug. Then again, maybe not. 'It's hard to explain; you had to be there.' Thoughtful for a moment. Shaking his head. Then, as if to convince himself, 'It wasn't right.'

His hand going to his packet of cigarettes. His touchstone. The slim, gold lighter balanced on top. Shunting them again around the table top.

'I never realised quite how bad she was. Not at first. Not for a while. She was always a bit flaky. A bit . . . ' pausing, 'wild, is what I thought. That's all. I mean, from when I first met her she did crazy things. But it all just seemed a bit of a laugh, y'know?' Another pause. A clearing of the throat. A swallow.

'When the boy came along she seemed to settle down.' Leaving the cigarettes, the lighter alone now. Looking up at Pearson. 'She was a good mum, y'know. Did all the feeds, the nappies, all that. So I didn't realise that she was properly sort of . . . off. Not until later.'

Cat felt a stab of irritation at the old man's appeal to Pearson. As if he'd been the one asking the question. Like she wasn't there. Morris looked down at the table, tracing a pattern on its surface. Fingertips squeaking. Leaving a greasy mark. A thin patina of sweat.

'As Michael – Mikey – grew up, I used to catch her looking at him occasionally. Some weird look on her face. Like she couldn't work him out?' Shrugging. A definite shrug this time. 'It got so I didn't trust her. I didn't like to leave her alone with him. I thought she might be hurting him.' He took a breath and said the next word slowly, drawing it out. 'Abusing him.'

Cat waited a beat. To be sure he wasn't going to say anything more. To be sure his attention would be back on her. 'So, what happened?'

'Linzi said some terrible things,' still talking to the table top, 'about the boy. She'd been having treatment for some time, as an outpatient initially. In and out of Rochford, a couple of days at a time.' Reaching for the gold lighter again, altering its position on the top of the packet of Marlboro. Then moving it again, putting it back, as far as Cat could tell, exactly where it had been. 'All the time accusing the boy of all kinds of really nasty stuff behind his back.' Moving the packet of cigarettes, the lighter balanced on top, aimlessly around on the scarred table. 'In the end – Mikey must have been about eleven or twelve – she had to be committed. He took it badly at the time. He'd problems of his own, y'know? He was getting all kinds of shit at school. Public school.' Sighing. 'You pay all that money, you'd think they could at least look after them. To top it all, me and Linzi were going through a bad patch – my fault, I'd been seeing someone else – Mikey wouldn't accept there was anything wrong with her, with her behaviour. So he thought his mother's problems were because of the affair. What could I do?' Rootling in his pocket, taking out a handkerchief. 'I couldn't let him think that it was because of him, could I? How would that've been? What kind of a father could do that?' Wiping his eyes. Putting the handkerchief away. 'So I let him believe that it was my fault for the way his mother was. He hated me. Wouldn't give me the time of day. When his mum went into the asylum, I wouldn't let him go and see her. I mean, what good would that have done? Seeing her like that, in that place?' A brief glance up at Cat. 'That was when he started running away.'

'So what did you do?' Cat asked.

131

'I would go out in the car. Drove around for hours. Called in a lot of favours. Eventually, someone would find him, let me know. I would go and get him, manage to persuade him to come home. But it got harder and harder the older he got, the more times he ran off. Finally he ran away, when he was . . . about fifteen? And I couldn't find him. I looked all over. Spent most of my money paying people for information. Nearly caught up with him a few times. But every time I just missed him. He'd been there last week, or yesterday. I was always just too late. So,' looking at Cat, a shrugging, a sagging of the shoulders, 'eventually, I gave up.'

'You haven't looked for Michael since then?' Cat asked.

Morris shook his head. 'Not really. Well, until recently, that is. Then I had this sort of . . . ' His hand strayed to the disfigurement on his neck. The skin red. Smooth. Almost polished in appearance. Tapping the unsightly scar with two fingers. 'Health scare.' Morris effected another shrug. 'Makes you think, something like that.' Even so, his eyes, his hands went back to the slim, gold lighter, the red and white packet of Marlboro. Then, looking at Cat. A half-smile. Answering her unasked question. 'Not enough to give up the fags, obviously.'

'But you never found him?' Cat asked.

'No.' Morris shook his head again, looking back down at the packet of cigarettes under his hand. 'At least, Tony didn't. He's the one who's been looking for him for me.'

'Tony?' Pearson asked, sitting forward in his chair. 'This is the same Tony who's been driving you around?'

18

'Anthony Derek Blake.'

'OK ...' Roberts said. Doubtfully: the adverb Cat would have chosen, if asked. Roberts put a Polo into his mouth. Crunching noisily. Offering the packet to Cat and Pearson in turn, both of whom, this time, shook their heads. Rewrapping them, he dropped the packet onto the desk. 'So, who's he?'

'Drives for Jack Morris,' said Pearson. 'His great-nephew, fancies himself as a bit of a hard man. Two counts of ABH, one of affray. Three cautions for drunk and disorderly.'

'Go on,' Roberts nodded, 'but make it quick. I've got a meeting in ten minutes about this afternoon's media conference. Seems the Chief Constable has decided that he's going to attend.'

'After all of Curtis's foot-dragging?'

'It appears my little comment about how we're perceived in the LGBT community may have hit home. Plus his nick is already "under a black cloud because of the Carragher business". He feels it's important that the most senior officer be present. Public relations are going to brief him on the correct terminology. And he wants to make sure he's got all the facts; in the meantime, I need to make sure that in going out of his way to appear to be helpful to the media he doesn't totally compromise the investigation.'

Cat was staring out of the window. At dank air suspended halfway between the sky and the ground. Fine droplets of water swirling in a chill flurry. A slick patina glistening on the triple black shards of the fountain, the red brickwork, the grey concrete of the square. The unkempt tarmac: leaf-littered, weed-strewn, sprouting clumps of discarded rubbish. Wet paper, fast food wrappers, cigarette packets ...

'And you know what it's like,' Roberts was saying. 'There's always some nosy fucker who wants to dig a bit deeper. And the more they're stonewalled, the more they'll want to dig.'

Cat was so tired of this little game. The pretence that, as a DCI, Roberts wasn't enmeshed in the same bureaucracy, party to the politics, the arse-covering that went on. Outside, water seemed to be seeping upwards from the earth. Gathering in small pools at the corners of the uneven paving stones. Even the concrete was incontinent. A damp patch spreading up the side of the tower block of the council offices like piss staining an old drunk's trousers ...

'If I can agree some kind of media strategy with Curtis and the CC that will help to keep a lid on things, at least for the moment, then we might have a chance of running some kind of autonomous, impartial investigation.'

The day still hadn't moved out of neutral. But the sky had at least broken up into patches of lighter and darker splotches. Across the road, behind the high-rise apartments of Skyline Plaza, it was almost luminous, casting the apartment block into a stark silhouette.

'So,' Roberts said, 'Tony Blake?'

'Morris *claims* he had a health scare,' Pearson said.

Again that note of antagonism, that ill-feeling, that Cat had picked up on in the interview. Definitely some previous there, that was obvious. But even if she asked what it was all about, Pearson would probably just brush it aside.

'And that he wanted to try and square things with his estranged son—'

'All right,' Roberts cut in. 'Spare me the soap opera. Where does this Blake fit in?'

'Tony Blake was supposedly looking for Morris's son for him.'

'"Supposedly"? You've got your doubts?'

'Blake told Morris that he couldn't find Michael,' Pearson said, 'but we've only got his word – Blake's, that is – that he was actually looking.'

'You think that maybe he could've decided that it wasn't really in his interests to find him? That maybe he didn't look too hard? In which case, why didn't Morris look for Michael himself?'

'For one thing, Jack Morris is an old man. And not a well one. Plus, Tony Blake and Michael Morris spent a lot of time together as kids apparently. So Morris has the idea that he'll have a better chance of knowing where Michael might be, who he might be hanging around with. He'd heard a rumour that Michael might be back in the area but no one knew, or was saying exactly where—'

'Hurry up and get to the point, Pearson,' Roberts said, casting a look at the clock on the wall. 'I haven't got all fucking day!' Slipping his arms into the sleeves of the jacket hanging on the back of his chair. Shrugging it on.

'OK, what if ... ' said Pearson, ' ... Blake already knew that Michael Morris was back in the area but didn't say anything? Even though he had been driving Morris round, spending hours at a time in his company ... '

'All right – why not?'

'Morris owns a couple of betting shops and minicab firms. Plus, word is he's got business interests in one or more of the clubs in town.'

'OK.' Roberts nodded. 'He's minted. The bookies have got to be a good little earner in themselves, right?' Picking up his packet of Polos from the desk, putting them in his jacket pocket.

'Meanwhile,' Pearson went on, 'Jack Morris's natural heir is nowhere to be found, Blake is his only family; he must figure he's due something, right?'

'OK,' said Roberts again, scanning the desk, picking up his mobile. 'Even if Blake does know where Michael is, I can see it *might* not be in his interests to tip Morris off – the last thing he needs is some tearful family reunion, right? Where the entire business is handed over to Morris's prodigal and he ends up with fuck all. In which case Blake *could* possibly have a motive for murder.' Standing up. 'All right, let's bring him in for a chat.'

19

Cat Russell was in Priory Park, standing in front of a crumbling granite obelisk about eight foot in height and gripped at its base by the bloodied fingers of three rusting iron bars. The words 'LON', presumably once signifying 'London', and 'MAYOR' barely decipherable, despite its rain-streaked surface. Unsure, now, whether this was such a good idea after all.

She'd had misgivings ever since the text message the previous evening. Had been in two minds even as she'd replied and arranged the time and place of the meeting. Staring distractedly out of the window in Roberts's office, barely half an hour or so ago, she'd experienced that familiar feeling of claustrophobia. The overcast, glowering sky. The looming concrete high-rise buildings. And she'd all but decided not to come after all. Yet, here she was. Early. But part of her still hoping it would start to rain again and that, even this late in the day, she could use the weather as an excuse to cry off. There was no one about. That fresh after-rain smell in the chill air. The lawn on which she stood – saturated. The only sound – the susurration of leaves in the nearby trees.

She wasn't very good at trees. The only one she recognised was the yew. And that only because of the berries. She began rifling through her handbag so she could find her phone and look them up—

'What is that thing?' The voice behind her was deep, soft, Geordie.

Cat turned to face the man she'd arranged to meet. John Hall was only about an inch or so taller than her. Not what you'd call handsome in the conventional sense of the word. Cropped mousy-brown hair. Going prematurely grey, she noticed. A broad, open face. The brown eyes soft, kind. But the brows above marred by past maltreatment. The right eyebrow bisected by a scar. The right eyelid with its slight droop. This, she remembered, became especially pronounced when he was tired. The record of his many bouts as an amateur boxer. *Never a very good one, pet. As you can see by the damage.* But even under his coat his body still bore the signs of his obsession with lifting heavy weights. If there was a word to sum up John Hall she had always thought that it would be 'solid'.

'The Crowstone,' Cat said, happy to break eye contact. She nodded at the stone column. 'This is the original, dating from seventeen fifty-five. There's another one, a replacement, on the beach at Chalkwell which dates from eighteen thirty-seven.'

'Same old Cat.' Glancing around she saw him shaking his head, the half-smile playing across his lips. 'Still the preoccupation with facts.'

Cat looked away again. 'This one was brought here in nineteen fifty,' she said. 'It's a boundary stone which marks—'

'I think you could manage a hug, Cat.' Hall had been the first to call her 'Cat'; it had always been 'Cathy' at school, 'Catherine' at home. 'Even people who are just "friends" hug, these days.'

They stood looking at each other for a moment. Ill at ease. Uncertain. Cat reluctant to bridge the gap between them. Finally, Hall took his hands from his pockets. Tentatively, almost apologetically, he opened his arms. And she moved towards him. But the embrace was clumsy. An ungainly, inelegant tangle of arms. The once-comfortable, and comforting, space now ill-fitting and troubling. That shared history somehow absent. After a moment, Hall stepped back and, hands still gripping her biceps, studied her face.

'You always were a bonny-looking lass, mind, Cat.' Doubt clouded his face momentarily and he ran his hand up and down her arms. 'Have you been—'

'Eating?' Cat asked. 'Yes.' Though she hadn't. Not really. Had been surviving for the most part on cigarettes and black coffee. The crayfish and mayonnaise bap she had only half-finished the day before had been the only thing she had eaten in the past few days.

Hall let his hands fall to his sides. Then, as if at a loss as to what else to do with them, he put them in his pockets.

'You look like you've lost weight, to me.'

'How would you know? You haven't seen me in … God, how long has it been?' Cat asked. Though she knew. Knew only too well.

Hall studied the grass for a moment, making a show of considering the question, then looked directly into her eyes. 'Seven years, two months and three days. Not that anyone's counting.'

Cat blinked, touched a dry top lip with her tongue. Breaking eye contact she nodded in the direction of the entrance to the formal gardens. 'Shall we walk?'

They walked in silence through the wooden gate and into the gardens. To the right, the overwhelming scent of rosemary from the bushes. Rosemary, Cat thought, for remembrance. To their left, the knot garden. The flowers gone. The earth newly turned over. Somewhere far off the plaintive caw of a solitary crow.

'The Morrigan,' Hall mused absently. 'The phantom queen of Irish mythology, often taking the form of a crow to fly over battlefields. The augur of imminent death.'

Mythology had been one of Hall's passions. Had been, had become, one of their shared passions.

'Are things as bad as that?' Cat asked.

'No.' He gave a small laugh. Self-deprecating. Embarrassed at his show of self-pity. Shook his head. 'It's not quite that black.'

After an awkward pause, Cat asked, 'So how is everything … everyone?'

Hands still in his coat pockets, Hall shrugged. 'Jean's much the same.' Sighing. 'Difficult, y'know?'

They paused beside an ornamental fish pond, bounded by two overhanging palm trees. It was octagonal in shape, had two barred rills leading off to the north and south. Cat wondered if it might be some arcane religious symbol, set as it was in the grounds of the ancient priory. But it was probably just a whimsy of the garden designer.

Neither spoke. Staring down, instead, into the dark pool. Watching as, in turn, goldfish of varied markings and diverse colours broke the surface then retreated back into its murky interior. Leaving, in their wake, a series of overlapping concentric circles rippling across the top of the water.

'And the girls?' Cat asked.

'Growing up fast. Samantha's in secondary now.'

'And Elizabeth?'

Glancing over, Cat saw pain etched briefly on Hall's face. Without looking at her, still studying the fish, he said, 'There's been quite a big improvement. She's in a really good special

140

school. The best in the area for children with autism. They've worked wonders really, she's hardly recognisable now.'

Cat looked away and across the gardens. Some way off, a faint mist rising from the damp grass. The smell of burning leaves on the air. Wind rustling the trees. Beyond the trees, the background hum of the traffic on the main road. The rumble and whine of building work on the site of what, many years ago, was the EKCO radio factory. The distant call, once again, of a lone crow.

'In Hindu mythology,' Cat said, 'crows were the bringers of information ...' When Hall didn't respond she asked, 'Why are you here, John?' Then, turning to face him, 'Actually, how did you even get my number?'

'Do you know Dougie Ettrick?' Hall asked. Finally looking at her. Cat didn't know Doug Ettrick. Not personally. But she'd heard of him. Ettrick was a former Detective Chief Super. Before her time, but Pearson had told her all about him. An outwardly persuasive and plausible senior officer who had been found wanting when put to the test. He had, nonetheless, managed to blag himself a string of promotions and was now the Assistant Chief Constable somewhere up north. He had recently given them a piece of key information which had helped resolve an ongoing case and had led to the arrest of an inspector from the Professional Standards Department.

'I've heard *of* him,' Cat said. 'Bit of a gossip, by all accounts.'

'Aye,' Hall smiled, 'that's Dougie. Anyway, I'd had to attend one of these residential police conferences —' He broke off when he saw the question on Cat's lips. 'I'm a DCI these days, goes with the territory, I'm afraid.'

'Oh, sorry,' Cat said, 'I forgot to ask. Congratulations.'

'No big deal,' Hall said. 'Jean's happy, keeps me off the streets, y'know? And the extra money's welcome. Anyway, I'm sitting having a quiet drink in the hotel bar and Dougie recognises me as one of the delegates. Sits down at my table. Well, he's a superior officer, it's not like I can say no, is it? He's going on about this and that nick and I'm not really paying attention ... until he happens to mention the name "Cat Russell". At first I'm thinking maybe it's just a coincidence, like. Then I thought, y'know, maybe it's the same Cat Russell?' He shrugged. 'Once I found out you were in the Job, well, it wasn't that hard to track you down ... '

Hall looked down into the water again. Started absent-mindedly scraping dirt and blades of grass into the pool with his shoe. Cat studied the man who had done so much for her. The man who had saved her life. Or, if not saved her life, had helped her to reclaim her sanity. It was because of him that she was who she was. What she was. It was because of him that she had joined the police.

'Why are you here, John?'

'Down south, you mean?' Not looking in her direction. Scraping more grass into the pool with his shoe. 'I'm down here for another seminar. Central London. A multi-agency workshop to do with the grooming of young teens. Dougie said you had something of the sort happening locally?' Looking at her again.

Cat realised that her jaw was aching. That she had been grinding her teeth.

'The Abigail Burnet children's home,' she said. Convinced Hall had wilfully misinterpreted the question, holding his gaze, she asked, 'No, John. Why are you here?' She spread her arms to indicate the gardens. Southend itself. But mostly his proximity to her. 'Why are you *here*? Why have you come all this way?'

'I told you,' Hall said, looking hurt now, shaking his head. 'I was in London.'

'That's still an eighty-mile round trip,' Cat insisted, then, relenting, she said, 'Why don't we go for a coffee? There's a café around the corner . . . '

Later, sitting at the table, the conversation dried up, their empty coffee cups in front of them, Cat had asked again, 'So, why did you come, John? I mean, after all . . . this *time*? Really? What exactly did you hope to achieve?'

Hall gazed down briefly into his cup, then up again to look at her. 'I wanted to see how you were. Make sure you were all right. That's all.'

'Nothing else?'

Hall took a deep breath. Looked past her. Was silent for a while. Blinked once. Twice. Finally looking at her. A smile. A concession.

'All right, I can't deny there might have been an element of desiderium.' A regretful shake of the head. 'I'm sorry, Cat. I see it was a mistake now. Really.' There was a tenderness in his touch as he brushed her cheek with his fingers. But also a definite distance, an awkwardness as they stood up to hug.

Cat made a point of not watching Hall leave, sitting back down in her chair. Reflecting on his final words. At first it had just been an attempt to improve their vocabulary. Each would come up with an interesting word, see if the other might know what it meant. In the end it became more like a competition. Cat dug her mobile out of her handbag, opening the web browser, typing the word in the search field. Then sat for a while, looking at the screen.

Desiderium (noun): A yearning, specifically for a thing one once had but has no more.

20

'Have you heard of ECT, Richard?' Dr Fitzgerald had asked. 'Electro ... convulsive ... therapy?'

Speaking slowly. Pronouncing each word carefully. Hoping that, this time, Richard Lennon might understand. Hoping that, this time, she might get some kind of response.

'Have you heard of it, Richard? Do you know what it is?'

But that time, like all the other times she had asked him the same questions, she got the same response. Which was no response at all. He'd just sat, hunched forward in his chair. Arms braced against the armrests. Concentrating on his hands, his fingers.

'I think that that is what has happened to you, Richard. I think you have had ECT. It's not so common these days, but they used to use it. In the sixties. I think you have experienced ECT at some time in your past, Richard, but I think that you received a dispro-portionate number of repetitions, and at an excessive voltage. Do you understand? Richard?'

A slow uncurling of arthritic hands. The straightening of the two tremulous fingers ... She glanced away. Looked down at her notes, to avoid seeing yet another iteration of his maddening ritual.

'Have you heard of St Thomas's, Richard? The hospital? Does that name mean anything at all to you?'

She looked up. Having just slid past each other, the hands were balled, once again, into tight fists. Lennon pausing momentarily before his next attempt.

'What about Waterloo, Richard? The Royal Waterloo? That's another hospital.'

Hands back in position. Forearms braced on the armrests of the chair. The index fingers pointing towards each other. She had asked these questions before, too. Received the same lack of response.

'Electro-convulsive therapy,' Fitzgerald had said into the phone earlier the same morning, 'in combination with induced insulin coma, was carried out at St Thomas's and its sister hospital, the Royal Waterloo, during the nineteen fifties and sixties—'

'Yes, yes,' said the voice at the other end of the line. Hugo Somerville. 'We've already established that it's the most likely place that he would have undergone these treatments, Angela. It's all a matter of public record. As is the short-term and long-term memory loss suffered by some of the patients. But, as I said before, you really are going to need more persuasive evidence in order to put forward the argument that this led to an attempt, and such an obviously unsuccessful attempt, at brainwashing.'

'Yes, Hugo, and I took that on board. I wrote down your points.' Fitzgerald eased out a sheet of notepaper from under a pile on her desk, started reading. 'What would have been the rationale behind it? On whose behalf would it have been carried out? Who would have sanctioned such a thing?'

Fitzgerald fell silent for a moment. Listening to the breathing in the earpiece. The lack of an objection.

146

'And you also said, "If you can answer the first question, maybe that will help you find the answers to the other two. Or at least point you in the right direction in which to start looking for the answers."'

Somerville sighed. 'OK.' Fitzgerald imagined him at the other end of the phone. Wearily kneading his temples between fingers and thumb. 'Go on.'

'So I went back to the internet—'

'Not the most reliable of resources.'

'No,' Fitzgerald conceded, 'but obviously I verified the facts, as far as I could, against official records and historical medical journals.' She paused, then, taking the lack of a response as tacit approval to continue, 'William Sargant, the head of the Department of Psychological Medicine at St Thomas's, was in correspondence with Donald Ewen Cameron of the Allan Memorial Hospital in Montreal. Cameron's work was—'

'Rumoured to have been covertly funded by the CIA,' Somerville cut in, 'and he was said to have contributed to the notorious Project MK Ultra mind control programme ...' Then, clearly irritated, 'I know all that, Angela. And your point is?'

Fitzgerald took a breath. 'Could someone in the British government have had the idea that they could do something along the lines of MK Ultra?'

'A collaboration, you mean?'

'In collaboration? In competition? But it's possible they might have wanted to shadow the experiments being carried out at the institute in Canada?'

Fitzgerald heard a noise at the other end of the phone. Somerville moving something on his desk perhaps. The thinning sandy hair dishevelled because of that habit he had of scratching at his scalp when he was agitated. Or perhaps he was just moving himself into a more comfortable position. 'Hugo?'

'Yes.' Curt. Impatient. 'It's possible. I'm listening.'

'I know on the face of it that it might seem absurd,' Fitzgerald said. 'Looking back, with the benefit of twenty-first-century knowledge and sensibilities, it seems, at best, naive ...'

'And, at worst, ill-informed and inhuman. Not to mention, at the very least, morally dubious – if not downright cruel and barbaric.'

Fitzgerald, the telephone pressed tightly to her ear, could hear in the background the sound of rain starting to hammer against glass. The squeaking of a chair. The suggestion that Somerville might be walking across the room. A window being closed. Finally, he spoke again.

'And you would have to wonder just how many people would have had to turn a blind eye, Angela.' Somerville's tone of voice softening. At least considering it now. 'How they'd managed to get away with it? Of course, it wouldn't be impossible, even these days. Complicated, yes. Unethical, certainly. But not impossible.'

Feeling herself back on the front foot, Fitzgerald began now to articulate a carefully rehearsed argument.

'And if you view it against the backdrop of the prevailing attitudes of the times, Hugo, when people were less well-informed. Less cynical. When post-war Britain was only just coming to terms with the assassination of an American president. The very public fall from grace of their own Minister of War as the result of a sex scandal?' Fitzgerald paused. 'Wouldn't the majority of the population still be clinging to their deep-seated belief in the established order?' She let the statement hang for a moment. 'And the established order would include not only government ministers and the instruments of national security, but also the medical profession.'

She had an image of him once again behind his desk, picking up a pen, rolling it between his fingers.

'OK,' Somerville agreed. 'Politically they could probably have got away with it.'

'By my calculations,' Fitzgerald said, 'the man we know as Richard Lennon was in St Thomas's sometime in nineteen sixty-six. The idea that brainwashing was possible would certainly have been validated in the public imagination at least a year earlier with the release of *The Ipcress File*.'

'The film?' Somerville asked. Unconvinced. The sceptical tone back in his voice.

'Just hear me out, Hugo ...' Silence, so Fitzgerald continued, 'Maybe some credulous government minister saw the film and was convinced enough to try and emulate it in real life? In retrospect it seems ridiculous, insane even. But as we know, Hugo, official policy, let alone speculative scientific experimentation, has been initiated by less rational notions.'

'But would they have believed it achievable, Angela? Even then? It seems to me to be stretching the bounds of possibility just a little too far. Don't you think? Even if we allow for some crackpot decision by a faceless government official—'

'So your only objection is that it should at least be based on some, if specious, scientific theory?'

'Not my only objection, Angela.'

Fitzgerald ignored him. 'What if someone in the government had read, say, *A Clockwork Orange* for instance? The "reclamation treatment", the fictitious "Ludovico technique" of the novella was supposedly inspired by B.F. Skinner's theory of "operant behaviour" ...'

She heard Somerville sigh again. Pictured him massaging his temples. Rubbing at his scalp.

'Wouldn't something like that, Hugo, if it proved to be success-ful, be worth doing? Just for the reduction on the prison budget alone? The cost of a few months' medical treatment set against the cost of keeping an individual incarcerated for life?'

'So, what you're asking me to believe, Angela,' Somerville said slowly, 'is that the destruction of this man's psyche could be the result of a scheme simply aimed at reducing government expenditure?'

Dr Fitzgerald opened the manila folder again. Looking down at the topmost sheet of paper. Considering what she actually knew. The facts. Or as near to the facts as she could get.

Her patient had spent some time at St Thomas's, or the Royal Waterloo, undergoing an intensive course of ECT and insulin coma therapy in order to alter his mind and implant a new personality. When this had proved unsuccessful he had been 'hidden' at Runwell Mental Institution where he had gone by the name of 'Richard Lennon'. He hadn't, of course, had any official documentation to verify this identity. Whether this was deliberate or the paperwork had simply been lost was impossible to say. Somehow overlooked or forgotten, he had been released as a result of the 'Care in the Community' programme when the hospital was closed. Since then he had been living in sheltered accommodation, before being referred to local mental health services when concern grew about his deteriorating mental state.

Who was he? And why had he been under the care of St Thomas's in the first place? They were questions she had been desperate to know the answer to. So Dr Fitzgerald had persisted. Had said, 'I think there's something else, Richard. I think if we can find out, you will feel much better.' And asked, at the end of each session, every session, 'Richard? You'd like to keep coming, wouldn't you?'

And, although he wouldn't answer, never answered, he had kept

150

coming back. Except for this time. This time he hadn't come back. She had other clients, of course, who didn't turn up. Nothing too strange about that, given the nature of the people she was dealing with. Except that during their last session together Richard Lennon, the man who never looked up, never looked directly at her, had done just that.

'The something else,' he had said.

'Yes?'

'You said there was something else.'

'Yes, Richard?'

'I think I know what it is.'

'OK, Richard, do you want to tell me?'

'I don't know.'

Head down again. Forearms braced. Stiff hands uncurling. Shaky fingers pointing at each other.

'It's up to you, Richard.' Turning away again, so she didn't have to watch. 'You don't have to tell me anything you don't want to.'

Turning back she saw it anyway. The spasm. The hands sliding past each other. The hands balled into tight fists. The momentary pause before he started again.

'It's just,' lifting his head, looking at her, the shaking worse this time, 'I think I may have done something . . . something truly evil.'

21

'Michael,' said Tony Blake, having taken off his black track-suit top to reveal a light blue vest; big shoulders. But running to fat, Cat noticed. And covered in tufts of orange hair. A moulting orangutan. 'Was always a conniving little cunt. Even as a kid.'

They were back in the same interview room – mercifully free from the bitter smell of yesterday's coffee dregs. Of day-old burgers, of rotting banana skins – Pearson having cleared the wastepaper bin. Or, more accurately, having swapped it with the empty one in the room next door.

'He was never happy, whatever he had.'

'Conniving?' asked Cat. 'With who?'

'Whoever.' Blake shrugged his big shoulders. Talking to Pearson. As if he'd asked the question. 'Whoever it suited him to pretend he was friends with at the time. The thing is, with Michael, he'd work out what you could do for him, take advantage of you, and then as soon as you weren't useful to him any more . . . that's it, he'd drop you.'

'That what he did with you?'

'That's what he did with everyone. Despite his mum, his old man, spoiling him rotten, giving him whatever he wanted, he always wanted more. He never thought he got what he deserved' – a curl of his lip – 'greedy little fucker.'

'You sound jealous,' said Cat.

'Listen,' Blake said, leaning forward, making a point of not looking at her, 'his mum loved him, right?' Looking down at the table. Rubbing at it with the side of his fist, as if he could erase the mark that Jack Morris's greasy fingers had made earlier, his words. 'Michael didn't care. Just saw it as another opportunity to get what he wanted. He's always played them off against each other.'

Cat had that feeling again. The feeling of being ignored. As if she wasn't in the room. She had felt it in Roberts's office a few hours earlier, during the interview with Jack Morris this morning.

'Jack claims,' Pearson said, 'that Michael's mum – Linzi? – had problems. Says he felt he couldn't trust her with him.'

'Proves my point,' Blake said. 'Jack's always going to take his side. Michael's got him wrapped around his little finger—'

'Had,' interrupted Pearson.

'What?' Looking up. Frowning.

'Had him. Had him wrapped around his little finger.'

Blake grudgingly conceded the point with a stony glare. 'So, anyway,' rooting around in an ear with a finger, 'when his mum cottoned on to what he was really like,' studying the result, 'what an evil little bastard he was, his old man wouldn't believe her,' rubbing his hand along the leg of his tracksuit bottoms. 'That's why he had her locked up. Michael made her life a fucking misery, then played the innocent. Made his old man believe it was all in her imagination.'

'So you and Michael spent a lot of time together as kids?'

'Yeah.' Blake leaned back, folding his arms. 'My parents weren't worth a wank. My old lady was out every night. Slagging around with any bloke who'd buy her a drink. Disappearing for days at a time, turning up so she could catch up on her kip or to borrow a few quid from the old man. When he wasn't there she'd sneak back for a change of clothes, a shower, then fuck off again.' A hand lifted briefly from a bicep to swat the memory away. 'Whatever. The old man was too frightened of losing her to say anything, so instead he'd stay home, get pissed, take it out on me.' Running his fingers absently over his nose, touching his front teeth. As if the nose had only recently been broken. The teeth newly loosened. The spectres of previous injuries, past beatings. The foreshadowing of violence yet to come. Cat noticed for the first time a defect in Blake's right eye. As if the black of the pupil had leaked into the brown of the iris and then pooled there.

'So I used to go round there instead. Knew where I was better off. And, yeah,' a nod, 'maybe I am jealous.' Unfolding, then spreading his arms. 'All I'm saying is, that his mum was a decent woman, right? I really liked her, and she was treated really badly. But then Jack treats everyone like shit.'

'Except for Michael,' Pearson prompted.

'Yeah, well, like I said, Michael had a way of getting people to do exactly what he wanted. He was the same as a kid. He'd be exactly what he needed to be, what he thought you wanted him to be, so he could get what he wanted. And he didn't give a monkey's if anyone else got hurt. I don't think he ever cared about anyone. I don't think he *could*, y'know? It's like there was something missing in him. Like he was empty inside.' He leaned forward again. This time putting his elbows on the table. Blake was beginning to sweat. Cat could smell him. The downy hair on his forearms damp.

155

As if he'd dabbed himself with glue and then rolled on a carpet recently vacated by a red setter.

'Did you know Michael was back in the area?' Pearson asked.

Richard Lennon stood now, staring out across the river. He wasn't sure how long he had been here. Only that it was a long time. The rain easing. The wind dying away. After a while he had been able to make out the constant hum of traffic at his back. Somewhere far off, the dull clanging of metal against metal. The light fading. The dark outline of the pier merging with the falling night. The silver tanks of the oil refinery receding into the gloom. The graceful, fairy-tale beasts tethered to its side becoming first indistinct, and then vanishing. There was something out there. He was sure. Something just out of reach. Something truly evil. Richard Lennon gradually became aware of lights coming on along the side of the pier. Glowing silver beads, extending towards the far bank. And reflected in spectral fingers stretching out across the saturated beach. The distant clanging of metal swelling to a maddening, insistent tattoo. A face slowly emerging on one of the tanks of the refinery. Opening blinking red eyes. Disapproving. Disparaging. Accusatory. A deafening grinding and screeching as bolts sheared, then gave way. The immense cables securing the giant beasts came loose, slapping against their long necks as they slowly turned to regard him . . .

Tony Blake wiped the sweat from his forehead with his hand. Staring at the inside of his palm, as if not quite believing what he was seeing. Then rubbed his hand on his tracksuit bottoms again.

'Did you know Michael was back in the area?' Pearson asked.

'I'd heard.'

156

'But you didn't tell Jack he was back.' Not a question, Cat noticed.

A negligent shake of the head. 'Nope.'

'Why not?'

Blake shrugged. 'I don't owe Jack anything.'

'He gave you a job.'

'Yeah, right.' Sneering. 'Some fucking job. I'm just a lackey. Get this, get that, make the tea, pick up the dry cleaning. I'm supposed to be family, right?' Blake gave another shake of his head. 'Who else but family would put up with him? Especially as since his little "dice with death"' – air expelled through his nose, dismissive – 'he's gone all fucking soppy and sentimental. Crying all the time about what a fuck up he's made of his life. How he misses Michael. How he should have done things differently.' Again, the hard stare at Pearson. 'It's a fucking nightmare driving him around.'

'You get paid.'

'Yeah,' scowling, 'I get paid. I get paid fuck all. What's your point?'

Pearson bristled at the sense of entitlement. It seemed to be this way with all the kids these days. They viewed the world as if they had some preordained right to anything they wanted. As if they needn't, shouldn't have to, work for anything. As if everything should be handed to them on a plate. Had he been like this as a young man? He didn't think so. He hoped not. He glanced across at Cat. Definitely irritated. Face tight. Drawing lines on her notebook. Pressing the biro between her fingers. Applying a little too much pressure. How long had it been since her last cigarette?

He turned back to Blake. 'My point is,' he said, slowly, as much to annoy the other man as to calm himself, 'you knew Michael was back. And you didn't tell Jack. Even though you're driving him around all day. You seem to think you're hard done by, that

157

Jack should treat you more like family, right? Jack's dying and he's worth a fair bit of money. He's got to leave it to someone. Family. So with Michael out of the way, why not you?'

'Dying?' asked Blake. 'What are you talking about?'

'His throat?' Pearson found himself aping the old man's movement. Tapping his neck with two fingers. And didn't much like the fact that he was doing it.

'That?' A half-smile. 'What did Jack say it was?' When Pearson didn't answer, his smile broadened. 'He didn't actually say, did he? Just gave you the impression that it was something serious. Like cancer or something.' Shaking his head. 'Some kind of cyst. Totally benign.' Miming with his fingers at the side of his neck. As if cupping something large, something heavy. 'To be fair, it did look fucking awful. Like he was growing a new head or something.' Letting his hand fall back to the table, knuckles rapping its surface. 'Only Jack's shitting himself, right? Absolutely convinced he's going to die. If not because of the growth on his neck, then because he's got to go into the local hospital. National Health. So, he decides to go private. And guess what? He catches MRSA or something. Some kind of superbug anyway. And the private hospital he's gone to can't deal with it. So he ends up under the NHS anyway. Twenty-four hours on AAU followed by three months on a ward. Fucking priceless.' Blake's smile faded. He shook his head again, 'And that's why you've got me in here?' Giving Pearson the dead eyes. 'You think I killed Michael so I could get my hands on Jack's money?' Sitting back, crossing his arms. 'Nah, you're looking at the wrong bloke. Jack's not going to give me fuck all. I told you, I'm not "family", I'm just the paid help. So I'm not going to get any of Jack's money whether Michael is out of the way or not. You think he's given me a job because I'm family?' A look to Cat. 'Out of the goodness of his heart?' And then back to Pearson.

'He's given me a job because he had to. Because he's got no other option. He's been done for drink-driving – not his first offence, so he's lost his licence.'

To Pearson, all of a sudden it made sense, the real reason Jack Morris had come forward. Or, let's be kind and give him the benefit of the doubt, one of the reasons. But a plausible reason all the same. Morris had only come forward because he was worried that they would get a match with him and Michael on the DNA database. A familial match. That was why he had been so interested during their conversation by the Crowstone a few days before. Jack Morris's DNA was already on the database. It would have been taken as a matter of course when he'd been done for drink-driving. So his hand had been forced. He had had to come forward and admit that Michael was his son. How would it have looked if he hadn't? The question was, though, why hadn't he come forward sooner? Why the reluctance to admit his connection to Michael? And, come to that, how had he known that the dead girl on the beach was Michael in the first place? There hadn't, as yet, been a photograph or e-fit released. So how had Morris made the link to his missing son?

22

Pearson stood under the overhang of the Chinese restaurant, contemplating the deserted street. His only company: two fabulous golden lions. The brown paper bag holding his takeaway already blotched and spotted with grease. The grey day, one of a seemingly endless succession of grey days, having ebbed into an equally miserable night. The earlier squally showers becoming little more than a heavy mist. He shot a cuff and checked his watch, though he knew what time it was. Knew it was already too late to visit his mother at the retirement home. Knew that, if he'd made the effort, if he'd really wanted to, he could have left work that little bit earlier. He watched for a while the haloing of the sodium street lamps. The drift and eddy of light reflected in the billowing damp air. It was the sort of fine drizzle, Pearson thought, that within a few minutes would somehow manage to insinuate itself into your clothes. To ooze up from the dank pavements and into your socks. To plaster your hair to your head and deposit a shroud of moisture across your face. He reached out a hand and patted the gilt-covered snout of the nearest statue. It was something he did, had become accustomed to doing, to bring him luck. Not that, up to now, it had done him much good.

Richard Lennon's feet hurt. As if he might have been walking for hours. He'd passed the Crowstone a few minutes ago, the slapping of the incoming tide a slow handclap on the cold, damp granite. The smell of the sea. The far-away thump-thump-thump of the Adventure Island amusement park. The rise and fall of the shrieking passengers on the rollercoaster. The girl's hot breath on his cheek ... the cartilage of her windpipe beneath his thumbs ... squeezing ... applying a steady pressure ... the light going out in her eyes ...

It's just, I think I might have done something ... something truly evil ...

Richard Lennon had passed under the railway bridge. The echo of his footsteps drowned by the sudden gust of wind. The rearing sheet of soggy newspaper. The skittering of a crumpled red-and-white Marlboro packet. Automatically turning left. The details of the memory, or the waking dream, or whatever it was were so vivid, so real at times that it might have happened yesterday ...

Turning up the collar of his overcoat Pearson set off towards his car, parked further up the Ridgeway. To his left: steam escaping from an extractor fan, the clatter of pots and pans from the kitchen, the smell of a deep-fat fryer – whether it was the chip shop or the Chinese, there was always that smell of the deep-fat fryer – the path down the side of the restaurant ...

Following the course of the railway. To Richard Lennon's right: the tennis club. Empty. Silent under the floodlights. An abandoned fluorescent yellow ball at the edge of one of the courts. At other times, it didn't feel real at all. Didn't feel like *his* memory. Felt like someone else's story. Or like he was watching a scene from a film. Or it was something that had been described to him so many times that he could remember it perfectly? Even though he might not have been there himself ...

As he walked Pearson felt in his left overcoat pocket for the key to the Mondeo. To his left now, a wire mesh fence, held in place by concrete posts. Beyond this the slope of the embankment, tangles of bramble and overgrown vegetation fading into long grass. The train tracks. Not finding the key, he swapped the bag containing his takeaway to the other hand, trying the right pocket. When he reached the car, he put the bag on its roof. Searching in the inside pocket of his overcoat. Poking around in the inside breast pocket of his jacket. Coming across his mobile, taking it out to check for messages. Sheer habit. There wouldn't be any. Not personal messages, anyway. Work, maybe. But then he hadn't heard it ring, hadn't felt it vibrate; even so he glanced down at the screen—

Something, someone, brushed past him. Bumping his arm, then grazing his sleeve. Pearson looked up, stifling the automatic urge to apologise. Was about to look down again ... when something stopped him. Something not quite right. Something that, if asked later, he wouldn't have been able to explain. But something just that little bit ... off. And somewhere deep in Pearson's subconscious an alarm bell started ringing. The old man walked with a sort of shambling limp. Threatening, at any second, to break into a run. Looking straight ahead. Eyes fixed on the middle distance.

Pearson followed the man's progress up the hill. Finally turning away when he disappeared into Chalkwell railway station.

Resuming his search for the car key. Unbuttoning his overcoat, trying the side pocket of his jacket. Glancing through the wire mesh of the fence. Past the embankment, the train tracks, the sea-front lit by sodium lamps. The estuary beyond. The tide in. The brown, salty water churning sluggishly. The occasional white fleck of foam breaking its surface. Fingertips finally closing around his errant key – outside handkerchief pocket of his jacket, God knows what it was doing there – Pearson caught a movement, down on the railway track. A deeper black against the darkness. The dark shape resolving itself into ... the figure of a man. The same old man that he had watched walking up the hill and disappearing into the station. The same fixed forward-looking stare. The same shuffling limp that threatened to break into a run. Walking along the middle of the westbound railway line. Pearson dropped the car key back into his pocket. Moving to the fence, gripping the wire mesh in his fingers, he shouted.

'Hello?'

Hello? Even to him this seemed a fairly stupid thing to say. But what was the correct form of address in this situation? What was the etiquette when you saw some suicidal lunatic intent on killing himself and you wanted to attract his attention? He tried again.

'Hey! You there!'

Not that much better. But his brain had frozen temporarily. Tiredness, hunger, the long day. The unreality of the situation, rendering him incapable of finding the right words. In any case, there'd been no reaction from the old man. He was beginning to doubt whether there *would* be ... whatever he said. Whatever he did. Pearson felt himself becoming more desperate. Panic rising, he rattled the fence.

'Oi! Oi!' No reaction. The same unhurried gait. Eyes fixed straight ahead. To himself now, 'Bollocks.' Slipping his phone into the inside pocket of his jacket. Dragging off his overcoat. Chucking it in the general direction of the car, he started running up the hill ...

Richard Lennon was on the track now. Gravel crunching underfoot. And at last he understood where he was going ... where he had been going all along ...

Pearson entered the railway station. Vaulting the barrier in the deserted ticket hall, the soles of his shoes sliding on the wet concrete. Cracking his head painfully on the wall opposite.

'Fuck!'

Turning left, then quickly right. Taking the stairs down, two and three at a time, jumping the last small flight. Landing awkwardly, turning his right ankle in the process.

'Bollocks!'

The eastbound platform. He checked quickly to his right that no trains were coming. Turning left again. Sprinting twenty yards along the platform. Down the slope. And into ...

Absolute dark. The sudden change in light from the starkly lit platform to the darkness of the track momentarily leaving him blind. He stood still for a moment, catching his breath, listening. The wind moaning down the staircase. The creaking of overhead lines. The susurration of agitated vegetation. And some distance off ... the crunch of feet on gravel. As Pearson's eyes finally became accustomed to the low light levels, he saw the man with the strange gait step out of the shadows, and into one of the pools of light cast by the overhead lamps along the side of the tracks. Pearson took off again. 'Hey! You there!' Crossing to the gap between the two train tracks, throwing a look back over his shoulder to make sure there was no train behind him. 'Hey! You!'

No response. No indication that the old man might have heard anything. Pearson sprinted between the tracks. His brain suddenly slipping into gear and, at last, he thought of something useful to say. 'Get off the track!' Still no response. The unhurried shambling gait. The eyes fixed straight ahead. 'Get off the fucking track!'

Then the overhead lines began to hum. Pearson looked over his shoulder, the track behind him flat. The view unobstructed for several hundred yards. Nothing. The rails started to rattle. The rails of the westbound track. The rails along which the man was walking. Pearson felt grit in his shoe. And – despite the drifting of fine rain, the chill of the night – the prickle of sweat on his skin. And cold air burning in his lungs. God, he was out of shape. He saw the old man emerging once again from a pool of shadow as a train rounded the bend ahead. Pearson tried to gauge how far away the man was ... maybe only twenty or thirty yards now. Increasing his pace, too out of breath now to call out, to do anything but gasp in the air. Time slowed. Pearson became acutely aware of the sound of his own footsteps in the gravel, the hum of the overhead lines, the rattle of the railway track. He wasn't going to reach him. He was going to watch as the man's body disappeared under the wheels of the train ...

Richard Lennon stared into the train's oncoming white headlamp. The overhead light in his kitchen ... the glint of light on the scissors as he put them down on the red Formica table top ...

The sick, helpless expression on the face of the train driver. The horn blaring. The screech of the brakes. Pearson threw himself at the man on the track. Desperately hoping for a handhold on his clothing ...

*

Richard Lennon headed towards the light. At last sure in his mind of something. He wasn't sure of who he was . . . or what he had or hadn't done . . . he wasn't sure what he was . . . but he knew what he wasn't. He wasn't 'Marks and Spencer'. He wasn't 'Made in China'. He wasn't 'Dry Clean Only'. He wasn't '100% Cotton'. And he wasn't . . . Richard Lennon.

Feeling the rough material of the coat. The weight of the body inside. Driving his shoulder into the small of the man's back in a frantic attempt at a rugby tackle. And, for that split second, Pearson was sure he'd done it. Believed they were safe. Thought his momentum would take them clear. Then they were clipped, the ground beneath them disappearing as they were sent spinning through the air. A metallic clang as they collided with something on the side of the track. Changing direction again. Falling through space. In turn his foot, leg, hip, arm hitting solid ground. Only for it to slide away. Gouging wet turf. Exposing the damp earth underneath. Tumbling down the embankment in a confusion of flailing limbs . . . before finally coming to rest.

Pearson lay on his back in a water-filled ditch. Gradually becoming aware of a night sky that was surprisingly free of stars. The orange glow of street lighting. The hum of the halted train on the track above. The crackle of radio static. The tick-tick of cooling metal. The sound of his own laboured and faltering breathing. Pain. Escalating, beginning to radiate throughout his body. A warm wetness starting to spread across his face. And the overwhelming, unmistakable, smell of blood . . .

PART TWO

Day Four

23

'Post-mortem?'

Pearson could hear the other man breathing into the phone. Slow, steady breaths. The Coroner's liaison officer. A constable from the British Transport Police, whose responsibility it was to deal with any non-suspicious fatalities on the railway. It had taken some time to track him down. And now, it seemed to Pearson, he was less than willing to help.

'I don't see why you would want to attend the post-mortem. I would have thought it would be fairly straightforward, wouldn't you? Given what happened. Sarge.'

Pearson didn't like the way the man said 'Sarge'. Or the slight hesitation before he said it. Despite his irritation, he made an effort to keep his voice neutral. Conciliatory.

'OK. When would you expect the PM results?' Again, Pearson could hear him breathing. And it was a few seconds before he replied.

'A couple of days, maybe. It isn't top priority, and the Coroner is backed up.'

'A couple of days,' Pearson repeated. The tone carefully judged to convey just the right level of dissatisfaction.

'It's a non-suspicious death. But I've been promised it will be done in the next day or two. In any case, we need fingerprints, DNA and dental for identification.'

'Didn't he have any ID on him?' Pearson heard another breath, possibly a sigh this time. There was another pause, this one slightly longer.

'No, Sarge. No ID. No phone, driving licence, no credit cards. Not even a library card. Nothing. Not even a set of house keys.'

'Nothing?'

'No. Sarge. We searched the whole area around the track, the embankment, even right back to the railway station itself. Nothing.'

'What about the clothing?' Pearson thought he heard the constable put his hand over the phone's mouthpiece. Possibly talk to someone else.

It was quiet for so long, Pearson wondered if the other man might have left his desk. Then, finally, 'With all due respect, Sarge, this is a British Transport Police matter. It's a routine, non-suspicious death. I really don't see why you should be so interested.'

Pearson hesitated for a moment and the constable continued. 'Has this got any connection to an ongoing investigation? Only I haven't heard as much. Usually your lot are only too quick to dump these cases on us. Sarge.'

'No,' admitted Pearson reluctantly, 'it's just that I was there, y'know? I feel a certain ... responsibility, an involvement.'

'I appreciate that, Sarge,' said the constable, sounding like he didn't appreciate it at all. 'But you must have phoned, going by the number of Post-It notes stuck to my PC, what, half a dozen times?'

'True,' said Pearson. Although, it wasn't. Three or four times, tops. 'But I didn't actually get to speak to you,' he pointed out.

'No, Sarge, but you have spoken to a number of my colleagues, as I understand it, and they've told you pretty much the same thing. Now, I've answered your questions out of courtesy to your involvement – and your rank. But it really is a routine incident, a non-suspicious death.'

'OK,' said Pearson, scratching his ear. 'Just answer me this one last question and I'll leave you in peace.'

The constable left it just long enough to make his point. 'And the question is?'

'The clothing?'

There was hesitation and then a sigh. 'OK then. The clothes are virtually untraceable. All high street brands, looks like, all bought fairly recently as far as we can work out. That is, they look new. But they all had their labels cut out.'

'Their labels cut out?' echoed Pearson. 'Doesn't that strike you as unusual?'

'Unusual? As opposed to what, for instance? Chucking yourself under the wheels of a train?'

'OK. Fair point. Have you ever bought anything from eBay?' asked Pearson. He heard the constable exhale. A long breath. A definite sigh this time. Making it obvious that he'd had enough.

'Is it relevant at all?'

'When you sell new clothes on eBay you're supposed to cut the labels out. It's a legal requirement.'

'Supposed to, yeah,' he said, 'but I doubt anyone ever does. I've never heard of it.'

'I'm just saying, it could be he bought the clothes off of eBay.'

'And that would help us how, exactly?'

Pearson considered this for a moment. 'Not sure really,' he conceded. 'Sorry, go on.'

'The fact that the labels are missing means we can't trace batch numbers and so on. But to be honest, we wouldn't normally bother too much in the case of a suicide.'

'So what would you do?' asked Pearson.

'If we get no joy with fingerprints or DNA we might appeal through the local and then national media. Might. In any case, the Coroner will be happy to sign it off whether we get an ID or not, as long as we follow the proper process. After that the deceased will get a cremation paid for by the local council.' The man paused again. 'Are we done here, Sarge?'

A long way from done, in Pearson's opinion. But he had pushed it as far as he could. 'OK, thanks for your help.' Adding, 'Sorry to be a nuisance.' But he was talking to the dial tone. The cord from the handset to the phone had become tangled. Pearson held the handset over the edge of the desk and let it spin until the coiled cord became unknotted.

Opposite him, Cat slipped into her seat. Booting up her PC. Pushing a coffee cup, sachet of sugar and stirrer across the desk. Flipping the lid off of her own coffee. Blowing across its surface. Looking at him for the first time.

'Christ, you look awful.'

'Thanks.'

'No, really, you look like shit.' Sipping her coffee. Studying him.

Pearson broke from her gaze, looking down at his hands. Palms flat on the desk. A slight tremor in the right index finger. It was only then that he realised how sore his hands were. And how pink.

'Are you sure you're OK?' she asked.

Pearson crossed his arms. Putting both hands under his armpits. 'I'm fine.'

Her eyes, though, stayed on him. After a few seconds, Pearson took the lid off his coffee. Careful not to look up. His attention fixed on preparing the drink. The actions slow. Deliberate.

Tearing the end off the sachet of sugar, shaking it in to the cup. Picking up the plastic stirrer. A perforated paddle with an intricate design of bars. How many months and hundreds of thousands of dollars had gone into its design? he wondered. Were the bars constructed to give the most efficient hydrodynamic flow? Watching the swirl of the coffee. Listening to the tick-tick of the stirrer as it hit the sides of the cup. Had the 'least number of stirs' to dissipate cream and sugar in various hot beverages been calculated by some complex mathematical algorithm? Tick. What was wrong with a spoon? Tick. After all, people had made do with it for hundreds of years up till now. Tick. How many of these stirrers were manufactured in a year? Tick. How much could you actually save if you factored up the difference in cost of producing the stirrer against the cost of producing the spoon? The ticking of cooling metal. The crackle of radio static, the smell of damp earth—

'Frank?'

Becoming vaguely aware of Cat's voice, he realised that he hadn't reacted to her last statement. Had the feeling that he may have been sitting there for a few minutes. Hearing nothing.

'Frank?'

Pearson made a show of running his hand over his chin, opened the bottom drawer of his desk, where he habitually kept an electric razor, toothpaste and toothbrush.

'I s'pose I'd better clean myself up a bit' – looking up, finally, at Cat – 'as I obviously look so rough.' Slamming the drawer shut again. Pushing his chair back. Standing up. Wanting to get away from her concerned, pitying gaze. Turning, though, his head swam. The incident room too hot. The background noise too loud. And he had to stand for a second or two to regain his balance.

*

175

'They say in your forties you get the face you deserve,' DS Laurence said, emerging from one of the cubicles ten minutes later. Addressing Pearson in the washroom mirror. Putting a folded copy of the *Racing Post* by the basin. Turning on the tap. Washing his hands. Because of the way the mirrors were arranged, both behind and to each side of the basins, Pearson and Laurence were reflected a thousand times among a thousand faux-marble sink tops and chrome taps stretching off into infinity. Pearson concentrated on his shave. Waiting for the pay-off. Pulling the skin taut with his left hand. A definite slackening under the jaw. Fat starting to gather. The beginnings of a double chin.

'You,' said Laurence, 'must have done some fucking terrible things in your life.'

Pearson had spent the night, and the early hours of the morning, dealing with the aftermath of the incident on the railway track. Giving statements. First to the uniform constables who arrived on the scene. Then to the British Transport Police. Reluctantly submitting to a medical examination from a first-response paramedic, ignoring her advice that he should go to hospital for a more thorough check-up. Finally going home and dumping his bloodied and ruined clothes into a black plastic rubbish bag. Taking a very hot, very long shower. Lying for an hour on his bed, staring at the ceiling, trying to sleep, before giving up and deciding to come into work.

Pearson thought it was your father you were supposed to look like as you got older. Of course, he didn't know his. Had never known him. And had no real desire to find out about him. Not at this point in his life. Besides, if he looked at his face, he could see a lot of his mother in it. Apart from the eyes. If he looked at his eyes, the area around his eyes, they put him in mind of ... Jack Morris. But that was impossible. Had to be impossible. Didn't it?

Laurence, still smiling to himself, finished drying his hands under the hot-air drier. Nodded to Pearson, picked up his paper and left. Pearson turned off the razor. He'd forgotten to replace his aftershave. Had to make do with washing his face in cold water. He dried himself on a paper towel, balling it and tossing it in the waste paper bin under the sink. Fiddled with the ring on his left hand, his wedding ring, trying to dig out some of the dried liquid soap from beneath it. Despite his shower, and having washed his hands at least a dozen times since, he could still see blood under his fingernails. Could still smell it, if he brought his fingers close to his nose and sniffed. He took out the nail file from his shaving kit and used the hooked tip of it to dig the dried blood out. Turned on the tap and put his hands under. Watching the reflection of the light from the overhead fluorescents in the running water. The blood from under his fingernails liquefying. Pink rivulets. Spiralling and swirling, before disappearing down the plughole. Pearson suddenly felt light-headed again. Leaning forward, he vomited into the basin.

Having locked himself inside one of the cubicles, Pearson put the toilet seat and lid down and sat on it. Feeling like he couldn't breathe. Like his heart was having to work too hard to pump blood around his body. Every third or fourth beat stronger, slightly out of time. The weight of the previous day. The weight of his life pressing down on him. He closed his eyes. Attempting to quell the images in his mind. Taking in deep breaths. Struggling to regain control. Clenching his fists, trying to stop his hands shaking. Bending forward then, putting his head between his knees. Gulping in great lungfuls of air.

After a time he felt better. His breathing becoming more regular. His pulse returning to normal. But he had the beginnings

177

of a headache. Could feel that his right arm, his side, his hip, were starting to stiffen badly. He pulled some tissue from the toilet roll by his side, wadded it up and wiped his clammy face. Standing up, he opened the toilet lid, dropped the tissue in and flushed.

24

'What the fuck's going on, Frank?'

Roberts got up from behind his desk. Going to the office door, closing it quietly. Pearson sat with his hands in his lap, saying nothing. Roberts sat back down. Leaning forward. Resting his hands on the desk, lacing the fingers. Looking down at them.

'I've just been on the phone with a DCI from the British Transport Police. I've been getting it in the neck because, apparently, you've been badgering one of their blokes about this train suicide last night. He reckons you're showing too much interest if it's only a normal non-suspicious death. Seems to think there's something else going on. So,' looking at Pearson now, 'is there something else going on, Frank?'

Pearson shook his head. 'No, guv. Not really. I just wanted to know what was happening. I just feel' – searching for the apposite phrase, finally settling on the same one he'd used with the constable from the BTP – 'a certain responsibility. Because I . . .' He trailed off. Thinking: failed to stop him killing himself. Saying, lamely, 'was there.'

'OK. That's pretty much what I told him. Simply a conscientious officer, maybe overstepping the mark a bit. Probably just a bit shook-up. Right?'

Not right. Not in Pearson's book. But he let it go. Nodded. Roberts relaxed. Sitting back in his chair, scratching his chin.

'I hear it wasn't too good?'

Shrugging it off, Pearson said, 'Not great, no.'

Roberts nodded at him. 'And you're OK?'

'Yeah,' Pearson said, rubbing a hand over his face. 'Just a bit tired, that's all.'

Roberts studied him for a minute. 'You sure you don't need some time off?' Not sounding *that* enthusiastic that Pearson should take him up on his offer.

There was a loud rap on the window of the half-glazed door. Roberts sighed, muttering, 'Fuck's sake,' before turning towards the door and shouting, 'Yes?'

DCS Andy Curtis came in, once again, carrying a sheath of paper. Pearson wondered how much of the day Curtis spent walking round the building with paper, ring binders, a box-file perhaps under his arm. Attempting to look like he was busy. In command. On top of things. In other words, interfering. He clocked Pearson, looked momentarily perplexed. Then, winkling out two sheets of A4 from the bundle he was carrying, did his looking-down-frowning thing again. Roberts expelled air quietly through his nostrils. Glancing briefly across at Pearson. Doing everything, in fact, but roll his eyes.

'Where are we on this Michael Morris thing?' Curtis asked, looking up from his paper. Before Roberts could say anything, Curtis answered for him, 'As I understand it, despite the fact that we've now got a positive ID, we're no further along. The forensics on the hair proved inconclusive; the father and his sidekick' – a

180

smirk here from Roberts – 'have been interviewed, and again, despite their both having criminal records, no charges have been brought. We cannot establish that they may have had any involvement in the death. Is that a fair summing up of the situation, Martin?'

'That is,' Roberts scratched under an armpit, 'a pretty accurate summing up of the situation up to this point, sir.'

'This Michael Morris thing is tying up resources, Martin. May I remind you, we have received some compelling intelligence that needs to be followed up regarding the truck hijacking.'

'Ah, yes,' Roberts said, barely hiding his amusement, his eyes sliding across to Pearson. 'The tip-off from your informant.'

'My Covert Human Intelligence Source, yes,' Curtis corrected. As if they might not know the accepted terminology.

Roberts looked across at Pearson again. Stony-faced. 'A whole truck-load of Jammy Dodgers.' Curtis eyed Pearson, curious as to why he was here. Roberts grabbed the opportunity to change the subject.

'Sergeant Pearson was involved in the incident on the train track at Chalkwell last night,' Roberts said.

'Ah.' Curtis nodded. 'I understand there was a fatality?'

'Sir,' admitted Pearson.

'I take it you'll be liaising with the Transport Police?'

'Sergeant Pearson has asked for a few days off,' Roberts cut in, blocking that particular route of conversation.

Curtis nodded again thoughtfully. 'Understood, but it's hardly the best timing.' Waggling the papers in his hand. 'As I said before, Martin, as far as the Chief Constable is concerned, the clock is ticking on this one.'

When the door closed behind Curtis, Roberts shook his head, rubbing at an eye and picking up a pen from his desk. 'You're a fucking idiot, Pearson. Here we are, slap bang in the middle of a murder investigation and now I lose one of my most senior officers.' Absent-mindedly rolling the pen back and forth under his palm, the lid of the biro click-clicking on the surface of the desk. As if Pearson had wilfully disobeyed an order. Click. Click. Got involved in something he needn't have, just to piss him off. Click. Click. Like it was Pearson's idea to have the time off in the first place ...

The tick-tick of cooling metal. The hum of the halted train on the tracks above. The crackle of radio static. On his back, winded and fighting for breath. In a water-filled ditch. Staring up at a night sky surprisingly free of stars and illuminated by the orange glow of street lighting. The smell of damp earth and vegetation. A drift of fine rain. A caul of moisture settling on his face. A cold dampness seeping up from the ground and into his clothes. Gradually becoming aware of where he was. What had happened.

Clambering to his knees, searching his pockets in the hope that he might still be in possession of his mobile phone and, amazingly, finding it in his inside jacket pocket. Dialling the emergency services. Reporting his location. Requesting police and ambulance.

Looking around frantically for the old man. A few yards away, lying on his back. Slipping the phone back into his jacket. Crawling over. Putting a hand to the man's chest. And finding no sign of breathing. Leaning across the face. Listening in vain at the open mouth for any faint sign of exhalation. Feeling the wrist for a pulse and finding none. Wondering then about CPR. The man was facing away. The head bent at an odd angle. Weighing up the risk of moving him. The possibility of spinal injury. Hesitating. Listening for the approach of an ambulance. No blue lights. No sirens in the distance. Just the crackle of radio static. The tick-tick of cooling metal. Considering the options. Death. Or a possibility of spinal injury. And in that moment the decision was made. Reaching across. Placing his hands on either side of the old man's face. Carefully turning the head. But the head turning too easily. With little or no resistance, as if there was nothing to keep it in place. As if it was barely attached to the neck. A spray of blood hitting his face, surging up from under the chin. The metallic smell of warm copper. The heat, the wetness, running over his hands. Through his fingers. Soaking the soggy turf beneath—

'Frank?'

For the second time that morning Pearson became aware that someone was talking to him. Had been talking to him for some time. Had been asking him a question. Had been expecting some kind of response. When he looked up, Roberts was staring at him.

'Are you sure you wouldn't benefit from some counselling?'

'Counselling?' echoed Pearson. Feeling panicked. The prospect of 'talking things over'; being encouraged to 'share'. The counsellor maybe deciding that he needed a few weeks off work.

'I don't think I need counselling.' Making a big thing of rubbing at his eyes. 'I probably just need some kip.'

Roberts looked doubtful, his eyes searching Pearson's face. Finally, he nodded. 'OK. It's your choice.'

Silence for a minute. Then, Pearson asked, 'So, what now?'

'Now, Pearson, you take some time off. Come back when you're of some use to me.' Taking some paper out of his in-tray, heaving a sigh. As if he had been severely put out, and without looking up, Roberts flapped a hand in Pearson's direction. 'Well – go on, then, fuck off.'

25

FRIDAY 11 MARCH, 1966

Beverly Marsh stood in front of the mirror in her bedroom, practising: drawing on the Peter Stuyvesant, trying to hold it just right, trying to look … 'interesting'. But then, spoiling it all by having to exhale the cigarette smoke out of the open window. So her dad wouldn't smell it in her room later. Once she'd finished, she'd wrap the dog-end in a bit of toilet paper and flush it. Eat a mint before she went down for her tea. So they wouldn't smell the cigarette on her breath. Because, smoking 'wasn't ladylike'. Even though her mum smoked. And her dad, come to that. Smoked like a bloody chimney, he did. Didn't actually do much else once he'd come home from work. Just smoked and sat in front of the television.

He'd built the telly himself. Bought the blueprints from the EKCO shop and spent every evening soldering in the components. She'd actually felt quite proud while he was doing that. Not everyone's dad could build their own telly. She'd sat up the table with him, sorting out all the bits and bobs. Reading all the little codes printed along the glass tubes of the valves. Just so she could pass what he needed to him exactly when he needed it. But now he'd finished the telly, it was like he couldn't bear to drag his eyes away from it. Even when they sat up the table for tea. She would be having a conversation with her mum. But he wouldn't be paying attention. He'd just grunt occasionally and reach blindly for the sauce or the condiments, or his cup of tea.

Was that what she had to look forward to? The same boring life as her mum? Working at EKCO for the next thirty years. Coming home and cooking tea for some bloke just like her dad. Spending the night in front of the television, being ignored, knitting something that nobody would ever wear? Watching *Coronation Street* or *Doctor Who*? Once or twice when she'd sat in the living room with her parents she'd glanced over to see her mum secretly staring across at her dad with a weird look on her face. Like any minute now she was going to get up out of her armchair, walk slowly across the room and ram one of her knitting needles into his eye socket.

That was why, her mum had said, they'd brought her up to be a 'lady'. So she'd have something 'better'. Why her dad had thumped her every time she swore, even though 'bloody' wasn't really swearing, was it? Not proper swearing anyway. That's why they'd got her private typing lessons. Paid for the boring bloody ballroom dancing lessons she endured every week in the Victor-bloody-Sylvester studio in the high street. *You'll need to be able to at least waltz and do a passable quickstep if you get invited to the bank's dinner-and-dance.* Barely sixteen, and her mum already had her married off to some bank manager. Living in a 'nice detached house'. 'Nothing too flashy,' her mum had said, some goofy look on her face. 'Classy, y'know? Gravel drive, climbing roses around the door ...' Christ, it wouldn't be long before she was suggesting names for the grandchildren!

186

They'd both gone mental when she'd dyed her hair. Black, like Cathy McGowan. At least, Cathy's looked black on their black-and-white telly.

'I don't know what's bloody got into you lately!' Her old man had shouted. And then turning on her mum, 'That's what you get for indulging her every bloody whim!'

Indulging her, meaning letting her order some clothes from the Kay's catalogue that her mum ran. Even though she paid for them weekly out of her own bloody money. She couldn't afford the decent stuff from London. So, instead, she bought her clothes mail order. She liked Kay's, because it had a range of clothes designed by Cathy McGowan. The trouble was, every sixteen-year-old girl's mum in Southend had the same catalogue.

She ran a few strands of her long, black hair through her fingers. The dye hadn't taken properly. The colour different along the length of the hair. Darker near the roots, getting lighter towards the ends. And it had left it in bad condition, too. Previously soft and silky, it now felt like string. It made her look ... 'cheap'. As her dad was only too happy to remind her.

What was the difference, anyway? Whether she married a bank manager or some factory worker like her dad, her life would still end up the same. Boring. And they'd all probably be out of work soon. Today at work, keeping her head down, pretending not to listen, she'd heard the other girls in the typing pool saying EKCO wasn't doing so well, that it had lost a lot of money. Millions, one of the girls said. There were even whispers, she said, that the whole place would have to be shut down. Beverly hadn't had the heart to tell anyone. It wasn't just her and her mum and dad that were employed by EKCO. Every-bloody-one in Southend worked there, or knew someone who did. So if it did shut down the whole town would be in trouble.

She ground out her cigarette in the saucer she was using for an ashtray. Took a piece of toilet paper out of her pocket and wiped it clean. Then put the dog-end in the toilet paper and wrapped it up. She'd drop it down the toilet on the way down for tea. She unwrapped a mint and put it in her mouth. Personally, she wouldn't miss working in that place. Typing stuff she didn't understand. Or had no interest in at all. Listening to the other girls planning their holidays. Their wedding. The whole rest of their lives. Home was no better. The same old tea every day, every week. Something with chips tonight. It was always bloody chips. Or mashed potato. Beef or chicken pie. Bacon. Sausages. Ham-and-bloody-egg. The occasional pork chop. Roast chicken or lamb on a Sunday. Served with the inevitable roast potatoes. Which were chips, just in a different shape.

At least it was Friday. The only part of the week she enjoyed, actually enjoyed, was Friday night. Starting with *Ready, Steady, Go!* on the telly. When her dad wasn't going on about how every single group were a 'bunch of yobbos' or a 'load of long-haired nancy-boys'. As if them being on his telly would infect it in some way.

After her tea she'd take her time getting ready to go out. Looking forward to Geoffrey picking her up at the front door on his flash scooter, so they could go dancing at the London or the Middleton Hotel. Her dad didn't like Geoffrey either. Even though he was always smart, wore really nice clothes, had his hair short and neat. Honestly, you just couldn't bloody win. A couple of nights ago Beverly and her mum had been talking about Geoffrey, or rather her mum had been giving her earache about him again, and her dad had managed to prise his eyes away from the telly – *Call-My*-bloody-boring-*Bluff*, his favourite programme – just long enough to say, 'Not right in the head . . .'

'Who?' her mum had asked.

'The lot of them,' he'd replied. Waving vaguely with his fork, flicking beans onto the carpet in the process. 'That Knowles family,' shaking his head, 'not right in the head.'

And her dad was always asking, 'Where does he get the money from for all those clothes?' And, 'That scooter can't have been cheap.' And her mum was forever saying, 'You watch yourself with him, my girl. Keep your hand on your ha'penny. He's up to no good, that one.' Well, they would say that, wouldn't they? Then again, about a month ago, in the dark, in the back row of the ABC. While they had been watching *Bunny Lake is Missing*, Geoffrey had tried to put his hand up her miniskirt and cop a feel. She had clamped her knees together. Because she was a good girl. Because she was a 'lady'. Later though, after three gin and oranges and a couple of pills, up against some pram sheds in some stinky little back street, she had finally given in. And put out. Despite the fact that she was terrified of getting pregnant. Despite the fact that Geoffrey hadn't had any johnnies. And she'd found out ... that she liked it. Found out that she wasn't a 'good girl' after all. Found out that she certainly wasn't any kind of 'lady'. Now, looking forward to her date with Geoffrey tonight, it was all she could think about.

After all, it wasn't as if her parents hadn't done it. She must've come from somewhere. And they still did it. Not that often, true. But the odd Saturday night after they'd been to the pub. She'd heard them in the bedroom next door. Despite burying her head under the pillow. The squeaking bedsprings. Her old man grunting and groaning. She'd never heard her mum make a sound, and at the end of it: the bedroom door opening, footsteps across the landing. Beverly had put her eye to the crack in her open door once and seen her mum, hunched in her ratty old dressing gown, shuffling across the hall. Had seen the bathroom light going on.

189

Heard the bolt being slid across. And, a few minutes later the flushing of the toilet . . .

Even now thinking about it made her feel . . . a little bit sick. And really, really sad. She'd told herself then, promised herself, that she wasn't going to end up like that. Like her mum.

Geoffrey had plans. He was always talking about how they could go to London. How they'd have 'some big, flashy gaff in Chelsea'. How he'd buy her the best clothes. How, eventually, they might even be able to have a baby together. And it was all going to happen, she knew it was. Just as soon as they had the money . . .

26

Pearson stepped into the Green Door Café. The atmosphere steamy. The inside of the windows condensation-fogged. Tear-streaked. The door swinging slowly shut on its spring behind him and closing with a soft click. There had been a recent effort at redecorating. A half-hearted attempt to clean the grease off the tongue-and-groove panelling, before it had been abandoned and painted over. Brush strokes reflected in the overhead fluorescent lighting. Here and there, dried dribbles of paint. The occasional bristle from a paintbrush. On the tables to his left a dozen shifty eyes shifted in his direction. Recognising him for what he was. The Old Bill. The Filth. The Enemy. There was a simultaneous, studiedly casual downing of last gulps of tea. Swallowing of last mouthfuls of greasy egg. Stuffing of bread into mouths. Folding of tabloid newspapers. Dropping of creased paper money and clattering small change onto table tops.

To his right, sitting alone at a square table covered with a mustard yellow plastic tablecloth, wearing a tired, brown tweed jacket over a blue V-neck jumper and shirt and tie: Ken Sawyer. By the time Pearson had walked over and squeezed himself into the chair opposite the journalist, the café was all but empty. Sawyer, stirring a third spoonful of sugar into his tea, nodded over Pearson's shoulder at the door.

'Mr Popular.'

'Yep,' agreed Pearson, moving a dirty plate to one side, 'that's me.' And a cup. And an egg-stained laminated menu. Reflexively rubbing his slippery fingers and thumb together.

'All-day breakfast today. Half price,' Sawyer said. By way of explanation, or apology, he added, 'Tea?'

'Thanks.' Pearson nodded. Sawyer raised his hand and signalled to the woman behind the counter. Red-headed, middle-aged, plump. 'Carole! Two teas.' He pointed to the empty space on the table in front of Pearson.

'Don't mind if I eat, do you?' Sawyer asked.

Pearson shook his head. 'No. You carry on.' Sawyer started to smother his food in salt and tomato sauce. 'Sure you don't want something to eat? They do a half decent bacon roll.'

Pearson looked at the fry-up on Sawyer's plate. Chips. Beans. A rubbery egg. Three blackened sausages in a spreading pool of grease and ketchup.

'Nah, you're all right.'

Sawyer picked up his cutlery. 'I hear you've got a name for that body on the beach.' Cutting up the rubbery egg. Adding it to a piece of sausage on his fork. Putting it in his mouth. 'Michael Morris, is that right?' Chewing. Looking at Pearson. Waiting for a reaction.

No use denying it. It would come out sooner or later. Sooner, would be Pearson's guess. 'That's right.'

'Any relation to Jack Morris?'

'His son,' Pearson admitted, 'halfway through gender

reassignment. And before you ask – no, you can't use it. I can't give you anything on that one, Ken. Sorry.'

Sawyer nodded. 'Fair enough.' Then, swallowing his food, said, 'Gender reassignment, eh? How did that go down with the old man?'

Pearson had been wondering about that himself. Whether it would have been enough of a motive for murder. Maybe Morris *had* met his son – despite what he'd told them in the interview. Hadn't known about the gender reassignment until that meeting. Maybe Michael had even flaunted the fact in front of him. Taunted him with it. Then, perhaps worse still, laughed in his face when Morris suggested he had wanted to hand over the businesses to him.

Carole arrived with the two cups of tea. Up close she looked older. Wore too much make-up. And way too much perfume. She placed the teas down on the table between them, spilling some in the process.

All speculation, of course. Not one piece of evidence to corroborate it. And, if he were honest, coloured by his own dislike of the old man. Pearson saw a look pass between the woman and Sawyer. The journalist watched the sway of her substantial backside all the way to the counter through narrowed eyes. Turning to Pearson with what he obviously hoped was a conspiratorial wink.

'Every man's fantasy, isn't it? A bird who owns a café?'

'A pub,' Pearson corrected. 'Anyway, I always thought Shaky owned this place. I've only ever seen *him* behind the counter.'

'Shaky?'

'Yeah, like the pop star? Last name Stevens. He was big in the eighties.'

'I know who you mean.' Sawyer's brow furrowed. 'Nah,' shaking his head, 'he just works here. Carole's brother. Alkie. Hence the nickname.'

'Then why's this place called the Green Door café?'

193

'Because' – Sawyer pointed with his fork over Pearson's shoulder; said, in a tone that suggested it should be perfectly obvious, even to an imbecile – 'it's got a green door?'

He began the process of piling up his fork again. Put the forkful of food into his mouth and chewed. Repeated the process. Speared some chips with his fork. Worked them into the ketchup. Red streaks and smudges across the plate. Pearson looked away, feeling nauseous. Picked up his tea. Took a sip. Already nearly cold. And waited.

Finally, through a mouthful of food, Sawyer asked, 'Know anything about this train suicide last night? I heard there was an off-duty copper involved.'

'Yeah,' staring into the remains of his cold cup of tea, 'you could say that. '

'Was it you?' He knew full well, thought Pearson, otherwise he wouldn't have brought it up. 'Rumour is, there's a story there. Something weird about it. But nobody's letting on what it is.'

It was, after all, why he'd come to the café in the first place. He knew there would be a good chance the journalist would be here. Why he'd sat down at this particular table. He knew Sawyer would get around to it eventually. Would have to ask. Even so, Pearson hesitated. He'd already been sent home. Been asking too many questions. Putting too many noses out of joint. But, why not? Nobody else seemed to be too bothered. He shrugged. Affected a casual tone.

'He had no ID.'

'That's not that unusual, is it?'

'Probably not. People are often found without a wallet, bank or credit cards. Robberies and the like. But this bloke had nothing, not even a library card.' Left it a beat, two. 'And he'd cut all the labels out of his clothes.'

Sawyer frowned. Picked up a paper napkin. Wiped his mouth. 'Sounds like he really didn't want anybody to know who he was.'

'Dunno,' shrugging, 'could be.'

'Can I use this one?' asked Sawyer.

Pearson pretended to consider it. Come to a decision. 'Suppose so. Just keep my name out of it, OK?'

Sawyer chewed ruminatively as he wiped the last of his breakfast around his plate and put the fork in his mouth.

'So, you've got a picture?' Looking up. Smiling. Pleased with himself at having sussed Pearson's little game. 'You wouldn't have come over otherwise.'

Pearson reached into his inside pocket and took out the photograph. Another morgue shot. One he'd managed to wheedle the mortuary assistant into emailing over this morning. Had managed to print out without anyone seeing. Just in case. He flipped it onto the table.

As he stood up to leave, Sawyer said, 'Do you remember I said the dead girl on the beach rang a vague bell?'

Reluctantly, Pearson sat slowly back down in his seat. Sawyer put his cutlery on the plate and took a mouthful of tea. 'Thursday the thirty-first of March, nineteen sixty-six. Girl of sixteen found dead on a Southend beach. Same place. Up by the Crowstone.'

'Can't say I've ever heard of it,' but taking his pen out of his jacket all the same. Patting his pockets. Finding nothing. Pulling out a clean paper napkin from the plastic holder on the table. Clicking his pen.

Sawyer shook his head. 'You wouldn't have. Same day as the general election. Labour won an unexpected landslide. Took their majority from one to ninety-six seats. I had to call in a favour from an old Fleet Street contact. Some bloke I used to work with on the *Telegraph*. Got him to go through the archives for the newspapers at the time. He could only find an NIB – News in Brief – for the Friday. Went through all the papers for the next couple of months. But there was no other mention of it.'

'Got a name?' asked Pearson.

'Beverly Marsh.'

Pearson wrote it down. 'Anything else?'

'Not a lot. Rumour was, police liked the boyfriend for it. But it was no more than a rumour.'

Pearson didn't bother to ask where Sawyer might have come across that little nugget of information. Or how he had discovered the girl's name. Besides, Sawyer wouldn't have told him anyway. 'Got a name for him?'

Sawyer shook his head. 'Nope. Sorry.'

'So what makes you think it has any connection with our girl?'

'Michael Morris?' Sawyer shrugged. 'Nothing. Just a coincidence. Right?'

Pearson had to agree. Slipped the pen back into his jacket. Stuffed the napkin into a side pocket. How could the two deaths be connected? They were fifty years apart for a start-off. And if you took any location at random you would probably be able to find any number of deaths, suspicious or otherwise, that had happened there. Probably. All the same, it didn't stop him slipping out his mobile before he had reached the door to the café and speed-dialling Cat's number.

27

Daryl Crawford pulled down the metal shutter on the front of the Double Carpet bookmakers. Clicking a padlock into place, giving it a little jiggle to make sure it was secure. Straightening up, he looked up and down the street. Empty. Even the makeshift skateboard ramps further up the road under the street lamps were deserted, the kids defeated by the day's blustery winds and on-off showers. He checked the sky. Black clouds holding the threat of a late downpour. The air cooler out here after a day spent in the back office.

Rubbing his eyes. Knackered. But no chance of any time off. Gambling was a seven-day-a-week business, what with televised Premiership football, all-weather horse racing, Test match cricket virtually all year round. And he couldn't trust anyone else to do his job. Not for more than a day. The paperwork always got fucked up. Or the books didn't balance. On one occasion money had gone missing and the girl he'd left in charge hadn't turned up for work the next day.

Slipping the pack of cigarettes and lighter from his shirt pocket, sliding out a cigarette, sparking up, Daryl took a deep, satisfying draw. Today was one day he hadn't minded working. Had stayed late. Later than he needed. Ploughing through the endless items of petty admin that he'd previously put off. Hanging around in the office. Finding things to do. Finding excuses. Until he couldn't postpone going home any longer.

He knew what was waiting. Tracy. In a negligee. Or nurse's uniform. Or dressed as a saucy French maid. Marvin Gaye on the CD player. Soft candlelight and a bottle of red wine already open and breathing on the coffee table. It was ridiculous. Here he was, thirty-nine years old, a veteran of Iraq and Afghanistan. And scared to go home.

It had been like this for the last six months now. Tracy, five years his junior, suddenly becoming acutely aware that her biological clock was ticking. Cutting back her hours behind the bar at the club. Bringing out the charts. The thermometer. The diary tracking her ovulation cycle. It had been fun at first. For the first three or four months. But then it had become – well, he had to admit – a chore. The science, the routine involved, the constant need to perform. It was just like being back in the army. 'Stand by your bed!' The real trouble was, he was beginning to wonder if it wasn't his little soldiers that were the problem.

Sometimes he missed the army, missed his mates. But as Tracy had said, all his mates, his good mates, were dead. Daryl took a last drag of his cigarette, dropped it on the pavement. Ground it out under his heel. So he had jacked it in. Traded in the army to become ... the manager of a betting shop. Still, he shouldn't really moan. He was better off than a lot of blokes coming out of the forces. At least he had a job. Such as it was. Had somewhere to live. Had readjusted reasonably well to civilian life. Wasn't suffering from PTSD. Wasn't homeless. Or in the nick.

Daryl glanced up at the sky again. Rotating his neck, trying to ease the stiffness a little. Turning back to the shop, he pulled the shutter above the front door down a few feet and stepped back inside to set the alarms. A sound behind him. The squeaking of a trainer on the wet pavement. An expulsion of breath. The sound of one material moving against another. Before he could turn, Daryl felt something hard and metallic pushed into the back of his neck.

'That's a double-barrel sawn-off shotgun. Turn your head and I'll blow it off.'

Daryl was shoved into the shop. Heard the door shutting behind him. The locks being applied. Heavy breathing. Could smell the acrid tang of sweat. Could sense the other man's agitation. He stood loose. Arms dangling at his sides. Trying not to make any sudden movements.

'Right, you bastard,' the gunman said. Breathless. Sounding like he was having trouble sucking in air. 'Get in the office.'

Daryl started walking. Slow, deliberate steps, 'Take it easy, man—'

'Shut up! Get in the office!'

Daryl opened the office door. Switching on the lights. Waiting on the threshold for the fluorescents to blink into life. The shotgun was jammed into his back. Propelling him inside.

'Where are the keys?' the gunman asked. 'Where are the keys?' The voice anxious. Flustered. Unnerved. The shotgun waving erratically around the room.

'Relax, man.' Daryl raised his arms. Showing the other man the back of his hands. Non-confrontational. Placatory. Talking slowly. 'Be cool. They're in my desk, OK? I'll get the keys and open the safe. You can have the money, man. I don't want any trouble.'

'Get a move on! And don't try anything.'

Daryl wasn't going to try anything. Why should he? It was all covered by insurance. He wasn't going to play the hero. Not for the sake of a few grand. A few grand of someone else's money. He slid open the top desk drawer and took out the keys. Moving slow and easy. Stepping to the back of the office. Putting the key into the lock.

'C'mon! C'mon!' The gunman almost shouting now. The voice shrill, overwrought. 'Stop fucking me about!'

Daryl half turned. About to tell the man, once again, to relax, when the gun went off. A deafening roar in the little room. Plaster showering down over them both. They stood for an instant. Paralysed. Daryl's ears ringing. The smell of cordite. Smoke from the shotgun barrel drifting in the air. He wondered, of the two of them, who had been the most surprised. He turned now to look at the other man. Some fat bloke. White trainers. Black tracksuit. A plastic clown mask. A red, curly nylon wig.

'Don't fucking look at me! Don't look at me!' he shouted, waving the shotgun. 'Turn round!'

Daryl raised his hands again. Slowly. Turning back to the safe. This guy, he thought, is fucking dangerous. A rank amateur. And his bottle's gone. He's likely to set that thing off again anytime. Shoot me. Or himself. Clicking the dial around to the four-digit combination. Taking out the canvas bags that contained the shop's takings. Putting them on the desk.

'Open it. Let me see inside,' the gunman said, waving the shotgun in the direction of the nearest bag. Daryl loosened the drawstring and tipped the bag towards him.

'There's about nine or ten grand. The other one's just coins.'

The gunman held out his hand. 'Give it to me.' Daryl passed it over. The gunman took a step forward. Raising the shotgun. Pressing it into Daryl's neck. 'Maybe I should blow your fucking head off anyway.'

Daryl pressed his neck against the barrels. Staring at the eyes behind the clown mask. Blinking now. Uncertain. The stupid grin. It was one thing being robbed by someone wielding a sawn-off double-barrelled shotgun. Quite another to be turned over by Ronald Mc-fucking-Donald. So, when he felt the pressure on the gun slacken slightly, Daryl moved forward. Grabbing the shotgun with his left hand. Nutting the clown. Inexpertly. Misjudging the positioning of the bridge of the nose behind the mask. A burst of white light exploding behind his eyes. Gripping the neck of the hooded tracksuit top, sweeping the man's feet from under him. Twisting his own hip, his momentum moving against the fat man's weight. The other man's head hitting the floor. The hollow sound of a coconut bouncing off concrete.

When Daryl looked back on it later there was a gap in his memory of events at this point. A period of missing time. A second. A few seconds. He wasn't sure. But . . . a definite absence. Then he found himself leaning over the figure on the floor. The red, curly wig beneath the man's head. Daryl's foot on his chest. Pressing the barrels of the shotgun into his forehead. The stupid-fucking-grinning clown mask only half on. The elastic cutting a groove into the flesh of the face beneath. A complexion like corned beef. The yellowing sclera of the single visible eye. The open pores on the cheek. The sheen of sweat on the skin. The blood and snot streaming from the ruined nose. Aware of the flexing tendons on the back of his hand. The tufts of hair on his knuckle. The tension in his finger as pressure was applied to the trigger. The dull gleam of the overhead lights along the shotgun's barrels. Daryl suddenly recognised him. The driver. The guy who stood by the Rolls-Royce when Jack Morris came to check the books. Leaning on the car, arms crossed. The guy who had stared him out when he had nipped out for a quick fag.

Tony Blake was whimpering. Mouthing something that Daryl couldn't hear. Knowing that he was about to die. Right here. Right now. In the dingy back office of some poxy little betting shop. His face and half his head blown away. And missed by no one. Daryl pushed the shotgun deeper into Blake's forehead. Bracing himself. Wanting, so much, to pull the trigger. Palms sweaty. Hand aching. Arm trembling. From the tension of not pulling the trigger. A bead of sweat popping from his hairline. Running down his forehead. Falling with a *plop!* onto the other man's face. One part of him, a small, logical, sane part of him, telling him not to do it. Telling him that the satisfaction of taking out this ... this ... wasn't worth the time in the nick. Wasn't worth giving up his own life. Wasn't worth losing what he had with Tracy. Seconds passed. Half a minute. A minute. Then Daryl took in a deep breath. Relaxed. Lowered the shotgun. Took his foot off the other man's chest. Stepped backwards. Sat on the edge of the desk. Reached into the top drawer and took out a can of Diet Coke. Popping the ring pull he held the can up in the direction of the crumpled figure on the floor. 'Cheers.'

Took a sip. Now he needed to make three phone calls. Each one more difficult than the last. First the police. Then his boss. And, finally, he would have to ring Tracy. Explain why he wasn't going to be able to make it home on time. Why he was probably going to be tied up for a while. Why it would be best if she didn't bother waiting up for him. On the positive side, though, it looked very much like his little soldiers might be able to stay in barracks tonight.

Day Five

Day Five

Pale hands, blood-slicked and trembling ... slowly reaching out ... The blood shines black under the moon ... a moon that has bleached out all colour ... has left the damp earth, the wet vegetation, stark and monochrome ... the oppressive pressure of an abrupt silence ... broken by ... the crackle of radio static ... the ticking of cooling metal ... the hum of an idling engine which quickens to become an insistent buzzing ... and then returns to a low-level murmur ... the feel of icy flesh under fingertips ... the skull beneath the skin ... the mouth opens ... a dry rattle ... a cough ... eyelids flutter ... then spring open to reveal—

Pearson woke with a start to the insistent buzzing of an alarm. Momentarily confused as to where he was. The weave of a vaguely familiar material. Blurry. Too close to his eye. He became slowly aware of the fabric of his settee. His coffee table. His television set: showing yet another in a seemingly never-ending series of programmes about amateur detectives. Solving crime, despite the hindrance of the cops. This one featured an ageing doctor who appeared to spend most of his time on roller skates. Hadn't he been in *Mary Poppins*? Dancing with penguins or some such? Try cracking a murder while doing that. Then again, maybe they were saving that for later in the series. The doorbell buzzed. Again, he realised. He checked the clock. Nearly half past two. He had spent the previous afternoon and night lying on his bed. Too uncomfortable, too restless, to sleep. Had finally taken a bath early this morning. Nodding off in front of breakfast TV. He swung his legs down from the settee. Feeling the stiffness, the bruising, in his shoulder, his side, his hip, his leg. Wincing, getting slowly to his feet. A slight head rush. And then it was gone. Limping down his hallway and opening the front door.

'Well,' said Cat, standing on his doorstep. Eyeing him up and down. 'It's a look, I suppose.' Pearson glanced down. Hooded bathrobe. White with broad red and blue stripes. Black ankle socks. 'Not necessarily a good one,' Cat added.

'I've just had a bath. Must've fallen asleep in front of the telly.'

She nodded at his hair. 'That would explain the barnet.' Pearson put his hand to his head. A ridge of hair running down the middle. The sides flattened. A geriatric Mohican.

'Bought you something,' Cat said. Hefting the paper bag in her right hand. Lifting the two paper cups, balanced precariously one on top of the other in her left.

After half a minute, staring at each other, neither making a move she asked, 'Are you going to let me in then, or what?'

Pearson yawned. 'Yeah, sorry, come in.'

'Love what you've done with the place,' Cat said, eyeing the hallway.

Pearson had decided to redecorate. Had got as far as starting to strip the wallpaper. Hadn't quite got as far as finishing the job. Here and there islands of the most recalcitrant and obstinate old textured anaglypta wallpaper still clung to the wall. Along the top edge nearest the ceiling. Around the light switch. Rising like stalagmites from the skirting board. Flecks of paper and dust on the bare boards underfoot.

'It reminds me of some kind of skin disease. Mind you, you might start a new fashion, "Decorative Eczema".'

'Yeah, all right,' said Pearson, 'when you've finished . . .'

They went into his living room. Cat sitting down on the settee, placing the cups and bag on the coffee table. When Pearson switched off the television and made a move as if to sit down himself, she said, 'Put some underwear on, Pearson, I don't fancy staring at your lunch all afternoon.'

When Pearson came back into the room – tracksuit bottoms, T-shirt, an attempt at dampening down his hair – Cat was sipping a black coffee. Had ripped open the bag to reveal three doughnuts.

'Three?'

'That's all they had left,' Cat said. 'It was either that, or an oatmeal flapjack.' Pearson wrinkled his nose. 'Yeah, that's what I thought.' Then, 'You're welcome, by the way.'

Pearson sat down in a chair. 'Yeah, sorry.' Picked up the other paper cup. 'Thanks.' Took off the lid. Blew across the top of the coffee. White. Took a sip.

'So, what's up?'

'Just thought I'd come round and see how you were,' Cat said. Picking up a doughnut.

'You sure Roberts hasn't sent you to see if I'm ready to come back yet?'

'Well,' Cat admitted reluctantly, 'he did say,' adopting a bad West Country accent, '"only if he's good and ready".'

'Yeah, right.'

'So,' Cat took a bite of the doughnut, asked, concerned, 'how are you?'

Pearson shrugged and made a face. 'Bored-fucking-stupid.'

'You've only been off half a day.'

'Yesterday afternoon,' Pearson said slowly, 'and this morning. That's a day.'

'You've slept through this morning,' Cat pointed out, taking another bite out of her doughnut. Nodding at him. 'You need a hobby.' Before he could protest, she said, 'One that you'll stick with.'

He'd tried hobbies. Hadn't really got on with any of them. Spent his days off – any time off – killing time until he could go back to work. What he needed was a life.

'So,' Pearson asked, 'what've *you* been up to?'

This time it was her turn to make a face. 'Answering calls, logging them into the system following the media appeal.'

'Anything?'

Cat shook her head. 'To top it all, Roberts has put me with Laurence – thought I might learn something.'

'And have you?'

'Yeah.' Cat sighed heavily. 'Who'd have thought that donkeys were quite so fascinating? Did you know that George Washington owned the first donkeys born in America? Or that they don't like the rain? Or that they utilise ninety-five per cent of what they eat so their manure is not very good as fertiliser—'

'A lot of useless shit, then.'

'Exactly.'

Pearson leaned forward and picked up a doughnut. Taking a bite. Looking at her questioningly.

'Cinnamon,' she said. For a minute they were quiet, sipping their coffee and eating. Then Cat asked, 'So what happened? Word around the nick is that you've had some kind of run-in with Curtis and you're suspended or something.'

'I'm just off sick,' said Pearson. 'Roberts "suggested" I took some time off.'

Cat nodded. 'Sounds like good advice.'

Pearson took a sip of his coffee. Staring down at the table. The remaining doughnut. Took another sip of his coffee.

'Go on,' Cat said, 'knock yourself out.' When he looked up, she shook her head. 'Anyone would think you were starving.' She wiped her fingers and lips with a napkin, dropped it on the coffee table. Then took a folded newspaper out of her bag. 'Have you seen this?' Passed it over.

He unfolded it whilst picking up the last doughnut. The early edition of the local paper, the headline reading 'Mystery of Train Suicide'. An 'artist's impression' of the man Pearson had tried, and failed, to stop killing himself on the train track two nights earlier. But it was obvious the drawing could only have been executed from the photograph that had come from the morgue. Taking a bite out of the doughnut, Pearson scanned the article. Mention of an 'off-duty policeman'. His unsuccessful attempt to save the mystery man's life. The lack of any items that might give a clue as to the man's identity. Including the lack of clothing labels. Something else that could only have come from someone close to the investigation. Another thing that might end up landing him in the shit.

Cat picked up her handbag. Putting it on her lap. Started fiddling with the clasp. Clicking it open and shut. Pearson sighed.

'Have a fag if you want one. Just don't sit there doing that.' He bit into the doughnut and chewed.

'Thanks,' Cat said, opening her handbag. Rummaging in it. 'This bastard bag! I can never find anything in it.' Taking things out one by one, putting them beside her on the settee. Finally fishing out her pack of cigarettes and lighting one.

Pearson asked, 'Did you follow that other thing up?'

Cat stopped putting things back in her handbag to look over. 'The girl's death in the sixties?' Sceptical. Exhaling smoke. 'The big tip from your fat mate? Yeah, thanks for that. You wouldn't believe the shit I got from Roberts over that.' Actually, Pearson would. 'Had the right hump with *me* because *you* were wasting *my* time. Work that one out. Said it was bollocks.'

'"Utter bollocks", probably. But you followed it up?'

Cat had followed it up. Had gone to the CID admin store at divisional headquarters that morning. A dusty concrete bunker. Yet somehow still smelling of damp, lit by low-wattage bare light bulbs. Row upon row of open metal racking containing stacks of perished and crumbling cardboard boxes held together with packing tape. After nearly an hour and a half of a frustrating search through collapsed and disintegrating boxes labelled with victims' names, the dates the victims were found, she had finally come across what she was looking for.

'Yeah,' said Cat, 'I followed it up.' She took another drag and then dropped the half-smoked cigarette into the dregs of her coffee cup. 'I found two boxes. But there's got to be more somewhere. There seems to be stuff missing. The whole thing was a mess.'

'In what way?' Pearson asked. Putting the last of the doughnut in his mouth. Chewing it slowly. Swallowing it. Gulping coffee to wash it down. Picking up a napkin. Wiping his mouth, his fingers. Dropping the balled-up paper back into the ripped bag on the coffee table.

'Incomplete statements,' Cat said. 'Dog-eared and screwed-up paperwork. Some of the cards in the card index system held

210

together with rubber bands, most just loose.' These held the 'nominals'. Each person, address, car registration deemed relevant would be held so that it could be cross-checked against any statement given. 'Your mate was right about one thing. Cause of death: manual strangulation. And I found the boyfriend. Geoffrey Knowles. Seventeen. Local boy.'

Cat's mobile began to ring. She took it out of her bag, checking the display.

'Roberts,' she said before answering it. Staring at him. Phone to her ear, nodding occasionally. Saying 'Guv,' every now and then. Finally, 'Guv, I'll let him know.' Ending the call. 'Apparently, Tony Blake has been arrested for the attempted armed robbery of a betting shop.'

'Attempted?'

Cat shook her head. 'That's all I know.'

'A betting shop? One of Jack Morris's?'

'So it seems.'

Pearson considered this for a while, then asked, 'So what happened to this Geoffrey Knowles?'

'No clue.' Cat shrugged. 'Presumably it's in the missing paperwork. One of the boxes contained the exhibits register. There was clothing. From the victim. According to the register it went off to the lab and was later signed back in. Seems to have been "misplaced" though. When I asked about it, everyone's just shrugging their shoulders, saying, "These things happen." The property officer told me it was probably at the lab. The lab told me it's probably in the property store somewhere. Meanwhile, the case is fifty years old. And solved to boot. So no one's in any great hurry to look for them.'

29

Pearson saw Cat to the front door. Then he went back into the living room, picked up the empty coffee cups and the bag in which she'd brought the doughnuts, took them into the kitchen and dropped them into the bin. Walking back into the living room, he checked his watch, wondering what he was going to do with the rest of the day. Flopping onto the settee. Picking up the remote control. Aiming it at the television set, his thumb hovering over the 'on' button. Quiz shows. Desperate people selling off their old crap. Reruns of thirty-year-old sitcoms. Pearson sighed. Although a sigh, he thought, was wasted if you were on your own. Surely the only purpose of a sigh was to show somebody else exactly how fed up you were? Fuck's sake, Pearson, pull yourself together. Things can't be that bad. You must be able to think of something to do to kill a few hours?

He placed the remote on the settee beside him. And his hand brushed something caught between the cushions. Prising it out, holding it up. Cat's mobile. An iPhone. The latest model. Probably. He was no great judge. Didn't really keep up with these things.

But it looked new. Almost pristine. His mobile, on the coffee table in front of him, by comparison, looked scruffy and out-of-date. The screen already scratched and difficult to read. Some of the keys loose. Others sticky, needing that little bit of extra pressure when pressed. Tape on the back to hold the battery in place where he had dropped it. He was just debating what to do with it when the doorbell rang again. When he opened the door, however, it wasn't Cat standing on his doorstep.

'You're a hard man to track down, Detective Sergeant. I've been halfway around the town looking for you.' Layla Gilchrist wore a white blouse and the skirt of an expensive-looking pinstriped business suit, the jacket of which was folded over one arm. 'First I went to the police station. Only to find you weren't in. Luckily, some nice man on the desk gave me your home address.' Pearson wondered who that was. He'd find out. And he'd be having words. She flapped the collar of her blouse, revealing the top of a black, lacy bra.

'Phew! We need some proper rain. It's so close. So then I went to what I thought was your house, spoke to your wife. Ruth, is it?'

Bet that went down well, Pearson thought. Said, 'Yeah,' dragging his eyes reluctantly away from her cleavage, 'Ruth.'

'She seems like a nice lady.'

'Ruth? Yeah, she is.'

Gilchrist arched an eyebrow, waiting for him to say more. When he didn't, she nodded over her shoulder. 'Is that yours?'

Pearson looked past her. To the cabin cruiser on its trailer: half-hidden under a blue tarpaulin; surrounded by long grass, weeds, various bits of windblown rubbish. 'Yeah, it seemed like a good idea at the time.'

Then again, all his hobbies seemed like a good idea. At the time. At the start. When it was still just a romantic notion. Before

214

reality kicked in. He'd meant to fix it up: to sand down the boards, diligently apply several layers of varnish, replace the old fittings. Preferably with ones reclaimed from a salvage yard, lovingly polished and made as new. After a few afternoons in the summer, though, he'd given up. Too much like hard work. A penance rather than a pastime.

'I've always loved boats,' said Gilchrist. Her tongue touching her small, white teeth on the 'l'. Lingering there for just a split-second too long. The tackiness of her lip gloss making her lips stick together fleetingly on the 'b' of 'boats' before parting. A tuft of hair at Pearson's crown, wetted down when Cat had called, chose that moment to dry out and spring up.

'Are you OK?' she asked. 'Only you don't look too good.'

'Yeah, I'm fine,' Pearson said. Though he didn't feel fine. Felt a little woozy, to tell the truth. The beginnings of a banging headache. And his leg and hip were starting to ache from standing in one position for so long.

'Do you mind if I come in?' Gilchrist asked.

Pearson hesitated. Wondering if that was such a good idea. She had, after all, been interviewed in relation to a murder case. She might yet have to be interviewed again. Might turn out to have vital evidence. How would it look later if this were to go to court and it was found that she'd visited him privately and there was no official record of what was said? On the other hand, she'd obviously gone to a lot of trouble to find him. Maybe she had something important to say. Something that might be of material interest to them. Something, more importantly, that might turn out to be time-critical.

He stepped to one side and, with an inclination of his head, indicated that she should come in. As she passed him, he caught a whiff of her perfume: flowers, musk, spice. He wondered fleetingly about his real motives for letting her in. Wondered, again, whether this was really such a good idea. Closing the door anyway. Turning. Following her along the hallway, he noticed her appraise the shabby walls. But she said nothing.

Sitting down in the armchair, laying her jacket on the floor beside her, Gilchrist asked,

'So, have you got a day off? I didn't think you got days off in the police when you were working on a case.'

Avoiding an explanation, Pearson asked, 'Do you want anything? I could make some tea.' Gilchrist shook her head, taking in his T-shirt and tracksuit bottoms, his socks.

'No, I'm fine thanks.'

Pearson sat down opposite her on the settee. 'So,' he said, 'you've tracked me down.'

Gilchrist looked down at her hands. 'It's so awful,' starting to pick at the nail polish on one of her fingernails, 'the dead girl on the beach, I mean.' Stopped picking, looked up at him. 'Except she wasn't a girl, right? Michael Morris, is it? The son of some shady local businessman, is that right?'

Pearson said nothing. Didn't take long these days for word to get around. A brief clip on local television. The death of an anonymous girl. Discussion on social media: Twitter, Facebook. Someone was bound to put a name to the face. Others would be only too willing to fill in the backstory. Add their own little bit of tittle-tattle. The more salacious it was, the quicker it got around.

'They say,' Gilchrist continued, 'that he was . . . '

Suddenly achy. Tired. Irritated by her feigned coyness, Pearson supplied, '"Working in the sex industry"' – wanting her to get to the point – 'is how it's termed these days.' Wanting her to leave so he could lie down. 'A prostitute. Rent boy. Whatever. Amounts to the same thing, whatever you want to call it.'

Gilchrist looked down, again, at her hands. 'I know maybe you've got an idea of what kind of person I am.' Her glance flicked up, gauging his reaction, back down again. Picking at her nail polish. 'Because of what I do. The business I'm in – a legitimate business these days, by the way. Just look at Ann Summers – but despite what you may think, it's not really about sex. It's just—'

'Economics?' Pearson cut in. Not attempting to hide the tone of scepticism.

Her face showed momentary surprise, then doubt, asking herself how much he actually knew, whether he'd done some kind of background check, before she crossed her legs. 'Business – exactly.'

'And no more disreputable,' Pearson said, 'than, say ... politics, for instance?'

Gilchrist met his gaze. Sure now of how much he knew. Calculating how much more she wanted to say. 'OK,' she said, 'you obviously know that I used to have an internship at the House of Commons and I studied Politics at uni. So you're wondering how I got from there to here, right?'

'Getting busted for possession of coke?'

Gilchrist nodded. 'In a way, I suppose.' She looked down briefly at her hands, making a move as if to start picking at the nail polish again. Then, annoyed with herself, she put one hand on top of the other, looking directly at him. 'Have you heard of the term "sugar baby"?'

'Like an escort, right?' Pearson asked. 'Young girls with older men? The other side of the "sugar daddy" thing?'

'Right.' Gilchrist said. 'Lots of girls put themselves through university by acting as escorts. Getting paid for it. It's all above board. Businessmen who want to be seen out in the company of younger, attractive women. No pressure on anyone to do anything they don't want to.'

After a pause Pearson asked, 'So?'

'So, I worked as a sugar baby to put myself through uni. And after, to do my masters, my doctorate. Only, I got to like the money. If I was asked to do a little … extra, I thought – why not? Got to like the parties, too. Caviar, champagne' – looking down again now – 'and cocaine. Ended up with quite a habit.'

Idly, Pearson's gaze slipped down to her cleavage. Her lacy, black bra. Then to her legs. Nice legs. Well-toned. The sheen of the recently waxed. His mind flashed back to the meeting with Sawyer in the café. The conspiratorial wink. Christ, he was starting to be as much of a lech as the fat journo.

'And that's what cost you your job?' he asked.

'No.' She shook her head. 'What cost me my job was being at a particular party. Seeing a certain government minister. A minister who had built his reputation on being the perfect husband, espousing the importance of family values, and doing … well, you can probably guess. Things that he wouldn't want to get out.'

'Why would that …' Pearson stopped himself from finishing the question. As the answer dawned. 'You knew him from the House of Commons?'

Gilchrist gave a bitter little laugh. 'You could say that.'

'Yeah well,' Pearson said, 'I can see that that wouldn't be the best career move.'

'The ironic thing,' Gilchrist said, 'is that I've seen the same junior MPs and civil servants that I met at the parties, recently on the telly. You know, in the back of shot, when they do a piece on the negotiations for Brexit? While I … I've ended up as the manager of some seedy little sex shop in the sticks. Still, some might say it's a natural progression, right?'

For a time they both said nothing. Then Gilchrist sighed. 'Look, the reason I came here is because I'm worried about

Courtney. She hasn't been to the shop for a couple of days. I can't get hold of her on her phone. I went around to her flat but couldn't get an answer ...'

'Any particular reason why you should be worried about her?'

She cleared her throat. 'She's been seeing this boy – well, man, really, I suppose – he's picked her up from the shop once or twice.'

'And, what? You don't like the look of him?'

'No.' She shook her head. 'He looks a bit ... rough, y'know?'

'And you think something might have happened to Courtney because of him?'

She nodded. But uncertainly. 'Maybe.'

'Have you got a name for him?'

'Tony.'

Suddenly, Pearson was interested. 'Got a last name?'

'Mmm, Blake?' She pursed her lips, appeared to think for a second or two, then nodded. 'Yeah, that's it, Blake.'

The doorbell rang. Without thinking, Pearson rose automatically to answer it.

'Left my bastard phone,' Cat said.

Cat watched Pearson dithering at the open door. Reluctant to let her in. Behind him, inside the house, she thought she heard a movement. Then scratching his ear, inclining his head, he said, 'You'd better come in.'

She followed him down the hallway. When they reached the living room, Layla Gilchrist was getting to her feet. Leaning forward to pick up her jacket. A few too many buttons unfastened on her blouse. Showing, in Cat's opinion, a little too much underwired, black underwear. She experienced a brief stab of jealousy. But there was a fine line between décolletage and having them hanging out. And Gilchrist was overstepping it. Her skirt was too short, too. A porn film secretary. Cat looked from Gilchrist to a guilty-looking Pearson.

'Blimey, Pearson. All these young women turning up on your doorstep. The neighbours will think you're running some kind of knocking shop.'

Gilchrist shot her a murderous glance. Made her excuses to Pearson. Made as if to leave. Cat standing her ground in the doorway, forcing Gilchrist to brush past her. When they heard the front door close, Cat said, 'What was all that about?'

'I need to go out,' Pearson said. 'D'you fancy coming with me?'

'Now?'

'Yeah.'

'You sure you don't want to have a cold shower first?'

30

Pearson rang the doorbell again. Glancing across to the bay window. Where a cat sat on the sill. Staring at them. Tail twitching irritably. Fat. White. With black patches on its forehead and under its nose. Pearson nudged Cat's elbow and nodded in its direction.

'What?' she asked.

'Don't you think,' he said, 'it bears an uncanny resemblance to Adolf Hitler?'

Just then, the front door opened, no more than a couple of inches. In the partial shadow behind it, an old man. Checked carpet slippers. A time-worn, grubby pair of trousers, into which he had made a half-hearted attempt to tuck a pyjama top. An equally grubby jacket of the same approximate original colour and material as the trousers. As if it had a vague memory of once being a suit. Glasses with black plastic frames hanging skew-whiff where the Sellotape on one of its arms was drying out. Pearson slipped his warrant card out of his inside jacket pocket and held it up to the crack in the door.

'Police. Can we come in?'

Opening the door, flicking on the hall light, taking a step back, the old man let them in. The inside held no surprises. Pearson had been in dozens of these Victorian houses. Subdivided into small flats and bedsits. Occupied, for the most part, by people on benefits. All of them basically the same. Narrow, dimly lit passageways. Frayed and threadbare carpets. Stained and peeling wallpaper. And that smell. Apathy. Surrender. Cat piss.

'We're looking for Courtney Woods?'

'Don't know her.'

'We have this as her address,' Pearson said. '3C?'

'Oh, upstairs,' flapping a hand in the general direction. 'Her, yeah. Never knew her name. Haven't really spoken to her, tell the truth. She in trouble, is she?'

'Trouble? Why should she be in trouble, Mr ... ?'

'Burrows. Ted Burrows. You know,' as if he knew as much as Pearson, sniffing, 'she's on the game, in't she?'

'What makes you say that?'

Shrugging. 'Dunno. Piercings and that? Miniskirt. No use to me though.' A pause. 'I've never got any fucking money.' He gave a wheezy cough.

Pearson looked over at Cat. Not impressed. Wondering, he suspected, if there was something she could charge the old man with. Regretting, by the look of it, being here at all. At the very least, questioning his motives. Pearson was, again, questioning them himself. Then he thought of Tony Blake. The shaved, ginger hair. The too-small suit. Sitting on the sea wall. Arms crossed. Staring him out. And already in custody for an attempted armed robbery. He started to move towards the stairs.

'I was just going to the offy,' the old man said, holding up a canvas shopping bag. 'Can you leave the door on the latch when you go? I can't find my keys.'

On the top landing. Two doors: one white, one orange. But both fibreboard. Cheap. And nasty. Someone had scrawled '3B' on the white door in felt tip. So the one next to it, presumably, was 3C.

'Maybe she's out,' Cat said.

After Pearson had knocked. Waited half a minute. Knocked. And waited again. Gone to 3B and knocked there. And likewise got no reply. Pearson ignored her. Pressing his ear instead to the thin door. Listening for any sound from inside. Rapping again, louder this time.

Cat suspected this would turn out to be a bad idea. A potential witness turning up at an officer's home address; an unofficial lead that had not been logged onto the system. Not to mention the fact that Pearson was supposed to be off sick. She had already been in two minds about it. Even as she sat in his living room, watching the light fade through the window, waiting for him to get dressed. But now she was convinced of it. Was ready to tell him that she was going to call it a day. Almost ready.

'Courtney!' Pearson's voice was raised, not quite shouting. Yet. But getting there. 'This is the police, can we have a word, please?' Pressing his ear to the door. Pounding this time. 'Courtney! Can you open up, please? We'd like a word.'

Finally, the door opened an inch. 'Yeah? What?'

Pearson took his warrant card out of his pocket and pressed it to the crack. 'Can we come in, please?'

The door opened. The girl turning away, wrapped in a duvet. Sitting down on the low bed. Cat followed Pearson in, leaving the door open. Partly in an effort not to spook her. Partly to fit them all in the cramped space. The room already claustrophobic. Cold – and damp.

Courtney Woods sat on the bed. The duvet over her shoulders. Holding it tight around her neck with one hand. Without make-up she looked younger than Cat remembered. Too young. She wore a crop top. A roll of flab hanging over the waistband of a miniskirt. Puppy fat. Plump legs, in need of a shave, the hair on them fine and downy. Her knees red and shiny. Carpet burns, Cat thought. Maybe. On the floor by the bed, several tinfoil ashtrays. Overflowing with cigarette ends, chewing gum wadded into wrappers. Next to these, drained cartons of Ribena, empty packets of jam tarts and Bakewell slices. The rest of the floor covered with piles of dirty clothes, wet wipes, cotton wool balls smeared with black mascara and ... God only knew what.

Concerned, Cat asked, 'Are you OK, Courtney?'

'Yeah, I've just been asleep.' Yawning to illustrate the point.

The air in the room was stale. The smell of cigarettes, old perfume, fruit juice and body odour.

'Asleep?' asked Pearson. 'Or hibernating?'

'I've been sick.'

'Sick?' asked Cat. 'With what?'

'Dunno, flu maybe.' Pulling the duvet up around her neck.

'Is that why you haven't been in to work?' Cat asked.

The girl said nothing. Her body moving under the duvet. A shrug maybe. Then again, maybe not.

'Your boss was worried about you, Courtney. She's been trying to contact you?'

'Yeah, I've lost my phone.'

'That's why we're here,' Cat said. 'She's worried about you seeing Tony. Tony Blake? He's your boyfriend, isn't he?' Again the girl said nothing.

'We came to the shop,' Pearson said. 'Do you remember?'

'We asked about some clothing?' Cat prompted.

Again Courtney gave no response. Fighting to keep her eyes open. Shifting on the bed.

224

Pearson dug into his pocket and brought out the photo of Michael once again, holding it in front of the girl's face. A few inches from her nose. She struggled to focus on it.

'We asked you if you recognised the person in this photograph,' he said, 'and you acted as if you'd never seen her before. Then we find out you're Tony Blake's girlfriend. And Tony Blake grew up with her. So, chances are, Courtney, you know exactly who this is—' Pearson paused. 'So, do you know who she is?'

Nodding. Her eyes suddenly brimming with tears. 'Him,' swallowing, 'him,' whispering, 'Linzi.'

'Linzi?' Pearson asked. When he glanced across at her, Cat could only raise an eyebrow. Courtney reached out tentatively to the picture, taking it from Pearson. 'Michael,' she said. 'That's his real name. Michael Morris. But he liked to be called Linzi. Like his mum. He was always talking about her. How when he was a kid he had always dreamed of making loads of money so he could bring her home, look after her properly.'

'Bring her home?' Cat asked. 'From where?'

'He said she was in some sort of private clinic. He said his old man was loaded and had paid to lock her away.'

'You didn't believe him?' Cat asked, catching the doubtful tone in her voice.

'If his old man was loaded, why would he be hanging around a shithole like this?' Courtney looked back down at the photograph. 'Anyway, we used to make up stories. Michael said you could be whoever you wanted to be. He said you could reinvent yourself anytime you wanted to. He said, why be someone you didn't like just because you were born that way?'

Cat waited for her to go on. When she didn't, she asked, 'How did you meet Michael?' The movement under the duvet again. The possible-shrug. 'Did Tony introduce you?'

Courtney looked up. Face pale. Podgy. Panda rings around her eyes where the mascara hadn't been removed properly. 'Not sure.' Pouting. Thinking. 'I don't really remember. He was just, sort of around? We just sort of clicked straight away. I'd only known him a few weeks, but it was like we'd known each other all our lives, y'know? We were like sisters. We spent all our time together. You know, just talking and stuff? Swapping clothes and that.'

Cat wondered how many of Michael's clothes would actually fit. Courtney appeared fat, lumpy in comparison to Michael's slim frame. Then felt instantly ashamed for thinking it.

'Do you have any pictures of Michael? You and him together, maybe?' As soon as Cat had asked the question, she knew the answer.

'They're on my phone.'

'You know we're investigating how Michael died?' Courtney nodded and her eyes went back to the photograph. 'We don't know at the moment if it was an accident or not, but it is possible that Michael might have been murdered.' The girl seemed to flinch, her eyes roving the photograph. 'Anything you can tell us about him,' Cat went on, 'might help us to find who hurt Michael. Or at least help us to find out what happened to him.'

'OK,' Courtney agreed, her eyes not leaving the picture.

'Did you think Michael might be mixed up in something dangerous?' Cat asked. The girl shrugged. 'Or that he might be running away from something? That he might be frightened of someone?'

'Like who?' When Cat didn't answer she said, 'No. Not really. He didn't seem frightened of anything.' She coughed into her hand. A smoker's cough.

'Do you think Michael could have been scared and not told you?'

'No.' An emphatic shake of the head. 'I told you, we used to tell each other everything.' Then, by way of confirmation, as if letting

226

them in on a confidence, 'After a while he even told me about his mum. The truth. That she was in a mental hospital? I told him he was lucky to have a mum who loved him.' Shaking her head. 'My mum fucked off when I was little,' looking up at Cat, the hurt still fresh in her eyes. 'I s'pose that's why I was so close to my stepdad. Until he got a new bird. Jealous bitch. Threw me out. Called me a nasty little whore.' She lapsed into silence, looking miserable. Looking down at the carpet.

'What sort of things did Michael and you do together?' Cat asked.

Courtney shrugged. 'Stuff.'

'It's very important that you're honest with us, Courtney,' Cat said, 'or we won't be able to find out who hurt Michael.'

Courtney sighed. 'We talked a lot, we found out we both liked the same kind of thing.' Reluctant. Evasive.

Cat shot a look at Pearson, then asked, 'What kind of thing?'

No answer.

'Drugs? Weed? E's? Coke, maybe?'

'Not drugs.'

'Sex, you mean?'

'Sex, yeah.' Courtney laughed, looked up at her. 'Fucking.' Looking for a reaction. The shock value. The stare a direct challenge.

Calmly, Cat asked, 'With who?'

'Whoever.' That movement again.

'Men?' Cat asked. 'Other men, I mean. Other than Tony?' No answer. 'And what about Tony? Didn't he mind?' Courtney looked at her, confused. 'About you having sex with other men?'

'We're not exclusive or anything.'

Not as far as you were concerned, Cat thought. The question is: did Tony Blake feel the same way? The girl started coughing again. The movement causing the duvet to slip momentarily from around her neck. Exposing an angry red mark. A scoring. An indentation. Where something – a ligature maybe? – had cut into the flesh of her neck. She glanced across at Pearson. Knew he'd seen it too.

'What happened to your neck, Courtney?' Cat asked. The girl shrugged. Pulled the duvet tight around her again. 'Did Tony do that to you?'

A knock on the door frame. They turned to find Layla Gilchrist standing half in the room.

'The front door was open? So I just came up.' Looking from Pearson to Cat, and then at the girl. 'You haven't been to the shop for a few days, Courtney, I was worried.'

Courtney shifted on the bed. Looking uncomfortable. Muttering, 'I've been sick?' Reaching to push some hair from her face.

'My God!' Gilchrist said. 'Look at you! What's happened to your neck? You look terrible.' Stepping across the room. Crouching. Obscuring their view. Whispering something. Pulling down the duvet, gently touching the bruise on the girl's neck. Saying something they couldn't quite catch. Then, standing up, she rounded on them.

'What are you doing, interrogating her? Look at the state of her. She ought to be in hospital!' Turning back to the girl. 'Put your shoes on, Courtney, I've got my car outside.' As Courtney stood up, letting the duvet slip to the bed, the crop top riding up, Cat saw with a shock what the girl had been trying so hard to hide. She made an attempt to pull her top back down. But too late to conceal the purple and black circles covering her ribcage, spread across her small breasts. It was as if, Cat thought, she had been beaten, with something like a knotted rope.

Day Six

31

'I take full responsibility,' said Pearson.

'Fucking right, you do!' Roberts said. 'You're the senior officer!' Looking from him to Cat, his gaze coming slowly back to Pearson. Lingering there a little too long for comfort.

'Whose bright idea was it to interrogate this girl in the first place?'

'To be fair, guv,' Cat said, 'I wouldn't exactly characterise it as an interrogation.'

Roberts' eyes stayed on Pearson. 'Well, we've had a complaint where it's "characterised" as just that.'

'A formal complaint?' Pearson asked.

'It hasn't gone that far. Yet. How old was this girl?'

'Sixteen?' hazarded Pearson. 'Seventeen? I'm not sure.' Seeing Roberts' jaw clench. In his mind Pearson picked up a shovel. Started to dig a hole for himself.

'So there's a potential issue about her being interviewed without an appropriate adult present as well?'

'At that point,' Pearson said, 'she hadn't been cautioned' – driving the blade into the soil – 'Gilchrist came to my house' – feeling the metal ridge of its shoulder under the sole of his foot, leaning forward and applying pressure – 'and said that she was worried about the girl—'

'Layla Gilchrist, right?' Roberts said. 'A witness you'd interviewed previously. Alone with you in your place of residence—'

Cat cleared her throat. 'I was there too.'

Roberts gave her a look. Half annoyance, half puzzlement. A look that said he didn't really want to go there. A look that told Cat that she hadn't exactly made it any better.

'This girl,' Roberts said, 'she's the girl you interviewed before, at the shop?'

'Courtney Woods.' Pearson nodded. 'Gilchrist said that she hadn't been into the shop for a couple of days. That she was the girlfriend of Tony Blake.'

'We just went round to check on her, guv,' Cat added. 'Make sure she was OK.'

Roberts' eyes were back on Pearson. 'According to Gilchrist, you showed Courtney Woods a picture of Michael Morris. The morgue shot?'

'We'd already showed her the picture when we visited the shop,' Pearson said. 'At that time she denied that she knew Michael Morris.'

'Gilchrist claims that when she turned up the girl was distressed. That she had an "obvious and serious" neck injury. She confronted you and asked you why you hadn't arranged for her to go to the hospital.' A look to Cat. Then back to Pearson. An opportunity for a denial. 'By ... the ... fucking ... book, I told you,' Roberts said. 'Everything by the fucking book, until this Carragher thing blows over.' Eyes slipping across to Cat momentarily. Picking up a biro from his desk. Then, softening slightly, 'You know Curtis is looking for any excuse.'

'Guv.' Pearson nodded.

'You,' Roberts said, waggling the biro at Pearson, 'weren't even supposed, officially, to be working. Off sick. That's what I told Curtis. To get you out of another load of shit, may I remind you.'

'Guv.' Pearson nodded again. Looking down at his hands, in his lap, fingers interlaced. Right thumb working the knuckle of the left.

'So,' Roberts went on, 'I expect you to have a day or two recuperating at home ...' *Apart from the fact you sent Cat round to get me back to work*, Pearson thought, '... instead of which, I get a phone call this morning from a member of the public complaining about your treatment of a vulnerable young girl. That's on top of—'

Roberts reached across and took something out of his in-tray, tossing it carelessly onto the desk – the early edition of yesterday's local newspaper. The same paper Cat had shown him the day before. The headline reading, 'Mystery of Train Suicide'. The drawing copied from the post-mortem photograph. The face of the man Pearson had tried, and failed, to stop from killing himself. The face that, during the day at least, he could reasonably successfully submerge under the minute-to-minute routine of his job. The face that, when he lay in bed, closed his eyes, and eventually did manage to get to sleep, would bob back to the surface. Like a turd in a swimming pool. Unwanted. Unpleasant. And ultimately, unavoidable. The face he had seen for the last two mornings burned on to his retina as he woke in a tangled of sweat-soaked bedsheets. Pearson looked up, intending to defend himself. Intending to deny any knowledge of it, but was stopped by Roberts' raised eyebrows.

'You're not going to try and tell me that that picture, that story, didn't come from you, are you? Where the fuck else could it have come from?'

Pearson shrugged, nibbled at a hangnail on his thumb. 'Nobody else seemed to be doing much.'

'So you thought it'd be all right to release that photograph without clearing it with anyone? Brief the press on the details of the case, a case you were already in the shit about? Because you'd already been treading on too many toes? I suppose that this is your fucking fat journo mate, is it?' Waiting a beat, two . . . 'Are you sure you didn't get a bang on the head on that train track? Because it certainly seems that way to me.'

Pearson didn't say anything. What could he say? He was, after all, in the wrong. Roberts tossed the pen onto the desk. Bollocking over, Pearson thought.

'In the event,' Roberts said, 'it seems to have worked. We've had a call from someone claiming to know the identity of your man.' Reaching across to the in-tray again. Taking out a dozen or so sheets of A4. Licking a finger, flipping through, stopping. 'Here we are, Dr Angela Fitzgerald. Psychiatrist. Apparently he was one of her patients.' Handing the sheet of paper over to Pearson. 'Address is on there. I've already arranged for you to go to see her. All right?' Looking from Cat to Pearson. 'By the time you've finished there, I'll have organised through prison liaison that you can visit Tony Blake at Chelmsford nick. If, as you say, Courtney Woods has been having sex with other men – possibly encouraged by Michael – and then she ends up badly beaten, to my mind, that puts Blake right back in the frame for Michael Morris's murder. Agreed?'

'Guv,' Pearson said.

'Well then. What are you waiting for?'

Giving an involuntary groan, Pearson stood up. Experiencing, not for the first time, the loud crack from a hip. The tight muscle in his thigh. The shooting pain in his leg. The slight head rush. The concerned look from Cat. And the steady scrutiny of Roberts.

32

'Brainwashing?' Cat asked.

From the corner of her eye she saw Pearson start. The room having fallen silent. The tape player stopping a minute or so earlier. Having asked the question, Cat was conscious of leaning forward in her seat. Not completely won over. Not entirely persuaded. But interested. Pearson, on the other hand, and despite the fact that they were only here in the first place because of him, was clearly bored. His attention quite obviously wandering during the last ten minutes or so the tape had been playing. But he was evidently coming to the slow realisation that he might have missed something. That the psychiatrist, Dr Angela Fitzgerald, had been speaking. Had been explaining something.

Aware of Pearson's renewed attention, Fitzgerald's hand drifted irresistibly to her face. Toying briefly with her hair. As if trying to shape it to the contour of her cheek. An unconscious attempt to mask the disfigurement there. A pitting of acne scars. It put Cat in mind of the peppering of pellets from a shotgun blast.

'I know it sounds ridiculous now,' Fitzgerald was saying, taking her hand away. A deliberately casual movement. Putting it on the desktop. Covering one hand with the other. Looking down. Sliding both hands beneath the desk. 'But we're talking about fifty years ago. It's now accepted that the CIA carried out so-called "mind control" experiments, such as Project Artichoke or MK Ultra.' The psychiatrist paused, looking between them. Getting no reaction from Pearson. But Cat nodding that she should carry on. 'Artichoke was an experiment carried out in the early fifties under the supervision of the Office of Scientific Intelligence—'

'The forerunner to the CIA,' Cat said.

'They used hypnosis, morphine addiction and forced withdrawal to supplement existing interrogation techniques. MK Ultra was an offshoot involving the administration of drugs to unwitting participants, such as giving LSD to members of the public without their knowledge or consent—'

'You think that Mr Lennon might be connected in some way to the American government?' Pearson asked. To Cat's mind being deliberately obtuse. Not trying very hard to keep up. Not trying too hard, either, to keep that note of cynicism out of his voice.

'Not necessarily,' said Fitzgerald, taking the question at face value. 'Our own government was conducting similar experiments at around about the same time. In fact, there is evidence that they may have started as early as the Second World War. Operation Paperclip, for instance . . . '

'Operation Paperclip was the systematic smuggling of Nazi scientists out of occupied Germany by Allied governments,' Cat said, turning to Pearson. 'Including, rumour has it, those scientists who carried out human experimentation in the death camps.'

'Evidence has recently come to light,' Fitzgerald said, clearly warming to her subject, 'regarding British interrogation centres in post-war Germany run under the auspices of the Ministry of

Defence, where prisoners arrested on suspicion of being communists were subjected to extremes of cold, systematic beating, starvation and sleep deprivation. The very same techniques which have been used at Guantanamo B—'

'Aren't we straying a little from the point here?' Pearson interrupted. 'What's this got to do with the tape we've just heard?'

Or, in his case, half-heard, Cat thought.

Fitzgerald nodded. 'You're right. I'm sorry. The point I was trying to make was that, as outlandish as it may seem now, these things may have, and quite probably did, happen in the past...'

Cat could see by Pearson's face that he was unimpressed, irritated by what he undoubtedly regarded as nonsense.

'The "London Cage", for example,' Fitzgerald went on, 'was a building in Kensington Palace Gardens where sensory deprivation experiments were carried out, resulting in extreme paranoia, memory loss and in some cases the complete disintegration of the subject's identity...'

Aware that Dr Fitzgerald was seriously trying Pearson's patience; that he was finding her zealotry, her strident tone, her – in his view – bizarre theories a little difficult to stomach, Cat made an effort to get back to the subject in hand.

'That's' – she nodded at the tape player – 'deep sleep therapy, right? Sometimes called insulin coma therapy?' Cat turned to Pearson again. 'Patients were given high doses of insulin which induced a sort of coma-like state and were periodically woken up to receive electro-convulsive therapy.'

'For what purpose?'

'It was seen as a cure for a number of psychological illnesses: anxiety, depression, psychosis, schizophrenia... but many patients experienced long-term or even permanent memory loss, to one degree or another—'

'Those,' Fitzgerald said, 'who did not suffer respiratory failure, in which case it often proved fatal.'

'And you're saying,' Pearson said, 'that this Richard Lennon had undergone deep sleep therapy and as a consequence had suffered memory loss. Is that right?'

Fitzgerald sighed. 'That's right, yes. And in Richard's case the damage to his memory was extreme ...'

Pearson opened the manila folder she had given him and started flipping through the sheets of paper inside. Reading each one. Passing each sheet across to Cat as he finished. A letter authorising the transfer of Geoffrey Knowles from Her Majesty's Prison Chelmsford. The photocopy extremely poor quality. The top cut off. The text blurred. The authoriser's signature all but illegible.

'The transfer was sanctioned by the Prison Service,' Cat mused.

'Looks like it.' Pearson nodded. 'Although that photocopy's pretty much useless as far as evidence that could be presented in court is concerned.'

'Wouldn't it have had to be authorised by the then Home Secretary?'

'I would've thought so.' Pearson handed across some more sheets of A4. A copy of a hospital admission form for St Thomas's. Medical notes on the hospital's headed paper. The typed transcripts of Fitzgerald's sessions with Lennon. Finally, some handwritten notes. Lots of question marks and underlinings. Scrawled addenda squeezed into the margins.

Cat gathered the papers together and passed them back to Pearson. Turning her attention to the psychiatrist she asked, 'You said that Mr Lennon said something to you on his last visit?'

'Yes,' Fitzgerald nodded, 'he said he'd done something ... "something truly evil".'

'But he didn't say what?'

Fitzgerald shook her head. 'No.'

Pearson looked down at the folder in his lap. Thinking. Then looked up again at the psychiatrist, tapping the folder. 'Why this particular patient?'

'I'm not sure what you mean.'

'Well, he must be, what, in his late sixties? You said yourself that you think that all this may have happened fifty years ago. The thing is, he's lived with it up to now, right? Maybe I'm missing something here, but what would be the benefit, to him, of his regaining his memory at this stage of his life?'

Fitzgerald looked down. Studying her desk. Starting to absently move a biro around its surface. Then, sighing, shaking her head. 'I have to admit, the motives weren't altogether altruistic. At first Richard – Geoffrey – came to me as a patient. Then as I looked further into his story, it became something more. During my researches online, I made contact with someone who said he might be able to help me. He said he was looking into similar cases ... '

Pearson slipped a pen out of his inside jacket pocket, opened his notebook. 'You got a name?'

Fitzgerald hesitated for a moment, then said, 'Hugo. Hugo Somerville.'

'Do you have an address?' he asked. 'And a telephone number?'

Fitzgerald told him and he wrote them down.

'You needed a face!" Cat said suddenly. 'The human interest angle ... ' Fitzgerald, shamed, looked down. Nodded at her desk. 'A modern-day freak show,' Cat continued. Disgusted. Then, puzzled, 'And all this for something that happened fifty years ago?'

'And might still be happening now,' Fitzgerald said by way of mitigation. Looking up, suddenly animated again. 'Iraq, Afghanistan, Guantanamo Bay. The extraordinary rendition of prisoners to black sites who then undergo sensory deprivation or are bombarded with noise. Sexual humiliation and beatings, the physical aspects of torture specifically calculated for their psychological effect, the lessons learnt from post-war experimentation recalibrated for the age of water-boarding—'

Pearson shook his head. 'The sort of wild conspiracy theories you see on the internet.'

'Exactly!' said Fitzgerald. 'Nowadays, everything will eventually appear on the internet. So what do you do? Leak the information, couch it in terms that seem implausible and far-fetched. Then everyone will do your job for you, there'll be dozens, hundreds queuing up to debunk whatever it is you put out there.'

'So, what about this?' Pearson asked, hefting the manila folder.

Fitzgerald shrugged, defeated. 'You might as well take it with you. Without Richard it's . . . ' she sighed, 'incomplete. There's so much documentation missing . . . there was a time when it was easy to suppress the truth. Slap a D-notice on something and it would never see the light of day. Even when historical documents *are* published they're worse than useless. Whole sections redacted in the interests of "national security". There have been cases where the Ministry of Defence have refused to release documents because they were supposedly contaminated by asbestos. Official reports shredded in "error". Claims of evidence simply misplaced or mislaid over time.'

Cat thought back to her visit to Pearson's home the previous day. The conversation about the missing clothing. His saying, 'After all this time? They could easily just have been lost. These things happen,' and Cat's reply, 'Yeah, so everyone kept telling me . . . meanwhile the case is fifty years old. And solved to boot. So no one's in any great hurry to look for them.'

Cat was unable to resist a glance in Pearson's direction, wondering if the same thought had just crossed his mind.

33

Cat glanced up from her phone to see Pearson turn the Mondeo off the country road, through a set of large, black wrought-iron gates and onto a long drive.

'All that stuff you came out with, when we were talking to Fitz-gerald,' Pearson said. 'I'm constantly surprised by the amount of...'

'Crap?'

'... Diverse...' Pearson said slowly, '... interesting... knowl-edge you have.' Gravel crunching beneath the tyres.

'That's almost a compliment,' Cat said. Thinking about the time she spent at home. On her own. On the internet.

'Almost?' Pearson asked. Passing sculptured conifers to either side. Manicured lawns beyond. Coming to a halt in front of a shab-bily elegant mansion reeking of old money.

'You don't actually believe any of it, though, do you?' he asked.

Disappointed, Cat shook her head, looking out through the windscreen. It was everything she'd imagined. A family estate in the Essex countryside. Successive generations hit by inheritance tax. Its upkeep too expensive. The staff gradually dwindling away over time. The property slowly going to rack and ruin. Until it was eventually signed over to a charitable trust in the nineteen sixties. Then became an annexe of a medical foundation.

Cat looked down at her mobile. 'Hugo Somerville's grandfather was also a psychiatrist,' she said. 'Sir Christopher Somerville. Quite a famous name in psychiatry. If a little controversial.'

'Have you come across him before?' Pearson asked. 'During your degree or whatever?'

'No.' Cat shook her head again. 'But according to this,' tapping the phone, 'he was "fully accredited by the British government . . . given high-level security clearance and during the early nineteen sixties part of his official duties saw him deployed at Porton Down." You've heard of Porton Down, right?'

Pearson nodded. 'It's a Ministry of Defence research facility.'

'Officially,' Cat said, 'it deals with the effects of, and development of counter-measures against, chemical and biological agents. But there have been rumours that, in the past, it was used for certain types of . . . questionable . . . psychological experiments on human subjects.'

'According to Wikipedia,' Pearson said sarcastically.

'According to Wikipedia,' Cat conceded.

Shaking his head, Pearson turned off the engine. They got out of the car, slamming the doors. Pearson engaged the locks with the electronic fob and they approached the house. Closer up. Cigarette butts in the flowerbeds. Crumbling brickwork. Flaking stone columns on each side of the mossy, worn steps. A warped and peeling front door. Only the shiny, brass plaque to one side was new.

Pearson rang the bell. A minute later the front door opened and Pearson held up his warrant card and said, 'Police. We've got an appointment with Hugo Somerville?'

*

The room they were shown into was a contradiction. The high ceilings, a few pieces of fine furniture: a desk, two visitors' chairs, a delicate bureau, ornate and antique. But the hardware on the desk: laptop, flat-screen monitor, mobile phone was very definitely state-of-the-art. In common with a lot of these rooms in a lot of these grand, old houses, though, it was cold.

Hugo Somerville had a cricket sweater tied around his neck, was wearing a long-sleeved white shirt and corduroy trousers. He had the physique of someone who once might have rowed for his college, Cat thought, played rugby for the first fifteen, but had obviously not done much exercise in the twenty or so years since. The thinning, sandy hair slightly tousled. The unblemished complexion of a baby. A weak mouth with full, red lips. Pearson showed his warrant card and introduced them. They shook hands and Somerville indicated that they should each take a seat.

'I've just been reading about your grandfather,' Cat said.

Pearson regarded the other man now across the cold room. The small hands laced on the desktop. The expression slightly superior. Mocking. Pearson had a fleeting impression of an oil painting. An old family portrait. Dull. Murky. Brown. The dissipated son and heir of a large estate. A supercilious dullard captured in hunting pinks by a skilled and perceptive artist. Committing to posterity his wicked and hedonistic nature.

'Not all this conspiracy nonsense from the internet again.' Somerville sighed.

'I read that he was seconded to Porton Down in the nineteen sixties?'

'And, entirely due to the internet, Porton Down has gained some unwarranted notoriety in recent years,' Somerville said, obviously irritated, 'because of uncorroborated allegations of unethical

243

human experimentation, when in fact it was purely a Ministry of Defence establishment that dealt with mitigating the effects of nerve agent and chemical and biological warfare.' Somerville rapped one of his small hands on the desk in punctuation. Leant forward in his chair.

'Grandfather had high-level security clearance. And he worked for a time at Porton. However, to say he was "seconded" there may be rather overstating the case. He attended Porton Down on a part-time basis. Acting as a consultant on the psychological consequences of various types of chemical and biological agents that might be employed by hostile foreign powers. And that's all.'

Somerville sat back in his chair. Giving ground, Cat thought. 'Nonetheless,' Somerville continued, 'in the nineteen fifties and sixties, psychiatrists – Grandfather among them – were prone to use many unfortunate people in rather academic exercises.'

He looked from Cat to Pearson and back. 'Even in mainstream psychiatric medicine, the needs of the patient were often secondary to the perceived furtherance of science.' Taking a breath. 'That, after all, is one of the reasons for this place.' He lifted one of his too-small hands to indicate the room – the house, the institute as a whole. 'Some quite heinous crimes have been perpetrated in the past in the name of medical progress. This place is, in part, my grandfather's attempt at some kind of reparation. Not just for what he'd done. Or might have done. But for the historic abuses of our profession as a whole.'

'What, exactly,' Cat said, 'is the purpose of the institute?'

'At present it's a residential centre for veterans suffering from the effects of combat.'

'So British troops suffering from PTSD?' Cat asked. 'Things like that?'

244

'That's part of it,' Somerville said, 'but it's not restricted to British troops alone. And we also deal with the effects of incarceration, interrogation and torture.'

While the other two had been talking, Pearson's phone had buzzed in his pocket, alerting him to an incoming text. Slipping it out, he'd read the message. The interview had been arranged with Tony Blake at HMP Chelmsford. Earlier than expected. They needed to get a move on. He said now, 'The reason we're here, Mr Somerville, is to ask you some questions regarding your relationship with Dr Angela Fitzgerald. I take it you do know her?'

'Yes.' Somerville's hand went to his forehead and he started to massage a temple with a thumb.

'She said she'd made contact with you on the internet? That you said you may be able to help her, that you'd dealt with similar cases?'

'Angela approached me,' Somerville said, 'because of the work we do here, or so I supposed at the time. She said she had a severely traumatised patient and wanted to know if we may be able to help with his therapy.'

'You said, "so I supposed"?' Pearson prompted.

Somerville sighed again. 'Yes, that was what I thought initially.' His hand disappeared into his hair, started to worry at his scalp. 'But it appears that she, too, had come across these ridiculous stories on the internet.'

'The stories regarding your grandfather?' Pearson clarified.

'That's right.' Somerville's hand left his hair and he placed it on the desktop, laced his fingers together. 'But I'd also given an interview to a psychiatric journal, along much the same lines as what I said to you earlier, how the institute's work was in part as reparation for what might have happened in the past . . .'

'So, what happened?'

'After a while,' Somerville looked down at his hands, pausing, the thumbs tapping each other, the tongue exploring the inside of his cheek, 'it became apparent that some of Angela's ideas were a little ... dangerous' – frowning – 'maybe, that's too strong a word for it. "Unconventional" is possibly a better way to put it.'

'When you say "dangerous",' Pearson asked, 'dangerous to whom?'

'As I said—'

'Yeah,' Pearson cut him off, 'maybe it's "too strong a word for it". Then again, maybe it's not. Did you know that this patient she was treating, Richard Lennon, right?' – the other man nodded – 'has since committed suicide?'

Somerville's head came up, a shocked expression on his face.

34

Tony Blake sniffed. Ineffectively. Ran his fingers tentatively over his nose: a split on the bridge starting to scab, smaller cuts and grazes surrounding it.

'You think I did that?' he asked. The voice slightly woolly. The nasal passages blocked. Some thick liquid congealed in the sinuses. He gingerly touched the area under his eyes: swollen and puffy, the skin having the sweaty, shiny look of imminent bruising, mauve circles already forming around the sockets. Felt his front teeth, as if they were a little loose.

But sitting across from him in the prison's visiting room, Pearson was staring at his forehead. Where there was an odd pattern, like a figure of eight. Or two letter 'O's set close together. Blake folded his arms. Sat back in his chair. Staring sullenly, first at Pearson, then at Cat. Shaking his head, as if he couldn't quite believe it.

'You think I did that? You think I beat up Courtney?'

'You saying you didn't?' asked Pearson.

'Yeah,' giving him the dead eyes, 'that's exactly what I'm saying.'

'So, who did?'

Blake shook his head again: as *if* he was going to say anything. Almost smiled; as *if* he was that stupid.

'Don't you care about what happened to Courtney?' Cat asked.

Blake turned slowly, giving her the hard stare. Cat stared back. The visiting room was bare. The walls whitewashed brick. The grey Formica table was bolted to the floor. The ubiquitous institutional chairs with their orange plastic seats and metal legs were not. To Pearson, it made no sense. Surely a prisoner would be less likely to pick up a table and hit someone with it than a chair?

'When we interviewed you before,' Pearson said, 'I asked you if you knew Michael was back in the area ... and you said, "I'd heard".'

Blake was wearing a black tracksuit. Had the top on this time. A concession to the coldness of the room. Sparing them, at least, the sight of his flabby arms with their down of ginger hair. While he was still on remand, Blake was allowed to wear what he liked. At least, Pearson thought, he won't find the transition too hard. After the court case. After he was found guilty. After he was sentenced, he would be straight back here. Once on one of the wings he would be allowed his own clothes. Within limits. No black or white. No designer logos. No slogans. Most ended up in grey or blue tracksuit bottoms and plain T-shirts.

At last, Blake asked, 'So?'

'So it was a bit more than that, wasn't it? When we spoke to Courtney yesterday she gave the impression that Michael had been around a while. A few weeks, at least. She said they "sort of clicked straight away".' Not taking his eyes off Pearson, Blake rooted in an ear with a little finger. '"Like sisters", according to Courtney,' Pearson went on. 'Spent all of their time together. Swapping clothes. Talking ... '

248

Blake removed his finger from his ear. Stared at it for a moment. Wiped it on his tracksuit bottoms. Sighed. Clearly unimpressed.

'And?'

'And, although you were supposed to be looking for Michael, you didn't tell Jack Morris that he was back.'

'Nope.'

'Why not?'

'I told you before. I don't owe Jack anything.'

'Yeah,' Pearson nodded, 'you're right, you did.' That sense of entitlement again. The idea that he shouldn't have to work for a living. 'What about Michael? Didn't you owe him anything either? You didn't think you should tell Michael that Jack might be looking for him?'

'What for?'

'Maybe to tell him that, what with Jack having his health scare, he might be in line for a payout?'

'Michael wouldn't have been interested in Jack's money,' Blake sneered. 'He didn't want anything to do with him.'

'And you knew this,' Pearson said, 'how, exactly?'

A negligent shrug. Nodding at Cat. 'She don't say much, does she?'

The prison officer who had shown them in – sitting on a stool against the wall, beer gut straining the short-sleeved blue shirt, occasionally readjusting the position of the keys in the ziplock bag on the belt loop of his black trousers, one shiny, steel-toecapped shoe on the rung of his chair; up to now feigning indifference, studying form in a tabloid paper – looked up briefly.

'How do you know Michael wouldn't have been interested in Jack Morris's money?' Cat asked.

Following the officer's fat neck down the corridors of the prison, Pearson had been taken back to school. In trouble. Being escorted

by one of the teachers down the run-down hallways of his old com-
prehensive to the headmaster's office. And it had struck Pearson
again, as it always did, how mundane, how ordinary, how normal
the whole idea of prison soon became to an inmate, especially the
repeat offenders. How quickly they acclimatised to the relentless
routine, the grinding process of it all. Pearson had wondered again
how many he'd put here over the years. It must number in the
dozens at least.

'How do you know Michael wouldn't have been interested in
Jack's money?' Pearson asked, repeating Cat's question.

Half-smiling again, Blake turned back to Pearson. 'Look,
Michael had his own thing going on ...'

Seeing Blake was still in his seat, behind the table, hadn't
moved, the prison officer went back to pretending to read his
newspaper. And earwigging.

'How do you know,' Pearson asked, 'that Michael had something going on?'

'That's what he told Courtney. And before you ask, I've got no
idea. He never said.'

'Or Courtney never told you,' Cat said.

'So, how did you feel,' Pearson asked, 'about Courtney and
Michael hanging out? Given that Michael was such a greedy little
fucker? That he'd take advantage of people and then just drop
them? That he didn't care about anyone? "Empty inside", you
said.'

'I warned her off of him,' Blake said. 'Told her to stay well clear.
Told her he was bad news.'

'But you didn't do anything about it,' Cat said. Halfway between
a question and a statement. Blake looked down at the table.
Shaking his head again. This time, though, Cat had the distinct
impression that it was out of ... what? Regret, maybe? Something

250

he'd wished he'd done, but hadn't? She looked across at Pearson. The slightest raising of his eyebrows. The look on his face saying, 'Your guess is as good as mine.'

'What I don't understand ...' Pearson said, a shift in tone, signalling a change of tack, a new subject, 'is, if you've got a job, why mess it up by trying to rob a betting shop? And one of Jack's betting shops, come to that? I mean, granted, you might not like the job. Maybe, you even hate it, right? But it's a steady income. That's got to be something ...'

Blake, actually looking embarrassed, Cat thought, genuinely embarrassed. For a moment he avoided Pearson's eyes, saying, 'I thought it would be easy, didn't I? I knew the routines. Knew where they kept the money.'

'Only you happened to pick the one betting shop where the manager was an ex-soldier, right?' Pearson asked. 'And, not just that, a decorated war hero. Or maybe that was the point? Maybe you wanted to prove something? That you had the beating of this guy?'

'Obviously,' Blake said, ' I'm a bit thick.' Tapping his temple with an index finger. 'Took one too many shots from my old man, I reckon.'

'And, maybe you thought it would be a good way to get back at Jack,' said Pearson, 'for treating you like shit? Like a lackey? When you thought you deserved better.'

Blake looked past Cat. Over to the prison officer – the screw – on his stool, still miming disinterest. A tiny blue pen in his hand now, marking out his horses in the racing pages. For Pearson, there were two types of prison officers: those who were nervous of visiting coppers, embarrassed to put them through the security searches, anxious to get through the paperwork and get them on their way; and others, like this one, who relished the power. Strung out the process of booking them in. Took as long as possible over the searches. The depositing of mobile phones and keys. The checking and signing of the various forms.

'Listen,' Blake leaned forward, lowering his voice, 'I went to him, right? I asked him for some money, a loan – very polite, very respectful. He just fucking laughed in my face.'

'Why should he give you a loan?'

'Look,' Blake said, 'yeah, I know.' Glancing across at the screw again. Leaning forward a bit more, lowering his voice even further. So that it was barely above a whisper. So that they had to crane forward to hear. 'It's his money, right? He doesn't have to loan me anything. I get that. And, chances are, I wouldn't have been able to pay it back. But I was desperate, OK? He knew that. He knew I'd have to be desperate to even ask. So I went to him, and I'm like' – another look across at the screw – 'nearly in tears, right? Begging the cunt. And, like I said,' shaking his head, 'he just laughs in my fucking face. I said to him "It's not for me, it's for Courtney. She's mixed up in something. In above her head. I need to get her away somewhere." And he's just laughing at me, saying, "You want to borrow money so you and your tart can go on holiday? What do you fucking take me for?"'

Blake gazed into the middle distance. Looking back. Shook his head free of the recollection. Wiped his hand down his face. Winced. Reminded, now, that it was swollen. Painful. He probed gently again around his nose with his fingertips.

'Listen,' – looking between them, an appeal, making an effort at including Cat for the first time – 'Courtney ... she's just a kid really, she hasn't got a fucking clue how she should behave.'

And, Cat had to admit, some of his cockiness, his swagger, had gone. Replaced with what seemed like real concern, sincere affection. Even blokes like Blake, she supposed, were capable of loving somebody. Or something. During her time on the job she had come across countless hard men, not averse to slapping their wives and girlfriends around, who were totally soppy when it came to their pet dogs. So why shouldn't Blake genuinely care about the girl?

'Courtney thinks that the way to get people to like her is to let them fuck her. That's what her stepdad did to her – dirty old bastard – made her like, I dunno, she's not worth anything? She's like' – shrugging his shoulders, mimicking the girl's movements, imitating her voice – '"Shit happens." As if it's what she expects?'

Leaning back now, resigned. 'Look, I know you don't give a fuck about me. Probably think I got what was coming to me,' shrugging. This time on his own behalf. Or for their benefit. Making a face. Like he wasn't bothered one way or the other. 'Maybe I did, who knows? But Courtney, serious, now' – looking between them again – 'she's mixed up in something nasty, right?'

'What?' Pearson asked. 'Mixed up in what? You talking about something she did with Michael?'

'She's in danger.'

'From who?' Pearson asked.

But Blake was shaking his head again. Staring past them. Had nothing more to say.

35

'So? What? Are you trying to tell me you've got women's problems?'

Pearson had an expression somewhere between appalled and embarrassed.

'M ... R ... T ...' Cat repeated slowly. 'Not HRT, you pillock!'

As Pearson smirked, Cat tutted and groaned. 'Oh, fuck off, Pearson!'

She turned to look out the rain-speckled side window of the car. And wishing she hadn't. The flyover leading out of Chelmsford. A single lane of tarmac. Three-foot-high crash barriers. Metal uprights every four to six feet supporting three square steel cross-bars. Beyond these, surrounded by railings and wooden hoardings, an abandoned and neglected concrete apron, punctured by straggly weeds. Cat experienced a momentary vertigo. She would never choose to drive this route. Certainly not when it was approaching rush hour. Nearing dusk. When it was raining. When half the time you couldn't see out of the front windscreen because the wipers weren't working properly. As it was, she always had an irrational fear that she'd drive off the side. Or the flyover itself would choose that exact moment to suffer structural weakening and tumble to the ground.

Refusing to close her eyes, just in case the action might be reflected in the side window, she focused instead on her annoyance. This was the thing about Pearson that irritated her the most. The childish wind-ups. Covering the fact that he didn't know something by making a joke of it. She gave it a moment or two. Just to prove to herself that the flyover didn't really bother her. Then turned back and said, 'Let's try again, shall we? What do you know about MRT? Memory recovery therapy?'

'Not a lot,' Pearson said. Face deadpan. Almost. She could swear there was still the ghost of a smile at the corner of his mouth. A tightness, at least. As if the bastard was trying hard to suppress a grin.

'Fitzgerald was treating this Richard Lennon, right?' Cat said. 'A vulnerable, confused man who, by her own admission, had long-term memory issues. In fact his memory was so badly damaged, or altered, that he wasn't even sure of his own identity.'

'And our Dr Fitzgerald?' *Our* Dr Fitzgerald. As if they'd been talking about other Dr Fitzgeralds. A verbal tic, she'd noticed, that Pearson had picked up from Robert. 'She's a bona-fide psychologist? Or psychiatrist? Or whatever it is she needs to be, to be doing this counselling?'

Cat leant forward, reaching into her handbag and retrieving her iPhone. Opening the web browser. Glancing out through the front windscreen. Essex Yeomanry Way. She had always thought that this part of the drive was one of the least interesting she'd ever done. Its most appealing feature was a nineteen-sixties housing estate to the right of the road. The rest of the view mostly obscured by trees and shrubs. The occasional break affording glimpses of the fields beyond.

Tapping in the information. 'Right, I'm on the Royal College of Psychiatrists website. They've got an online public members list.' Then, a few seconds later, 'And here she is, "Angela Fitzgerald, MRC Psych—"'

'OK,' Pearson cut her off, 'she's properly accredited. So what about this Richard Lennon?'

'I've been thinking about these dates,' Cat said, opening the manila folder on her lap, flicking to the relevant page. 'According to this, Geoffrey Knowles was admitted to St Thomas's on the twenty-third of June, nineteen sixty-six. Three months after the body of Beverly Marsh was found on the beach by the Crowstone—'

'"According to this"?' interrupted Pearson.

Cat looked up from the sheet of paper and over at him. 'What?'

'You said "according to this",' Pearson said, 'as if you had some doubts.'

'Well, after what Hugo Somerville had to say . . . '

'And the way Fitzgerald presents herself doesn't exactly add credence to any theories she might have.'

'All right. Anyway,' Cat said, 'from what I've read about this on the internet' – before Pearson could say anything – 'I know, I know. But, apparently, most of the patient notes from this time – St Thomas's, the Royal Waterloo – seem to have disappeared.'

'It's not beyond the realms of probability that patient notes might have gone missing, is it?' Pearson asked. 'Even for the most innocent of reasons?'

'No,' Cat said, accepting the point, 'it's not. But it just sort of begs the question as to how Fitzgerald might have laid her hands on them.'

'Are you saying you think she might have fabricated them?'

Cat shook her head. 'I'm not saying that. But this,' tapping the papers, 'is all we've got to go on at the moment. Until we can corroborate it, I think it's right to be a little cautious.' Needled by his interruption. Waiting for him to raise another objection. Riffling through the pages again. Then, picking up her interrupted sentence, 'Having been transferred from Chelmsford nick where he was, according to Fitzgerald' – a pointed look in Pearson's direction; left hand on the gear stick, right hand on the steering wheel, Pearson said nothing – 'on remand for some unspecified crime.'

'Presumably, the murder of Beverly Marsh.'

'If this Richard Lennon *is* Geoffrey Knowles,' Cat said. '*If* what we have here,' tapping the folder again, 'is to be believed.'

'Wouldn't that imply some kind of arrangement? Between the prison governor and the Home Office? Some kind of kickback for the prison governor, maybe?'

'It needn't be quite as venal as that,' Cat said. 'It could have been something as simple as a promise of improvements to the prison? More warders? Less prisoners? Buildings being refurbished. Whatever ...' She took a breath. 'Can we just agree, for the time being, that Fitzgerald is convinced that that's why he was there?' A look to Pearson again, who nodded. 'So, in the course of this psychiatric counselling, she introduces the idea in the sessions that he murdered this girl.'

'Through this memory recovery therapy.'

'Right.'

'Which is what, exactly?'

'Well, it's not a specific single treatment as such. More, a group of therapies that you can draw on.'

'Such as?'

'Hypnosis—'

'Hypnosis?' Pearson cut her off again. 'I thought hypnotherapy was used mainly for things like ... dunno ... weight loss? Quitting smoking? That sort of stuff.'

'It can be,' Cat agreed. Glancing out of the window into the dark. Trees. Shrubs. Electricity pylons in the fields to their left. 'It is. But it can also be used for relaxation, pain relief ... '

'I sort of mainly equate it with those stage shows. You know where they get people to do embarrassing things? Like pretending to be chickens ... '

'Well, yeah, that's part of it. But it's been accepted these days as a genuine, effective treatment. There's standard qualifications, professional bodies ... ' Tapping into her iPhone again. Reading, 'The UK Confederation of Hypnotherapy Organisations – hmmm ... who also have a public online register,' and a moment later, 'And here's our girl!' Our girl. She was fucking doing it now. Pausing. 'Having said all that, hypnosis is still a contentious treatment with some mental health professionals.'

'Especially if the subject might be susceptible to suggestion, I imagine.'

'Exactly,' Cat said. Leaning forward again, dropping the mobile into her handbag.

'OK,' said Pearson, 'so, hypnotism. What else?'

Above their heads the powerlines crossed the road, the pylons on the right now.

'Relaxation training, drug-assisted recall, guided visualis- ation ... As I said, it's a sort of umbrella term for a lot of different treatments.'

'Drug-assisted recall. You mean like truth serums, like – what is it, sodium pentothal?'

'Amytal.'

Pearson nodded. 'And is there anything in those notes to say that she was giving Richard Lennon sodium amytal?'

'Not specifically,' Cat conceded, 'but she was definitely treating him with hypnotism and guided visualisation.'

'Which means what?'

'Walking the subject through scenarios. Getting them to "see" it in their mind's eye.'

As they breasted a hill and came down the other side, Cat glanced past Pearson and into the night. Beyond the banked verge. Past the trees and shrubs on its top, Cat knew, was the site of the old Runwell hospital.

'Getting them to imagine that they'd murdered someone?' Pearson asked.

'It doesn't have to be as straightforward as that. You could get them to imagine different aspects of the situation? Maybe a few seconds at a time. What can you see? What can you smell? What can you hear and feel? And you could spread it over more than one session. So the impressions build up over time. Asking about what he remembers at the next session, then seeing each thing he comes out with as corroboration of your theory, pushing it that little bit further each time?' She could see by Pearson's expression that he wasn't buying it. 'There *are* documented cases of psychiatrists introducing ideas to patients in this way. Convincing them that something happened to them in the past when nothing of the sort took place. It's called "false memory syndrome".' As if Pearson was going to ask. Though he probably wasn't. But, what the fuck, she'd started now. So Cat explained it anyway. 'False memory syndrome is a condition where a person's relationships or, as in this case, their identity revolves around a traumatic experience that is totally real to them, but is actually untrue.'

Far off, Cat could see, by some optical illusion, a foreshortening of distance, some trick of perspective: a disquieting, huddled flock of electric pylons.

'We've all had memories that we've believed all our lives but later find out are completely wrong,' she said.

'Like remembering a situation from when you were very little? And then you find out you've constructed it from looking at photographs and listening to other people talking about it?'

'Yeah, except it's more than that. It's believing in an experience that is so important, so entrenched, that it dominates the whole way you behave, colours how you interact with other people. False memory syndrome is usually associated with memories of sexual abuse as a child. Having a vivid recollection of specific occasions when it happened. When in reality nothing of the sort took place.'

'Like those cases where children were taken from their parents by social services?' Pearson asked.

'Exactly. Children convinced that they suffered sexual abuse, even took part in satanic rituals, and then later it is found out that it had all been implanted in the children's minds by psychological counselling.'

Pearson nodded slowly. 'Yeah. I vaguely recall reading about it. So what are you saying? That our Dr Fitzgerald got it into her head that Richard Lennon is Geoffrey Knowles? And that she was so convinced of the fact that she "implanted" the idea that he killed Beverly Marsh in his subconscious? Made him think that somehow he had either suppressed the memory or his memory had been lost as a result of insulin coma treatment? But all the time she believes that she is helping him recover this traumatic experience, she's actually putting the whole false memory in his mind? Then, when he finally remembers – or thinks he remembers – he is so disturbed by it all that he decides to commit suicide by chucking himself under a train?'

After a minute, Cat said weakly, 'It's just a theory.'

They took a left onto a slip road, then down under the road

261

bridge, onto the Fairglen Interchange. Catching a green light for once. Swinging a right off the roundabout and onto the slip road taking them onto the A127. Where, as usual at this time of day, they came to a standstill.

Pearson wound down his side window. 'Rather than going straight back to the nick, d'you fancy dropping in on Courtney Woods?'

'Because of what Tony Blake said?'

'Yeah, we should really check it out.'

'Really?' Cat asked. 'After the bollocking we got from Roberts last time?'

Pearson took his fingers off the steering wheel. A small gesture of surrender, 'I'm not saying interview her. We'll just talk to her. Make sure she's OK.'

After a moment, Cat sighed. 'All right.'

They spent the next ten minutes crawling forward a few feet every now and then, stopping, crawling forward again. It wasn't until they reached Rayleigh Weir that Pearson spoke again.

'Or . . . ' one hand on the wheel, the other elbow leaning on the open side window, rubbing gently at his forehead, 'maybe Richard Lennon *is* Geoffrey Knowles. Maybe he *did* kill Beverly Marsh and then had his memory wiped. Maybe it's all true and our Dr Fitzgerald has got it all right. Maybe it was remembering what he'd actually done that drove him to kill himself.'

Cat had thought that this particular conversation was over, that Pearson hadn't really been that interested.

'As you said,' Pearson shrugged, 'it's just a theory.'

36

FRIDAY 18 MARCH, 1966

Geoffrey Knowles stood by his scooter in a dimly lit side street. Next to him, doubled over, hands on her knees. Swaying slightly from side to side. Coughing and retching over the gutter: Beverly Marsh. Geoffrey, holding her hair, looked up, through the tears welling in his eyes, through the starburst of orange street lights. The smear of pink and blue neon. To a sky illuminated by white light pulsing in rhythm to the thump-thump-thump of the music from the amusements by the pier.

Was it always going to be like this? The last few times they'd been out, the night had ended in the same way. Beverly doubled over, him holding her hair. Trying not to look. Holding his breath in case she threw up again. This was supposed to be the best part. They were young. They were supposed to be having 'fun'. Having the 'time of their lives'. After this, things just got worse . . .

His mind went back to their first meeting. In the typing pool. He'd been selling cigarettes out of a carton of Peter Stuyvesant and he'd asked her out. Because he'd thought she was a bit of a mouse. Because, in spite of all the winking, the cheekiness, the chat, the truth was he'd been a virgin. Worse than that, he hadn't really had a steady girlfriend up to that point. Hadn't even kissed more than one or two girls in his entire life. Beverly had seemed a safe bet. He'd made a big show of asking her to the pictures. With no expectation of her saying 'yes'. Assuming that she would just be embarrassed by the whole thing and he could have a bit of a chuckle about it with the rest of the girls. He'd been as surprised as anyone when she'd said she'd go. Now, though, he was beginning to think the whole thing had been a mistake. Was starting to suspect she might be a bit unhinged. That maybe she had something properly wrong with her. It was like she had all these different people living in her head. You never really knew where you were with her from one minute to the next. And once she'd had a drink or popped a few pills ... she was wild. Crazy. Uncontrollable. And you couldn't tell her 'No.' Not if you had pills on you, not if you had a few bob for a drink. She'd just go on and on at you until you had to give in.

And the mouth on her, the language! When they'd first been going out she wouldn't – what was that expression his nan used? – wouldn't have said boo to a goose. The worse she'd say was 'bloody'. And that only occasionally. Had had that beaten out of her by her old man. But now? Christ, *he* swore, but not like that. Sometimes when she was in that mood she genuinely scared him. Tonight, she'd been in that other mood. Still manic. Still reckless. But more self-destructive than aggressive. They'd been to the Middleton. Dancing. The music in there mainly Stax. Which was fine by him. Tamla was only OK for the slow stuff towards the end of the night anyway. But they hadn't got that far.

Even at the start of the night, Beverly had been dancing a little too hard, a little too fast. Drinking too quick. Pestering him for one too many pills. Altogether too intense. Coming on strong during the occasional slow number that had been played. He'd known

264

all along that it wasn't going to end well. So, it had been a relief more than anything when she'd said she felt sick and wanted to go outside . . .

'I'm sorry,' Beverly was saying now. 'I'm sorry,' Beverly kept on saying. 'I'm sorry,' Beverly always fucking said.

'It's all right,' Geoffrey said. Though if she spewed on another one of his suits, it wouldn't be. He'd only just finished paying this one off. He'd only worn it for the first time tonight. Seventeen and a half quid from the Burton's in the high street. Six weekly instalments while he waited for it to be made up. Three separate fittings to get it just the way he wanted it. And all this after deliberating for ages about the right material, finally deciding on a grey and blue two-tone. Beverly tried to hawk. Attempted to spit. But it just came out as a long string of drool that dangled from her open mouth. She groaned and shook her head. A little bit of spittle landing on Geoffrey's trouser leg. 'Sorry,' she mumbled, dabbing at it ineffectually with two fingers. Losing her balance in the process, stumbling forward into the scooter. Making it rock precariously on its stand for a moment so that it threatened to topple over. He grabbed her shoulder so that she didn't end up flat on her face. Beverly shrieked hysterically. Geoffrey cringed. Jesus, that laugh, it went straight through you.

Her face was flushed, blotchy. Her eyes half shut, as if she were having trouble staying awake. She hiccoughed, putting the back of her hand to her mouth.

'Now you're angry with me.' Beverly pouted pathetically. Sulky. But close to tears too. Then she swallowed, put her hand to her mouth again. 'Urrh, I don't feel very well . . . ' She bent over again.

'It's all right,' Geoffrey Knowles said. Although it wasn't. It wasn't fucking all right at all. Desperate, is what it was. Desperate, is how he felt right now. How he felt most of the time lately.

Desperate to get out of this place, to find something better. And sometimes, like tonight, desperate and sad and tearful. Like everything was too much. Like he just couldn't cope any more. As if everything was about to go wrong. As if something really bad was about to happen. 'It's all right,' he said again, starting to rub her lower back. 'It's all right, babe.'

'Oh, you're so sweet,' Beverly said. Belching loudly. 'Ooh, Jesus!' Giggling again.

'Have you thought any more about what we were talking about?' he asked.

'Uh, what's that?'

'You know . . .' he insisted. Pressing harder. Making little circles with his palm at the base of her spine.

'We could get away from this place,' he'd said. 'Go to London. Get a nice flat and that. You could get yourself some nice – nicer – clothes.'

'And it's not like I'd be doing it for ever, is it?' she'd asked. 'It's not like you'd be asking me to do something I don't like.'

She'd seemed OK with the idea. Sort of . . . enthusiastic . . . even. And she'd said, 'It's no different from being married, is it? Not that different from what my mum does?'

Looking to him for confirmation. Or trying to convince herself. Or had she said these things at all? Had he said them to her? Tried to convince *her* that it was all right? Persuading himself in the process that she'd been the one to bring up the idea in the first place?

'And you like shagging, don't you?' he'd said. 'So, in a way, it'd be like a bit of a bonus. Getting paid as well.'

He remembered saying that, anyway. Felt bad about it now. 'And you wouldn't get pregnant,' he'd said. 'We'd make sure they all wore a johnnie. I can get them for you.'

*

266

Felt bad about that too. He started to rub Beverly's back, from the base of her spine, up between her shoulder blades. She flapped a hand. Trying to bat his away. 'Don't! It's not helping. You're making me feel sick!'

He stopped rubbing. Sighed. Thought, then, about leaning over. Moving her hair tenderly away from her face. Saying, 'You said you loved me. You said you'd do anything for me.' But her face was flushed. Her eyeliner smudged. Her nose running. And her breath would smell. Cigarettes. Gin. And sick, probably. Besides, he wasn't certain himself now that it was what he wanted. Wasn't sure he could ask her to do something like that. That it was even right to ask her. It was just ... sometimes ... it was all ... so ... bloody ... hard ...

'I've thought about it,' Beverly admitted. 'Don't go on, eh? Not tonight. I feel really sick. I'm sorry. I just want to go home ...'

'All right,' Geoffrey conceded. 'You going to be OK on the scooter?'

Beverly swallowed again, nodded slowly. 'I think so.'

Looking across the road, Geoffrey Knowles saw a man in a handmade suit. An expensive raincoat. A grey fedora. Sliding a silver cigarette case out of his inside pocket. Taking out a cigarette. Snapping the lid shut. Tapping the cigarette on the lid. Retrieving a lighter from his overcoat pocket. Catching Geoffrey's eye. The man he'd seen in the room above the Shrubbery coffee bar. The man who, later the same night, had watched him from across the street. As he lit his cigarette he gave a curt nod of acknowledgement. In the light of the flame, an expression on his face of ... recognition, annoyance—

Beverly threw up in a violent explosion of gin and stomach acid. Geoffrey heard it hit the pavement, felt it splatter across his shoes, imagined it splashing back off the kerb. And, looking down, he saw the regurgitated gin across his suede winkle pickers. The partly digested remains of a sausage sandwich she'd eaten earlier at the Black Cat café spattered over the bottom of his new two-tone trousers. Gritting his teeth, Geoffrey shook his head. There were times, he swore, when he could just about fucking strangle her . . .

37

The door opened and Pearson recoiled. Gagging.

'That's my moggy,' said the old man; Ted, the same old man from the day before. 'Her litter tray needs emptying.' And, judging by his breath, Ted had recently been eating from it. Beyond him, further up the hall, the Hitler-cat sat in a partly open doorway. Staring malevolently. Tail swishing in irritation.

'Adolf!' the old man shouted, flapping a hand in its direction. 'Get indoors!' Turning back to Pearson. 'Adolf!' Squeezing out a wheezy laugh. 'Get it?' He tapped the area under his nose. 'Adolf. She fucking looks just like him, don't she?'

'We're here to see Courtney Woods,' Pearson said.

'Who?'

'Three C?' Pearson prompted.

'Oh, her. Don't think she's in. Haven't seen her for a couple of days.'

'She was here yesterday,' Pearson said. 'We spoke to her.'

'Oh, yeah, yeah.' Noticing the warrant card in Pearson's hand for the first time. Squinting at it. 'Old Bill, right?'

'Yeah,' Pearson said, 'Old Bill.' Gesturing with the card towards the stairs. 'Mind if we go up?'

'Nah,' Ted sniffed, readjusted his broken glasses, 'but, I told you, she's not in.'

On the top landing. The door to 3B, the door next to Courtney's room, was off its hinges. An indentation, the imprint of a boot, at about the height of the door lock. Pearson shared a look with Cat and then gave the door a gentle push. Rather than swinging, it fell flat onto the floor. Or it would have done, if there had been any floor for it to fall onto. The small room, like the one next door, was no bigger than an average-sized living room in an average-sized house. It had been turned upside down. A single mattress stood up against the wall, its ticking slashed, its stuffing spread about the room amongst the other debris: overturned drawers, clothes, books, a broken porcelain figurine. The carpet ripped up and in one corner some of the floorboards lifted.

'I'll have a word downstairs,' Pearson said, 'see if the old boy knows anything.'

The door opened on the second knock. The telly too loud. The heating up too high. The smell of fried food. And the litter tray.

'The flat upstairs has been burgled,' Pearson said.

'Yeah?' Ted asked. Not surprised. Not particularly interested either.

'You hear anything?'

'Nah.' Then, by way of an excuse, 'I'm a bit mutton, plus I drink, y'know?'

Pearson knew. Could smell it on him. Tennent's Extra. In the time it had taken them to go upstairs and find the flat turned over, he'd opened a can. And drunk quite a bit of it, if Pearson was any judge.

'D'you know who lives there? The flat next to Courtney? Three B?' Pearson felt something brush against his trousers. Glancing down he saw the Hitler-cat twining itself in and out of his legs.

'Yeah, a friend of . . . the other bird?'

'Courtney?' Pearson eased the cat away with the instep of his shoe. 'The girl in Three C?'

'Yeah, that's it.'

'Got a description?' Then, when the old man looked confused, 'The girl in Three B. Do you know what she looked like?' The cat was back again. Brushing up against his trouser leg. Maybe it was on heat or something.

Ted wrinkled his nose. Thinking. 'Strange-looking thing.' Pearson again eased the cat away. More forcefully this time. 'Pretty though,' the old man said, 'black hair,' – touching his shoulder to indicate the length. 'Long, y'know. Tiny thing' – a little snort – 'compared to the other one anyway.'

Pearson fished in his inside pocket again. Took out the photo of Michael. 'This her?'

The old man peered at the photograph. Tilted his head. 'Yeah,' but unconvinced. Looking at Pearson. Trying to work out the answer he was expected to give. Trying to gauge how much trouble he could be putting himself in. 'Dunno. Could be.'

'When was the last time you saw her?'

'Dunno. A while. I don't really take much notice. I told you—'

'Yeah,' Pearson said, 'you drink.'

On the way back up, Pearson felt again the ache in his thigh. Deep in the muscle. Something like a dead-leg. The stiffness in his joints. The sharp pain in his hip. The result, no doubt, of the long drive. And climbing up and down these bloody stairs.

Reaching the landing, he said, 'According to our mate downstairs, a girl lived here. Description fits Michael Morris ... vaguely.' He indicated the other door with his chin. 'Did you try Courtney?'

'Yeah, no answer. So what now? Call in the SOCOs?'

'Yeah.'

As Cat took her mobile from her handbag, keyed in a number and put it to her ear, Pearson checked his watch. Another night he wouldn't get round to visiting his mum. Then, looking around, he considered the layout of the house. In common with most of the places of this type it was built in a sort of L-shape. One bedroom, 3C, and the bathroom on the longer leg. One of the bedrooms, this bedroom, set at a right angle. It brought to mind something that had happened on a previous case.

'Won't be a minute,' he said. 'I just want to check something out.'

Walking further along the landing. Finding a partly open door inset with frosted glass panels. Giving it a nudge with his elbow, it opened onto a bathroom. The toilet filthy. He doubted it had ever been cleaned. A crooked plastic seat. No lid. A knotted piece of string hanging from the cistern in place of a toilet chain. A pedestal basin covered with limescale. The plughole starting to rust. The soap in the dish grey and cracked, ingrained with something, the nature of which he wouldn't like to hazard a guess at. Over the basin, the window so dirty and smeared that he could barely see through. An overgrown back garden. A brick wall in need of repointing. White goods abandoned among the foliage. A window to his left open an inch or so. Flat 3B, Michael's room. He squinted through the filthy pane. Tempted to get some wetted toilet roll and clear an opening. But this, after all, could be a potential crime scene. Staring instead. His eyes starting to ache. Next to the window opposite, just below the level of the window ledge itself, ran a downpipe. Broken. Pearson leant forward, his nose almost pressing the glass. Was that a piece of string? He looked at the window ledge. The drainpipe. Back to the window ledge. Yeah. A piece of string. Secured under the window ledge with some kind of hook and running into the drainpipe. He went back along the landing.

'SOCOs are on their way,' Cat said.

'OK, you got any gloves?'

Cat shot him a quizzical look, before rooting around in her bag. Pulling out a pair of latex gloves in a sealed plastic bag. Handing them to him.

'Thanks,' Pearson said. Slipping them on, he entered the room. Side-stepping the door. Walking, as carefully as he could, across the debris-strewn floor to the window.

'The SOCOs will love you,' Cat said, hovering in the doorway.

'I doubt they'll find much. Anything useful will be long gone by now.'

'The boot print on the door? Fingerprints?'

'How long since this place was cleaned, d'you reckon? I'd say a couple of years at least. How many fingerprints d'you think are in here?'

'Fair point.'

Cat was right. This room could turn out to be the murder scene. All the same, this had to be weighed against what he might find hidden in the drainpipe. He pushed aside a tatty, orange nylon curtain and yanked at a partly opened window warped into its frame. After a few seconds it budged with a teeth-grating shriek. Pearson leaned out, pulling carefully at the piece of string in the drainpipe. When it emerged, the other end held a small cloth bag, the sort Pearson used to use at primary school for carrying his plimsolls. But there was a distinct lack of

weight as he brought it in. Loosened the drawstring. Felt inside.
'Shit!'

'What is it?' asked Cat.

'Empty.'

Pearson pulled the car door closed but didn't start the engine.
Cat, sitting in the passenger seat, seat belt on, handbag on her lap,
waited.

'D'you fancy trying Layla Gilchrist's place?' Pearson asked.

'For Courtney?' Cat asked. Shaking her head. 'I just knew you
were going to say that.'

Pearson ran a hand absently over the top of the steering wheel,
looking out through the front windscreen as a white-suited SOCO
unloaded metal cases from a van, slammed the doors and disappeared inside the house. 'You worried about Roberts?'

Gobsmacked, Cat turned towards him. 'Well, yeah, I'm worried
about Roberts. This morning, Pearson, this ... morning ... he
hauls us over the coals about talking to Courtney Woods without
an appropriate adult present and without issuing a caution. This ...
morning ... he tells us that Layla Gilchrist has phoned him personally and is,' she held her hand up, index finger almost touching
a thumb, 'this close to making a formal complaint.'

Pearson's hand settled on the rim of the steering wheel. 'OK.'
He nodded. Talking slowly. Adopting a 'reasonable' tone. A tone
that only served to infuriate Cat all the more.

'Look,' Cat said, exasperated, 'I agreed to seeing if Courtney
was all right because ... that was all it was going to be, just a quick
check on her. Just to make sure she was home safe.'

'Which she's not,' Pearson pointed out. He turned to her. 'Tony
Blake has told us she's mixed up in something. Right? We go
round there to see her and find that not only is she not at home,

but the flat next to hers has been turned over?' He lifted his hand from the wheel, made a gesture as if to indicate that it was self-evident. That he'd proved his point.

Cat looked away and into the street. Well, maybe he had. Maybe.

'If you are really that worried,' Pearson said, 'I can give Roberts a call, clear it with him.'

But making no move, she noticed, to actually take his mobile out of his pocket.

After a minute Cat heaved a sigh. 'Oh, why not?' Relenting. 'It's not as if I've actually got a career to jeopardise.'

Entering the street, the downstairs lights in the house were on. Pearson found a free parking space just outside.

'Looks like we're in luck,' he said. Pulling up, applying the handbrake, taking the keys from the ignition. Cat unclipped her seat belt, opened the passenger-side door, got out. Standing on the pavement: tired, fed up, sweaty. Needing a fag. But wanting to get this over and done with. Wanting to go home, wanting a shower, wanting her bed. So much wanting her bed.

Layla Gilchrist opened the door wearing a pink jumper: soft, expensive – angora, maybe. PVC trousers over high-heeled boots. But at least, Cat thought, she was actually dressed this time.

'We're a little concerned for Courtney,' Pearson said. 'We've been round to her flat, but she's not in. We were wondering whether you may have any idea of her whereabouts?'

For a moment, Gilchrist didn't move, didn't say anything. Ignoring Cat again. Appraising Pearson. Coming to a decision, saying, 'You'd better come in,' then turning away.

The girl looked out of place in the twee sitting-room: plain amongst the Laura Ashley flowers, graceless in the company of the

275

Lalique dancers. Shapeless in an over-large, pink dressing gown. Her hair had been washed. An attempt made to backcomb it into a style. But it just looked messy. Her face was clean, though still pale. Devoid of make-up, apart from some black eyeliner. As if that were the only make-up she just couldn't do without. Or as if she'd started to put her face on, but had given up. They took the armchairs again and Gilchrist sat next to the girl on the settee. Stroking her hair.

'The officers have come to see that you're all right, Courtney.'

'How are you doing, Courtney?' Cat asked.

Looking down, not meeting their eyes, the girl shrugged. 'OK, I suppose.'

'We've just been to see Tony,' Cat said, 'at the prison. Did you know he's in prison? What he did?'

'I thought I'd better tell her,' Gilchrist said, 'before she saw it on the news.'

Courtney said nothing, one hand worrying at the other.

'It's all right, Courtney,' Cat said, 'you're not in trouble. Is it OK if we ask you a few questions?' A look to Gilchrist.

The girl nodded, still not looking up. Started gnawing at the skin around a thumbnail.

'Can I ask you about Michael?' Cat asked. Then after a pause, a silence, 'How did Tony feel about Michael?'

Taking her thumb from her mouth. Putting her hands in her lap. Courtney asked, 'How do you mean?'

'Did he like Michael?'

'S'pose so.'

'So he didn't say anything to make you think he *didn't* like Michael?'

'Like what?'

'Well, I don't know really. He was OK that you and Michael were friends though?'

276

'Yeah,' Courtney said. Looking at her thumb, starting to chew it again. 'Sometimes he got a bit jealous, I suppose, that we spent so much time together ... ' Shrugging.

'What made you think Tony was jealous?' No answer. 'Did he say something?'

'He said that he was just trying to look after me, that he didn't want me to get hurt.'

'OK,' Cat said slowly. 'And you told us that you'd been sleeping with other men? What did he say about that?'

Courtney looked at Gilchrist and then down at her hands again. Gilchrist shuffled closer.

'Courtney?' Cat prompted.

Courtney started to worry at one hand with the other again. Gilchrist reached across and put her hand over. Stilling them. And then giving a little squeeze.

'I think,' she said, 'that Courtney doesn't want Tony to get in more trouble than he's in already.'

'What happened to your neck, Courtney?' Cat asked. 'Who hurt you? Was it Tony?' Courtney said nothing. Looking down, shaking her head. 'You told us about these other men, Courtney – is that where you got the injury to your neck?'

Courtney was still shaking her head. Gilchrist gave her hand another little squeeze. The girl's shoulders started to shudder. Gilchrist removed her hand from Courtney's long enough to get a tissue from her pocket and hand it to her. Then put her hand back on top of the girl's. Crying now, finally Courtney looked up. Shaking her head. Panic in her eyes.

'If I say anything ... ' Mascara running. Black blobs in the lower lashes. Cheeks streaked with dirty tears. Tissue balled in a fist. 'Tony will be in even more trouble.'

'More trouble?' Cat asked. 'Tony's been arrested for attempted armed robbery. That's pretty serious, Courtney. Are you saying Tony's been involved in something else?'

But the girl looked away again. Down at the tissue balled in her fist. Squeezing it. Sniffing. Shaking her head.

Gilchrist spoke to Cat. 'Look, you said you wanted to make sure Courtney was OK. You can see that she is.' And then to Pearson, 'I think she's had enough, don't you?'

38

Hands thrust deep into the pockets of his overcoat, Pearson stood at the top of the concrete stairs. Wind slapping his ears. The rattling of the metal kiosk shutters. The shushing and fizzing of surf against the wooden planks of a breakwater. His sight slowly adjusting to the light cast by a jaundiced and gibbous moon. The distant amber beads of the street lights on the far shore. Out in the estuary, the blinking red, white and green lights on bobbing cabin cruisers. Overhead, the reverberation of an aeroplane engine. Looking up, Pearson saw its red and white lights winking a response. On the seafront below: the flare of a lighter, the tip of a cigarette glowing, and then dimming. The smell of tobacco smoke drifting on the breeze.

Jack Morris stood hunched into his camel-hair overcoat. The thin shoulders, the bony back, clearly visible. Pearson followed the other man's gaze. Out past the granite obelisk of the Crowstone. And into a cold, still darkness. The beach where six days ago Jack Morris's son had been found dead. Pearson descended the steps.

Feeling again the deep, dull ache in his hip. The stiffness in his thigh. Limping over, he joined the old man.

'No Roller, Jack? Only I didn't see it in the car park.'

'Nah, I cabbed it.'

'Right,' Pearson said, nodding slowly. 'I suppose you'll be needing a new driver now, eh?'

'Already got one,' Morris said. 'Phoned an agency. Starts tomorrow. Some middle-aged bird. What I should've done in the first place.'

'You know,' Pearson said, 'what I've never understood, Jack. You own a minicab place, right? So why pay for someone else to drive you about?'

'One of my cabbies?' Morris asked. 'You seen the sort of cars they use? Fucking rust-buckets the lot of them. Poxy little Skodas and Nissans. Catch me in one of them!' Seeing the look on Pearson's face. Shaking his head. 'You don't think much of me, do you, son?'

Pearson looked away. 'Son'. It was just an expression, right? A figure of speech. Something people of Morris's generation said whenever they referred to anyone – anyone – younger than themselves.

'Besides, I've asked one or other of them to drive me round in the past,' Morris went on, 'but they end up getting the idea they're the one doing you a favour. Plus, they're forever fucking rabbiting, wanting to know your business.'

As Pearson turned back to face him, Morris added, 'Look, all that stuff, the Roller, all that – you know it's all bollocks. I know it's all bollocks. Right? But these people' – lifting his chin, but to indicate who, Pearson wasn't exactly sure – 'they expect it, y'know? It's like proof you're doing all right for yourself.'

They stood in silence for a few minutes. Morris finishing

his cigarette. Taking the packet of Marlboro out of his pocket. Crushing the cigarette on its side. Opening the box and dropping the dog-end in. About to put the box back in his pocket, he had second thoughts and took out another. Sparking up the gold lighter. Cupping the cigarette in his hands. Pearson studied the other man's profile in the shifting light of its flame. There was something. A fleeting expression. A certain set of the features. Something about the eyes that was all too familiar. Something he'd glimpsed briefly in the washroom mirror in the nick. Something that he'd been only vaguely aware of before—

'That offer's still open,' Morris said. Adding, as if Pearson might be uncertain as to exactly what offer he was talking about, 'To pay for your mum to go into a better place?'

Pearson sighed, suddenly annoyed. 'I might have known that's why you wanted to meet. I told you, Jack. I'll sort it out.'

Pearson watched Morris take an irritated draw on his cigarette. The pause no doubt calculated to calm himself. Could this man have killed Michael? He probably wouldn't have relied on Tony Blake to find him. Thick, in Morris's estimation, and lazy with it. Plus Blake had no real reason to find Michael. So he could have made a few enquiries of his own. Asked people to keep an eye out. Promised good money to anyone who tipped him off. That, at least, would explain how Morris had made the connection between the dead girl found on the beach and his missing son. It wouldn't really take that long for someone to come up with Michael's whereabouts, would it? To tell him all about Michael. That he was a girl. Or was going to be a girl. He wouldn't believe it, of course. Wouldn't want to believe it. Would want to see it for himself. He'd have his pick of cars. Driving ban or not. Could use a different one each night. Something unobtrusive. Dark blue. Black. Some little Ford, or whatever. Maybe he'd just parked up opposite the house. Watching. Just wanting to talk. Trying to work out how he'd approach Michael. So he'd have seen Tony going in and out. Would have known then that the fucker had found Michael and chosen not to tell him. Had he made up his mind, gone in and tried to talk to Michael, to try and patch things up? Had Michael thrown it back in his face? Told Jack that his transition was a direct rejection of him? Laughed when Jack said he wanted to hand over his business interests to Michael? Had Jack lost his temper?

Nah, he couldn't see it. And besides, even if he had killed Michael, there was the question of the disposal of the body. Pearson doubted Morris would be strong enough to move the body alone. And doubted even more that Tony Blake would be in any great hurry to help him out.

So, maybe he was actually as upset by Michael's death as, at least superficially, he seemed. In that case, after Michael died he could have gone back to see if he could find out anything. Anything to tell him what might have happened. Sitting outside again. Watching the house. The woman turning up. The woman who he'd have later found out was Courtney Woods' boss, Layla Gilchrist. Leaving after a few minutes, not happy. Pearson arriving an hour or so later. The policewoman in tow. Gilchrist returning ten or so minutes later. The door left open. The door was probably always being left open while Ted nipped out to the off licence. Gilchrist coming out with the girl and driving away. The two coppers following. The old man downstairs coming back. Forgetting to shut the door. Morris taking his opportunity. If he'd been watching the house he'd have known that Michael's flat was at the front. Kicking in the flimsy door. Ransacking the place: lifting the carpets and floorboards, slitting open the mattress, turning out the drawers. Finding nothing. Then, standing in the middle of the

282

room, amid the chaos. Wouldn't he have twigged where Michael would hide something? In the very same place he'd always hidden things as a kid? If Morris had found the bag, he would definitely have taken whatever was inside . . .

'I suppose you've heard Tony's girl took a bad beating?' Pearson asked. 'Nothing to do with you, I suppose?'

'Me?' Morris turned to look at him. 'Why should I give her a doing?'

'I don't know, maybe you think she got Michael involved in something and that's why he ended up dead. So maybe you see it as partly her fault.'

Morris took a long drag on the cigarette. Narrowing his eyes.

'Maybe.' As if it was the first time he'd considered the idea. Pearson studied the old man's profile again. Not really Morris's style. A beating? Yes. But the ligature around the neck?

'If she did get Michael into something,' Morris said, 'then maybe it was partly her fault. But bashing little girls around?' Shaking his head. 'Nah. What do you take me for? Now, don't know about you, but I'm fucking freezing! I'm going to call a cab. Head home.' But his face told a different story. Morris had made what he would consider a perfectly reasonable proposal. And he wouldn't quite be able to leave it at that. Now, thought Pearson, Morris would point out that Pearson hadn't sorted it out. Before trying one more time. Adopting a conciliatory tone, making an appeal to common sense. Playing on the fact of his past relationship with Pearson's mother.

'This thing about your mum,' Morris said, exhaling a plume of smoke from his nose, 'you haven't sorted it out up till now.'

'I've been kind of busy, Jack,' Pearson said pointedly. 'On a murder case?'

Morris acknowledged this with a curt nod. Then said, 'Listen, son. I appreciate you've got your pride. But I've got the money, so why not let me spend it? I'd just like to do something nice for your mum, it's no big deal.'

'I told you, Jack, I'll sort it.'

Day Seven

Day Seven

39

Cat was sitting in one of the public shelters on the seafront. The very same shelter, had she but known it, where Pearson had met Jack Morris four days before. Normally, on the days she left home early enough, on the days she didn't accept a lift from Pearson and drove to work in her own car, she would take the opportunity to walk on the beach. Maybe pick up some sea glass. In the summer. This time of the year: wet shoes, damp sand clinging to the lower half of your trousers, skin sandblasted and chapped, hair so windblown and full of salt that it was like toffee. Plus, in the winter months, people were free to walk their dogs on the beach. Which meant, more than likely, some fat lab or cocker spaniel bounding across, jumping up at you and nearly knocking you over. The owner shouting, 'Don't worry! He's only being friendly!' As if that were the problem. Not the trail of slobber up your leg, the dirty paw prints on your jacket. Besides, it had started to spit with rain. So she'd had to content herself this morning with sitting in the shelter. Getting her fags out of her handbag. Lighting up. Having a quiet, contemplative smoke. Idly watching a pair of bickering crows circling each other. Exchanging grated warnings. Jet plumage reflecting iridescent trails of oily light. Then, an over-stepping of boundaries. The flare of a malevolent black eye. An agitated 'Krrah!' The flapping of wings. And Cat's mind had gone back to . . . Roberts. Standing in front of one of the white incident boards. Crime-scene photos. The prone form of another dead girl. Waggling his arms into the sleeves of a black jacket. Picking over the bones . . .

Cat had tensed, had been about to stand up to get a better look to see what, exactly, the birds were squabbling over. For the briefest of moments imagining them pecking at the decomposing remnants of a severed limb, a decapitated human head. Probably only seaweed, she told herself. Taking a slow drag on her cigarette, she'd managed to get herself to relax. To let it go. She'd taken that as a positive sign, an indication that her mood might be lifting. After all, it wasn't that long ago that she'd convinced herself that a seal swimming in the estuary was the bloated corpse of a drowned woman . . .

Her mobile began to ring. She put her handbag on her lap and dug out her phone, checking the caller display. Pearson. Accepting the call. Putting it to her ear. Saying, 'What's up?' Slinging her handbag over her shoulder. Standing up. Pulling up the hood of her anorak.

'We've got to go back to Chelmsford nick.'

Walking over to the bins. 'Oh, for fuck's sake!'

'Yeah, Tony Blake has asked to see us. Well, me actually. But Roberts wants you there too. He's got something important to tell us. Apparently.'

'Couldn't he have said yesterday?' Taking one last drag of her cigarette, grinding it out on the top of the metal bin.

'Yeah, you'd have thought so. Where are you?'

'I'll be about ten minutes.' She poked the dog-end through the hole in the lid of the bin.

After she ended the call, Cat stood for a minute looking out over the estuary. Listening to the pattering of the rain on her anorak. She'd picked it because of the colour. Powder blue. And because it felt nice to the touch. Soft. 'Showerproof', it had said on the label. But it was nothing of the fucking sort ...

Cat followed Pearson and the prison officer into the visiting room. The officer, the same pain-in-the-arse who had given them such a hard time before – and had given them a hard time again – picked up a discarded tabloid newspaper from the table and took his place on the stool next to the wall. Cat and Pearson pulled out the two orange plastic chairs and sat down opposite Blake. They sat there for a while, Blake picking distractedly at the scab on the bridge of his nose, no one saying anything. The silence in the room broken only by the sound of the screw turning the pages of his paper.

Finally, Blake gestured at Cat with his chin. 'I hope she ain't going to sit there giving me evils again.'

'Maybe,' Cat said, '"she" doesn't much like you. Maybe "she" doesn't like the way you treat women. Maybe "she" doesn't believe yet that it wasn't you who beat and strangled Courtney Woods.'

Blake folded his arms. Sat back in his chair. Uninterested. Bored.

'So, what is it you want?' Pearson asked. 'You asked us to come here, after all. You could have said whatever it is you have to say when we were here yesterday.'

Blake expelled air from his nostrils. As if he was the one who was put out.

'We've gone to a lot of trouble to come here this morning,' Pearson said, 'organising things through prison liaison, getting the OK from the governor. Arranging for an officer to be available.' He nodded in the direction of the screw, turning the pages of his paper. Cat suspected that he was only too happy for any opportunity to sit around for a while doing fuck all. Pearson, though, she noticed, was starting to get annoyed. 'Plus, the traffic's a fucking nightmare this time of day,' he said, 'out of Southend *and* into Chelmsford.'

When Blake still said nothing Cat said, 'Just to put your mind at rest, Tony' – making it plain from her tone of voice that she still didn't believe him – 'about Courtney? We went to her flat last night, after we left here. Because of what you said. Because you seemed worried about her ...'

She trailed off. Blake hadn't reacted, so maybe he wasn't that bothered after all. Didn't really want to know ...

Blake unfolded his arms, resting his elbows on the table, putting his hands on the side of his face. As if the effort of holding his head up was almost too much for him.

'Well?' he asked. Eventually.

Pearson sighed. 'The point is, she's fine. She's staying with her boss at the shop. Layla Gilchrist?'

When he said it. When Pearson told him. When the words left his mouth. There was a moment, a few seconds maybe, when it was obvious the meaning hadn't quite registered. Then Tony Blake's head, supported up until now, hands on either side of his face, elbows on the small table, seemed to Cat to slip between his fingers. Gather momentum. And crash onto the table top. The prison officer – nose in his newspaper, miles away – jolted upright. Half leaving his stool. Pearson looked over. Gave one short shake of his head. The officer, hesitating, touching the bunch of keys hanging from the belt loop on a pair of black trousers straining under his impressive beer gut, not quite sure if he had missed something. Eyeing Pearson suspiciously for a moment. As if he might have grabbed the prisoner behind the neck and smashed his head on the table while he wasn't looking.

'I told you!' Blake said. Talking into the grey Formica. Lifting his head. Butting the table once more. 'I fucking told you she was in danger!'

Pearson glanced over once again at the prison officer: frozen, one foot on the floor, one arse-cheek still on the stool, and shook his head again. The screw, wavering. Uncertain as to what to do. Not quite sure of the procedure in this situation.

'I fucking,' Blake hit his head on the table again, 'told you!'

The screw was staring at Pearson. His mind – almost – made up to move. If Blake did it again, Cat thought, the interview would be over.

'How could you let that happen? I fucking told you ...' Blake's forehead now resting on the table. Talking into its surface ...

Cat was staring at the back of Blake's head. 'What is it, Tony?' she asked. 'What are you so worried about?'

His hands went to his ears. Blocking out her words, his back and shoulders heaving. Cat wondered for a moment whether he was crying.

Blake was muttering to himself, 'Gilchrist? Shit! Gilchrist.' Still not lifting his head from the table. 'I tell them Courtney is in danger ... and they let her go off with fucking Gilchrist!'

Confused, Cat looked to Pearson. He gave a shake of his head. A shake of his head that said he didn't know what was going on either. A shake of his head that told her not to say anything. They sat for a minute or so in silence. Staring at the back of Blake's head ...

Abruptly, he sat up, his fingertips squeaking over the surface of the table.

40

'I killed Michael,' Blake said.

His voice calm. Quiet. When Blake sat up, Pearson had half expected to see the wet tracks of tears on his cheeks. But his eyes were dry, though red-rimmed. The small scratches, the remnants of the grazes between them, scarlet. His face blotchy and flushed. The cut on the bridge of his nose reopened. An angry welt beginning to appear on his forehead, already partly obscuring the double 'O' bruise, the artefact of the force applied from the shotgun barrels.

Another passage of time. Nobody speaking. The room silent. The only sound: the screw settling his other arse-cheek back on his stool, folding back a page of his tabloid.

'Is that why you asked us here?' Pearson said. 'To tell us that?'

Blake glanced over at the screw. His nose back in his newspaper; for him, clearly, the immediate drama was over. Now, he was back to not paying too much attention to what was going on. Or doing a good impersonation.

'That bird Courtney works for ...' Blake said.

'Layla Gilchrist?' Cat asked.

'Yeah, her, you know anything about her?'

'Like what?'

'Like she used to work at the House of Commons? Like she got busted for possession of coke? Anyway, it's all over the net, look it up. So, I tell Courtney, because I got fed up with her going on about what a great boss she had, how she admired her, how much she'd like to be like her when she was older . . . '

'As opposed to your opinion of *your* boss . . . ' Pearson said.

'Yeah, whatever,' Blake said, giving him the dead eyes again. 'So the silly cow only went and asked her about it. And she comes back and she's all like,' mimicking Courtney's voice again, breathless, gushing, '"She was really cool about it, and she told me all about how she ended up on the game, and going to some dodgy parties, and saw the wrong people, and that's why she really lost her job!"'

'So?'

'So,' Blake said, 'Michael turns up out of the blue one day. Like, I go round there, to Courtney's flat, and guess who's sitting on the bed? So then Michael's there all the time? Like every time I go round there? And one day they're there talking and Courtney's on about her boss – and I get the impression that it's not the first time they've talked about her – and Michael's all interested? Saying to Courtney how he thought the parties sounded like a lot of fun. Fun!' Blake spat the word. 'And how he bet you could make a lot of money . . . so, after that, I go round there a few times and each time they're both out.'

'And you think that maybe they've started doing – what?' Cat asked.

Blake shrugged. 'Stands to reason . . . '

'But you don't know,' she pointed out.

'I don't know, not for sure, but it's obvious, isn't it? Gilchrist got her into the same sort of parties,' Blake insisted, 'and Michael encouraged it. Encouraged her to ...' He trailed off into a scowl.

'What?' Cat asked.

"Look,' Blake said, 'a couple of weeks before Michael died, I got a call from Courtney, right? Hysterical; said there'd been some kind of accident, Michael was hurt, could I come round. When I got there, to Courtney's bedsit, it was obvious straight away that it was serious. Michael was lying on the floor unconscious, not breathing, his lips blue. Some kind of sick game they were playing that went too far. Somehow we, I, managed to get Michael breathing again ...'

'So what happened then?'

'Nothing. After a few days they just treated it all as some big fucking joke. Seemed to make them closer, if anything. Like, when I was there they were all like,' rubbing at a cheekbone, 'I dunno. Like sitting with their heads together. Whispering. Giggling, y'know? Like they had a little secret between them.'

'And you thought it was what?' Pearson asked. 'These parties?'

'I pleaded with her to stay in, to stop hanging around with Michael.'

'So why didn't she?' Cat asked.

A muscle twitched beneath Blake's eye. 'I told you, she's fucked up. She thinks she deserves to be hurt. She's like "It's only a bit of fun, what's your problem?"'

'But you didn't, right?' Pearson said. 'Think it was fun, I mean.'

'You saw her neck,' Blake said. 'Is that what you'd call fun? And the bruises on her chest ...' Sniffing. Shrugging again. 'It's not the first time it's happened, that's all.'

'She's been beaten before?' Pearson asked. 'Strangled? At these parties she was going to with Michael?'

'Parties organised by Layla Gilchrist?' Cat asked.

Blake heaved an exasperated sigh. 'That's what I'm telling you ...'

'OK,' Pearson said, 'so tell us what happened. The day Michael died.'

Blake sighed. 'It was the same as the other time.' Lifting his hand to his face. About to rub under his eyes. Hesitating. His hand hovering in front of his nose, finally he put it back down on the table.

'I get a call from Courtney. Proper hysterical. "Michael's in trouble ... I think he's really dead this time ... I don't know what to do." So I told her to stay put. Not to open the door to anyone. Not to do anything till I get there ...'

'And then what?' Pearson prompted.

'Same as before. I gave him CPR, all the time she's screaming in my ear how Michael's dead, how it's an accident, how it's not her fault because Michael did it himself ... So, anyway, I'm doing chest compressions, checking his breathing, then after a while I think I can feel a faint pulse. I told Courtney I'd better get him to hospital.'

'You didn't think of phoning an ambulance?'

'I didn't want them coming to the house. Didn't want Courtney involved. Besides, you got any idea how long they take to turn up? Anyway, I thought if I took Michael to hospital, maybe I could just leave him there. Or give a false name, I dunno – listen, I wasn't thinking straight.'

'Fair enough,' Pearson said. 'Then what?'

'I've been using one of Jack's cars – some crappy

estate – ferrying shit around? Anyway, I had the back seats folded down? So I put Michael in the back. And on the way, he starts coming round. Like moaning and groaning and that. So I'm looking in the rear-view mirror and I start to think about things. About what'll happen if Michael pulls through, goes back to hanging round Courtney. How they'd be like before? Like it was some big fucking joke? Only worse. How they'd be back at those parties . . .'

'With Courtney getting hurt again,' Cat prompted.

Blake looked down. Rubbing at the table top with the side of a balled fist. A heavy breath. 'So I thought, why not? Why not finish the job? Top him. Dump the body. No big loss to anyone, as I see it.' Looking up. 'Wasn't that hard, as it happens.' Matter-of-fact. No sign of remorse. But no sign of pleasure either at what he'd done. 'I mean, he was halfway there already. All I had to do was apply a little pressure.'

'You strangled him?' Pearson asked. 'With your hands?'

'Had a coat in the car,' Blake said, 'like a nylon sports coat thing? So, anyway, I held that against his neck, then squeezed. Thought you lot might have been able to do fingerprints or something.' A laugh. More a breath through his clogged nose. 'I mean, who knows? Probably shit, right? The stuff they have on the telly?'

Pearson said nothing. Waited.

'So then I had to get rid of him. Hadn't quite thought that one through. Thought of maybe dumping him in the woods. Driving out into the country a bit, putting him in a field or something?' Eyes on the table top again. Brushing away some imaginary dust.

'But your bottle went, right?' Pearson asked. 'You panicked.'

Blake didn't look up, didn't deny it. 'I was down by the seafront, and, now I'd done it, I didn't really want him in the car any more. Wanted rid of him as soon as.' Shrugging, 'Like I said, I'd been carting some shit around? I had some gloves in the car and I put on the sports coat ... slung Michael over a shoulder, fireman's lift, y'know? Thought if I dumped him on the beach the tide might take him. Or at least the salt water might mess things up a bit, forensics and that ...'

41

'What did you make of that?' Cat asked.

They were in the prison car park. Pearson ending the call to Roberts. Arranging for the car that Blake had been using to be impounded for forensic examination. A warrant to be issued to gain access to his home and a search to be implemented for the gloves and nylon sports coat that had been used to move Michael's body. Pearson, hesitating by the driver's door, key fob in hand, looked across the roof of the Mondeo at her.

'Exactly what it was. Blake confessing to the murder of Michael Morris. Why, you got doubts?'

Cat took a last drag on her cigarette, thinking for a moment, then shook her head. 'Dunno.'

'Why confess to a murder you didn't commit?' Pearson asked.

Cat nodded, reluctantly. Dropped her cigarette on the floor and ground it out under her heel.

They had been quiet on the journey back. The radio off. The drumming of rain on the windscreen, the laboured clunk and squeal of the car's faulty wiper the only accompaniment to Cat's thoughts. Staring out of the side window. Testing herself again on the flyover. The Mondeo, buffeted by a sudden gust of wind, momentarily veering across the rain-slick tarmac towards the metal crash barriers. Essex Yeomanry Way. Even more dreary and dismal – as if she'd ever thought that possible – in a premature twilight illuminated by the headlights of passing cars. The spectre of the old Runwell hospital lurking out of sight behind the banked verge topped by shrubs and trees. It wasn't until they swung a right off the roundabout at the Fairglen Interchange and onto the slip road taking them onto the A127 that she finally turned to Pearson and asked, 'The thing is – why confess at all?'

'You're doing that thing again ...' Pearson said as the traffic ground, predictably, to a halt.

'What "thing" is that?'

'That thing where you've been having a long conversation in your head, then you decide to include me, and I have to try and catch up.'

'Well technically,' Cat said, 'I'm actually doing that other thing? The thing where I pick up the thread of something we were talking about an hour ago and then carry on as if there hadn't been any break in the conversation? So ... Tony Blake is already looking at seven to twelve for armed robbery, right?'

'Yeah,' Pearson nodded, 'depending on how the judge applies the sentencing guidelines. My guess is his brief will make a plea of mitigating circumstances, that he was doing it out of a misguided attempt to help Courtney. But then you've got to take into account the level of violence involved.'

'By him?' Cat asked. 'Or *on* him?'

'Yeah.' Pearson gave a wry smile, nodded. 'There is that.'

'Let's say he's hoping for seven,' Cat said, 'and thinking he'll be out in half that. In which case, why hold your hands up for another – worse – crime?'

'Unless it's to protect Courtney Woods?' Pearson ventured. 'Maybe Blake was lying about Courtney telling him that Michael had done it himself. Maybe she was the one who killed Michael, an accidental strangulation as a result of some sick game that had gone a little too far? Maybe Michael was already dead when Blake turned up at the house and he just dumped the body? Maybe he's just taking the blame in order that she can avoid being implicated in Michael's death?'

'Maybe,' Cat said. Not persuaded. 'But that would depend on Blake being capable of an act of pure selflessness, wouldn't it? And his reaction, didn't it strike you as a little extreme?'

Pearson's mind went back to the interview. When Blake had banged his head on the table; the anger, the desperation, had appeared real. He pictured Blake: his forehead on the grey Formica, his shoulders heaving. All of that, too, had seemed authentic. 'His feelings for the girl came across as genuine enough,' he said.

'Yeah, I suppose,' Cat agreed, but with a degree of reticence.

Pearson stared out of the windscreen at the immobile traffic. Shifted in his seat. Leaning an elbow on the door sill. Resting his head on a hand. Settling himself in for a long wait.

'I've been asking myself,' Cat said, 'if confessing to Michael's murder was Blake's initial intention when he asked us – you – to go to Chelmsford?'

She turned to face him and Pearson nodded for her to carry on.

'I've been wondering,' Cat said, 'whether all that head-banging wasn't all some kind of distraction to give him time to think? And if he only made up his mind to confess to Michael's murder during

301

the minute or so his head was on the table? Which was *after* you'd told him that Courtney Woods was with your girlfriend ...'

'Layla Gilchrist?'

Cat gave him a look that said: *Like you've got other girlfriends?*

Pearson wound down the side window, leant his elbow back on the sill, stared out of the front windscreen at the tail-lights of the car in front.

Layla Gilchrist had turned up unannounced at his place, claiming to be concerned about Courtney Woods. Saying that she hadn't been to the shop for a few days, that she hadn't answered her door or returned any of Gilchrist's calls. Saying that she was concerned because of the girl's relationship with Tony Blake, who by this time was already in custody for the attempted armed robbery of the betting shop. Had she gambled on the fact that Pearson would take it on himself to check that Courtney was all right? Had she, even, sat outside Courtney's flat and waited for them to arrive? Giving them a few minutes, during which time she'd assume that they had got to see the girl. Entering through a front door that had been carelessly left open. Had she waited on the stairs, overhearing their conversation? Even then the timing of her arrival had seemed a little opportune, to say the least.

At the bedsit. Gilchrist saying, 'You haven't been to the shop for a few days, Courtney, I was worried.'

Had that been out of concern for the girl? An innocent enquiry? Or an accusation? Courtney shifting on the bed. At the time, just a repositioning for the sake of comfort. But looking back: had she seemed slightly cowed?

Could Courtney have told Blake something that put him, put them both, at risk? Was Courtney being held as some kind of surety in order that Blake kept his mouth shut? Had Gilchrist's phone call to Roberts, the threat of a formal complaint, been just another attempt to throw them off the scent? A way of discrediting any investigation that might follow?

At Gilchrist's house. When they had tried to question the girl. Gilchrist saying, 'I think that Courtney doesn't want Tony to get in more trouble than he's in already.' Courtney worrying at one hand with the other. Gilchrist reaching across and putting her hand over. Stilling them. And then giving a little squeeze. But what, at the time, might have been interpreted as a comfort could now, just as easily, be viewed as a warning. Or a reminder of a warning.

But if you looked back at any encounter with anyone, he supposed – and viewed them in a particular way, looking for lies, looking for anything that may now strike you as suspicious – actions and motivation you might previously have judged as entirely innocent could quite easily become questionable ...

'Maybe,' Cat said, 'Blake simply decided that if he confessed to the murder of Michael Morris, that would be the end of it. That the circumstances of the death, Layla Gilchrist's involvement, and, in particular, Courtney's part in it, wouldn't be probed too deeply.'

'Or,' said Pearson, 'if it *was* Courtney who killed Michael, perhaps Gilchrist knew. Blake said Courtney looked up to her. So she might see her as someone she could confide in. That would give Gilchrist leverage over Blake. "Hold your hands up to Michael's murder, or I'll dob Courtney in."'

'Which would mean, again, a degree of self-sacrifice on Blake's part.'

Any answer that Pearson might have been about to give was interrupted by the ringing of his phone. The car's Bluetooth system kicked in. 'Unknown caller' on the dashboard display. He accepted the call, said, 'Pearson.'

'Ah, Detective Sergeant ...'

Pearson looked across at Cat, raising his eyebrows.

'Where are you?' Layla Gilchrist asked.

'In the car,' Pearson hedged.

'Listen,' Gilchrist said, 'I'm at the police station. Or, outside it, actually. How long do you think you'll be?'

'Well,' Pearson sighed, 'we're currently in a traffic jam on the A127, so it's anybody's bloody guess.'

From the car's speakers: moving traffic, the sound of wind on the phone's mouthpiece.

Finally, 'I've got Courtney with me.' A deadening of sound – a hand over the mouthpiece – muffled voices, then, 'I'm going to leave her in the reception. She's promised to stay there till you get back.'

'You're not staying?'

'On balance,' Gilchrist said, 'I'm not sure that's the best idea—'

'There are questions we need answers to . . .'

'Then ask them now, but be quick.'

'Courtney's injuries, for a start.'

'That's something you can ask her,' Gilchrist said. 'She's promised me that she'll tell you everything.'

'Tony Blake seems to think,' Pearson pressed, 'that Courtney got those injuries at parties that she and Michael attended, and he implied these parties were arranged by you.'

A long silence. At least, Gilchrist said nothing. Just the background hum of traffic, the wind again, against the phone's mouthpiece. Then, 'It seems that some people can never escape their past. Let's hope, for her sake, that for Courtney it's different.'

The call ended.

42

'Have you heard of iatrogenesis?' Cat asked.

Waiting for ... the studied pause, the deadpan face, the 'Never much liked Phil Collins myself.' They were sitting in the empty rest area, each with a drink from the vending machine on the table in front of them. Pearson dabbed a forefinger on the surface of his coffee. Fishing something out. Rubbing his thumb and finger together. Taking a sip. Nodding.

'It means a doctor unintentionally harming a patient in the course of their treatment, right?'

On second thoughts, this was probably what irritated her most about Pearson. You asked him a question and he knew a lot more about it than you thought he did. Even, on some occasions, a lot more than you knew yourself. Which only made the other times worse. That deadpan expression, so you weren't ever quite sure. Letting you think you were imparting a unique and innovative piece of information. Some pearl of wisdom. When all the time you were just banging on. And he was humouring you.

'It can also be applied to a psychiatrist,' Cat said, 'who, over a series of consultations, might unknowingly implant a false memory into a patient.'

Cat licked her lips. Hesitating. They had grabbed a table near the entrance. Pearson only switching some of the lights on. Directly beyond the table they occupied lay pools of darkness. Above their heads, one of the fluorescent lights was on the blink. Buzzing noisily. Flickering into life every few seconds. Before almost immediately going out again.

'Are we back on our Dr Fitzgerald?' Pearson asked. Not, quite, rolling his eyes. Cat nodded, uncertain now if she really wanted to go on.

'So,' she said, 'initially I thought that this Richard Lennon business was something to do with iatrogenesis. That "our" Dr Fitzgerald had somehow implanted a false memory into Richard Lennon by the use of MRT. And this is before we went to Chelmsford and spoke to Tony Blake, remember. But then I got to wondering whether there might not be something to your theory . . .'

Pearson looked puzzled. Obviously had no idea that he'd had a theory. Cat cleared her throat.

'You know' – nodding encouragement – 'about Richard Lennon, or Geoffrey Knowles as he was then, having actually killed Beverly Marsh?' Still no sign of recognition from him. Cat wished she had the manila folder. Wished she could open it now, check her facts. Point to the places in the notes she felt would back up her hypothesis. Give substance to what now seemed like mere supposition. They didn't have it, of course. They hadn't known what to do with it. So they'd given it to Roberts the previous evening. What he would do with it, neither of them had been quite sure. Sit on it, more than likely.

'You remember,' she insisted, though, clearly, he didn't. 'We were talking in the car?' Slowly, as if he were feeble-minded. 'You said that Fitzgerald could be right? That Richard Lennon was Geoffrey Knowles? That he killed Beverly Marsh and then suppressed the memory, or had it wiped? That the counselling he underwent with Fitzgerald enabled him to remember what he'd done and that's what drove him to commit suicide?'

Pearson sighed. Cleared his throat. 'Oh, yeah, right.' Looking down into his cup again. His expression saying that he remembered what he'd said now, but . . .

'So.' Cat took a sip of her own coffee. Looking down – it was contagious – turning the plastic cup on the table top. 'I'd been thinking, what if, this "something truly evil" that Lennon thought he'd done wasn't the murder of Beverly Marsh? What if it was the murder of Michael Morris?'

To give him his due, Pearson didn't laugh in her face. Didn't even smile. Didn't just knock it back straight away. He did, however, do an almost comical kind of double-take. 'On what evidence?'

'We have documentary evidence that Geoffrey Knowles was on remand in Chelmsford nick. Presumably for the murder of Beverly Marsh. Let's also take it as read that Geoffrey Knowles is Richard Lennon—' She held up a palm. 'Bear with me for a moment, OK?'

'OK,' Pearson agreed. Without enthusiasm.

'Deep sleep therapy was usually prescribed for depression or schizophrenia,' Cat said. 'Let's also assume that Geoffrey-Knowles-stroke-Richard-Lennon had, say, paranoid schizophrenia?'

'Can't we just stick with one name? To save any confusion? We're assuming that Geoffrey Knowles is Richard Lennon, right? And Richard Lennon is the name he went by at the time of his death. So why don't we just refer to him as Richard Lennon?'

'Fair enough. Richard Lennon it is. So, in the course of Richard

307

Lennon's therapy with Fitzgerald, rather than her implanting the idea that he'd killed Beverly Marsh, she actually recovers his memory? And his previous personality . . . ' Cat took a mouthful of her black coffee. Letting Pearson mull it over.

'And you had the idea that this would account for our two murders occurring fifty years apart?' Pearson asked. 'That Geoffrey Knowles killed Beverly Marsh. Had his memory erased. And then fifty years later – as Richard Lennon – Dr Fitzgerald reawakens this paranoid schizophrenia – or whatever it is – by hypnosis? Right?'

Cat nodded.

'He then,' Pearson went on, 'meets Michael Morris at some time – and we've got absolutely no evidence of this happening – and for some unknown reason decides to kill him? Why? What's his motive?' Waiting a beat. Then, 'Come on, bit of a stretch, isn't it?'

'Yep,' Cat agreed, 'that's where it all fell down. Which is why I didn't say anything. I could just guess what Roberts would have said.'

'You're not a fan, are you?'

'Of Roberts? You could say that.'

'He's a fan of yours.'

'Yeah, right.'

'He is. I know he doesn't always show it.'

'Never. Never shows it.'

'All right. Never shows it. But that's just his way. He's always been a bit . . . irascible.' Pearson nodded, pleased with his choice of word. 'Irascible. Yeah, prickly – you know?'

'I know what it means.'

'But he really does like you. In fact . . . '

'What?'

'Nothing.'

'In fact – what? Come on, you can't say "in fact" and then just leave it hanging.'

Pearson sighed again. Pulled at an earlobe. 'All right. In fact, it's thanks to him that you've still got a job.'

'What?'

'After all that Carragher business, Curtis was all for pushing you out.'

'On what grounds?' It was a stupid question. If they really wanted to get rid of you, they'd find a reason. Or, if they couldn't find a reason, they'd make your life in the Job so unbearable, so intolerable, that you'd eventually just jack it in anyway.

Pearson swallowed the last mouthful of coffee. It was foul. But the tea was worse, and by the time the hot chocolate had cooled enough to drink it had usually formed a skin on top, the rest separating, causing a thick sludge to coagulate in the bottom. He put the cup down on the table, turning it, watching a droplet of coffee slide from one side to the other.

'Do you have to keep doing that?' Cat asked. Pearson looked up. 'Rattling that cup?' she said. 'It's getting on my bastard nerves.'

He pushed the cup away. 'So, does this explain your scepticism regarding Blake's confession?'

Cat gave this some thought, then shook her head. 'Not really. And now we've spoken to Courtney Woods I'm not sure I believe either of their stories completely.'

They had interviewed Courtney Woods earlier. Given her age – sixteen, as it turned out – it had been a brief, hastily arranged, informal 'chat' in front of a social worker acting as an 'appropriate adult'. It had been agreed that afterwards she would be handed over to the Child Protection team and they would have an opportunity of a more formal interview in 'due course'. Her version of the events surrounding Michael's death were a little confused. And although she insisted that Michael had lost consciousness after a *self-administered* strangulation, this had had the air of something rehearsed. However, when they told her that Blake had confessed to the murder of Michael Morris, she had seemed genuinely bewildered. Finally, the social worker had cleared his throat and turned his wrist to show his watch. Their time was up.

'Just a few more questions?' Cat had asked.

The social worker had nodded.

'Who did that to your neck?' Cat asked.

Hesitantly, not meeting anyone's eyes, Courtney said, 'Michael.'

'And the bruises to your body? Was that Michael too?'

The girl nodded.

'Why, Courtney?' Cat asked. 'Why did Michael do that? Why did you let him? Did you let him?'

The girl nodded again.

'Why did you let him do that to you? Why let him hurt you like that?'

The girl shrugged. 'It was like a game,' and then, 'at first.'

'But not later?'

Courtney swallowed. Shook her head.

'Tony seems to think,' Cat said slowly, 'that you and Michael used to go to parties together? Is that right?'

'S'pose.'

'And that's where you got hurt, where you got the bruises?'

The girl was shaking her head.

'And that these parties were organised by Layla Gilchrist.'

The girl looked up, met Cat's gaze, shook her head again. Emphatic this time. Adamant, she said, 'No!'

'You're saying Layla didn't organise these parties that you went to?'

'They weren't really parties. Not organised parties.' She shrugged. 'Just, like, at people's houses?'

'But,' Cat said, 'nothing to do with Layla? She didn't make you do anything you didn't want to?'

'No,' the girl had insisted, 'she's always been good to me.'

'OK,' Pearson said, 'just for the sake of argument – and it's a pretty flimsy argument – let's consider the two murders. Both victims found on the same beach—'

'And in roughly the same place,' Cat said. 'Both dying in a similar manner. Beverly Marsh by manual strangulation. Michael Morris ... well, that's less certain ... but manual strangulation hasn't actually been ruled out.'

'It's not just the fifty-year gap that's the stumbling block,' Pearson said. 'You heard the tape. Do you think the man on that tape sounded capable of murder?'

'Yeah,' Cat conceded finally, 'you're right. In all probability, Blake *must* be the person who killed Michael Morris.'

'Which still leaves us with the murder in the sixties,' Pearson said. 'So, firstly, we need to establish precisely why Geoffrey Knowles was in Chelmsford nick—'

'And we can only do that,' Cat said, 'if the official records still exist.'

'Then, we need to prove that Knowles is actually Richard Lennon. Then we have to prove that he killed Beverly Marsh.'

'We have DNA from Lennon's post-mortem.'

'But,' Pearson pointed out, 'it's of absolutely no use unless we turn up some DNA from the Beverly Marsh case.'

'And that still means turning up those missing clothes, right?'

311

43

'What's that?' Cat asked, pointing at Pearson's tie.

He held it out, scratching at it with a fingernail. 'Egg, maybe?'

'You had a toasted egg sandwich this morning. That must've been there all day.'

'Could be,' said Pearson. 'Then again, I think I had egg yesterday as well.'

Having managed to scratch off most, but not all, of the egg from his tie he gave up and let it fall back into place. Looking past her to see Roberts, standing in the open doorway. Crooking a finger. 'You two!'

Entering the DCI's office they sat in the three visitors' chairs. Cat taking her customary position nearest the window. Roberts, the seat to the left. Pearson, trailing in behind, closing the door, was left with the middle one. The broken one. The moulded plastic top having come away from the metal legs, it wobbled unsteadily under him. And he had to plant his feet firmly on the floor to keep it from tipping him out. There was a woman behind

Roberts' desk. Mid- to late-thirties, maybe. Frizzy brown hair pulled back in a severe pony tail. A pair of striking violet eyes behind glasses with thin metal frames. A light dusting of freckles on her forehead and nose. Bright orange lipstick.

'My name is Graham,' she said.

She didn't look much like a Graham. But, then again, the only Graham Pearson knew wore a cardigan and worked in the library, forty-five years old and still living with his mum. 'I work for the British government . . . '

'Which department?' asked Pearson. After a suitable pause. A pause in which she could have elaborated. But chose not to. Obviously deciding that they didn't merit any further explanation. Graham blinked. Otherwise, her face didn't move. Perhaps this was how she showed annoyance.

'My department deals with counter-intelligence and security.'

'So, what?' asked Pearson. 'MI5 then?'

She gave the faintest of nods in response. Not exactly what you'd have been expecting when you thought of a spook. Older, maybe. Male, probably. Educated at public school. Recruited at Cambridge. Almost certainly gay. Things were changing. But not, Pearson suspected, at the very top level. A fair guess then that she was reasonably junior. A dogsbody, sent to clear up what was viewed as a minor inconvenience.

'I have spoken to your Chief Constable,' Graham was saying, 'and he asked me to talk to DCI Roberts. As a further concession to courtesy, the Chief Inspector has asked me to include you two.' A reluctant concession, by the sound of it. She might be junior, but she still wasn't too happy about having to move this far down the food chain. Dealing with the lower ranks. The bottom-feeders. Pearson looked across to Roberts. Sitting stiffly in his chair, staring at the woman. Colour rising up his neck and into his cheeks. Embarrassment? Fury? Pearson wasn't sure. Maybe both.

'It is my understanding that you visited HMP Chelmsford earlier today' – looking from Pearson to Cat and back again – 'where Anthony Derek Blake, currently on remand for armed robbery, confessed to the murder of Michael Jason Morris.'

Who had she heard this from? Pearson's eyes cut across to Roberts. Judging by the look on his face, not him. The screw, had to be. Sitting on the stool. Pretending to cock a deaf 'un. Clearly earwigging. Reporting back to the governor, no doubt. And from there . . .

'Is that correct?' Graham asked.

'He claimed he murdered Michael Morris,' Pearson said, 'yeah.'

'"Claimed"?' Lacing her fingers. Resting her hands on the desk. On top of . . . a manila folder, which had gone unnoticed until now. A folder Pearson recognised only too well. The very same folder given to them by Dr Fitzgerald the previous day. The folder they'd passed on to Roberts.

'We're still pursuing other lines of enquiry,' Pearson hedged.

'Really?' Graham asked. Amused. Almost. Clearly dubious. 'Such as?'

'Well,' – nonchalantly picking a non-existent strand of cotton from his trouser leg – 'we have another potential suspect' – rubbing his thumb and forefinger together, letting the imaginary thread drop to the floor – 'who is linked to a previous murder.' Looking up, he continued, 'Namely, the manual strangulation of Beverly Marsh, on Thursday the thirty-first of March, nineteen sixty-six.'

Pearson wasn't really sure why he was doing this. When a government official turns up – a government official who knows about your murder investigation, clearly knows just a little too much about your murder investigation – the prudent thing to do would be to keep your head down. Keep your mouth shut. But, somehow, he just couldn't. And, if he'd been asked, he'd have had no explanation as to why not. Other than just sheer bloody-mindedness. There was no evidence. Just a theory. And a pretty shaky one at that. A theory that, when presented by Cat only a few minutes earlier, he had all but dismissed. Pearson could feel Cat looking at him now. Made an effort not to catch her eye.

'We believe that Beverly Marsh was killed by Geoffrey Knowles. And then, while on remand in HMP Chelmsford, Knowles was selected for psychological depatterning by the British government.' Pearson crossed his arms and sat back. The chair teetering precariously beneath him. Slow and steady, Pearson, he told himself. Or you'll end up falling on your arse. 'Unfortunately,' he continued, 'this depatterning proved unsuccessful, resulting in a severely damaged personality. Knowles was "hidden" in the health system under the name Richard Lennon. Where he was forgotten, until he was released under the "care in the community" programme.' Studiously avoiding Roberts' gaze, even though he'd noticed, from the corner of his eye, the DCI turn in his direction. Had seen the look on his face. 'He has subsequently undergone psychiatric counselling and, we believe, that somehow this may have led to him murdering Michael Morris.'

Graham blinked. Perhaps this was how she showed surprise, too. Perhaps this was how she showed all her feelings. The gamut of human emotion, conveyed in four hundred milliseconds.

'As a line of enquiry, Sergeant,' she said, 'it seems extremely speculative. Wouldn't you agree?'

Pearson said nothing, one way or the other.

'As it is, you are unable to confirm any of this by interviewing Richard Lennon because, subsequent to this treatment, he committed suicide on the westbound train line just outside Chalkwell station. Isn't that correct?'

Reluctantly, Pearson admitted, 'Correct.'

'So what other evidence do you have?' Pearson looked pointedly at the folder on the desk. 'Oh yes. This.' Looking down. Tapping the manila folder. 'I could claim that it comes under the auspices of the Official Secrets Act,' she stared directly at Pearson, 'but that would only serve to confirm your suspicions. Am I right, Detective Sergeant?'

Looking down again. Drumming on the folder with orange-painted fingernails. As if considering. 'Of course, there's no real hard evidence in here, is there? Just the ramblings of a confused old man, garnered under the influence of various unconventional therapies, together with the flights of fancy of an oddball psychiatrist. At least, that is how she'll be viewed by the wider public' – pausing. Looking up – 'and reputations are so important, don't you think? But, by all means, take a photocopy if you so wish ... '

Pearson, about to lean forward, about to hold out his hand for the folder, about to do just that, glanced across at Roberts ... and changed his mind.

44

'Can we get back to Michael Morris?' Roberts asked, slowly unclenching his hand. 'As that's the real reason you're here. That thing,' he nodded at the manila folder, 'is just a bonus as far as you're concerned.'

Sitting by the window, Cat experienced a sudden blast of chill, damp air. The street lights, the world outside, disappearing as rain started to speckle the dark glass. A whistling tinnitus as the wind explored the gaps in the ill-fitting frame and water began to pool on the sill ...

'I think, Ms Graham,' Roberts continued, 'that we at least deserve some sort of explanation for your interest in the investigation. Everybody in this room is, after all, bound by the Official Secrets Act.'

Graham lifted a hand to the side of her glasses. Making a micro-adjustment. Stalling for time, considering her options. Then, clearing her throat, 'Michael Morris—'

'Was working for you,' Roberts cut in. Impatient. As if it was all patently obvious.

'For MI5?' Cat asked.

Curtis's interest, his interference in the case, now making a little more sense. Turning up at the dump site. Raising objections about manpower. Even the initial reluctance to do a media appeal. Not all, then, about budgets and expenditure. It had been a factor. But it hadn't been the only, or overriding, reason. Clearly, he had been approached – got at – and been asked to shut down the investigation, or at least to do his best to obstruct it, in order to safeguard the British government's interests.

'To say Michael Morris worked for us,' Graham said, 'may be overstating matters somewhat. But it is true that he had received payment from us in the past for certain services—'

'From what we have learned in the last few days,' Cat said, 'Michael Morris was a compulsive liar, lacked remorse or empathy for other people, had a history of poor behaviour even in child-hood, and he was promiscuous. All of which point to him possibly suffering from antisocial personality disorder.' Pearson and Roberts were looking across at her. 'He was a sociopath,' she explained.

'That's a rather simplistic interpretation, Constable Russell,' Graham said. 'As you are no doubt aware, having gained a first in Psychology, these disorders exist within a complex spectrum of conditions, and it is therefore quite difficult in most cases to pro-vide a definitive clinical diagnosis. In fact, according to our own retrospective evaluation, Michael Morris scored very highly indeed when rated on the Hare Psychopathy Checklist—'

'Re-evaluation,' Roberts said coldly, 'a retrospective re-evaluation. As this is down to a cock-up. And I'm not just talking about that.' He indicated the folder. 'That's your job, after all, isn't it? That's why you're here. To make sure that the British govern-ment's part in the hiring and subsequent death of Michael Morris doesn't become public knowledge.' Roberts wagged a finger at

Graham. 'And I'm giving you the benefit of the doubt here. I'm assuming that you didn't know this about Michael *before* you hired him?'

'But you must have done some kind of initial assessment?' Cat asked.

Graham said nothing. Cat took this as a tacit admission. Though it might have been nothing of the sort.

'And you still used him?'

Graham addressed the room. 'Of course. He was remarkably well-suited to our purposes: along with the characteristics Constable Russell has already listed, Michael was also charming and manipulative, a born role-player and deceiver—'

'And totally immoral,' Pearson said.

'Amoral,' Cat corrected. 'That is: Michael operated outside of conventional social norms. I'm not trying to condone the way he behaved; just to explain it. I think that to Michael there was no fixed concept of "good" or "evil"; these were in a constant state of flux. Just as in Michael's case there was no fixed idea of identity.' She turned to Pearson. 'Remember what Courtney Woods told us what Michael said? "Why be someone you didn't like just because you were born that way?"' Pearson nodded and Cat turned back to the room. 'The fact of Michael's gender-fluidity for instance—' She broke off as she sensed, to her left, Pearson shift in his chair. She turned to him again. 'Someone who is gender-fluid regards themself as neither definitively of one gender or the other.' She searched his face for a sign he had any idea what she was talking about. Didn't find any. 'The gender to which a particular person associates themself changes in regard to the situation they are in at the time.'

'I think,' she addressed the room again, 'that this assumption that Michael was part-way through gender reassignment is wrong.'

More likely, the incomplete transition was a conscious choice. While associating mainly to female, Michael would also have lived as "man" or "woman" at different times. If you wanted to categorise Michael, it would be as a "gender-fluid transwoman"—'

'Let's save the philosophical discussion for another time,' Roberts broke in. Obviously irritated. 'We're straying from the point here, which is that Michael had worked for you before, right?' he asked Graham. 'So, why employ him again? Apart from the obvious: that he knows the area.'

'Because,' Pearson said, 'they made the same mistake as Tony Blake.'

Rain began to hammer on the windowpane. Wind rattling it violently in its frame. As if something outside, impatient, frustrated, angry, might be trying to gain entrance.

'Layla Gilchrist told us,' Pearson said to Roberts, 'that while employed as an intern at the House of Commons, she serviced a cocaine habit by working in the sex industry and was later convicted of possession of class-A drugs and lost her job. This is all common knowledge, or at least it's easily accessible on the internet' – a look to Cat – 'but she also claimed to have attended a number of parties where certain MPs and high-ranking civil servants were present.'

Graham said nothing. The tip of a pink tongue briefly touched a top lip and then retreated.

'Then,' Pearson went on, 'Layla Gilchrist turns up in Southend, running the local sex shop—'

'At the same time,' Roberts said, 'that the tabloids are running articles containing salacious allegations about "parties" and sexual exploitation of minors from the Abigail Burnett children's home.'

'Right,' said Pearson, 'so it doesn't take much to put the two together, right? It's what Tony Blake did, after all.'

Cat glanced across the room. Graham, eyes downcast, was drumming absent-mindedly on the manila folder with her orange-painted fingernails. As if practising the piano. Or tapping out her evasions, her excuses, in Braille.

'We know,' Pearson continued, 'that Michael befriended Courtney Woods. The question we've always asked ourselves is: why?' He took a breath. 'She'd been having sex with older men—'

'So Michael Morris,' Roberts interrupted again, clearly wanting to move the conversation on, 'would see it as a good way of getting close to Gilchrist. To try and find out what she might have, if anything, on these MPs and civil servants she attended parties with.'

Graham sighed, said, 'This is all just speculation on your part, isn't it? Do you have *any* evidence at all to substantiate any of these claims?' She looked slowly from Roberts to Pearson and then to Cat. Then she looked deliberately at her watch. As if she'd already wasted quite enough time on this.

'Like I said,' Roberts insisted, 'just an enormous cock-up. Two, in fact. First, jumping to the conclusion that Gilchrist might be involved with this sexual exploitation; second, employing Michael Morris to find out what she knew. Without properly evaluating whether he was psychologically fit for the task.'

'As a direct result of which,' Pearson said, 'Courtney Woods, a vulnerable young girl, was lured by Michael Morris into a lifestyle where she was severely beaten and strangled.'

'On top of which, let's not forget,' Roberts said, 'another young person has lost their life.'

For a few seconds nobody spoke. Then Graham said, 'Unless there is anything else?'

Pearson was about to ask about the burglary of Michael's flat. Had he had something in that bag that MI5 wanted? Is that why the flat had been ransacked? And that was where that particular line of thought came to an abrupt halt. Not a professional job. If it had been MI5 they would have been in and out. And no one would have been any the wiser.

Instead, he said, 'There's still the matter of the murder of Beverly Marsh. In my view, we've raised enough questions for it to be recommended for a cold case review.' Even as he said it he knew he was clutching at straws. There was little or no chance Roberts would sanction it.

Graham picked up her briefcase from the floor. Laying it on the desk. Snapping open the catches. Pearson watched as she dropped the manila folder, the scant evidence they had, inside. She shut the lid and, closing the briefcase again, she said, 'If, and when, a cold case review is authorised, feel free to apply to us for the release of any relevant information we may have. But as I understand it, for a cold case review to be initiated some compelling new piece of evidence must be forthcoming?'

'Correct,' Pearson said, 'and this usually arises out of some advance in forensic science. Which is all very well, except that, in this case, in the fifty years since her murder, the girl's clothing has mysteriously disappeared. And, along with it, any potential DNA evidence.' For only the second time, Graham's face showed some emotion. Her brow creasing slightly, she looked down. Rubbing ruminatively at the leather of the briefcase, she said, 'I'm sure they'll turn up.' Snapping the catches of the briefcase shut. Looking up again: 'And my guess is, within the next forty-eight hours?'

The door closed behind Graham; Roberts wiped his hands down his face. Exhaling. Standing up. Not saying anything. Making to retake his seat behind the desk. His trouser leg snagging on the bottom drawer. The sound of ripping material. The drawer being pulled fully open. For five, maybe ten, seconds, Roberts didn't move. Just stared at the desk. Then . . . he totally lost it.

'Fuck!'

Roberts kicked the open bottom drawer so hard the desk itself jerked and moved across the room.

'Fuck! Fuck! Fuck!'

Each time he swore he kicked the drawer. The desk moving so far, turning on its axis, that Cat, in danger of being squashed, had to jump up out of her chair.

There was a gentle knock on the door. When it opened, Laurence poked his head round and asked, 'Everything all right, guv?'

Roberts glared. Shaking his head. Said, almost apologetically, 'Fuck off, Laurence.' But the anger had subsided.

Laurence retreated quickly, the door shutting again. The DCI pulled the desk back into its usual position. Resignation already setting in. Slumping into his seat. Looking down at his desk drawer. He tried to push it back in, getting more and more irritated that the buckled metal drawer would no longer fit.

'Three fucking pairs of trousers, this thing has cost me!'

Finally pulling the drawer out and tossing it into the corner of the room. As it landed, two clear biros, one cap blue, one red, jumped out and rolled a little way off. Roberts wiped his hands down his face again. Sighing deeply.

'I don't know about you two; personally, I'm too tired to think any more. I'm going to go home. Get some kip. I suggest you do the same.'

Pearson's phone, switched to silent, began to buzz in his pocket. Taking it out, he checked the caller display . . .

Ten Days Later

45

It had rained the previous night. Most of the morning, too. A torrential downpour, bringing with it the smell of the sea. Now, on his front drive, the time nearly midday, Pearson unlocked the Mondeo with the electronic fob. Looking up, hoping for a change in the weather. An end to the cycle of overcast skies, on-off drizzle and torrential downpours which had persisted for the last couple of months. But he found only the same grey, monotonous clouds. He pulled open the driver's door, its handle beaded with water, wiped his hand on the seat of his trousers. Throwing his overcoat onto the passenger seat. Feeling, still, a residual low-level ache in his hip. A stubborn tightness in his thigh as he climbed in, started the engine and drove away. The side roads were flooded. Brown leaves clogging the gutters and drains, gathering on the pavements in drifts, their mulch, greasy and treacherous underfoot; a black, almost sooty deposit that made the streets look grimy and industrial.

A few minutes later, Pearson pulled up in the car park on the Western Esplanade. Turning off the engine. Sitting for a moment, staring out through the windscreen. Wondering what he was feeling. Not grief. Not exactly. More a kind of pervasive melancholy. A sense of general low spirits bordering on depression. It had been like this since that phone call. Received in Roberts' office. A phone call from the retirement home. A phone call telling him that his mother had unexpectedly passed away. Simply gone to her room after lunch and not come back down. She hadn't been missed until dinner time. Had been found lying on her bed, on top of the covers, fully dressed, having slipped quietly away with the minimum of fuss. He'd taken compassionate leave, plus a few days of his annual holiday entitlement to deal with the legalities, make the arrangements. The registrar. The council tax. The utilities. The building society savings account. The bank. Probate.

Pearson hadn't had a clue who to invite to the funeral. Hadn't known who her friends were. If she had any friends. Had gone through his mother's address book, not recognising any of the names. Phoned them all. The ones who didn't want to know. The ones who had moved away years ago. The ones who had died themselves long since. In the end it had been a reasonable turnout at the crematorium. Including, surprisingly – given their spiky relationship – his wife. His soon-to-be ex-wife . . .

'Hello, Frank.' Ruth. A little thinner. A bit more grey in the black pixie-cut hair. The bags under her eyes more pronounced. Pearson automatically looking past her. Scanning the car park for Terry.

'I came by cab,' Ruth said. Pearson nodded. He'd had the distinct impression that his brother-in-law might be deliberately avoiding him for a while now. Ruth leaning forward to kiss him. The smell of cigarettes on her breath. The dry, papery lips brushing his cheek. Leaning back. Looking him over.

'How are you doing?' A cold hand on his.

Pearson shrugging. 'OK, I suppose.'

Ruth lifting his left hand to study it. The indentation, the ghost of the missing wedding ring, still in evidence. Giving him a thin, tired smile.

'It's good that you're moving on, Frank.' Pearson wasn't so sure.

At the reception afterwards, held in his mother's small bungalow in Leigh-on-Sea, Pearson had busied himself with making the tea, handing out the drinks, the sandwiches he had ordered in from Waitrose. Once or twice catching a glimpse of Cat, as he made polite conversation with total strangers. Or stared into an empty glass. They had only managed an initial nod, the occasional shared look. Somehow they hadn't found the time to actually talk. At one point, Jack Morris had come over. Had made a point of coming over, of taking his hand. Patting him on the arm; Pearson trying his hardest not to flinch, not to shrink away from the old man's touch. His hand in Pearson's just a little too long. Morris saying, 'I'm sorry for your loss, son.' Looking old. Older. Frail, even. Holding him with a steady gaze. Those fucking eyes again. Saying, 'It's a terrible thing, Frank, to lose flesh and blood. When it comes down to it, family's the most important thing, the only thing that really matters.'

Pearson slammed the heel of his hand into the steering wheel.

'Shit!' The word flaring momentarily. Then fading away in the gloomy interior of the car. He got out of the Mondeo, shrugged on his overcoat. There'd been a definite drop in temperature that, hopefully, might augur a period of crisp, bright autumn sunshine. He clicked the electronic fob to lock the car doors, jammed his hands into his pockets. Then made his way down the steps onto the seafront. And caught sight of the Crowstone.

Tony Blake had now acknowledged his guilt in a formal, written statement and been charged with the murder by manual strangulation of Michael Morris and his subsequent effort to dispose of the body. The estate car he'd been driving and the nylon sports coat and gloves he'd used had been recovered and were currently undergoing forensic examination.

Cat had felt, at the time, that Blake's confession was a little too convenient. 'Why confess to a murder you didn't commit?' Pearson had asked.

And she'd had no real answer. As to the question of why he'd confessed at all, well, that was something they'd probably never find out. The same could be said of the exact relationship between, and involvement of, Courtney Woods and Layla Gilchrist.

Pearson had wondered if Cat had also been a little uneasy that the case seemed to have been wrapped up too easily. But, in his experience, most were. The majority of investigations were reasonably straightforward. Even the murders. A domestic dispute. An argument between two junkies in a flat over drugs, or the money to buy drugs. A drunken fight in the street or a club that got out of hand. On many occasions the culprit would be at the scene, or easily found. Bloodstained. In shock. The course of events witnessed, or easily reconstructed through the use of CCTV footage. Most of their time was actually spent preparing the case to go to the CPS and then court. There were the odd unsolved deaths, of course. A body found that could not be identified. No hits on the DNA database. No one coming forward after a public appeal. No traceable forensic evidence. No obvious cause of death. But, in reality, these were pretty few and far between. Blake was already on remand and awaiting trial for the attempted armed robbery of the Double Carpet betting shop. Given that they had the eyewitness account of the shop manager, Daryl Crawford – a decorated war hero – and the shotgun in the possession of Blake had been matched to a cartridge discharged into the ceiling, the Crown

Prosecution Service were quite confident of guilty verdicts on both counts.

According to Cat, the 'misplaced' clothing of Beverly Marsh had miraculously come to light, just as Graham had predicted. But despite the advances in forensic science in the intervening years, it had not been possible to secure any specimens of DNA. Even at the time, Pearson had suspected that this had already been known. That the clothing had already been tested and found to contain no useful evidence. Otherwise, why would she have been so ready to hand them over? It was a tacit admission of their involvement in the clothing's apparent 'disappearance', but it didn't matter. Nothing could be matched with the samples of DNA collected from Richard Lennon at his post-mortem so they could not establish a link between Richard Lennon and the murderer. They couldn't even prove conclusively that the murderer was Geoffrey Knowles, given that their own records of the case were incomplete and the documentary evidence Dr Angela Fitzgerald had compiled was now in the hands of MI5.

The Beverly Marsh murder had, as a consequence, not been passed on to the Cold Case team for review. Even if it had been, a fifty-year-old investigation with no fresh DNA evidence and no obvious lines of enquiry would at best have been marked low priority. So, any prospects of getting to the truth now seem pretty remote.

46

D r Angela Fitzgerald stared down at the sheets of A4 in her hand. The paper covered in her small, meticulous handwriting. The impressions and commentary added during numerous reassessments since the actual sessions had been taped. The only notes she had chosen not to hand over to the two detectives. The only ones from the folder that weren't photocopied, rendered into monochrome, the stark black and white lending them a weight. A solidity. A seriousness. By contrast, these, with their many different colours of ink – black, blue, green, red – now seemed of less consequence. The conclusions drawn less plausible. The scientific method less rigorous.

The transcription of the final session with Richard Lennon. A session which had taken them back even further into his past. As a result, the recall had been even sketchier. The thought processes even more chaotic. The language even more confused. The transcript from the session where Richard Lennon had finally remembered that he had once been Geoffrey Knowles. The session before he'd thrown himself under a train on the tracks outside Chalkwell station . . .

. . . The spasm. The hands sliding past each other. The tightly balled fists. And in the momentary pause before he started the ritual again, the shaking as bad as she'd ever seen, the old man lifting his head, looking at her . . .

Fitzgerald selected the corresponding audio tape from the top drawer of her desk and fitted it into the player. As the old man's voice could be heard from the speakers, halting, unsteady, even she had to admit that a degree of creativity might need to be applied. A fair measure of imagination employed. She had never been inside a prison. Had no real idea what one might look like in the nineteen sixties. Could only ever bring it to life as if it were a scene from a TV drama. Stranger still, whenever she played this specific tape, pictured this particular meeting, she never imagined it through the eyes of Geoffrey Knowles. But rather through the eyes of the man he'd met . . .

The room. Cold. Damp. Whitewashed brick walls. A small semi-circular window set high up behind metal bars. The slate grey of an afternoon sky visible outside. A bare pendant light bulb offering only meagre illumination. The wooden chair heavy as he slides it out. Removing his raincoat. Something expensive. British-made. A Burberry. Folding it carefully and placing it on the scuffed, green linoleum floor. Removing his hat. A trilby. Or something a little less sober, perhaps. A fedora, grey. Placing it carefully on the scratched, wooden table. Seating himself. Shuffling the chair forwards an inch or two.

Looking up now. Taking in the person opposite for the first

time. Light blue shirt. Thin black tie. A jacket of some coarse, grey material. Wool, perhaps. A pretty face. High cheekbones. A straight nose. Full lips. The single green eye quick. Nervous. The skin clear despite his time inside. The prison diet. In those clothes, this environment, seeming smaller than he remembered. Slighter ... diminished somehow. An altogether less threatening figure than the one he'd interviewed several times in the consulting room in Wimpole Street. Not much more, really, than a boy. All this time there had been no sound. Save for the laboured breathing of the prison guard who'd shown him in, and now stood behind him in a corner of the room. His own movements as he settled himself into place. Finally, he addressed the boy.

'You know, Geoffrey, in a way, you're quite fortunate.'

Geoffrey, his right eye puffy. Starting to shut. The cheekbone underneath swollen and grazed. Obviously didn't feel lucky, but said nothing.

'Last year, the manual strangulation of a sixteen-year-old girl would have meant a death sentence. However, a law was passed in October, the Murder Act, which resulted in the abolition of capital punishment. Which means, Geoffrey, that you can no longer be hanged.'

Some of the tension left the boy. There was a slight slumping of the shoulders. A relaxation of the facial muscles. Scanning the table top. As if he'd momentarily misplaced something. Then, frowning. Puzzled. Saying, 'But I didn't kill her, Mr Somerville.'

'Christopher. I told you before, Geoffrey, you can call me Christopher.' Geoffrey, still frowning. Staring across the table at him. 'Of course, for you, Geoffrey, it does still mean a sentence of life imprisonment. Now, it's true that in some cases a prisoner might be able to apply for parole after ten or fifteen years. But unfortunately, in your case it's likely that the Crown will insist on a life sentence without parole. You will, Geoffrey, be in prison for the rest of your life.'

Christopher Somerville carelessly stroking the area under his right eye with two fingertips. The same area where the boy's face was swollen. In imitation of a natural action. Something unthinking. The effete mannerism of a cultured man. The boy flicking a nervous glance towards the guard. The Adam's apple bobbing up and down as he swallowed.

Somerville asking, 'How old are you now, Geoffrey?'

The green eye going down to the table. Shoulders coming up towards his ears. Geoffrey mumbling.

'Seventeen?' As if this might not be the right answer. As if giving the wrong answer might result in some ... unpleasant eventuality.

Somerville nodding, as if in confirmation, saying, 'Seventeen.' Slipping a cigarette case from an inside breast pocket. Silver. Antique. Flipping it open. Selecting a cigarette. Snapping the case closed again. Tapping the cigarette on the lid. The boy's hungry eye following each movement. An ashtray appearing on the table in front of them. And as Somerville put the cigarette to his lips, the flame of a lighter. Turning to the guard. Somerville nodding his thanks. Then saying, 'I think you can leave us alone now, George.' George. Always useful to learn people's names. Even the seemingly unimportant ones. Especially the seemingly unimportant ones. George, a big man. Now running to fat. The upright bearing of an ex-serviceman. Navy, judging by the fading blue tattoos on his forearms. Looking uncertainly between Somerville and the boy.

Somerville saying, 'I don't think Mr Knowles is going to be any trouble. We're old friends. Aren't we, Geoffrey?'

The guard asking, 'Is that right, Knowles?' Looking at the boy again. 'Can I trust you to behave?'

Geoffrey Knowles nodding. 'Yes, Mr Underwood.'

The guard giving a last look at the boy. Turning back to Somerville.

'OK, sir. I'll just be outside if you need me.' Uncertain now as to what to do. Hesitating. Looking for one absurd moment as if he might salute. Then turning on his heel and leaving the room. The door closing.

Somerville turning back to the boy. Taking out the cigarette case again. Flipping it open. Offering it across the table. The boy uncertain.

'It's all right, Geoffrey. Take one for later as well.'

Geoffrey Knowles taking two cigarettes, one disappearing immediately somewhere under his grey jacket. Putting the other between his lips. Somerville taking out the gold lighter from his inside breast pocket. Leaning across the table. Conspiratorial. Friendly. Lighting the cigarette. Knowles taking a long drag. Coughing. Laughing, embarrassed.

'I'm used to roll-ups. Old Holborn. I don't suppose you've heard of it.'

Somerville snapping the case shut. A dip of the head. A half-smile. Deliberately not answering the boy's question, instead saying, 'Actually, I get these from a little shop in Holborn,' and by way of explanation, 'London. Do you know London at all, Geoffrey?'

The boy shaking his head. 'Only up Carnaby Street. Other than that, I've never really been out of Southend.'

Somerville taking the cigarette from his mouth. Regarding it for a moment. Looking at Knowles. Holding the cigarette up.

'These are roll-ups. Of a sort. Handmade. The tobacco's exclusively imported from France. They use a special little machine to roll the cigarettes. Did you notice how tight the paper is? That it's all of a uniform consistency?'

Geoffrey Knowles taking another drag. Coughing again. Taking the cigarette out of his mouth to examine it. Somerville realising that Knowles didn't like it. Wasn't enjoying it. But was impressed that it was 'exclusive', 'special'. Mostly, that it was expensive.

Somerville saying then, 'Now, Geoffrey, you are going to be presented with a unique opportunity' – flicking the ash from his cigarette into the ashtray – 'an opportunity, not only to further the cause of medical science, but to save the British government an untold amount of money. Both now, and into the future.' Pausing. 'Most importantly to you, at the same time, you can avoid spending the rest of your life in prison. Now how does that sound, Geoffrey?'

Knowles drawing on the cigarette. Eyes narrowing. But saying nothing.

'Wouldn't you rather spend two or three months in hospital? Undergo this new treatment? Rather than spend your whole life in this place?'

Geoffrey Knowles looking past him. To the door through which the prison guard had left. Leaning forward. Lowering his voice, 'But I didn't kill her, Mr Somerville!' Shaking his head as if to emphasise the point. 'Beverly.' As if there might be some confusion as to which murdered girl they were talking about. 'I didn't kill her!'

'The point is, Geoffrey, who's going to believe it?'

'You *know* me, Mr Somerville, from ...' Not wanting to say more. Not knowing how much to say. What to say. '... from before ...'

'Now, now, Geoffrey.'

'But I didn't do it, Mr Somerville!' Insistent. 'You *know* me. You ... know—'

Somerville cutting him off. 'Nobody's going to be looking for anyone else, Geoffrey.' Saying, coldly, 'Nobody's ... interested ... in looking for anybody else. And with your reputation, Geoffrey? You won't stand a chance. Once you're in that court ... you'll be found guilty. Come on, you know that.'

The boy thinking. Sagging a little. Shaking his head nervously. 'I don't like hospitals, Mr Somerville. Never have done—'

'A young girl's been murdered, Geoffrey. The public will want someone to pay. Someone nasty, Geoffrey. Someone wicked. Someone like you. Someone who befriends young girls ...' Somerville drawing on his cigarette. Holding in the smoke for a while. Rolling it against his tongue, his palate. As if the flavour of the fine tobacco blend, the undertone of liquorice, might be enough to mask the bad taste in his mouth from the words he was about to speak.

'Someone who befriends young girls, Geoffrey, and then persuades them to fuck older men for money. A pimp. Someone who lives off these earnings. That's you, Geoffrey. A ... nasty ... little ... ponce.'

The boy staring back. Shocked into silence.

Somerville saying, 'Even if you didn't actually kill Beverly Marsh yourself' – taking a last drag on the cigarette, grinding it out in the ashtray – 'you still took advantage of a sweet, vulnerable young girl. You turned her into a whore. You put her in a position where she could be killed. So, however you might choose to look at it, Geoffrey, you are directly responsible for her death. You still did something ... something truly evil.'

47

Cat Russell slammed her car door. Engaged the central locking system with the electronic fob. Thorpe Bay, by the Tram Stop Shelter. Although, according to the internet, no trams or trolleybuses had run along the Eastern Esplanade since before the Second World War. And all that actually remained of the original shelter was a concrete platform which now formed the roof of a toilet block. But names stuck. A name would become connected with a place and in spite of everyone's best efforts to call it something different, would somehow for ever be associated with it. The White Horse would always be the White Horse, despite the fact that the pub had now been renamed as Old Walnut Tree – not even *THE* Old Walnut Tree. Even the etymology of the Crowstone had been lost. One theory was that the name derived from an existing tenement in the fifteen hundreds, called Crowes; another was that the ubiquitous and ever-present birds had always used the stone pillar as a perch, but nobody was really sure.

Cat took the slope down onto the beach, turned right and started towards the pier. It was just far enough from the Ness Road

park, at one and a third miles, that she could walk here and not
ɪmatically flash back to Sean Carragher's incinerated body in
the burnt-out Audi A8.

Besides, this stretch of the foreshore was the best for sea glass.
Presumably because the incoming tide was strongest here, the
water more churned up. Although there was surprisingly little
to be found about the estuary on the web and she'd found no
scientific evidence to back up this theory. Most of the sea glass
she'd found up to now was white. Occasionally she'd come across
some green and, less frequently, brown. She'd heard that people
had found the odd piece of cobalt blue. But she'd never heard
of anyone finding red. At least along this beach, this part of the
coast. Looking for sea glass had started as just an excuse to walk
on the beach. Just something to do to help clear her mind. Now,
she realised, like so many other things, it was starting to become
a bit of an obsession.

John Hall saying, 'Same old Cat.' A half-smile, a shake of the
head. 'Still the preoccupation with facts.'

Cat picked something up off the beach, feeling a stab of guilt.
Looking for sea glass was one of the few interests she hadn't
derived from her time with Hall. In almost every other way he
had shaped the person she was now. It wasn't just her interests:
her choice of career, her world view, her whole moral code was in
no small part due to him. She held the object in her hand, rubbing
the sand from its surface with a thumb, examining it. And how had
she repaid him? By treating his sudden reappearance in her life as
an unwanted irritation, an inconvenience. A stone. She pitched
it back onto the beach. She owed him better than that. Even if
she had sought to consign him, that part of her life, to history. An
apology, at the very least. She had considered whether she should
text him. Was still considering whether to text him. But she wasn't

quite sure what to say. And whether letting him back into her life now would be such a good idea ...

Hearing a gargling sound, Cat looked up to see a flock of about a hundred Brent geese flying upriver in unruly V formations. The autumn migration. Last year, enjoying an early evening drink with her sister outside the Peterboat at Leigh, there had been vast flocks of them gathered on the mud flats. Black heads dipping in the shallow water for eel grass. The air thick with the guttural 'rhut' of their calls. Cat recalled their most recent meeting.

Vicky saying, 'My big sister, in the police!' A smile on her face, fleeting, self-conscious. 'Mind you, you were always bloody bossy! But, Cat, you ... you made something of yourself ...'

And across the table, Vicky looking down into her glass, a tear running down her face.

Cat felt now as if she owed her sister something. As if any failure mattered as much to Vicky as to Cat herself. As if she owed it, also, to her nieces to try. Owed it to all the others. The dead girls. The girls who *would* die. She hadn't, she realised, thought much about her stalled career in the past few days, caught up as she was in the excitement of the investigation. The opportunity to apply the knowledge she had gained during her Psychology degree. And even, she was loath to admit, Roberts' approval had gone some way to reinvigorate her. 'It's thanks to him that you've still got a job,' Pearson had said when they were in the rest area. 'After all that Carragher business, Curtis was all for pushing you out.'

Pearson had said no more. Then again, he hadn't really needed to. The implication was there. Roberts had had to fight to keep her in the Job. Had had to stand his ground against a senior officer. Maybe more than one senior officer. Perhaps, a hint had even come down from the Chief Constable that if there was a method of easing her out, with the minimum of fuss, without bringing too much attention on a force already in the public eye, then it should be exercised. How much, then, had Roberts had to put on the line to go against their wishes? 'Irascible', as Pearson put it. Annoying, certainly. Even downright bloody rude sometimes. Quite a lot of the time. But, despite the constant fidgeting: the fiddling with pens and elastic bands, the face-wiping, the retucking of shirts into trousers, the armpit scratching, Roberts was undoubtedly a bloody good copper. And more importantly he seemed to actually, genuinely, care.

Cat saw Pearson coming down one of the sets of concrete steps onto the beach. Still limping, she noted. Not overly pronounced, but if you knew him, spent a lot of time every day with the man, it was definitely noticeable. The leg held slightly stiffly. The face set. She hadn't walked on the beach, she realised, hadn't spent time in search of sea glass since the last time they were on the beach together, when she'd confided in Pearson that she was having doubts about her future in the Job, about her role in the death of Sean Carragher.

'You're thinking maybe if you'd said something earlier, Sean might be alive?' Pearson had asked, and later, 'Whatever Carragher was involved in, it was his choice. His responsibility. Not yours. Or anybody else's. If you want my advice, don't go making any rash decisions.'

So she had taken his advice. Well, in as much as she hadn't done anything anyway. Now she—

'Morning,' Pearson said.

'Morning,' Cat said. 'How's the leg?'

'Yeah, OK.'

'Sorry, I didn't get to talk to you at the funeral yesterday, it just never seemed the right time.'

'No problem,' Pearson said. 'It was nice of you to come.'

346

Looking away. Subject closed. Neither spoke for a while. Then, he asked, 'So what's happening?'

'Paperwork, mostly,' Cat said. 'Oh, one mystery's been solved ...'

'Yeah?' Pearson turned back. 'What's that?'

'The break-in at Michael's flat? Turns out it was the old man downstairs.'

'Ted ...' Pearson groped for a last name.

'Edward Albert Burrows. Apparently, Burrows had overheard them on the stairs, coming in late. Laughing and joking about what they'd been up to. That's where he got the idea that they were both "on the game". Burrows saw Michael with a load of cash ... Anyway, Burrows is skint, Michael and Courtney are out, at least as far as he's concerned. Obviously, by this time, Michael's dead, Courtney's ill in her flat. So, he decides he's going to turn the flat over. Finding the bag was just a lucky guess. He says he saw the curtain flapping, so he decided to have a look on the off chance. Claims there was just a couple of hundred quid in there.'

'Right.' Pearson nodded. Looking away again up the beach. They lapsed, once more, into silence ...

'Mediterranean,' Cat said.

Pearson turned, confused.

'The bird,' Cat said, nodding past him.

Pearson followed her gaze. 'I thought it was a seagull.'

When he turned back Cat was shaking her head. 'No such thing as *sea*gulls. Gulls. Those,' pointing in the direction of the birds, 'are Mediterranean gulls. We get loads of different types just on this beach.'

'They all look the same to me. How do you tell them apart?' Pearson asked. Then, by the look on his face, immediately regretted it.

347

'The colour of their legs,' Cat said, 'the rings around their eyes, the colour of their heads. Mediterranean gulls have a black head. Although, the black-headed gull's head is more of a chocolate brown.'

Pearson studied the birds on the beach. Looking from one to another. 'None of those have got black heads.'

Cat sighed. 'They're in winter plumage.' Her tone of voice implied that that was something he really should have known. As if it was something that everybody knew. Though, to be fair, it was something she had only found out herself recently online. 'Their heads are only black or brown in the late spring and summer. We also get herring gulls, which are much bigger. The lesser black-backed gull, which has a dark grey back. And the common gull which, strangely, isn't that common at all, at least not round here.'

'Well,' Pearson said sarcastically, 'I'm so glad you've cleared that one up for me.'

Then he slipped his hands into his pockets. Looked down at the beach. No doubt, Cat thought, wondering if now might be the right time to ask the question. Digging the toe of his shoe in the sand. The question that had so obviously been on his mind for the last couple of months. Finally, he said, 'So have you made your mind up what you're going to do?'

'About the Job?' Cat asked.

Pearson turned. Nodded. 'Yeah, that.'

It was out. Almost before Cat realised. Before she was aware of making a conscious decision. Circumventing the Broca area in the frontal lobe of the left hemisphere of her brain. Bypassing the language centre. Appearing fully fledged from her mouth. 'Yeah, I'm going to stay.'

48

The tape player clicked off. Dr Angela Fitzgerald ejected the cassette from the machine and put it into a plastic case. Put that into the box along with the others. Slipped the sheets of paper into the manila folder. Closed the cover. But she was in no great rush to hand any of it over.

'Is that all of it?'

Or to look up and make eye contact with the person on the other side of the desk. Still not quite wanting to believe it was true.

'You were indiscreet, Angela,' Hugo Somerville said. 'Asking the wrong questions, of the wrong people. Posting your ideas on the internet, visiting chatrooms—'

'So, it's all been a lie, Hugo?' Fitzgerald asked angrily. 'From the very start?'

'Not from the start, Angela,' Somerville said, adopting a placatory tone. 'Not until that telephone call. But when you started talking about the remodelling of aberrant personalities in order to effect cost savings in the penal system? Well, I knew then that you were possibly getting a little too close to the truth.'

Fitzgerald looked away, down at the desk, feeling betrayed. Feeling angry. Feeling hot tears welling in her eyes.

'I couldn't see Grandfather's reputation destroyed, Angela,' Somerville said. 'You have to understand, the grandfather I knew was a kind and compassionate man—'

'Really, Hugo?' Fitzgerald asked, hurt. 'Really?' Furious. Swiping the tears from her cheek with the back of a hand. 'Does a "kind and compassionate man" coerce a teenage boy into taking part in a dangerous, immoral and, at best, speculative treatment? A vulnerable teenage boy, Hugo. Who just happened to fit the profile your grandfather had previously identified as a suitable subject for his experiment. Does a "kind and compassionate man" oversee an unsuccessful attempt to implant a new personality into an unwitting subject? Does a "kind and compassionate man" collude in the concealment of the psychologically damaged subject of such an experiment in the mental health system—'

'It wasn't something he was proud of, Angela. On the contrary, it was something that caused him a deep and lasting shame. Something that haunted him for the rest of his life.'

'All the weeks spent talking to Richard Lennon,' Fitzgerald said, 'all the internet research. All the effort hunting down the official documents. All the ... ' She trailed off weakly. The anger suddenly replaced with a feeling of utter defeat. 'And all the time, you knew?'

'Grandfather had confided in me,' Somerville said softly, 'in his later years. He wasn't a well man. Towards the end, we spent a lot of time together, just talking. He was a brilliant man, Angela. I couldn't see all the valuable research, all the good work he'd done, overshadowed by what amounts to no more than murky insinuation.'

A guttering ember of outrage unexpectedly flared in Fitzgerald's chest. 'Did you know about the murder of Beverly Marsh?'

'I had my suspicions.' Somerville sighed. 'But I had no real proof of how deeply Grandfather might have been involved.'

'Until now.'

'I haven't heard any real evidence—'

They both turned to the other woman as she spoke. The woman introduced simply as 'Graham'. The woman who had sat there through the playing of the tapes. Throughout Fitzgerald's explanation, her theories. Up until now saying nothing. Impassive. Unmoving. Unmoved.

'—that Sir Christopher Somerville killed the girl. All I've heard is the confused testimony of a mentally unstable old man. And even that was elicited in the most dubious of circumstances. Now, I trust we are finished?'

Fitzgerald and Somerville said nothing.

'Good.' Graham nodded. 'So, if that really is *all* of it . . .' She held out her hand towards the manila folder, the box containing the tapes on the desk.

Pearson stood by the pier, looking across the estuary, low tide, the featureless silt of the deserted mudflats. Further out, the brown, brackish water of the Thames. In the distance, a container ship heading out to sea. Above the chimney of the disused power station on the far shore, the sky was beginning to darken. Shifting position to ease the ache in his leg his fingers brushed something in his coat pocket. He took out the piece of sea glass, holding it up between his thumb and index finger. Red. The shape of a teardrop. It put him in mind of another ruby teardrop. Layla Gilchrist had disappeared, seemingly, without a trace. He had visited her house, only to find it locked up and empty. Peering through the windows front and rear he'd seen only empty rooms. Little or no sign that anyone was living there. The sex shop, too, had a Closed sign at the window. He'd tried to get a look in. But could not see beyond the discreet curtaining of the shop front.

He weighed the sea glass in his palm. He'd looked it up on the internet during his time off. For something to do. Because he was bored. Nothing more. Had bought some too. For no particular reason. And now he had it, he wasn't sure what to do with it. He could give it to Cat, he supposed; he was back at work tomorrow. But that wasn't really the point, was it? Some things you had to discover by yourself. It was why he hadn't pressed her since Sean Carragher's death. Had let her come to a decision on her future by herself. Almost. Had finally had to ask. And been secretly delighted, and not a little relieved when she'd said, 'Yeah, I'm going to stay.'

Hearing the reverberation of a jet engine, or the distant rumble of thunder, Pearson looked up. Surprised to see that the light level had dropped without him noticing. A bank of heavy black rain-clouds had rolled in. A fine drizzle started to fall. Time to go. He dropped the sea glass into his pocket and pushed himself off from the railing he'd been leaning against. Walking back towards the car. As for Pearson himself? He was a copper. Whatever happened, he would carry on being a copper. As Ruth had once said, it's what he did. What he was.

After the funeral, after everyone had left, Pearson had dug out the photos he'd found while clearing out his mother's bungalow. Had stacked up the leather albums. Had sifted through the dusty cardboard shoeboxes. Unbound the elastic bands from the over-stuffed envelopes. Tipping them out across the living room floor. Sorting them chronologically, his task made easier by the place, date and time noted beneath, or on the back of, each photograph in his mother's neat block capitals. Working forward from the earliest, the small format glossy black-and-white images of the fifties and sixties. His mother as a young woman, posing in front of a sports car, on a beach, looking surprisingly glamorous. Smiling for the person behind the camera. The colour snaps, their emulsion now bleached in places, faces, figures and sometimes entire buildings fading away to nothingness. As if their memory, too, had become faulty somehow with the passage of time. There were the usual domestic snaps. Pearson as a young boy. On various family holidays. In school plays. At children's parties. Houses they had lived in. Cars they had owned.

When he had finished he'd made himself a cup of tea. Drank it sitting on his mother's sofa, staring at the images of her past laid out across the carpet. Realising for the first time that he'd never considered his parents', his mother's, life before him. Never thought of her as young and attractive, fashionable, full of hope. The black-and-white images sharp and clear. Having no signs of the fading of the colour pictures featuring Pearson as a young boy. As if her life before him was somehow more distinct. More defined. More real. Turning to the last page of the most recent album he'd found a photo of himself. A fresh-faced Francis Pearson. In his new police uniform. On the eve of starting his training as an Essex police cadet in Ashford. It was the last photo his mother had been bothered enough to put in an album.

To his right, just like on that first day, the restaurants under the arches were shut tight, the chairs and tables put away, their metal shutters down.

It was as if the day his life in the police had started, her life had ended. In a way, he supposed, it had. His mother coming from that generation before women had careers, had even considered the possibility of having a career. His mother's generation, and

353

class, he reminded himself, had been content to be housewives and mothers. What happened to them, though, when there was no longer a husband to cook and clean for, when their children had grown up and left home? They did what his mother had, he assumed: they worked as cleaners, behind the tills in corner shops or supermarkets, took any number of lowly paid menial jobs.

A jogger passed. Hooded waterproof jacket. Shorts, head down against the rain and wind. He loved the town out of season. Closed down. The holidaymakers, the day trippers gone. To be replaced with the joggers. The strolling elderly couples. And, of course, the dog walkers.

Pearson had found no pictures of his father. Of course, it might be that his father had taken the majority of the photos, so you might expect him not to appear in many. But none at all? Not a single one? Not even a blurred image of him on the periphery of another scene? Some partial likeness where he might have been caught accidentally? It just didn't make sense. The thing was, he'd never known his father. Or, at least, didn't remember him. Hadn't really wanted to know about him. He'd asked about him when he was little. Why he wasn't around. Where he was. What he might be doing. What he was like. Had been fobbed off. Diverted. Finally, angrily told to stop bloody well asking so many questions. So he had dropped the subject. Forgotten about him. Until now. Now it was too late to find out anything. Too late to ask his mother any questions . . .

But, if he was honest with himself, he didn't really want to know who his father was, did he? Just – that he wasn't Jack Morris.

At the bottom of the steps leading to the car park, Pearson stopped. Turning to look out at the beach. The Crowstone. As if on cue, there was a deafening crack of thunder. And the heavens opened . . .

Epilogue

THURSDAY 31 MARCH, 1966

The tide was coming in. His feet sinking as the silt became softer, less definite. Rivulets of advancing water reflecting the sickly dawn over the estuary. The air damp and chill, the haze yet to be burnt off by the warmth of the sun. So his stinging and streaming eyes could not make out the other side of the river, although he knew its contours and dimensions by heart. The county of Essex at his back. Somewhere in front of him, beyond the mist, lay Kent. In the occasional lull between gusts of a buffeting wind which had numbed and frozen his ears, came the distant clanging of halyards on masts. The screech of seagulls ...

It was that laugh that had first attracted his attention. The Kursaal ballroom. A break between numbers by the band. The girl audible, even above the sudden clamour of voices in the smoky bar. He'd watched her then. Slowly sipping his drink. A brandy. The band starting up again. A half-empty glass in front of her. An elbow resting on the counter. A cigarette between fingers in a limp-wristed hand. Tilting her head back and shooting a plume of smoke towards the ceiling. The mimicking of some Hollywood actress for the benefit of the fleshy, red-faced man at her side. Picking up the glass and waggling it at her companion. The fat man shaking his head, pulling at her arm, trying to get her to leave. The girl breaking free, turning away. The man standing for a moment, at a loss as to what to do next. Then melting away into the crowd. The girl catching his eye across the horseshoe-shaped bar. Winking. Picking up her glass. Staring across at him over its rim. He'd watched her place the empty glass carefully back on the counter. Look up meaningfully. Nod in the direction of the exit. Finishing his brandy in a single gulp he'd followed her outside.

Out in the night. Hugging the shadows. The air cool. The garish illumination of the pier and amusement arcades. The hum of passing conversation. The screams of the passengers on the two nearby rollercoasters. The smell of beer. Hot vinegar on chips. Frying onions. But the girl herself was nowhere to be found. He'd lit a cigarette then. Feeling a mixture of emotions. Disappointment. Frustration. But mostly ... relief. He'd barely smoked half of it before the girl had reappeared at his side. Close up, by the light of the street lamps, she looked different somehow. The long, black hair dull. Out of a bottle. Too much make-up. The skin coarse. The delicate features vulgar. Although, underneath it, she still looked ... too young. Too young to be—

'Ten quid.'

The voice. Behind him. Close to his ear, had startled him. Spinning round he came face to face with someone he recognised.

'Ten quid,' he said again. Geoffrey Knowles. He might have known it would have something to do with Geoffrey Knowles. Everybody knew Geoffrey Knowles. Knew what he did. What he was. Uncertainly, he turned back to the girl. She was half smiling.

356

As if the price were a point of pride. As if it showed how much Geoffrey valued her. Knowles circled behind the girl. Put an arm round the front of her, running a hand over her grey satin top. Whispering into her ear. The girl nodding. Saying something. Resting a hand on his. Moving it to cup one of her small breasts, giving it a hard squeeze. Then leaning into him. Reaching a hand behind her to stroke the back of his head. 'Her name's Beverly,' said Knowles, 'and she's ten quid.'

He had taken out his wallet as Knowles snaked his other arm round the girl, reaching down and putting his hand on her stomach. Fumbled out the note as Knowles pulled the girl to him. Whispering in her ear again, shooting a look in his direction. The girl giving a little laugh. Nodding. Giving him the once-over. A re-evaluation. A downgrading. Knowles relaxing his grip then, and holding out his hand . . .

They'd walked along the seafront, past the boating lake. The replica of the *Golden Hind*. The prone figure of the disembowelled man. Bloody guts hanging out behind the glass. 'Torture through the ages.' They walked away from the pier. The entrance to Peter Pan's Playground. The open air lido. Away from the bustle. The noise. The people. And west, towards the quiet, the seclusion, the darkness. The girl always trailing a few yards behind. Him occasionally glancing back over his shoulder. Half hoping she hadn't followed him. Once they passed the lido he'd scrambled down onto the beach. Across the pebbles and shingle. Onto the hard sand left behind by the tide. Glancing behind again. The girl still following. Shoes in her hand now. Eventually the beach had run out, and they couldn't walk any further. He'd turned then. To look out into the darkness. Sweating into his suit, despite the chill. Listening to the distant shushing of the water. The pounding blood in his ears. His own ragged breath. Passing him, dropping her shoes in the sand, the girl spoke for the first time.

'Can we stop walking now? My feet are fucking killing me.'

'What is that thing?' he'd asked.

'It's called the Crowstone,' the girl said.

'What's it for?'

'What's it *for*?' she echoed. 'I don't bloody know! But you know what it reminds me of?' A lascivious look. A low, guttural chuckle. Then, running a suggestive hand up and down the granite surface of the stone column, she asked, 'What's the matter? Ain't I worth ten quid?'

Fumbling with his belt then. The girl lying down on the beach. Lifting her skirt to reveal that she wasn't wearing any underwear. Dropping his trousers. Kneeling down. Her saying softly into his ear, 'You're not going to disappoint me, are you?' Stroking his hair. The smell of damp sand. Seaweed. The gin and cigarettes on her breath. The cold flesh of her splayed legs under the black miniskirt. The grit of the beach beneath his knees. His trousers bunched around his ankles . . .

After the third attempt, lying on top. Pressing desperately against her to no effect. He leant back. Face burning. Cock dangling limply beneath his shirt. It wasn't that he couldn't. It wasn't. It was that he didn't want to. Not here. Not with her. She laughed. That laugh. The screech of a seagull across the silent mudflats.

'Jesus, all that fucking walking, and for what? Sand up the crack of my arse and sore bloody feet!' She laughed again.

Wouldn't stop laughing. He'd just wanted it to stop. That's all. Just wanted to shut her up. So, he'd put a hand over her mouth. Leant close. Hissed, 'Be quiet.' She snorted a laugh. Snot exploding out of her nose. And onto the back of his hand. He glanced nervously up and down the beach. 'Be quiet. Someone'll hear us!'

Looking back down at her, he'd seen something in her eyes. Amusement? Excitement? A challenge? Under his hand her mouth opened. A sound against his palm. A whimper, maybe. Or a groan. As if she might be enjoying this. Being held down. His weight pressing on top of her. Beneath his hand. The parted lips. The sharp teeth. The slithering wetness of her tongue. He yanked his hand away.

She'd thrown her head back and laughed.

'What's the matter? You scared?'

Slipping his hand loosely around her neck then. Tightening his grip. Ever so slightly, 'Shut . . . up . . . I . . . said!'

'Go on, then,' she whispered. Mocking him. But there was something else in her voice. Compliance? A request? Or a command? He'd felt himself starting to become aroused. Her thighs clamping around his hips. Starting to move against him. 'Go on,' she urged.

His erection faded and she fell back again. 'Oh, for fuck's sake,' she laughed. 'Come on! We haven't got all night!'

He'd felt the warmth of her neck beneath his hands, the sinews, the cartilage of her windpipe under his thumbs. Had her head moved? Was that a nod? Was that a breath? Or had he heard her say 'Yes'? Her eyes focusing on his. Too bright for the gloom. As if they were drawing light in from somewhere else. The expression unreadable. Then . . . they began to cloud and fade, her breath faltering. Stertorous. He saw himself. Reflected in the receding pupils as he applied more pressure, her thrusts beneath him becoming more powerful. Less controlled. Panic creeping in. Before, finally, she shuddered, and then went still . . .

He'd sat for hours. Just staring at the dead girl. The long, black hair fanned out, framing her delicate features. At some point in the night he'd come to his senses. Pulled up his underpants and trousers. Zipped up his fly. Refastened his belt. Making some attempt to bury her in the sand. Managing to cover most of the body. Until … it had come to the face. After a few handfuls he'd stopped. Unable to go any further. He'd sat down again then. Sat for a long time. Smoking cigarette after cigarette …

The figure lay half-submerged in the mud. The eyes and mouth open. Grey silt gathering and then cracking on the skin so that now it seemed more like a statue than a human being. Sandflies already hovering over the face. A tiny translucent crab scuttling from the mouth, grains of sand dislodged by its claws.

Finally, he stood. Slipping the packet of Marlboro and the gold lighter back into his jacket pocket. Then, taking a deep breath, Jack Morris stepped closer. Putting the sole of his boot on the face …

Acknowledgements

My sincere thanks to the following people who helped with the edit of this book: Sarah Armstrong, Phil Tucker, Juliet Mahony, Jade Chandler and Lucy Dauman.

Special thanks to Jade who gave me a kick in the pants when it was sorely needed.

I'd also like to thank the team at Sphere: Catherine Burke, Kirsteen Astor, Clara Diaz, Emma Williams, Thalia Proctor and Liz Hatherell. Many apologies if I've missed anyone out – I have had so much help from so many people that it is sometimes hard to keep track! Your assistance is nonetheless greatly appreciated.

Phil once again offered advice on police procedure, terminology and attitudes. Any inaccuracies, or liberties taken, are completely my own. Cheers, mate!

Many thanks also to Stephen Tucker who kindly helped with the passages involving the British Transport Police.

Thanks to my fabulous and long-suffering agent, Juliet Mahony from the Lutyens & Rubinstein Literary Agency, for putting up with my moaning and whingeing.

Thanks and much love to Kirsty Hardie, Joseph Hardie and James Hardie who helped at various stages with both *Truly Evil* and *Burned and Broken*.

Thanks to my in-laws, Valerie and Arthur Ayres, for their unfailing generosity and support.

And, of course, Debbie, without whom nothing would be possible and everything attained would be meaningless.